**India Grey**'s qualifications ⬚⬚⬚⬚⬚⬚⬚⬚⬚⬚⬚⬚⬚⬚⬚⬚
in English Language and ⬚⬚⬚⬚⬚⬚⬚⬚⬚⬚⬚⬚⬚⬚⬚⬚
stationery and an inexhaus⬚⬚⬚⬚⬚⬚⬚⬚⬚⬚⬚⬚⬚⬚⬚⬚
grew up—and still lives—in a⬚⬚⬚⬚⬚⬚⬚⬚⬚⬚⬚⬚⬚⬚⬚⬚
with her husband and three ⬚⬚⬚⬚⬚⬚⬚⬚⬚⬚⬚⬚⬚⬚⬚⬚
stuff and is a firm believer in ⬚⬚⬚⬚⬚⬚⬚⬚⬚⬚⬚⬚⬚⬚⬚⬚

You can visit her website at www.indiagrey.com, check out her blog at www.indiagrey.blogspot.com or find her on Twitter.

# Champagne Summer

## INDIA GREY

MILLS & BOON

All the characters in this book have no existence outside the imagination of the author, and have no relation whatsoever to anyone bearing the same name or names. They are not even distantly inspired by any individual known or unknown to the author, and all the incidents are pure invention.

All Rights Reserved including the right of reproduction in whole or in part in any form. This edition is published by arrangement with Harlequin Enterprises II B.V./S.à.r.l. The text of this publication or any part thereof may not be reproduced or transmitted in any form or by any means, electronic or mechanical, including photocopying, recording, storage in an information retrieval system, or otherwise, without the written permission of the publisher.

This book is sold subject to the condition that it shall not, by way of trade or otherwise, be lent, resold, hired out or otherwise circulated without the prior consent of the publisher in any form of binding or cover other than that in which it is published and without a similar condition including this condition being imposed on the subsequent purchaser.

® and ™ are trademarks owned and used by the trademark owner and/or its licensee. Trademarks marked with ® are registered with the United Kingdom Patent Office and/or the Office for Harmonisation in the Internal Market and in other countries.

Mills & Boon, an imprint of Harlequin (UK) Limited,
Eton House, 18-24 Paradise Road, Richmond, Surrey TW9 1SR

CHAMPAGNE SUMMER © Harlequin Enterprises II B.V./S.à.r.l. 2012

Originally published as *At the Argentinean Billionaire's Bidding* © Harlequin Books SA 2009 (Special thanks and acknowledgement to India Grey) and *Powerful Italian, Penniless Housekeeper* © by India Grey 2009

ISBN: 978 0 263 90172 6

010-0712

Printed and bound by
CPI Group (UK) Ltd, Croydon, CR0 4YY

# Tamsin

For my dad (1940–1981), who loved rugby so much,
and for my mum, who supports me with the same
unfailing enthusiasm as she supports Scotland.
With love and thanks.

# PROLOGUE

TAMSIN paused in front of the mirror, the lipstick held in one hand and the magazine article on 'How to seduce the man of your dreams' in the other.

*Subtlety*, the article said, *is just another word for failure.* But, even so, her stomach gave a nervous dip as she realised she hardly recognised the heavy-lidded, glittering eyes, the sharply defined cheekbones and sultry, pouting mouth as her own.

That was a good thing, right? Because three years of adoring Alejandro D'Arienzo from afar had taught her that there wasn't much chance of getting beyond 'hello' with the man of her dreams without some drastic action.

There was a quiet knock at the door, and then Serena's blonde head appeared. 'Tam, you've been ages, surely you must be ready by—' There was a pause. 'Oh my God. What in hell's name have you done to yourself?'

Tamsin waved the magazine at her sister. 'It says here I shouldn't leave anything to chance.'

Serena advanced slowly into the room. 'Does it specify you shouldn't leave much to the imagination, either?' she croaked. 'Where did you get that outrageous dress? It's completely see-through.'

'I altered my Leaver's Ball dress a bit, that's all,' said Tamsin defensively.

'That's your *ball dress*?' Serena gasped. 'Blimey, Tamsin, if Mama finds out she'll go mental—you haven't altered it, you've *butchered* it.'

Shrugging, Tamsin tossed back her dark-blonde hair and, holding out the thigh-skimming layers of black net, executed an insouciant twirl. 'So? I just took the silk overskirt off, that's all.'

'That's *all*?'

'Well, I shortened the net petticoat a bit, too. Looks much better, doesn't it?'

'It certainly looks different,' said Serena faintly. The strapless, laced bodice of the dress, which had looked reasonably demure when paired with a full, ankle-length skirt, suddenly took on an outrageous bondage vibe when combined with above-the-knee net, black stockings, and the cropped black cardigan her sister was now putting on over the top.

'Good,' said Tamsin firmly. 'Because tonight I do *not* want to be the coach's pathetic teenage daughter, fresh out of boarding school and never been kissed. Tonight I want to be…' She broke off to read from the magazine. '"Mysterious yet direct, sophisticated yet sexy".'

From downstairs they could hear the muffled din of laughter and loud voices, and distant music wound its way through Harcourt Manor's draughty stone passages. The party to announce the official England international team for the new rugby season was already underway, and Alejandro was there somewhere. Just knowing he was in the same building made Tamsin's stomach tighten and her heart pound.

'Be careful, Tam,' Serena warned quietly. 'Alejandro's gorgeous, but he's also…'

She faltered, glancing round at the pictures that covered Tamsin's walls, as if for inspiration. Mostly cut from the sports pages of newspapers and from old England rugby programmes, they showed Alejandro D'Arienzo's dark, brooding beauty from every angle. Serena shivered. Gorgeous certainly, but ruthless too.

'What, out of my league? You don't think this is going to work, do you?' said Tamsin with an edge of despair. 'You don't think he's going to fancy me at all.'

Serena looked down into her sister's face. Tamsin's green eyes glowed as if lit by some internal sunlight and her cheeks were flushed with nervous excitement.

'That's not it at all. Of course he'll fancy you.' She sighed. 'And that's exactly what's bothering me.'

Above the majestic carved fireplace in the entrance hall of Harcourt Manor was a portrait of some seventeenth-century Calthorpe, smiling smugly against a backdrop of galleons on a stormy sea. Across the top, in flamboyantly embellished script, was written: *God blew and they were scattered.*

Alejandro D'Arienzo felt his face set in an expression of sardonic amusement as he looked into the cold, hooded eyes of Henry Calthorpe's forebear. There was no discernible resemblance between the two men, although they obviously shared a mutual hatred of the Spanish. Alejandro could just remember his father's stories, as a child in Argentina, of how their distant ancestors had been amongst the original *conquistadors* who had sailed from Spain to the New World. Those stories were one of the few tiny fragments of family identity that he had.

Moving restlessly away from the portrait, he ran a finger inside the stiff collar of his shirt and looked around at the impressive hallway, with its miles of intricate plasterwork ceiling and acres of polished wooden panelling. His team-mates stood in groups, laughing and drinking with dignitaries from the Rugby Football Union and the few sports journalists lucky enough to make the guest list, while the same assortment of blonde, well-bred rugby groupies circulated amongst them, flirting and flattering.

Henry Calthorpe, the England rugby coach, had made a big deal about holding the party to announce the new squad at his stunning ancestral home, claiming it showed that they were a team, a unit, a *family*. Remembering this now, Alejandro couldn't stop his lips curling into a sneer of savage, cynical amusement.

Everything about Harcourt Manor could have been specifically designed to emphasise exactly how much of an outsider Alejandro was. And he was damned sure that Henry Calthorpe had reckoned on that very thing.

At first Alejandro had thought he was being overly sensitive, that years in the English public school system had made him too quick to be on the defensive against bullying and victimization—but lately the coach's animosity had become too obvious to ignore. Alejandro was playing better than he'd ever done, too well to be dropped from the team without reason, but the fact was that Calthorpe wanted him out. He was just waiting for Alejandro to slip up.

Alejandro hoped Calthorpe was a patient man, because he had no intention of obliging. He was at the top of his game and he planned to stay there.

Draining the champagne in one go, he put the glass down on a particularly expensive-looking carved chest and glanced disdainfully around the room. There was not a single person he wanted to talk to, he thought wearily. The girls were identikit blondes with cut-glass accents and Riviera suntans, whose conversation ranged from clothes to the hilarious exploits of people they'd gone to school with, and whom they assumed Alejandro would know. Several times at parties like these he'd ended up sleeping with one just to shut her up.

But tonight it all seemed too much effort. The England tie felt like a noose around his neck, and suddenly he needed to be outside in the cool air, out of this suffocating atmosphere of complacency and privilege. Adrenalin pounded through him as he pushed his way impatiently through the groups of people towards the door.

And that was when he saw her.

She was standing in the doorway, her head lowered slightly, one hand gripping the doorframe for support, giving her an air of shyness and uncertainty that was totally at odds with her short black dress and very high heels. But he didn't notice the details of what she was wearing. It was her eyes that held him.

They were beautiful—green perhaps, almond shaped, slanting—but that was almost incidental. What made the breath catch in his throat was the laser-beam intensity of her gaze, which he could feel even from this distance.

His footsteps slowed as he got closer to her, but her gaze didn't waver. She straightened slightly, as if she had been waiting for him, and her hand fell from the doorframe and smoothed down her short skirt.

'You're not leaving?'

Her voice was so low and hesitant, and her words halfway between a question and a statement. He gave a twisted smile.

'I think it would be best if I did.'

He made to push past her. Close up, he could see that behind the smoky eye make up and the shiny inviting lip gloss she was younger than he'd at first thought. Her skin was clear and golden, and he noticed the frantic jump of the pulse in her throat. She was trembling slightly.

'No,' she said fiercely. 'Please. Don't leave.'

Interest flared up inside him, sudden and hot. He stopped, looking down at her sexy, rebellious dress, and then let his gaze move slowly back up to her face. Her cheeks were lightly stained with pink, and the eyes that looked up at him from under a fan of long, black lashes were dark and glittering. Seductive, but pleading.

'Why not?'

Lowering her chin, she kept them fixed on his, while she took his hand and stepped backwards, pulling him with her. Her hand felt small in his, and her touch sent a small shower of shooting stars up his arm.

'Because I want you.' She smiled shyly, dropping her gaze. 'I want you to stay.'

# CHAPTER ONE

*Six years later.*

LEANING against the wall of the players' tunnel at Twickenham when the final whistle went was a bit like being trapped inside the body of a giant beast in pain. Tamsin hadn't been able to face watching the game, but she knew from the great, roaring groan that shook the ground beneath her feet and vibrated through her whole body that England had just fallen.

St George might have slain the dragon, but he'd certainly met his match in the mighty Barbarians.

Not that Tamsin was bothered about that. The team could have lost to a bunch of squealing six-year-old girls for all she cared, as long as they looked good while they were doing it.

She let out a shaky breath, pushing herself up and away from the wall, and discovering that her legs felt almost too weak to hold her up. This was the moment when she had to find out whether all the work of the past few months—and the frantic damage-limitation panic of the last eighteen hours—had paid off.

Like a sleepwalker she moved hesitantly to the mouth of the tunnel and looked out into the stadium, which stretched around her like some vast gladiatorial arena. Heads bent against the thin drizzle, shoulders stooped in defeat, the England team was making its way back towards the dressing room. Tamsin looked anxiously from one player to the next and, oblivious to the dejection and bewilderment on their exhausted faces, felt nothing but relief.

The players might not have performed brilliantly, but as far as she could see their shirts had, and to Tamsin—designer of the new and much-publicised England strip—that was all that mattered. She had already been on the receiving end of numerous barbed comments about what a coincidence it was that such a prestigious commission had been landed by the daughter of the new RFU chairman, so any whisper of failure on her part would be professional suicide.

Wearily, she dragged a hand through her short platinum-blonde hair and rubbed her tired eyes. *That was why it was kind of important that news of last night's little crisis with the pink shirts didn't get out.*

At the entrance to the tunnel, the bitter east wind that had made kicking so difficult for the players all afternoon almost knocked her over, slicing straight through her long ex-army greatcoat to the flimsy cocktail dress she wore beneath it. She'd left last night's charity fashion-gala early and gone straight to the factory, and hadn't had time to go home and change. Ten hours, numerous therapeutic phone-rants to Serena and a lot of very black coffee later, they'd had just enough newly printed shirts for the squad, but she'd spent the whole match praying there would be no substitutions. Only now did she feel she could breathe more easily.

The feeling lasted all of ten seconds.

Then she felt her mouth open in wordless horror. Looking up at the huge screen at the top of the south stand, the air was squeezed from her lungs and replaced with something that felt like napalm.

It was *him*.

So that was why the England squad had lost.

Alejandro D'Arienzo was back. And this time he was playing for the opposition. Tamsin's heart seemed to have jumped out of her ribcage and lodged somewhere in her throat. How often in the last six years since that wonderful, devastating night at Harcourt had she thought she'd seen Alejandro D'Arienzo? Even though in her head she knew that he'd gone back to Argentina, how many times had she found herself turning round to look again at a tall, dark-haired man on a London street? Or felt her pulse start to race as she caught a glimpse of a sculpted profile through the tinted windows of a sportscar, only to experience a sickening thud of disappointment and simultaneous relief when she'd seen that it was some less charismatic stranger?

Now, staring up at the vast screen, she knew there was no such respite, and no mistaking that powerfully elegant body, the broad, muscular shoulders beneath the black-and-white Barbarians' shirt, and the arrogant tilt of that dark, dark head.

The crowd broke out in spontaneous applause as the TV cameras closed in on him, and the image of his beautiful, unsmiling face filled the screen, above the words *Man of the Match*. He was still wearing a gum shield which accentuated the sensual fullness of his contemptuous mouth—bloodied from the game—and the hollows beneath his high cheekbones. A red bandana held back his damp black hair, and for a second his restless, gold-flecked eyes glanced into the camera.

It felt like he was looking straight at her.

She wanted to take her eyes from the screen, but some inbuilt masochistic streak prevented her, and she was left staring helplessly up at him. Six years dissolved away and she was eighteen again, incandescent with fear and excitement as his eyes had met hers and he had walked across the hall at Harcourt towards her...

The England players had lined up on either side of the tunnel and were clapping the Barbarians in, but suddenly Ben Saunders, a young England player who'd been playing in the number-ten position for the first time, broke away and began to walk back across the field. Numbly Tamsin watched as he pulled his shirt over his head and held it out to Alejandro in a gesture of respect.

For a second the proud Argentinean didn't move. A tense hush seemed to fall over the stadium as the crowd watched. It was as if they were holding their breath, waiting to see whether Alejandro D'Arienzo, former England golden-boy, would accept the shirt he had played in with such glorious finesse before turning his back on the team so suddenly all those years ago.

The cameras zoomed in, but the sinister stillness of his face gave nothing away.

And then a huge roar of delight and excitement went up as Alejandro took hold of the hem of his own shirt and brought it slowly upwards over his head. Every hollow, every perfectly defined muscle beneath the bronze, sweat-sheened skin of his taut stomach filled the huge screens at both ends of the ground. And then, as he pulled the Barbarians shirt right off, the crowd screamed and whistled as they saw the tattoo of the sun—the symbol on the Argentine flag—right over his heart.

Vaguely aware that her chest hurt with the effort of breathing, and her fists were clenched so tightly that the fingernails were digging into her palms, Tamsin turned away with a snort of disgust.

Sure, Alejandro D'Arienzo was gorgeous. That was indisputable. But so was the fact that he was the coldest, most arrogant bastard who had ever breathed. It was just that most people hadn't been unlucky enough to see that side of him.

She had. And she still bore the scars. So why was she turning round again, and staring like some moon-struck adolescent as he walked back across the pitch, pulling on the white shirt? The crowd were on their feet, turning the stands into a rippling sea of red and white as they waved their flags joyously at seeing their unforgotten hero back in an England shirt.

And suddenly it hit her; the implication of what she had just witnessed finally penetrated her dazed brain.

An England shirt.

Alejandro D'Arienzo in an *England* shirt.

A precious, produced-at-the-last-minute, paid-for-in-blood-sweat-and-tears England shirt... One of the ones she absolutely couldn't afford to lose.

'*No!*'

With a horrified gasp, Tamsin leapt forward, her four-inch heels sinking into the mud as she desperately tried to push her way through the crush of journalists, coaches, physios and groupies to reach the mouth of the tunnel before he did.

'Please, I have to...'

It was as if she was invisible. There were too many people, and the noise from the ecstatic crowd was too great. The moment he stepped from the pitch, journalists closed around Alejandro like iron filings around a magnet, and Tamsin was forced backwards by an impenetrable wall of bodies. Her heart was hammering, her body suddenly pulsing with heat beneath her heavy coat, and all thoughts but one had been driven from her shocked brain.

The shirt. She had to get the shirt back, or else...

With a whimper of horror, she tried again, taking advantage of her relative slightness to duck beneath the arm of a muscular ground official in a fluorescent jacket. Someone behind grabbed her coat and tried to pull her back, but panic gave her strength, and with a desperate lunge Tamsin broke free.

The England number two in front of her turned round and, recognising her, moved aside to let her through. At the same moment Alejandro finished talking to a journalist and stepped forwards.

There was hardly time to register what was happening, much less to stop it. Already unsteady on last night's killer heels, Tamsin felt herself hurtling forwards into open space, where she'd expected to encounter a solid and immovable row of muscular bodies, but just as she was falling strong arms seized her and she was lifted off her feet.

'Tamsin! Steady, darlin'.' It was Matt Fitzpatrick, the England number five. He grinned at her good-naturedly, revealing a missing front tooth. 'Don't tell me—when you saw my glorious try in the first half you finally realised you couldn't live without me?'

She shook her head. 'I'm...I need...' Her voice came out as a breathless croak, and she looked wildly around, just in time to see Alejandro disappearing into the tunnel. 'Him,' she said in a hoarse whisper.

Matt shrugged his shoulders and gave a theatrical sigh of regret. 'I see. Can't argue with that, I suppose.' And with that he hoisted her into his muscular arms and pushed easily through the crowd before she could protest. 'D'Arienzo!'

Horror flooded her and she let out a squeal, which bounced off the walls of the tunnel. 'Matt, no!' she shrieked, wriggling frantically in his giant's arms, aware that her coat had fallen off her shoulders and the skirt of her tight black-satin cocktail dress was riding up to mid-thigh, showing the lacy tops of her stockings. But it was too late. As if in slow motion, she watched Alejandro stop.

Turn.

Look at her.

And then look away, without the slightest flicker of interest or recognition.

'Yes?'

He was talking to Matt, his eyebrows raised slightly.

'Someone wants you,' grinned Matt, setting her down on her feet. Tamsin ducked her head. Her blood felt like it had been diluted with five parts of vodka as misery churned inside her, mixing uneasily with wild relief. He didn't recognise her. Of course he didn't—her hair had been darker then, and longer. She'd been younger.

And she'd meant absolutely nothing to him.

It was fine. It was good. The humiliation of facing him again if he'd remembered that night would have been terminally appalling. Some in-built instinct for self-preservation told her not to look up, not to meet the eyes of the man who had blown her world to smithereens and walked away without a scratch, to keep her head down.

Oh, God. Her self-preservation instinct hadn't reckoned on the effect of looking at the length of his bare, muscular thighs.

'Really?' he said in a quiet, steel-edged voice. 'And what could Lady Tamsin Calthorpe possibly want with me?'

Adrenalin scorched through her like wildfire, and she felt her head jerk backwards. Towering above her, he was smiling slightly, but the expression in his eyes was as cold and bleak as the North Sea.

She raised her chin and forced herself to meet his gaze. So he *did* remember. And he had the nerve to look at her as if she was the one who had done something wrong. *Like what, for example—not being attractive enough?* Pressing her lips together, she pushed back the questions she had asked herself a million times since that awful night at Harcourt and simply said, 'Not you. The shirt. Could you take it off, please?'

Looking up into his face was like torment. She should have been used to it—she'd seen it in her dreams often enough in the last six years—but even the most vivid of them hadn't done justice to the brutal beauty of him as he stood only a foot away. Bruised and bloodied, he was every inch the conquering Barbarian.

'Oh, dear,' he drawled. 'What's it been—five years? And clearly nothing's changed.'

Oh, Lord; his voice. The melodic Spanish lilt that he'd all but lost growing up in England was stronger again now. Unfortunately.

Tamsin swallowed. 'Six,' she snapped, and instantly wanted to bite out her tongue for giving him the satisfaction of knowing that she cared enough to remember. 'Anyway, I don't know what you mean. From where I'm standing, plenty has changed.'

*Like I'm not naïve enough any more to think that the face*

*of an angel and the body of a living god make a shallow, callous bastard into a hero.* She didn't say the words, but just thinking them, and remembering what he'd done, made the strength seep back into her trembling body.

'Really?' He nodded slowly, reaching out a strong, tanned hand and smoothing it over the wing of pale-gold hair that fell over one eye. 'Well, there's this, of course, but I'm not talking about superficial things. It's what's underneath that I'm more interested in.' Guilty, humiliating heat flared in the pit of her stomach as his gaze flickered over her, taking in the black-satin cocktail dress beneath the huge overcoat, and the muddied skyscraper shoes that clearly said she hadn't been home last night. 'I'm sure that line about taking the shirt off usually enjoys a very high success rate, especially since your daddy is now so high up in the RFU, but that cuts absolutely no ice with me these days. I'm out of all that—' He broke off, and laughed. 'Though, of course, I don't have to tell you that, do I?'

She would not melt. She would not succumb to his voice or his touch, or his questions, or anything. Looking over his right shoulder at the red cross of St George painted on the wall of the tunnel, she affected a tone of deep boredom.

'Whatever. I just want the shirt back, please.'

Wordlessly, as if he were weighing up what to do next, Alejandro took a step towards her, closing the gap between them. The other players were filing past them and the tunnel echoed with their shouts and the clatter of their studs on the floor, but the noise seemed to be coming from miles away. Tamsin felt her flimsy façade slipping. The physical reality of his closeness was acting on her senses like a drug, giving her a painfully heightened awareness of his broad, sculpted chest beneath the tightly fitting shirt, the scent of damp grass and mud that clung to him, and its undertone of raw masculinity.

'I'm sure you do,' he said thoughtfully. 'I'm sure the last thing your father wants is to see me back in an England shirt. After all, he tried hard enough to get me out of one six years ago.'

'Yes, well, you have to agree that the Barbarians strip is much more appropriate, Alejandro. Given that you behave like one.'

A lazy smile pulled the corners of his sexy, swollen mouth. With a nonchalant lift of his shoulders, he turned and began to walk away from her, his massive shoulders filling the narrow space. He called the shots here, and he knew it.

'Wait!'

Fury welled inside her and she ran after him, suddenly finding that without the distraction of his closeness she could think clearly again, and fuelled by a renewed sense of urgency to reclaim the shirt. Slipping past him, she placed herself defiantly in the doorway of the visitors' changing room, blocking his way.

'The shirt, Alejandro.'

She saw the dangerous gleam in the depths of his tiger's eyes, and for a split second wondered if he was going to push her out of the way. Given the relative size of them, he'd hardly have to try, but something in him seemed to prevent him. If she didn't know any better she'd think it was some sense of inherent chivalry, but that would be ridiculous, because she knew better than anyone that there wasn't an atom of decency in the whole of Alejandro D'Arienzo's magnificent body.

He stood back, raising both his hands as if in surrender, but his face bore a look of subdued triumph.

'OK—go on, then. Take it.'

She cast a furtive look around. The tunnel was emptier now, but there were still officials, a few cameramen and journalists hovering outside the press room. '*Me?* Take it off *you?* Don't be ridiculous. I can't.'

Alejandro gave a small shrug and dropped his hands. 'I think we both know that you can, because you've done it before. But if you don't *want* to…' He came towards her and she found herself automatically stepping aside. 'Obviously it's not that important.'

'It is.'

She spoke through gritted teeth, trying to keep back the scream of frustration and fury that was gathering in her chest. Alejandro's hand was on the door and she reached out and grabbed his arm.

It was as if she'd touched a bolt of lightning. White-hot tongues of electricity sizzled up her arm and exploded inside her, simply from the contact of his body beneath the shirt. How come in six years this had never happened with anyone else, even when she'd wanted it to?

He stopped, then slowly turned round so he was standing with his back against the door. 'OK, then. If it matters so much, you'd better take it.'

He was challenging her, she realised, and Tamsin Calthorpe was a girl who could never resist a challenge. Her eyes were pinned to his as she moved towards him, her heart pounding painfully in her chest. *Just do it*, she thought wildly. *You're a big girl now, not that gauche and gullible teenager. Show him that he can't intimidate you...*

She made a short exhalation of exasperation and disgust. Quickly, so he couldn't see how much her hands were shaking, she took hold of the hem of the shirt and tugged it roughly upwards, while he stood unhelpfully motionless, his gaze fixed mockingly on her face.

'You're enjoying this, aren't you?' she hissed.

'Being undressed so tenderly by a beautiful woman?' he drawled with heavy irony. 'Who wouldn't?'

Viciously she yanked his arms up, standing on her tiptoes to pull the shirt over them, her breath coming in uneven gasps with the effort of manhandling his immensely powerful body, and of hiding the screaming, treacherous desire that it aroused in her. But as she reached up he made a sudden, sharp move backwards so that the door swung open and she fell against his chest with a cry of anguish and surprise.

A raucous cheer and a volley of wolf-whistles rang around the Barbarians' dressing room. Tamsin froze in horror, her hands still entangled in the rugby shirt which was now midway over Alejandro's chest, realising exactly how it must look.

Exactly how Alejandro had intended it to look.

'Don't tell me you're not enjoying it too,' he murmured. The amusement in his voice was unmistakable.

As she disengaged herself and stepped back, Tamsin felt an eerie calm descend on her. It was as if, in those few seconds, she was selecting an emotion from a range displayed before her: the murderous rage was tempting, or the cathartic, hysterical indignation... But, no. It might be difficult to carry off, but she was going to go for something a little more sophisticated.

She felt her mouth curve into a languid, slightly patronising smile as she took the bottom of the shirt gingerly between her finger and thumb, and pulled it disdainfully down, covering up the sinuous convex sweep of Alejandro's stomach.

'Cover yourself up, D'Arienzo,' she said scathingly. 'When I said "nice strip" I was referring to the shirt.'

The changing room erupted in whoops and whistles of appreciation as Tamsin turned on her heel and, casting a last, pitying glance at Alejandro, swept out. Her rush of triumph and elation lasted just long enough for the door to slam behind her, and then she collapsed, shaking, against the wall.

Suddenly the shirt seemed like the least of her problems.

Ignoring the boisterous cheers of his team-mates, Alejandro pulled off the shirt and tossed it contemptuously down on the bench before grabbing a towel and heading grimly towards the bathroom beyond the changing area. He felt none of the physical exhaustion that usually descended on him in the immediate aftermath of a game. Thanks to that close encounter with the High Priestess of Seduction and Betrayal, his mind was racing, his body still pulsing with adrenalin.

*Adrenalin and other more inconvenient hormones.*

The bathroom was a spartan white-tiled room with six huge claw-footed baths arranged facing each other in two rows, each filled with iced water. Research showed that an ice bath immediately after a game minimised the impact of injury, and shocked the body into a quicker recovery, but this didn't make the practice any more popular with players. In the nearest tub the blond Australian giant, Dean Randall, sat still in full kit, grim-faced and shivering with cold. He glanced up as Alejandro came in.

'Welcome to the Twickenham spa, mate,' he joked weakly through chattering teeth. 'I'd have kept that shirt on if I were you. It doesn't make much difference, but, by God, anything's better than nothing.'

Alejandro didn't flinch as he stepped into the bath.

'I think I'll take my chances with the cold rather than wear an England shirt for any longer than necessary,' he said brutally, closing his eyes briefly as the icy water tore into him like the teeth of some savage animal. For a second his body screamed with exquisite agony before numbness took hold, mercifully obliterating the insistent pulse of desire that had been reverberating through him since Tamsin had tried to strip the shirt from him.

Randall forced a laugh. 'No plans to come back, then?'

'No.' Alejandro's gritted teeth had nothing to do with the freezing water. 'It would take a whole lot more than a fancy new strip to make me come back and play for England.'

*Like an apology from Henry Calthorpe. And his daughter.*

Randall nodded. 'You came to settle old scores?'

'Nothing so dramatic,' said Alejandro tersely. 'It's business. I'm one of the sponsors of the Argentine rugby team.'

'Los Pumas?' Randall gave a low, shaky whistle of respect and Alejandro smiled bleakly. 'I'm here because, with another

World Cup looming, it's time everyone was reminded that Argentina are major contenders.'

'I wish I could argue with that, mate.' At the physio's nod the huge Australian stood up and vaulted over the side of the bath, wrapping his arms around his body and jumping from foot to foot to bring the circulation back to his frozen legs. 'You certainly showed them today, at any rate. They'd have walked all over us if it hadn't been for you. I owe you a drink at the party tonight. You'll be there?'

Alejandro nodded. Just thinking about the last England team party he'd attended made the agony of the iced water fade into insignificance. He frowned, resting his elbows on the sides of the bath, and bringing his clenched fists up to his temples as unwelcome memories of that night came flooding back: the damp, earthy smell of the conservatory at Harcourt and the warm scent of her hair, the velvety feel of her skin beneath his shaking fingers as he'd undone the laced bodice of her dress.

'OK, Alejandro, time's up,' said the physio.

Alejandro didn't move. A muscle hammered in his cheek as he remembered pulling away from her, struggling to fight back the rampaging lust she had unleashed in him long enough to find someone to lend him a condom. Telling her he wouldn't be long, he had rushed out into the corridor...and straight into Henry Calthorpe.

The expression of murderous rage on his face had told Alejandro instantly who the girl in the conservatory was. And exactly what it would mean to his career. In one swift, devastatingly masochistic stroke, Alejandro had handed Henry Calthorpe the justification he'd been looking for. An excuse so perfect...

'You some kind of masochist, D'Arienzo? I said, time's up.'

*An excuse so perfect it was impossible to believe it had happened by chance.* Alejandro stood up, letting the iced water cascade down his numb body for a second before stepping out of the bath. That explained the directness of her approach. He'd thought there was something honest about her, something refreshingly open, but in fact it had been exactly the opposite.

She had deliberately set him up.

Back in the dressing room, he picked up the discarded England shirt and looked at it as he brutally rubbed the feeling back into his frozen limbs. The new design was visually arresting and technologically ground-breaking, and, in spite of himself, he was grudgingly impressed. Impressed and intrigued. Applying similar design principles and fabric technology to his polo-team kit would make playing in the heat of the Argentinean summer he had just left behind so much more bearable. Thoughtfully he picked it up and was just about to put it into his kit-bag when his eye was caught by the number on the back.

Number ten.

It all came crashing back. For a moment he'd allowed himself to forget that this was so much more than just a cleverly designed piece of sports kit. This shirt, the England number ten, was what he had spent so many miserable, lonely years striving for. When it had felt like there was nothing else to live for, this had been his goal, his destiny, his holy grail, and through his own hard work, his own blood and sweat, he'd achieved it.

Only to have had it snatched away from him, thanks to Tamsin Calthorpe.

In one swift, savage movement he threw the shirt into his bag and swore viciously. So she wanted this back, did she? Well, it would be interesting to see how far she would go to get it this time, because Alejandro didn't intend to relinquish it easily.

Tamsin Calthorpe had been directly and knowingly responsible for him being stripped of his England shirt six years ago. She owed him this.

And a lot more besides.

# CHAPTER TWO

'HUMILIATING doesn't even begin to describe it,' Tamsin moaned, clutching the phone and sinking down into the steaming bathwater. 'I mean, it would have been bad enough if he hadn't remembered me, but it was a million times worse when he did...'

Sticking a foot out of the water, she used it to turn on the hot tap with a dexterity born of long practice and added, 'Obviously I can't go to the party now.'

'Don't be silly,' said Serena mildly. 'You've got to. You can't let him get to you like that.'

'I've got a splitting headache, anyway,' Tamsin said sulkily. 'It's probably the start of a really bad migraine.'

'You don't get migraines.'

'Yes, well, there's always a first time. Look, Serena, it's all very well to say I shouldn't let him get to me, but it's a bit late for that, wouldn't you agree? It's not just about what happened today; it's about the fact that Alejandro D'Arienzo got to me six years ago and completely—'

'Exactly. Six years.' Her sister's calm logic was beginning to wind Tamsin up. 'You were a teenager, for goodness' sake—we all make mistakes and do things we regret when we're young.'

'You didn't,' Tamsin snapped, making islands of bubbles on

the surface of the water. 'You played it so cool that Simon was virtually on his knees with a ring before you'd kissed him. I, on the other hand, was so deranged with infatuation for Alejandro that I dressed like I was charging for it and didn't even take the time to tell him my name before I threw myself at him.'

'So? It's in the past. Like I said, we make mistakes, and we *move on*.'

'I know, but...' Tamsin knew Serena was right. In theory. 'Moving on' sounded so simple and logical. So why had she never been able to do it? Even Serena had no idea of the extent to which what had happened that night had affected her in the years that followed. And was still affecting her now. 'I can't.'

'I'm sorry, I'm going to have to stop you right there. I thought tonight was about your work not our sex life.' *Ouch*. 'I thought that you were going to the party to unveil the England team suits?' Serena gave a breezy laugh. 'Gosh, just think: all those people who said you were flaky and you only got the commission because of Dad will *love* it if you don't turn up because of some bloke!'

Tamsin stood up in a rush of water.

'*What?* Who said that?'

'Oh, well, no one in particular,' soothed Serena. 'Not in so many words, anyway, although Simon said that article in last week's *Sports Journal* sort of implied—'

'God, I *hate* that!' Snatching a towel, Tamsin stepped out of the bath and stormed into the bedroom, stepping over the chaos of discarded clothes and piles of magazines, and leaving a trail of wet footprints on her polished wooden floorboards. 'How *dare* they say that? Don't they do their research? Don't they know I have a first-class degree in textiles, and that I was up against some of the stiffest competition in the business to get this commission? Don't they know that Coronet won "best new label" at last year's British Fashion Awards?'

'I'm not sure, but *I* do,' said Serena placidly. 'It's the press pack at the party that you need to be haranguing, not me.

Although, of course, if you're not there I don't suppose you can. You'll just have to let the clothes speak for themselves. The suits are exquisite, and from what I gathered from Simon the new shirts were very—'

Tamsin, who had flung herself down on top of the mountain of clothes piled on her un-made bed, gave a cry of dismay and slithered to her feet. 'Oh, my God, the *shirt*! I'd almost forgotten about that. I have to get it back. If I don't, by the end of tomorrow's press conference my reputation is going to be toast, and on top of everything else that's the last thing I need.'

'How are things at Coronet?' asked Serena carefully.

'Bad. While I was dealing with the shirt crisis, Sally left a message on my answerphone to say that another buyer had pulled out because of loss of exclusivity, since the designs have been so widely copied on the high street.'

'Imitation is the sincerest form of flattery, darling,' Serena said weakly. 'And the shirt crisis wasn't your fault. The factory messed up the dye process, and it's entirely to your credit that you thought to test the shirts for colour-fastness ahead of the game.' Serena giggled. 'Otherwise England would have been playing in pink by half time.'

'Given that the press are out for my blood already, I don't think they'll see it that way.' Tamsin threw open her wardrobe and began to rifle through the rails. 'Which is why I can't afford for it to get out.'

'What's that noise? What are you doing?'

'Looking for something to wear.'

'Ah. Does that mean you're going?'

'Oh yes, I'm going all right,' Tamsin said grimly, pulling out a sea-green silk dress, grimacing and putting it back. 'I'm fed up of being taken advantage of. Alejandro bloody D'Arienzo picked the wrong day to mess with me. He screwed me up enough last time, and I'm not going to give him the satisfaction of doing it again. He took something that belongs to me.' She paused, frowning. 'And I intend to take it back.'

'Are we talking about the England shirt now?' said Serena gently.

'Amongst other things.' *Let's see: my pride, my sense of worth, my self-confidence...* 'God, Serena, when I think about that night—about how it felt when I realised he wasn't coming back... I thought nothing could be worse than knowing that he found me so unattractive back then, but you should have seen the expression on his face this afternoon. It's like he *hates* me, like he has nothing but contempt for me. Like I'm *worthless*.'

'Don't say that, Tam.' Serena's voice hardened slightly. 'He was the one in the wrong back then. You're brilliant. And beautiful.'

Tamsin stopped, catching sight of herself suddenly in the wardrobe mirror. Wrapped only in a towel, her newly washed hair was slicked back from a face that was flushed from the bath. So far, so OK, but her eyes automatically travelled downwards to her right arm.

She grimaced and turned away.

'Yeah, right. And you're clearly suffering from pregnancy hormones,' Tamsin said with a rueful grin. 'Go and eat another pickled onion and chocolate-spread sandwich and leave me alone. Don't you know I have a party to get ready for?'

'Not so fast. I need to know what you're wearing first. You can keep your weird sandwich combinations; now that I know I'm condemned to spending the next six months in a maternity smock, my only craving is for tailored clothes, so I'll have to indulge myself through you. You need something that screams *"successful, glamorous, assured, mysterious, sexy, but completely unavailable"*.'

Tamsin pulled out a narrow slither of light-as-air ash-grey chiffon and looked at it thoughtfully. 'Exactly.'

'You look lovely, darling,' Henry Calthorpe said stiffly, barely glancing up from the evening paper in his hand as Tamsin slid into the back of the car beside him. 'Nice dress.'

'Thank you, Daddy.'

Tamsin suppressed a smile. She was grateful for the sentiment—sort of—but it would be great if for once he'd actually looked. Then he would have seen that the dress wasn't *nice*—it was a triumph. It was her favourite design for the new season's collection; the whisper-fine chiffon was generously gathered from a low V-neck, crisscrossed by bands of silver ribbon which fitted snugly under the bust and swept downwards at the back, giving the whole thing a slightly Greek feel. The long semi-sheer sleeves fell down over her hands, covering her arms. Of course; fashion wasn't her father's thing, but he certainly would have noticed if she'd left her arms bare.

'Initial comment on the strip seems to be fairly positive, you'll be pleased to know,' Henry continued acidly. 'It's just a shame they didn't manage to get a picture of one of our players wearing it.'

He closed the paper and put it down quickly, but not before Tamsin had caught a glimpse of a full-page photograph of Alejandro walking from the pitch in the England shirt beneath the headline: *Barbarian Conqueror*.

She picked up the newspaper and opened it. In the hushed interior of the Mercedes, her heart was beating so loudly she was surprised her father couldn't hear it. Trying to keep her hand from shaking as she held the paper, she began to read.

*Former England hero Alejandro D'Arienzo made a welcome return to Twickenham this afternoon in a closely fought match between England and the Barbarians. In a stunning display of skill, the Argentine Adonis helped the Barbarians to a surprise 36-32 victory, after which an outclassed Ben Saunders handed D'Arienzo his new shirt in a gesture of well-deserved respect.*

*The crowd were clearly delighted to see D'Arienzo back in the England number ten shirt, the position he famously made his own in his three years in the England squad. His international career came to an abrupt and mysterious end six years ago amid rumours of a personality clash with then-coach Sir Henry Calthorpe, and D'Arienzo returned to his homeland where he has earned a formidable reputation in the polo world, as both patron and player for the high-goal San Silvana team.*

*Both sides have always maintained a steely silence on events that led to this defection, but his dazzling performance today, coupled with reports that he is closely involved with Los Pumas, must make Calthorpe wonder if he would have been better swallowing his pride and keeping him on...*

'Utter rubbish,' said Henry tartly as Tamsin folded the paper with exaggerated care and put it down on the seat between them. Picking idly at a bead on the sleeve of her dress, Tamsin kept her voice neutral as she said, 'You never liked him, though, did you?'

Henry suddenly seemed hugely interested in the featureless black landscape beyond the car window. 'I didn't trust him,' he said with quiet bitterness. Then, turning back to Tamsin, he gave a bland smile. 'He was dangerous. A loose cannon. No loyalty to the team with that...that God-awful tattoo on his chest. The press conveniently forget all that now, don't they?'

Tamsin felt the breath catch painfully in her throat as the image of Alejandro's chest, with the Argentine sun blazing on the hard plane of muscle over his heart, filled her head. As a teenager she had cut a picture from a magazine that had showed him stripped to the waist during one hot summer training session for the World Cup. Even now, all these years later, she could still recall the sensation of terrible, churning longing she'd felt whenever she looked at that tattoo.

The car slowed, and a scattering of flashbulbs from the other side of the darkened glass told her they'd arrived at the very exclusive hotel where the post-match party was being held. Tamsin blinked, dragging in a shaky breath and forcing herself back into the present as the car glided smoothly down the drive towards a solid-looking, square stone house half-covered with glossy creeper.

Even before the driver had opened the car door, the noise of the party was already clearly audible.

'After this afternoon's shameful performance, heaven knows what they think they've got to celebrate,' said Henry cuttingly, getting out of the car. 'You'd better do the photo-call straight away while there's still some hope of the team doing justice to your elegant suits. If you leave it any later, they'll all be rolling drunk and singing obscene songs. Come on.'

Henry held out his arm. Absently, she took it. 'Oh, dear, you're right. And, since the photographer wants all those cheesy and predictable shots of the team holding me up like a rugby ball, I'd rather I was in sober hands.'

Instantly she felt Henry bristle. He stopped, and Tamsin instantly cursed herself for walking right into that one. It was all Alejandro D'Arienzo's fault. She wasn't thinking clearly, otherwise she would have been all too aware that her father's legendary and highly annoying protective streak was about to reveal itself. 'That's ridiculous,' he snapped. 'I'm not having my daughter mauled around by the entire team like some Playboy bunny. I'll have a word with the photographer and make it perfectly clear that—'

'No! Don't you dare! I got this commission on my own merit, and I'll handle the PR on my own terms.'

For a second they glared at each other in the light of the carriage lamps on either side of the front door. Then Henry withdrew his arm from hers and walked stiffly up the stone steps into the brightly lit reception hall, the set of his very straight back conveying his utter disapproval. Left alone outside, Tamsin gritted her teeth and stamped her foot.

Hell, he was *impossible*. It was all right for Serena; she'd always been able to wrap Henry round her little finger with a flash of her dimples and a flutter of her big blue eyes. Whereas Tamsin had always argued, and—

She paused.

Then, running quickly up the steps in her father's wake, she caught up with him in the centre of the panelled reception area.

'Please, Daddy.' She caught hold of his arm, forcing him to stop.

Picturing Serena's lovely face in her mind's eye, and trying desperately to assume the same gentle, beseeching expression, Tamsin looked up at her father. 'It's only a couple of photographs,' she said persuasively.

It worked like a charm. Instantly she saw the slight softening in Henry's chilly grey gaze, and he nodded almost imperceptibly. 'All right,' he said gruffly. 'You know best. I'll let you get on with it.'

Relief flooded her, and impulsively she reached up to kiss his cheek. 'Thank you, Daddy.'

Turning, she ran lightly across the hallway, just about managing to resist punching the air, but unable to stop a most un-Serenalike smile of elation breaking across her face.

Alejandro froze at the top of the stairs, his face as cold and impassive as the rows of portraits on the oak-panelled walls around him as he took in the touching little scene below.

He saw her cross the hallway in a ripple of silvery grey chiffon, her pale hair gleaming in the light from the chandelier above. He watched her tilt her face up to her father, looking up at him from under her dark lashes, and heard the persuasive, pleading tone in her husky voice as she spoke.

*Please, Daddy... Thank you, Daddy...* It was as much as he could do not to laugh out loud at the saccharine sweetness in her voice, but a second later his sardonic amusement evaporated as she turned away, and the melting look on her face gave way to a smile of pure triumph.

The calculating bitch.

Nothing had changed, he thought bitterly, carrying on down the corridor to his room. Not deep down, anyway. She'd cut her hair and gone blonde big style, but the glittering green eyes, the attitude and the rich-girl arrogance were still the same.

Back in his room he checked his watch and picked up the phone. It was just after five p.m. in Argentina, and the grooms would be turning the ponies out for the night. Two promising mares—a chestnut, and a pretty palomino that he'd bought last month in America for the new polo season—had been delivered yesterday and he was impatient to hear how they were settling in.

Giselle, his PA back at San Silvana, reassured him that the horses were doing fine. They'd recovered well from the journey, and the vet was happy that they would both be rested and ready to use on his return.

Alejandro felt better once he'd spoken to her. Nothing to do with the husky warmth in her voice, but simply because it was good to be reminded that San Silvana, with its rolling lawns, its stables, poolhouse and acres of lush paddock filled with ponies, was still there. Was real. Was his.

Coming back to England had dredged up insecurities he had long forgotten, he thought wryly, catching a glimpse of his reflection in the mirror as he went to the door. He'd come a long way, but beneath the bespoke dinner suit, the Savile Row shirt and silk bow-tie, there apparently still lurked the displaced boy who didn't belong.

Out on the galleried landing the sounds of the party drifted up to him. Glancing down on his way to the stairs, he could see the England players, standing shoulder to shoulder in identical dark suits as they lined up for a photograph. They had their backs to him, and were standing in two rows while a photographer wearing tight leather-trousers and an expression of extreme harassment tried to get them all to stop messing around and keep still.

'Fifty quid to swap places with Matt Fitzpatrick!' someone called from the back row, and there was a huge guffaw of laughter, followed by someone else shouting, 'A hundred!'

'Sensible offers only, please, gentlemen,' grinned Fitzpatrick.

For a second Alejandro didn't understand the joke, but then he moved further along the shadowed gallery and looked down, feeling his sore shoulders stiffen and ice-cold disgust flood him.

Tamsin Calthorpe, her cheeks glowing and her honeyed hair shining like the sun beneath the photographer's lights, was stretched out horizontally in the arms of the front row of players, facing out towards the camera. Matt Fitzpatrick, exuding Neanderthal pride, supported her body, one huge hand cupped around her left breast.

The photographer's flash exploded as he took a volley of shots. Her bare legs and feet, held in the meaty hands of one of the England forwards, looked as delicate as the stem of some exotic flower, and next to the coarse, battered faces of the players Tamsin's skin gleamed like pale-gold satin.

'How come you get the best position anyway, Fitzpatrick?' shouted one of the younger players at the back.

Tamsin laughed, and to Alejandro the sound was like fingernails on a blackboard. 'He's more experienced than you, Jones. And his handling skills are better.' As Jones blushed to the roots of his hair, the team erupted into more rowdy laughter and cheers.

So that was what she'd been asking her father for: permission to appear in the team photo. He remembered her soft, pleading tone as she'd put her hand on his arm and said 'only a couple of photographs'.

Had she no pride at all? Alejandro's face felt stiff with contempt as he leaned against one of the gallery's carved wooden posts and watched. What was she, some kind of unofficial team mascot? It was perfectly clear that she knew all the players pretty well.

*How many had she slept with?*

The thought slipped into his head without warning, but he had to brace himself against the lash of unexpected bitterness that accompanied it.

There was much clapping and shouting below as two of the players, under direction from the photographer, lifted her onto their shoulders. Laughing, Tamsin tipped back her head and looked up.

He watched the smile die on her glossy lips as her eyes met his.

In that moment Alejandro realised who it was she reminded him of: the blondes who'd populated the rugby parties he used to attend. The girl he'd thought was so different had grown up into one of those women he'd so despised at the party at Harcourt. A polished, hard-society blonde whose satiny skin concealed a ruthless streak a mile wide. A professional flirt, a consummate party girl, a shallow, manipulative man-user whose every flattering word was meaningless and every smile was a lie.

And, judging from the look on her face now, she was all too aware she'd been found out.

No.

*No, no no.*

It couldn't be possible. Even her luck wasn't that bad. As the two props set her back on her feet, Tamsin shook her fringe from her eyes and looked back up into the minstrels' gallery where a figure in the shadows had caught her eye. A figure she'd thought for one nasty moment was…

Oh, God. It was. *Him.*

He was leaning insolently against a carved wooden post, looking down. Though his face was in shadow, every line of his elegant, powerful body seemed to communicate contemptuous amusement, and she could feel his eyes searing her with their intensity and their disdain.

The photographer clapped his hands and trilled, 'OK, people—are we ready? Now, if the two guys on either side of Miss Calthorpe could look down at her, please?'

Why? Why couldn't he just go?

Dimly Tamsin was aware of laughing banter breaking out around her again, and of Matt pulling her towards him and making some joking comment to the player on her other side. But, as she looked up into Matt's appreciative blue eyes, it was Alejandro's cold, contemptuous stare that she saw.

The photographer's flash exploded in her face as fury erupted inside her.

That was what he'd done to her *that* night.

'That's fabulous,' gushed the photographer. 'Really fabulous. Gorgeous, sexy pout, Miss Calthorpe. Now, shoulders straighter, Matt... Lovely.'

*He'd broken something inside her, so that no matter how much men like Matt flattered her and flirted with her...*

'Tamsin, you're looking *de*licious. Just put your hand on Matt's chest...yes, like that...'

*...she could never quite make herself believe that they meant it.*

'Now, let's make sure we get the nice rose-patterned lining of the jacket in the shot. Just slip your hand underneath his jacket, and sort of half-push it off his shoulder. Yeah, like that. That's gorgeous.'

*Maybe it was time she proved to Alejandro Arrogant D'Arienzo, and herself, that not all men found her such a turn-off?*

The shutter rattled like machine-gun fire. High on adrenalin, fuelled by fury, Tamsin let instinct take over. For six years she had surrounded herself with a forest of thorns, keeping men at bay with her endless succession of barbed comments and razor-sharp retorts, all because he had robbed her of the belief that she was desirable. But she would show him that she was attractive, she was sexy... Her spine arched reflexively as she slid her hand over Matt's shoulder, but it wasn't Matt she was thinking of. Turning her head towards the bright lights and the camera, lifting her chin in silent, brazen challenge, she looked into the shadows, straight into Alejandro's eyes.

It was like a steel trap closing around her—cold, hard, unyielding. He was looking down at her, the lights from below accentuating the sharp planes of his face, which were wholly at odds with the sensual swell of his mouth. And then, as she watched, he shook his head in an attitude of incredulous, pitying amusement.

He turned and walked away. Just as he had six years ago. He walked away, without a backwards glance, leaving the hot throb of desire ebbing from her and nothing but icy desolation and humiliation in its place.

# CHAPTER THREE

*Blue ball, top-left pocket.*

With narrowed eyes Alejandro looked thoughtfully at the billiard table. It was a difficult shot, and in his own personal game of dare this was sudden death.

If he got it in, he would play on. If he missed, he had to go back out and rejoin the party. He had to go out there and watch Tamsin Calthorpe tease and flirt her way around the rest of the England team. And, he thought with a grimace of scorn, judging by her earlier performance, probably most of the Barbarians as well.

It was probably just as well he never missed.

Lazily he bent to line up the shot. From the other side of the massive polished-wood door he could hear the raucous sounds of the party. As a major investor in Argentine rugby he ought to be out there; after today's game he was the man everyone wanted to talk to and he should be capitalising on that to get publicity for Los Pumas. That was, after all, what he'd come back for.

Unhurriedly he adjusted the balance of the cue. To even up the odds a little he closed his left eye, leaving only the bruised and swollen right one to judge the angle of the shot.

With a sharp, insouciant jab the blue fell neatly into the top-left pocket.

Alejandro straightened up, smiling ruefully as a sting of perverse disappointment sliced through him. He had no desire to go out there and mix with the great and the good of the rugby world, but there was a part of him that would have rather enjoyed the chance to watch the amazing Lady Calthorpe in operation some more, for no other reason than to marvel at how much more polished the routine had become in the last six years. Back then there had been a gawky awkwardness about her, a trembling sort of defiance, but it had affected him far more powerfully than tonight's virtuoso display of sexual invitation.

Powerful enough to cloud his judgement and get beneath his defences, he thought acidly.

She'd upped her game considerably since then, and as a result it seemed that she was no longer kept in the background as a handmaid for her father's sordid, secret schemes. Now she was much higher profile, which of course made perfect sense. Henry Calthorpe was now chairman of the RFU, and, judging by the photoshoot Alejandro had just witnessed, the organisation had become one big, indulgent playground for his spoiled daughter. He wondered how far her influence spread now.

With sudden violence he threw down the cue and went to stand in front of the fire.

Henry Calthorpe was obviously too important these days to invite the riff-raff into his own home, but the hotel had apparently been chosen to provide a very similar setting. The billiard room was a gentleman's retreat in typical English country-house style, with leather wing-backed chairs and oil paintings of hunting scenes on the walls. The long, fringed lamp hanging low over the table made the billiard balls glow like jewels in a pool of emerald green, and firelight glinted on a tray of cut-glass decanters beside him.

He reached for one and splashed a generous measure into a crystal tumbler, and had just thrown himself into one of the high-backed chairs facing the fire when there was a sudden rush of noise behind him as the door opened and then closed again quickly. Alejandro didn't move, but his hand tightened around the glass as, reflected in the mirror above the fireplace, he saw her.

She went straight to the billiard table and leaned against it, dropping her head and breathing hard, as if she was trying to steady herself or regain control. His first thought was that she was waiting for someone to follow her into the room, and he glanced towards the door again. But it stayed shut, and a moment later Tamsin Calthorpe lifted her head and he saw that the laboured breathing, the bright spots of colour on her cheeks, weren't caused by desire but by anger.

Picking up the cue he had so recently thrown down, she barely glanced at the table before stooping, and, with a snarl of fury, took a vicious shot which sent the balls cannoning wildly across the table.

In the mirror Alejandro watched the white rebound off the top cushion, just missing the pink and the black and sending the brown ball cannoning into the middle pocket. Still completely oblivious to his presence, Tamsin punched the air and gave a low hiss of triumph.

'Lucky shot,' he said sardonically.

In the mirror he saw her freeze, the billiard cue held across her body like a weapon.

'Who said luck had anything to do with it?'

Her voice was cool and haughty, but he caught the nervous dart of her eyes as she looked around to see who had spoken. Her blonde head was held high, her shoulders tense and alert. She looked oddly vulnerable, like a startled deer.

'It was a difficult one.' Alejandro stood up and turned slowly towards her, feeling a flicker of satisfaction as he watched her eyes widen in shock and the colour leave her face. She recovered quickly, shrugging as she walked towards the curtained windows.

'Precisely. What would have been the point in taking it if it was easy?'

It was Alejandro's turn to be stunned. As she walked away from him he saw that the dress that had looked so demure from the front was completely backless, showing a downwards sweep of flawless, peachy skin.

He made a sharp, scornful sound—halfway between a laugh and a sneer, which sent a tide of heat flooding into Tamsin's face and a torrent of boiling fury erupting inside her. Her heart was beating very hard as she whipped round to face him again.

'You don't believe me?'

'Frankly, no.' He moved around the chair and came towards her. He'd taken off his dinner jacket and undone the top two buttons of his shirt. His silk bow-tie lay loosely around his neck, giving him an air of infuriating relaxation that was completely at odds with the icy hardness of his face. She was pleased to notice that there was a muscle flickering in the hollowed plane of his cheek.

'You don't strike me as a girl who likes to try too hard to get what she wants,' he said scathingly.

The injustice of the statement was so magnificent she almost laughed. Pressing her lips together, she had to look down for a second while she fought to keep a hold on her composure. 'Don't I?' Her voice was polite, deceptively soft as she met his gaze. 'Well, may I suggest that your assumption says more about you than it does about me, Alejandro?'

He flinched slightly, almost imperceptibly, as she said his name, and for a moment some unfathomable emotion flared in his eyes. But it was gone before she could read it or understand its meaning, and she was left staring into hard, golden emptiness. It was mesmerizing, like meeting the eyes of a panther at close range. A scarred, hungry predator.

'What does it say about me?'

He spoke quietly, but there was something sinister about his calmness. Above the immaculate, hand-made dress shirt his black eye and swollen mouth gave his raw masculinity a dangerous edge. Tamsin felt fear prickle on the back of her neck, and was aware that she was shaking.

Which was ridiculous. She wasn't *afraid* of Alejandro D'Arienzo. She was *angry* with him. Clenching her jaw, she managed a saccharine smile. 'Let me see,' she said with sugared venom. 'It says that you're an arrogant, misogynist bastard who thinks that women are for one purpose and one purpose only.'

His mouth, his bruised, sexy mouth, curled slightly in the barest, most insolent expression of disdain. 'And don't you rather perpetuate that stereotype?'

Tamsin felt the ground shift beneath her feet. The panelled walls seemed to be closing in on her, leaving her no chance of escape, no alternative but to confront the image he was holding before her of herself the girl who dressed like a slut and had thrown herself at him without even bothering to tell him her name.

'That was six years ago,' she protested hoarsely. 'One night, six years ago!'

'And how many times has it happened since then?' he said, draining his glass and picking up another cue.

Surreptitiously holding the edge of the green-baize table, Tamsin took a quick, shaky breath and made herself hold her head high as she gave a nonchalant shrug. The entire contents of the Cartier shop window wouldn't induce her to let him see how much his rejection had hurt her, how far-reaching its consequences had been. She managed a gratifyingly breezy laugh.

'I don't know, it's hardly a big deal. Don't try to tell me you've lived a life of monastic purity and celibacy for the last six years?'

He didn't look at her. 'I'm not going to.'

'Well, don't you think it's a bit much to expect that I have? What did you think, Alejandro, that I would have hung up my high heels and filled my wardrobe with sackcloth and ashes just because you weren't interested?' She laughed, to show the utter preposterousness of the idea. 'God, no. I moved on.'

'So I saw. A number of times, evidently,' he drawled quietly, bending down and lining up a shot. 'The England squad seems to be your personal escort-agency.'

Idly he jabbed the cue against the white ball, sending it hurtling across the table. Tamsin felt like it was her heart. 'Wrong, Alejandro,' she said stiffly. 'The England squad are my *clients*.'

His eyebrows shot up; he gave a twisted smile. 'Indeed? My mistake. I got it the wrong way round.'

'Don't be stupid,' she snapped. 'They're my clients because I'm the designer who handled the commission for the England kit. The new strip, the suits and the off-pitch clothing.'

Just for the briefest second she saw a look of surprise pass across his deadpan face, but it was quickly replaced by cynicism again.

'Did you, indeed?' he drawled, somehow managing to make those three small, innocuous words convey his utter disbelief. But before Tamsin had a chance to think up a suitably impressive response the door burst open and Ben Saunders appeared, swaying slightly. His unfocused gaze flitted from Alejandro to Tamsin.

'Oops. Sorry... Interrupting.' Grinning, obviously misreading the tension that crackled in the quiet room, he began to back out again with exaggerated care, but Tamsin leapt forward, grabbing his arm.

'Ben, wait!' she said grimly. 'Tell *him*—' she jerked her head sharply in Alejandro's direction '—about the new strip. Tell him who designed it.'

Frowning, Ben looked drunkenly at her as if she'd just asked him to work out the square root of nine hundred and forty two in binary.

'Uh...you?' he said uncertainly.

*Great*, thought Tamsin hysterically. *Brilliant. Hugely convincing.*

'Yes. Of course it was me,' she said with desperate patience.

Ben nodded and grinned inanely, obviously relieved to have got the right answer. 'And the shoots,' he slurred, turning around clumsily to show off his suit, and almost overbalancing. 'You did the shoots too, didn't you? Lovely shoot.' He beamed across at Alejandro. 'Very clever, Tamsin. Very good at measuring the inside leg...'

Alejandro glanced at her, his face a study of sadistic amusement. 'I'm sure,' he said icily. 'That takes a lot of skill.'

Tamsin clenched her teeth. 'Thanks, Ben,' she said, turning him around and steering him towards the door. 'Now, maybe you'd better go and find some water, or some coffee or something.' When the door had closed behind him she turned back to Alejandro with a haughty glance. 'There. Now do you believe that I'm not just some airhead heiress with time on her hands?'

'It proves nothing.' Malice glinted in the golden depths of Alejandro's eyes as he picked up his glass again. 'I'm sure it makes great PR sense for you to be used as a front for the new strip, but surely you don't expect me to believe that you actually designed it? Sportswear design is an incredibly competitive business, you know.'

'Yes.' Tamsin spoke through gritted teeth. 'Astonishingly enough, I do know, because I got the job.'

Nodding thoughtfully, Alejandro took an unhurried mouthful of his drink. 'And what qualified you for that, Lady Calthorpe—your father's position in the RFU? Or your own extensive research into rugby players' bodies?'

'No,' she said as soon as she could trust herself to open her mouth without screaming. 'My first class honours degree in textiles and my final year project on techno-fabrics.' Looking up at him, she gave an icy smile. 'I had to compete for this commission and I got it entirely on *merit*.'

His dark brows arched in cynical disbelief. 'Really?' he drawled. 'You must be good.'

'I am.'

It was no use. If she stayed a moment longer, she wouldn't be able to keep the rip tide of vitriol that was swelling and surging inside her from smashing through her flimsy defences. She put down the cue and threw him what she hoped was the kind of distant, distracted smile that would convey total indifference as she turned to reach for the doorknob. 'You don't have to take my word for it, though. If you look at my work, it should speak for itself.'

'I have, and it does. For the rugby shirts, at least.' He laughed softly and she froze, her hand halfway to the door as a bolt of horrified remembrance shot through her. 'I have one, remember?'

Her fingers curled into a fist and she let it fall to her side, the nails digging painfully into her palm. She could have sunk down onto the thick, wine-red carpet and wept. Instead she steeled herself to turn back and face him.

'Of course,' she said, unable to keep the edge of bitterness from her voice. 'How could I forget?'

He came slowly towards her, his head slightly to one side, an expression of quiet triumph on his face. 'I really don't know, since you seemed pretty keen to get it back earlier,' he said quietly. 'Obviously it can't be that important, after all. To you, anyway.'

Tamsin swallowed. He had come to a halt right in front of her, and it was hard to marshal the thoughts swirling in her head when it suddenly seemed to be filled with *him*. She closed her eyes, trying to squeeze him out, but the darkness only made her more aware of his closeness, the warm, dry scent of his skin. She opened them again, looking deliberately away from him, beyond him, anywhere but at him.

'It *is* important, I'm afraid. I need it back.'

'You *need* it?' he said softly. 'If you're the designer, you must have lots of them. Surely you can spare that one?'

'It's not that simple. I...'

The mirror above the fireplace reflected the broad sweep of his shoulders, the silk of his hair, dark against the collar of his white shirt. She stared at the image, mesmerised by its powerful beauty as the words dried up in her mouth.

'No. I thought not,' he cut in, a harsh edge of bitterness undercutting the softness of his tone, like a knife blade wrapped in velvet. 'It's not about the shirt, is it? It's about the principle—just as it always was. It's about your father not wanting the English rose on an Argentine chest, isn't it?'

Argentine chest. *Alejandro's chest.*

'No,' she whispered.

Gently, caressingly, he reached out and slid his warm hand along her jaw, cupping her face, stroking his thumb over her cheek. A violent shudder of reluctant desire rippled through her. She felt herself melt against him for a second before his fingers closed around her chin, forcing her head back so she was looking straight into his hypnotic eyes.

'I hope you're a better designer than you are a liar.'

'I'm not lying,' she hissed, jerking her head free. Her hand automatically went to the place where his had just been, rubbing the skin as if he had burned her. 'This has nothing to do with my father. There was a—a problem with the production of the shirts. I only found out yesterday when I suddenly thought to test one, and found out the red dye on the roses wasn't colourfast. I had to contact the manufacturers and get them to open up the factory and start from scratch on a new batch of shirts, but there was only time to make one for each player. *That's* why I need yours back, otherwise on the photoshoot at Twickenham tomorrow Ben Saunders will be half-naked, as well as hungover,' she finished savagely, feeling her blood pressure soar as he gave a short, cruel laugh. 'What's so funny?'

'I thought you were supposed to be good: "I had to compete for this commission and I got it entirely on merit",' he mocked. 'So who exactly were you competing against, Tamsin? Primary school children?'

'Oh, I can compete with the best, make no mistake about that,' she said with quiet ferocity, which melted seamlessly into biting sarcasm as she added, 'Now, it's been just *fabulous* to see you again, Alejandro, but I really ought to be getting back to the party. So if you could just give me back the shirt?'

She was walking towards the door as she spoke, but suddenly he was in front of her, blocking her path. Looking up, Tamsin saw with a shudder that all trace of amusement had vanished from his face. His eyes were as cold and hard as Spanish gold.

'Sorry. The spoiled-diva routine won't work with me.'

Misery and resentment flared up inside her, and for a moment she could do nothing but look at him. 'What do you want me to do? Beg?'

Kicking the door shut, he took a step towards her and she shrank backwards, pressing herself against the billiard table. 'It's quite a nice idea,' he said thoughtfully. 'But I think not, on this occasion.' He leaned forward, as if he were about to touch her. She flinched away with a low hiss of animosity, but he was only reaching for something behind her.

'So, you reckon you can compete with the best, do you?' he said softly. 'Let's see if you were telling the truth about that, at least.'

He handed her the billiard cue he had picked up from the table. Hesitantly, Tamsin took it, looking up at him in mute uncertainty.

'I don't understand. What are you saying?'

'You want your shirt back? You have to win it.'

## CHAPTER FOUR

FOR just the briefest second he saw panic flare in her eyes, and felt an answering surge of grim satisfaction.

'Don't be ridiculous,' she snapped, looking at the cue as if it was a loaded gun. 'Play now? With *you*?' She gave a harsh, scornful laugh. 'Forget it.'

Chips of ice crystallised in Alejandro's heart. He was offering her a chance to prove herself. She couldn't hope to win, of course; he was far too skilled a player for that. But he would have given her credit—and the shirt back—just for trying.

And giving Tamsin Calthorpe credit for anything went very much against the grain.

'Afraid of losing?' he said scathingly. 'I don't blame you. I don't suppose you're used to it, and, believe me, I won't make allowances for who you are—or who your father is.'

Brimstone sparked in the depths of her green eyes. 'It's not the thought of losing that bothers me,' she hissed. 'It's the prospect of spending the next hour in your company.'

'Oh, don't worry,' he said, his voice a languid drawl. 'It won't take that long for me to thrash you.'

He was only inches away from her. Close enough to hear her little shivering gasp, close enough to see the instant darkening of her eyes as his words hit her and the flashing anger was swallowed by spreading pools of desire at their centre.

'Thrash me?' She gave a hoarse laugh. 'I don't think so.'

His eyebrows rose. 'You're walking away?'

'Oh no,' she breathed. Reaching out, she curled her fingers around the cue he held and for a moment came so close to him that he could feel the warm whisper of her breath on his neck. 'I'm not going anywhere. Not until I have my shirt back.'

Languidly she turned and walked away from him to the other end of the table. Alejandro frowned, feeling his chest, and his trousers tighten as he watched the sinuous movement of her bare back. He hadn't expected this.

'So, what are we playing?' she said, whipping round to face him again. 'Bar-room pool?'

The low light from the billiard lamp fell onto her short platinum-blonde hair, making her look like a rebellious angel. She was looking at him steadily, insolently, her head lowered slightly and her slanting green eyes unblinking.

'If that's what you want.'

She shrugged. 'I'm easy. I just thought it might be what you're used to.'

For a fleeting second Alejandro felt almost lightheaded with hatred at her casual, calculated viciousness. To her, he was still the boy from nowhere, the imposter in the charmed circle of privileged English youth that made up the team, and her social circle.

'I can play anything, anywhere, *Lady* Calthorpe. Would you prefer English billiards perhaps?'

His voiced dripped with contempt and his eyes raked over her, cold and assessing. Holding the cue upright in front of her, Tamsin clung to it tightly, glad of its support. English billiards? How the hell did you play that?

'No. Bar-room pool is fine with me,' she said, trying to make it sound of little consequence to her, but secretly hoping that all those smoky afternoons spent playing pool in the student bar at college were about to pay off.

She was in danger of getting seriously out of her depth here.

With the lamplight casting hollows beneath his razor-sharp cheekbones and the bruising on his lip, he looked like some kind of avenging warrior, primed for battle. Her hands were damp as she watched him move easily around the table. *I can play anything, anywhere,* he'd said, and she knew with a sick, churning mixture of fear and excitement that he was right. He would be just as at home playing pool in the back-street bars of Buenos Aires as playing billiards in an upmarket gentlemen's club in Mayfair. He exuded an effortless confidence that transcended all boundaries and singled him out as a natural winner.

Which was unfortunate, considering her reputation kind of rested on getting this shirt back.

'You first.'

Placing her right hand firmly on the table, Tamsin hoped he couldn't see how much it was shaking.

'You're left-handed?'

'In some things.'

She took the shot, mis-hitting wildly so that the balls scattered crazily over the table.

'You're sure this is one of those things?' Behind her his was voice cold and mocking. 'Maybe you might be better with your right hand.'

She turned, colour seeping into her cheeks as a slow pulse of anger beat in her veins. 'Thanks for the tip, but can we assume that if I want your help I'll ask for it?'

'I thought I'd already made it clear that, even if you did, you wouldn't get it,' he said smoothly, moving around the table and potting balls with a swift, lethal efficiency that made Tamsin's heart plummet. 'Although maybe I could make it a little fairer.' He smiled lazily across the table, moving his cue to the other hand. 'Since you're playing left-handed, I will too. Number ten. To you.'

Tamsin opened her mouth to make some stinging retort, but found her throat was dry and no words came. Helplessly her gaze fixed itself on the strong, tanned hand Alejandro placed on the table, splaying his lean, long fingers.

The room was very quiet and very still. A clock ticked on the mantelpiece, below which the fire had sunk to an amber glow. His narrow, focused stare was exactly level with her knicker line, and it was intense enough to feel like he could see right through the flimsy grey chiffon.

The thought sent a gush of arousal crashing through her.

The sudden sharp crack of the balls colliding made her jump, and she watched, mesmerized, as the yellow ball rolled gently across the green baize towards the pocket beside her thigh. A shiver rippled through her as she suddenly, unaccountably, found herself thinking not of the movement of the ball across the table, but of Alejandro's fingers over her skin...

Guiltily she wrenched her head up as the ball came to a halt. Alejandro was watching her, the expression on his dark, bruised face unreadable.

'There,' he said with exaggerated courtesy. 'Your turn.'

Tamsin blinked. He'd missed the shot. That was good news, but somehow the knowledge that he'd only missed because he'd taken it with his left hand took any sense of triumph she might have felt and turned it right on its head.

'I don't need favours, Alejandro, and I don't need special treatment,' she snapped, walking briskly towards him to take the shot. 'In fact, let's be honest, I don't need any of this. Wouldn't it be better for both of us if you just did the decent thing for once in your life and gave the shirt back to me now? Or are you on some kind of personal mission to make my life as unpleasant and difficult as possible?'

'You want to concede defeat?'

There was a sinister, watchful stillness about him, and his tone was carefully neutral, but she heard the challenge in his words.

She smiled slowly, sweetly. Adrenalin was pulsing through her like pure alcohol, dilating her blood vessels, making her heart beat faster. She felt high, but at the same time perfectly lucid and oddly calm as she turned her body towards his, mirroring his position, leaning with one hip propped against the edge of the table. 'You'd love that, wouldn't you?' she said softly. 'Which is exactly why it's the last thing I'd ever do.'

He didn't smile back. His swollen upper lip accentuated the beauty of his face while making him look twice as dangerous. Standing there, with the lamplight making the hair that fell over his face blue-black, he was every inch the Spanish *conquistador*.

'You're sure about that?' he said quietly, almost apologetically. 'You have to know that you don't have a snowball's chance in hell of winning this?'

He held her in his gaze. It was like drowning slowly in warm syrup…delicious…but no less terrifying for it. She blinked. Drowning was drowning, after all.

'Let's see, shall we?' she said in a low voice, and moved round so that she was facing the table again. She was acutely, painfully aware of him beside her, towering over her as she bent to take her shot, looking down on her bare back with that hard, golden gaze that seemed to warm her skin like evening sun.

She had to get a grip. Concentrate.

There was no hurry. She flexed her shoulders slightly, steadying herself. Above her she heard a low rasping sound as Alejandro dragged a hand across his stubble-roughened jaw. She clamped her own mouth shut against the whimper of excitement that rose up in her at the sound, and took the shot.

With a series of satisfying staccato clicks, the balls ricocheted around the table, the orange she'd lined up cannoning neatly into the top pocket. She threw him a quick glance from under her lashes as she moved around to the other side of the table.

'I hope you're keeping score.'

Alejandro gave a low, ironic laugh. 'Don't worry about that.

And you still have a long way to go before the shirt is yours. Don't get complacent.'

The look she gave him was full of fire and loathing. Alejandro watched with interest as she bent forward over the table to take the next shot, his eyes automatically travelling to the shadowed hollow between her breasts. Being so relentlessly spoiled for a lifetime had obviously given her a completely unrealistic grasp of her own limitations, he mused, forcing himself to shift his gaze upwards to her face. In the glow of the lamp above, the green baize of the table intensified the colour of her eyes to a vivid emerald. He watched them flicker, dart, measuring the distance as a tiny frown of concentration appeared between them.

She hesitated, completely focused, the tip of her pink tongue appearing between her plump lips. She moved, and with one swift flick of her wrist the ball dropped into the pocket. As it fell, Alejandro realised he'd been holding his breath. His whole body felt tense.

Well, that was one word for it. And some parts felt more 'tense' than others.

*Damn her.* As she straightened up he saw the same look of self-satisfied triumph on her face as he'd seen earlier in the hallway with her father when she'd got her own way. She was playing him, he thought acidly. She was perfectly aware of how sexy she looked, leaning over that table with her dress falling forward, and her green eyes right on a level with his crotch. She was manipulating him as ruthlessly as she had that night at Harcourt Manor all those years ago, but with twice as much finesse.

'This isn't complacency, Mr D'Arienzo,' she said huskily. 'This is confidence.'

Lust gripped him, making him feel dizzy. Leaning against the wall, tipping his head back, he watched through narrowed eyes as she undulated around the table, taking shot after shot. In the quiet room, everything seemed distorted, exaggerated, so that he was almost painfully aware of the soft sigh of her breathing, the whisper of chiffon against her velvet skin.

She straightened up. 'How many times do I have to tell you I don't want special treatment?' she said coldly. 'I missed. It's your turn.'

Scowling, he levered himself upright and walked stiffly around the table. His mind had been so occupied with other things he'd almost forgotten about the game, and he was surprised to see how few balls remained now. She was more skilled than he'd thought. As he leaned over the table he was aware of her picking up the small cube of chalk and rubbing it across the tip of her cue. He looked up. She was holding the cue in both hands in front of her, like a pornographic prop, and as he watched she put it by her mouth and blew softly, getting rid of the excess chalk.

It was deliberate torment.

'I have to congratulate you. You're quite a player.'

He spoke with lethal calm, but the careless savagery of his shot gave some hint of the choking rage inside him. The few remaining balls ricocheted violently from cushion to cushion and then stilled.

'Thank you.'

Alejandro took a step backwards, out of the pool of light, and leaned against the wood-panelled wall. Tensing his jaw, he looked away as she stood with her back to him to take her turn. 'It wasn't a comment on your sporting ability.'

Inexorably he found his head moving round to look at her again. In the lamplight from above her bare skin gleamed, as smooth and flawless as thick cream. The bones of her spine showed through, making him want to run his fingers down them to where they disappeared beneath the grey satin band of her dress. She shifted her position slightly, pressing her hips against the table and adjusting her weight in the high heels.

'No?' Her voice was cool and detached as she parted her legs to gain better balance and stretched forward over the table. He'd thought her legs were bare, but now he could see that he'd been wrong. She was wearing stockings of the sheerest silk. Stockings with wide, lace tops which were visible as she bent forward.

Alejandro felt his breath stop and his muscles tighten, as if he'd just been tackled and brought down. Hard.

She turned back to him and her eyes were very dark. 'What was it, then, Alejandro?'

'I was referring more to your match technique,' he said with quiet brutality. 'Though the theory behind it is fatally flawed. If you think that after last time there's even the smallest chance that I'd be interested—'

'You *bastard*!'

He caught her by the wrist as she raised her hand to hit him and wrenched her arm back to her side. Her breathing was very rapid, and he could feel the rise and fall of her chest against his own. 'Oh no,' she breathed, her voice trembling slightly. 'I wouldn't think that after last time there's any chance of that, Alejandro. Your lack of *interest* then was sufficiently spectacular to leave me in no doubt about that. But don't worry,' she went on, her emerald eyes glittering with feverish defiance, 'I'm sure that to most people all that hugging and kissing on the pitch when you score a try just looks like the camaraderie of the game.'

His grip tightened on her wrist, and he saw her wince. 'Be careful, Tamsin.'

She laughed, a low, breathy, mocking laugh. 'Why? Because you don't want—'

She didn't get any further. In one decisive movement Alejandro had closed the small gap that separated them and brought his mouth down on hers, so that the rest of her stupid, childish taunting was lost in the wildfire of his brutal kiss.

It was like falling off a cliff and finding she could fly. The ground beneath her feet melted away. Gravity ceased to exist. There was nothing but darkness and fire, and the roar of blood in her head. His fingers dug into her shoulders, pulling her against the hardness of his body. Of his arousal.

His rigid, obvious arousal.

Oh, God...

She wasn't aware of dropping the billiard cue, but she must have done, because suddenly her hands were sliding across the rock-hard contours of his shoulders, moving up the column of his neck to tangle into his hair. The taste of him, the scent of him, filled her—dry and masculine, earthy and clean. His mouth ground down on hers, violent, desperate, brilliant, searing his brand on her forever.

The billiard table pressed hard into her bottom and instinctively, with a hitch of her hips, she raised herself up so that she was sitting up on it, parting her thighs and pulling him into her. The bittersweet taste of blood was on her lips, metallic and warm, and his fingers bruised her skin. She didn't care.

If he stopped now she knew she would scream.

She wriggled back on the table, grabbing the open collar of his evening shirt, pulling him with her. Suddenly she was aware of the sound of their breathing, harsh and laboured. Her whole body vibrated with want, arching towards him, opening like some exotic, fleshy flower, oozing nectar. Reality was irrelevant. The past was meaningless and the future incomprehensible. All that mattered was now, and this—the glorious incarnation of every one of her guilty, luscious teenage fantasies.

She was in the arms of Alejandro D'Arienzo, and his mouth was crushing hers, his hands holding her, sliding downwards, his thumbs caressing the underside of her breasts.

Alejandro lifted his head and looked at her. His eyes were as dark as vintage cognac, glinting dully in the low light, and his mouth was full and crimson where the ferocity of their kiss had opened up the cut in his lip.

He moved his thumbs upwards, brushing them over the hardened tips of her swollen, tingling breasts. She stiffened, her head falling backwards. Instinctively, helplessly, she felt her legs wrap around his body, tightening and drawing him into her, wriggling against him as the straining peak of his arousal pushed against the damp silk of her pants.

Her mouth opened in silent bliss, her eyes were wide, dazed, and her breathing shallow as, frozen on the brink of some terrifying, tempting abyss, she stared up into his bruised face.

His bruised, cold, totally emotionless face.

Before she could move or speak he had let her go, stepping sharply away from the table where she was sprawled backwards, turning so she could no longer see his face.

'I think we've proved that your cheap shots were wide of the mark, sweetheart,' he said mockingly. 'It's not that I'm not interested in women, *per se*. It's just that spoiled little girls who use sex as a bargaining tool don't really do it for me. Sorry.'

Points of light danced in front of Tamsin's eyes and for a desperate, horror-struck moment she thought she might faint. Or be sick.

She closed her eyes, fighting the feeling, focusing all of her fading energy on holding onto that small scrap of tattered dignity which would enable her to hold up her head and look him in the eye as she told him exactly what she thought about men who treated women like laboratory rats to be experimented on.

But when she opened her eyes again he was gone.

## CHAPTER FIVE

Tamsin gave a low moan of despair as she looked at her reflection in the big, cruelly lit mirror.

The lighting in the ladies' loo at Twickenham might be designed for functionality rather than flattery, but there was no doubt that the face that looked back at her was a mess. Mortuary-pale, with matching white lips, the only hint of colour came from the bluish shadows beneath her bloodshot eyes. It wasn't a good look.

Right at that moment she would rather face a firing squad—than photographers and journalists from the sports desk of every major national and special-interest publication in the country, but she didn't have much choice. Her father, along with members of the England management, was waiting for her, and he would expect her presentation to be seamless.

With a shaking hand she dabbed some lipstick onto her pale, numb lips and pressed them together, remembering with a slice of sudden breathtaking pain how they'd swelled and burned beneath Alejandro's kiss last night as the blood from his torn mouth had crimsoned them.

*No.*

She couldn't go there now, not when she had to get out there and look like a poised professional instead of the creature from the crypt. It was absolutely not the time to revisit the ground she had worn bare throughout the long hours of the night as she had asked herself the same question over and over again.

*Why had she been so stupid?*

Letting him humiliate and reject her once was bad enough. Giving him the opportunity to do it a *second* time... Well, that was nothing short of insanity. And yet, at the time she had been powerless to stop it. It was as if, the moment he'd left her shivering in the freezing darkness of the orangery at Harcourt, she had shut down and had gone into a state of mental suspended-animation. She remembered reading somewhere that extreme shock could do that to people. For six years she had gone about her life, looking for all the world like a normal person, a perfectly healthy, successful young woman, so that even those closest to her—even Serena—had no idea that beneath the surface she was frozen. A stopped clock.

Until last night.

Putting the lid back on the lipstick, she threw it into her bag and pressed her palms to her cheeks as tears smarted in her eyes again. *Big girls don't cry*: that was what her father always said. By the time Tamsin had been born Serena, two years older, had already cornered the market on 'pretty and feminine'. Tamsin did 'tough' instead, and Henry had accepted her as the son he'd never had. Tears were for babies, he'd told her, and Tamsin had learned very early to hold them in.

Last night had been a minor blip—well, quite a major blip, actually—but she was back on track today. She stepped back, taking a deep breath and giving herself one last look in the mirror before heading back out there. As a designer, her clothes were about so much more than fashion, both mirroring her mood and influencing it. The way she dressed always made a statement, and today's severe black trouser-suit said very loudly 'don't mess with me'. The four-inch heels she wore with it added, 'or I'll smash your face in'.

The noise from the press room spilled out along the corridor as she left the sanctuary of the ladies', a loud babble of conversation, as rowdy and excited as the bar on match day. Tamsin shuddered. Right now it sounded good-natured enough, but she had a horrible feeling that in a few minutes it could turn into the sound of a pack of journalists baying for her blood.

'Ah, there you are, Tamsin. We were waiting.' Henry Calthorpe looked at his watch as he came towards her. 'Is everything all right?'

Tamsin summoned a smile. It felt like strapping on armour plating. 'Everything's fine, Daddy,' she said ruefully. 'Why wouldn't it be?'

'No reason.' Henry was already moving away. 'You look pale, that's all. But if you're ready let's get started.'

The noise level in the press room rocketed as they filed in. The cameras started whirring and journalists got to their feet, keen to get their questions answered.

Boards showing life-size images of the players lined up at the start of yesterday's game had been placed behind the long table at the front of the room. Taking a seat right in front of Matt Fitzpatrick's hulking figure in the picture, Tamsin found herself sitting between her father and Alan Moss, the team physio. He was there to comment on the effect the techno-fabric of the new strip was expected to have on the players' physical performance, but he'd also come in very handy if she passed out, Tamsin thought shakily, picking up the pen that had been left on the table in front of her and starting to sketch.

Henry introduced them all, saying a few brief words about each person's role in the new team. When he reached Tamsin, the reporters seemed to strain forwards, like greyhounds in the stalls the moment before the start of the race.

'As you may be aware, Tamsin Calthorpe won the commission to design the new strip, as well as the off-field formal attire of the team.'

'Surprise, surprise!' shouted someone from the back. 'I wonder how that happened?'

Outrage fizzed through Tamsin's bloodstream. Instantly

her spine was ramrod straight, her fingers tightening convulsively around the pen in her hand as her body's primitive 'fight or flight' instinct homed in on the former option. Forcing a grim smile, she looked into the glittering dazzle of flashbulbs in front of her.

'It happened thanks to my degree in textiles and my experience designing for my own label, Coronet.' She didn't quite manage to keep the edge of steel from her voice. 'I believe there were three other designers competing for the commission, and the selection process was entirely based on ideas submitted for the brief.'

'But why did you put yourself forward?' someone at the front persisted. 'You're best known for designing evening dresses worn by celebrities on the red carpet. It's quite a leap from that to top-level sports kit, wouldn't you say?'

She'd been expecting this question, and yet the hostility of the tone in which it was asked seriously got to her. She wondered if the microphone just in front of her was picking up the ominous thud of her heart.

'Absolutely,' she said through clenched teeth. 'And that was exactly why I wanted the commission. I'd built up my own label from nothing, and I was ready for the next challenge.'

'Was it the challenge you wanted, or the money? Rumour has it that the recent spate of high-street copies has hit Coronet hard.'

Tamsin felt like she'd been punched in the stomach. The bright lights of the cameras made it hard to see anything beyond the front row, but that was probably just as well. Lying was easier if you didn't have to make eye contact.

'Coronet's designs are as in demand as ever,' she said coldly. 'My business partner, Sally Fielding, is already handling requests for next year's Oscars and BAFTAs.'

All that was true. Sally had been approached by several stylists in Hollywood and London, but, since all of them expected dresses to be donated for nothing more than the kudos of seeing them on the red carpet, it didn't help Coronet's cash flow. But there was no time to dwell on that now. If she let her focus lapse for a second this lot would tear her limb from limb.

'Would you agree that your background as a womenswear designer had an obvious influence on this commission?' another voice asked.

*Thank goodness; a straightforward question.*

Tamsin was just about to answer when the speaker continued, assuming an outrageously camp tone. 'The oversized rose-motif and the dewdrops on the rugby shirts are simply to die for, aren't they?'

A ripple of laughter went around the room. Tamsin's patience was stretched almost to its limit.

'Maybe it might be an issue for any guys who aren't quite confident about their masculinity,' she said sweetly. 'Fortunately, that doesn't include any of the team. The dewdrops, as you call them, are small rubberised dots that maximize grip for line-outs and scrums. But you're right—my background in couture has been influential. The starting point for any design is the fabric, and this was no different. Working in association with Alan here, and experts in the States, we sourced some of the most technologically advanced fabrics in the world.'

The room was quieter now. People were listening, scribbling things down as she spoke. A bolt of elation shot through her. 'We started with tightly fitting base-layer garments beneath the outer kit,' she continued, her voice gaining strength. This was safe ground. Whatever poisonous comments people could make about who she was or where she came from, no one could say she didn't know her subject. 'These are made from a fabric which actually improves the oxygenation of the blood by absorbing negative ions from the player's skin. It also prevents lactic acid build up, improving performance and stamina.'

'So why did England lose yesterday?' someone sneered from the back.

*Because Alejandro D'Arienzo was playing for the opposition.*

Tamsin's mouth was open, and for a terrible moment she thought she'd actually said that out loud. Casting a surreptitious, panicky glance around, she realised that the cameras were now pointing at the coach, who was talking about form, injury and training. Thank goodness. She picked up the mini bottle of water from the table in front of her and took a long mouthful, grateful for a moment of reprieve. On the pad in front of her she'd unconsciously been sketching the outline of an elongated female figure, and looking at it now she felt a wave of anguish. All the critics were right, she thought miserably, adding a drapey flourish of fabric falling from one shoulder of the figure. She didn't belong here. She should be back in the studio with all the team, working on next autumn's collection.

The pen faltered in her hand as dread prickled the back of her neck. If the business was still going then. The RFU commission had helped appease the bank a bit, but...

She gave a small start, dimly aware of Alan's gentle nudge. 'Tamsin? This one's for you.'

She blinked and looked ahead into the gloom beyond the dazzle of the camera lights. 'Sorry? Could you repeat the question, please?'

'Of course. I wondered—' the voice was leisurely, unhurried. '—did you encounter any particular problems in the production of the strip?'

A hand seemed to close around her throat so that for a moment she could hardly breathe, much less answer. There was no mistaking that deep, mocking, husky voice with its hint of Spanish sensuality. 'No,' she said sharply, her eyes raking the darkness, trying to locate him.

'None at all?'

He stepped forward, people standing around the edges of the room beyond the rows of chairs moving aside to let him through. His eyes, bruised and shadowed, burned into hers with laser-like intensity that belied the lazy challenge in his voice, and Tamsin noticed with a thud of sheer horror that in his hand he held the shirt.

The missing number-ten shirt.

The treacherous, sadistic, ruthless, vindictive *bastard*. For a moment she was speechless with loathing. He was trying to force her to admit, in front of people who were already cynical enough about her ability, that she had messed up.

As if he hadn't humiliated her enough.

'No,' she repeated coolly, lifting her chin and meeting his gaze head-on. 'I was lucky that the manufacturing team was excellent, and the whole production process was very straightforward. When working with very specialised fabrics like these, technical problems with dye or finishes are almost to be expected, but in this instance I managed to anticipate all potential issues and as a result there were no problems at all.'

*There.* She stared defiantly at him, daring him to say anything to the contrary. After all, if he did, that would betray the fact that he had inside information, which would be an extremely unwise move to make in front of a room full of journalists.

Tamsin's heart was pounding. She watched him glance down at the shirt in his hand, and back up again. Back at her. His face was like stone.

'I see. You had an excellent team. Does that mean that your involvement in this commission was merely nominal?'

'No, it does not,' she said in a low, fierce voice. Beside her, Tamsin heard her father make a sharp sound of impatience and disgust, and was aware of him leaning over to whisper something to the RFU official on his other side. She knew that at the smallest signal from her he would summon security to remove Alejandro D'Arienzo from the room, but the knowledge gave her no satisfaction. She didn't want him to go anywhere before she'd made him see that she was more than just a dizzy, vacant heiress playing at having a grown-up job.

'In that case,' said Alejandro smoothly, 'may I assume that you're available for other commissions of a similar kind?'

'What do you mean?'

The rest of the room was watching—waiting with the same morbid fascination that make people slow down when they passed a road accident, Tamsin thought bitterly. She felt like a cat who had been lured into the lion's cage at the zoo and was about to be devoured in front of a crowd of avid onlookers.

'Miss Calthorpe—sorry, *Lady* Calthorpe.' Alejandro's voice was husky, seductive, eminently reasonable. Only she could sense the barbs beneath the silk. 'You've convinced us all that you won this contract fairly and have been single-handedly responsible for seeing it through every stage from design to completion. I'm sure I'm not alone in admiring the results of your work.' There was a murmur of grudging assent from the rows of reporters. Tamsin felt irritation prickle up her spine as she noticed the rapt expressions on their faces as they looked up at Alejandro. 'I'm one of the sponsors of Los Pumas—the Argentine rugby team,' he was saying, 'And I'd like to invite you to redesign their strip for their relaunch next season.'

*A moment ago they'd been preparing to lynch her, but one word from their hero and they were rolling over like puppies. It was sickening.*

'I—sorry?'

Tamsin's head snapped round to look in bewilderment at her father as her mouth opened in astonishment. She should have been paying closer attention. For a moment there she thought he'd just asked her to design the Pumas strip, but surely she'd misheard?

Henry Calthorpe cleared his throat importantly. His voice was utterly dismissive. 'I'm afraid that would be impossible. Tamsin's schedule is booked up for months in advance, although I'm sure if you put your request in writing...'

A low, derisive murmur went around the room as the reporters shifted in their seats and looked meaningfully at each other, sensing carnage. But Tamsin was oblivious to everything but Alejandro. His dark, handsome face wore the look of a pirate king who had just forced the damsel in distress to walk right to the end of the plank.

There was nowhere for her to go, and he knew it. It was a case of give in, or give up. If she refused him now, it would make everything she'd just said sound like a lie.

Tamsin didn't give in easily, but she knew when she was outmanoeuvred. She forced herself to look straight at him, but it was more than she was capable of to manage a smile as well.

'I'd be absolutely delighted, Mr D'Arienzo.'

So, Tamsin Calthorpe had talent, of that there was no doubt. Whether it extended into the field of design, or was simply confined to deception and dishonesty remained to be seen.

Alejandro pushed through the crowd of journalists, many of whom had now turned in his direction to pick up on the unexpectedly juicy twist the story had just taken. Ignoring them, he made straight for the door through which the RFU officials, with Tamsin amongst them, had just disappeared.

He saw her straight away, deep in conversation with her father at the far end of the room where croissants and coffee were set out on a table. If that severe black trouser-suit was supposed to make her look grown up and professional, she'd got it completely wrong, he thought sourly. She just seemed absurdly young; far too thin and somehow...

Ah. Of course.

*Vulnerable.*

Silly of him to be so slow on the uptake. That was exactly the effect she must have been going for.

As he crossed the room towards them, he watched her put a hand on her father's arm, as if restraining him. Deliberately he avoided looking at Henry Calthorpe, instead focusing on his daughter. She was very pale—he'd thought before that was just the harsh TV lighting—but he could see now that she looked as if she were about to pass out. Could it be that he'd finally managed to shake the oh-so-secure world of Lady Tamsin?

Leaving Henry's side, she came over to him. She was trembling, he noticed with a twisting sensation deep in his gut.

'I hope you're satisfied.'

'Extremely,' he said in an offhand tone. 'I've just secured the services of an extremely talented designer who's apparently booked up for the foreseeable future. Now all I need is a cup of coffee and my day would be made.'

Her fine eyebrows rose. He could almost see the sparks of hostility that seemed to electrify the air around her. 'Secured? I'm sorry—shouldn't that be *blackmailed*?'

Alejandro laughed. 'You've been watching too many films. Or did I miss the part when someone held a knife to your throat?'

'You know what I mean,' she hissed, looking swiftly around her, as if checking to see if anyone was listening, and taking a step towards him. 'You know that there's no way I could refuse out there, with the world's press just waiting for a chance to tear me to ribbons.'

With some effort Alejandro kept his face and his voice completely blank. Her clean, floral scent as she moved closer gave him a sudden flashback to last night, and how it had felt to kiss her. His lip, swollen and bruised this morning, throbbed at the memory.

'Refuse? Now why would you want to do that?'

'Because I cannot and will not work for someone I don't respect.'

He moved past her, and with complete insouciance began pouring coffee from the cafetière on the table into a china cup. 'Oh dear,' he drawled. 'Well, you'd better get over the artistic-diva tantrums, because by tomorrow morning every paper is going to be carrying the story of how England's up and coming celebrity designer is off to Argentina to work her creative magic on the Pumas.' He turned back to her, leaning against the table as he took a thoughtful sip of coffee. 'Unless of course you'd like me to call some contacts and tell them you've reconsidered—'

*'Argentina?'* Her eyes widened in horror, 'Who said anything about Argentina?'

For a split second she looked so scared that Alejandro almost felt sorry for her. Almost. But the memory of what she'd done to him six years ago burned like his split lip. It was her turn to be sorry now.

'Did you really think I would bring the whole team over here? That may be how people in Tamsin's world usually operate, but you're going to have to get used to a whole new way of doing things, sweetheart.'

Watching her eyes darken from emerald to the dark, opaque green of yew trees in winter, he waited for the storm to break. He had seen from the little firework display last night when she'd tried to hit him that Lady Tamsin had a formidable temper, and wondered what she would do now. Scream? Throw something? Or turn to Daddy for help?

She tilted her chin, her blistering hostility cleverly cloaked in ice-cold nonchalance. Alejandro was grudgingly impressed at her restraint.

'Why are you doing this to me?'

'To you?' he said very quietly. 'Oh no, Tamsin, I'm doing it *for* you. I'm giving you a chance to prove yourself. I'm giving you a chance to showcase your talents and seal your reputation. You should be grateful. I thought you liked a challenge.'

She laughed softly then, almost as if she was relieved. It sounded breathy and musical. 'I get it. You think that I've had my hand held and all the hard work done for me here, don't you? You think that I'm going to be absolutely clueless out there on my own, and you just can't wait to watch me fail.' She looked up at him, her soft, pink mouth curved into a smile.

'Well, Alejandro, I won't fail. I did it all myself, and I can do it again—better, more easily this time—so, if you're dragging me over to the other side of the world just so you can have the pleasure of watching me screw up, you're wasting your time.'

'Fighting talk. Very impressive,' he drawled sardonically. 'But I warn you, Tamsin, this isn't a game. This isn't like last night, where you can flirt and seduce your way through when the going gets tough. This is work.'

A rosy tide flooded her cheeks and the smile evaporated instantly. 'And you're the boss, right?' she said with quiet venom. 'Good. I'm so glad we got that straight, because if you so much as lay a finger on me I'll have you for sexual harassment faster than you can say "hotshot lawyer".'

Before Alejandro could respond, a member of the grounds team in an England tracksuit and baseball cap had appeared beside them, looking anxious. 'Miss Calthorpe?' he said nervously. 'The photographer's ready to start the photo-shoot down on the pitch. But, er, unfortunately we seem to be missing one shirt...'

For a moment she didn't move. And then, still keeping her gaze fixed to his, she said, 'Thank you. I'm bringing it right now.'

Alejandro smiled as much as his swollen lip would allow. 'A car will come for you tomorrow morning,' he said with exaggerated courtesy. 'Please be ready by eleven o'clock.'

'Tomorrow? But—' She stopped abruptly, visibly struggling to rein in the furious protest that had sprung to her lips. Finally, pressing her lips together, she gave a curt nod and turned on her heel to follow the grounds official.

Alejandro watched her go, her narrow back ramrod-straight, her blonde head held very high. She was hanging onto that fiery temper by a thread, he thought wryly. She seemed very confident that she could handle the professional aspect of the next couple of weeks—but how would she do on the personal? Would the spoiled little diva be able to cope?

He waited until she was almost at the door before calling, 'Oh—and Tamsin?'

She turned, her face set into a mask of politeness. 'Yes, Mr D'Arienzo? Or, now I'm working for you, should I call you "sir"?'

'Alejandro is fine. We'll be flying on my private jet tomorrow. It's only a small plane, so bring one bag only, please. I know what women are like for packing ridiculous amounts of unnecessary clothes.'

The look she shot him was ice-cool. 'You're saying clothes will be unnecessary? Careful, Mr D'Arienzo—this is business, remember?'

And then she was gone. Alejandro was left staring after her, his coffee cooling in his hand, his mind swirling with disturbing thoughts of Tamsin Calthorpe sprawled naked on the leather seats of his jet, and the unwelcome suspicion that she'd just scored some victory over him.

He'd take her advice. He would be careful.

He had an uneasy feeling that this was going to be a whole lot more trouble than he'd bargained for.

# CHAPTER SIX

'ONE bag! How the hell am I supposed to get everything I need into one stupid bag?' Wedging the phone against her shoulder, Tamsin picked up a soft jacket, the colour of dark chocolate, and looked at it longingly. 'Should I take my army coat or the brown cashmere jacket?'

'Cashmere,' said Serena firmly. 'The other one makes you look like you're in the Hitler Youth. So, tell me, how's Daddy about all this?'

'Well, that's another annoying thing, actually. He's *furious*. Which is particularly unfair, considering he knows I had absolutely no choice.'

She squashed the jacket onto the top of her already bulging leather holdall. It was half-past ten, and the bedroom looked like the scene of a police raid, with drawers pulled open and spilling out silken wisps of underwear, cardigans and dresses in every colour.

'Darling, since when has Pa been rational where his best beloved daughter is concerned? He thought he'd dealt with this problem once and for all, so you can't blame him for being a bit fed up.'

'What?' said Tamsin vaguely, looking around the room. 'Do you think three sweaters will be enough?'

'Sweaters?' There was a long silence at the other end of the phone. Eventually Serena said in a strangled voice, 'Tamsin, just run by me what else you've packed.'

Tamsin picked up a thick leather belt with a heavy jewelled buckle and threw it back into a drawer. 'Look, I know you're going to say that I should take lots of dressy stuff, and that Alejandro Playboy D'Arienzo probably holds A-list parties every night or whatever, but I don't care, because I'm not getting involved in *any* of that. I'm not interested in him. I'm there to work.'

'It's not that. Just tell me you haven't packed for winter? Darling, it's the height of summer over there just now. The temperature is in the thirties!'

In the middle of the chaos Tamsin stopped and went very still, her mouth suddenly dry. Her eyes darted to the big, old-fashioned schoolroom clock on the wall by the window, and then to the miserable London greyness outside. She gave a small whimper.

'Oh, God. Oh, *no*! I didn't think…"

'OK. Don't panic. Let's be rational about this. First you have to take everything out of the bag.'

'Everything out,' repeated Tamsin desperately, pulling out armfuls of cashmere and wool and trying not to cry. 'OK. Now wh—?'

She stopped suddenly as she heard the sound of a car engine in the mews below.

He wasn't due for another fifteen minutes yet, and surely he wouldn't be so inconsiderate as to—?

A door slammed. Footsteps echoed on the frosty pavement.

'Oh, Serena. He's here,' she whimpered into the phone as the doorbell rang. 'What am I going to do?'

'OK,' said Serena urgently. 'You're going to be cool and professional. You're going to bear in mind at all times that he is absolutely not to be trusted, and most importantly of all—' the doorbell rang again '—you are *not* going to sleep with him.' She sighed. 'But first, you're going to let him in.'

\* \* \*

'Finally.' Alejandro walked past her into the narrow hallway and looked around with barely concealed impatience. 'I was just about to leave. I assumed you'd had second thoughts.'

'About such a—what was it?—generous opportunity to prove myself?' Tamsin said sweetly. 'Now why would I do that?'

'You tell me,' he replied with heavy irony. 'Are you ready?'

She was halfway up the narrow stairs. 'Nope. Come up.'

Gritting his teeth in irritation, Alejandro followed her, trying not to look at her rear in the skinny black jeans she wore.

'This better not take long. My driver's waiting.'

'Really?' she said lightly. 'Can you drive to Argentina? I thought we'd be going by plane.'

He found himself in a large living space with windows all along one wall and warm old pine floorboards. There was a kitchen area at one end with peacock-blue cupboards and an enormous French baker's rack groaning under the weight of china and pans. The other end was taken up with a huge sofa upholstered in shocking pink brocade and a white furry rug. The whole space was painted in a creamy off-white, and even on the greyest winter morning it was airy and bright.

It was also incredibly messy.

'Have you been burgled, or is it always like this?' he asked, looking around. On the table beside the telephone was a pile of unopened brown envelopes, many of them printed in red and marked 'urgent'.

Stepping over piles of clothes, magazines, discarded shoes and scraps of fabric, he made his way to the door through which Tamsin had just disappeared and felt a dart of heat as he realised it was her bedroom.

'No, and no,' she said haughtily, picking up an armful of bulky winter clothes and shoving them into the bottom drawer of an enormous old *armoire.* 'It's like this because some annoying person forced me to travel halfway across the world at a moment's notice, and then arrived early to pick me up.'

Alejandro glanced at his watch. 'Ten minutes. That's hardly *early*. I assumed you would have packed last night.'

'Oh, did you?' she snapped. 'Well, I think that's one of the many things I find annoying about you, Alejandro. You have no right to assume anything. How do you know that I didn't have other plans last night? Why should I turn my life upside down and cancel everything when you snap your fingers?'

Without letting a flicker of the emotion that suddenly licked up through him at the thought of what her 'other plans' for last night had been, Alejandro bent down and picked up a scrap of fuchsia-pink silk from the floor beside the bed and held it up. It was a suspender belt.

'It doesn't look as if you cancelled anything last night,' he said sardonically, feeling a twist of grim satisfaction as he watched her eyes widen in outrage. For a moment she stared mutely at him as he turned the delicate band of silk and lace around in his hands before tossing it casually onto the bed.

'If you must know I spent last night in my design studio, alone, getting together all the stuff I need to bring with me for work. That's why I haven't had time to tidy up, or pack, because *that's why* I thought you'd hired me—to design your rugby strip for you. If you'd wanted someone with the domestic skills of Snow White, you should have gone to Disneyland.'

She had a point. Maybe he should have, because from what he'd found out last night it seemed likely that Snow White would be about as capable of designing sportswear as Lady Tamsin Calthorpe, and would probably be a lot less scared of hard work.

Leaning against the doorframe, Alejandro shoved his hands into his pockets and watched her thoughtfully. He knew from the press conference yesterday when she had so convincingly denied that there had been any problems with the production of the shirts that she was a virtuoso liar. In fact, identifying when she was telling the truth and when she was making it up was going to be very entertaining. The flight to Buenos Aires was fifteen hours. A challenge like that would pass the time nicely.

He sighed impatiently, letting his gaze wander around the room. The bed was an old Edwardian brass one, piled high with lace pillows and silk cushions, both its head- and-footboards draped with sequined scarves, bead necklaces and bras. The intimate femininity of the place made him uncomfortable. It reminded him of things that he'd resolved to forget. A bottle of perfume on the antique dressing-table instantly brought back the warm, fresh scent of her body; a lidless lipstick beside it conjured an image in his mind of her lips, plump and pink in the moments before he'd kissed her, engorged with desire and scarlet with his own blood as he'd pulled away.

Levering himself away from the doorway in one sharp, aggressive movement, he crossed impatiently to the window. 'I suppose it's pointless telling you to hurry up.'

Tamsin gritted her teeth and very deliberately carried on folding the long linen shirt on the bed. 'If you helped it would be quicker,' she said with exaggerated patience. 'Or is helping anyone an entirely alien concept?'

Alejandro turned round. 'It depends,' he said slowly in a voice that dripped acid, 'whether the person you help is then going to claim they did it all themselves.'

The barb found its mark with cruel accuracy. Tamsin bit back a small gasp of pain and grabbed another plain-white linen shirt from the wardrobe, followed by a faded pair of cut-off jeans and an Indian-print tunic top. 'Forget it,' she muttered through clenched teeth. 'Just don't bother.'

'Don't forget this.' Alejandro picked up the suspender belt from where he'd thrown it on the bed and held it out to her. His eyes glittered with malicious amusement. Tamsin snatched it and shoved it viciously back in the drawer.

'I don't think I'll be needing that,' she said icily, gathering up a pale-blue satin bra and another one in pink candy-striped silk and throwing them in on top of the suspender belt. 'Or these. It's work, remember, Alejandro. I thought we made that perfectly clear.'

Ostentatiously she pulled out three pairs of plain-white cotton knickers, and a white cotton bra and, casting a defiant glance at Alejandro, threw them into the bag. Then she zipped it up.

'There. I'm done.'

'That's all you're taking?'

She saw him glance incredulously down at the bag, and shrugged nonchalantly to cover up her own sense of unease. Half an hour earlier it had been bursting at the seams, now it was half empty. But having Mr Disapproving there had really cramped her style. There was no way she was going to let him watch her pack anything that could remotely be considered frivolous or alluring.

'I think it's enough, since I don't intend to stay long, and I certainly don't intend to—'

He laughed. 'Enjoy yourself?'

'Absolutely.'

'Well, if you're sure you don't want to change your mind—add anything?'

'No. Let's just go.'

# CHAPTER SEVEN

'SOME wine, Lady Calthorpe?'

Tamsin gave a stiff nod of assent. Squashing down a leap of annoyance at the use of her title, she watched Alberto, the uniformed steward, pour pale-gold wine into two long-stemmed glasses.

They'd been airborne for just over an hour, but in spite of the exceptional luxury of Alejandro's private jet she felt nervous and jittery. She'd spent all of the time so far gazing vacantly at a magazine, but couldn't remember a single detail of anything in it. She did, however, seem to have become oddly familiar with the cover of the share report which Alejandro was reading opposite her.

Alberto gave a courteous murmur and melted away, and Tamsin picked up her glass.

'Could you please inform your staff that there's absolutely no need to bother with the whole "Lady Calthorpe" thing?' she said brusquely. 'I never use the title myself, and I prefer it if other people just address me by my name.'

Alejandro looked up from the share report. 'Of course. If that's what you prefer, I'll pass it on.'

His face didn't betray a flicker of emotion, so why did Tamsin get the distinct impression that he was laughing at her? The irritation that had been simmering inside her for the last hour now came bubbling up, like milk coming to the boil.

'Do you have a problem with that?'

He leaned back in his seat, apparently totally relaxed, but his hooded gaze stayed fixed to her face with a sharpness that belied his laid-back body language. 'Not at all,' he said smoothly, throwing the report onto the seat beside him and unfolding a snowy-white linen napkin. 'I just find it slightly... ironic that you're suddenly so keen to play down your aristocratic connections.'

'Ironic?' she snapped. 'In what way *ironic*?'

Alejandro took an unhurried mouthful of wine. 'Well, you clearly have no problem with using them when it suits you, to get what you want.'

Alberto appeared again, carrying two white plates as big as satellite dishes, each bearing a delicate arrangement of pale-pink lobster and emerald-green salad leaves in its centre. He set these down on the table with elaborate care, giving Tamsin the chance to beat back the fury that instantly flamed inside her. She waited until Alberto had retreated again before answering.

'Let's get this straight from the outset, shall we? I love my family. I'm proud of who I am and where I come from, but I have *never* used it in any way to open doors for me in my professional life.'

Toying lazily with a rocket leaf, Alejandro reflected that that wasn't what the guy he'd had dinner with last night had said. A board member of the RFU, he had confided over an extremely good port that there had been no other contenders for the England-strip commission, that the design brief from the chairman's daughter had been the only one under consideration.

'You don't believe me, do you?'

He smiled. 'Not really. I'm prepared to believe that you might *think* that because you have a flat and a job that your life is just like everyone else's. But your family background—'

She cut him off with an incredulous gasp. 'You hypocrite! We're having this conversation on board your *private jet*, for God's sake! What do you know about living like everyone else?'

He felt himself tense, giving a small indrawn hiss of warning. 'The difference is,' he said with quiet venom, 'I've worked for this. For everything I have. I came from nothing, remember.'

He expected her to back down then, to understand that she—the pampered heiress who had never known what it was like to be without anything, particularly not an identity—was on very, very dangerous ground here. But she didn't. Instead she laid down her fork and looked at him through narrowed eyes.

'OK,' she said softly, pausing to suck mayonnaise off her thumb. 'You had it tough. So that made you need to prove yourself, didn't it?'

Her words were like a punch in the solar plexus. A very hard, accurate and unexpected punch.

'Which I'd say,' she went on in the same quiet, even tone, 'means that you're just as much shaped by your family background as I am.'

'Wrong. I have no "family background".'

His voice was like gravel, and the warning in it was blatant. She ignored it. A small frown creased her forehead beneath her sleek platinum hair, but other than that her expression was completely calm as she said, 'Of course you do. Everyone does.'

He gave an icy smile. 'Maybe in your world, but my *family background* was wiped out when I was five years old, when I came to England.'

Her frown deepened. 'Why did you come?'

The pressurised, climate-controlled air seemed suddenly to be charged with tension. Tapping one finger against the polished table top, Alejandro looked out at the blue infinity beyond the window of the plane. He wanted to tell her to back off, that she had strayed into territory that he kept locked, barred and guarded with razor wire, but somehow to do so felt like a denial of who he was and where he'd come from; a betrayal of his father.

And hadn't his mother betrayed Ignacio D'Arienzo enough for both of them?

He kept his tone neutral and his explanation brief. 'Argentina was a troubled country at the time that I was born. There was a military dictatorship. My father and uncles were taken for their involvement with a trade union, and my mother was afraid that we might be next. She was half English, on her father's side, and she booked us on a flight to London the next day. We took nothing with us.'

'What happened to your father?'

The pure, clear sunlight filtering in through the moisture-beaded window of the plane lit up Tamsin's face, turning her skin to translucent gold. She leaned forward, resting her elbows on the table and propping her chin upon them. Her eyes were the cool, shady green of an English woodland in summertime, and they seemed to draw him into their quiet depths.

'Who knows? He's one of thousands of *los desaparecidos*: the disappeared. Neither living nor dead.'

'That's an awful thing to have had to live with,' Tamsin said softly. 'Not knowing...'

He shrugged. 'It allowed me to believe that he was alive.' His smile was brutal. 'Unfortunately my mother didn't share that view. She remarried quite quickly—the man she worked for as a housekeeper in Oxfordshire.'

'Oh,' Tamsin said, and it was more of a whispered sigh than a word. She hesitated, biting her lip. 'But it can't have been easy for her.'

Alejandro rubbed a hand across his forehead. Of course, he should have realised that Tamsin Calthorpe would see it from his mother's side. They were two of a kind. Loyalty and faithfulness weren't on the program. It was all about expedience.

'Oh, I think it was,' he said with brittle, flinty nonchalance. 'I think it was very easy, in the end, to completely reinvent herself and behave as though the past had never happened. The only thing that was difficult was living with the reminder of where she'd come from. Which was where my long incarceration in the British public-school system began.'

While he was speaking she'd been playing absently with the stem of her wine glass, but suddenly she wasn't doing that any more, and her hand was covering his. Her touch seemed to burn him, to sear flesh that already felt exposed and flayed raw.

'I'm sorry,' she said in a quiet voice.

He'd waited six years for that, and the irony of the circumstances in which he was finally hearing it took his breath away. What was she sorry about—his mother's betrayal, or her own?

He moved his hand from beneath hers.

'I doubt it,' he said getting up and giving her a twisted smile. 'Yet.'

Well, actually, he was *wrong*. She was sorry. Very sorry.

Sorry she'd agreed to come with him, sorry she'd ever set eyes on him, sorry she'd made the mistake of responding to him like he was a decent, well-adjusted human being. It wouldn't happen again any time soon.

She was only trying to break down the awkwardness that seemed to exist perpetually between them. She was trying to be *nice*. She couldn't help it if he was bitter, emotionally arrested and had major trust issues.

Tamsin sighed and looked out of the window into nothingness. Major and perfectly understandable trust issues, she thought miserably. His revelations had touched her deeply, and she'd seen his pain behind the hard, cynical façade. She understood why he had so fiercely maintained his Argentine identity during his time in England, even though it had infuriated the management of the England team and had ultimately cost him his place on it. But it was all he had left of his father, and of his old life. He had been trying to stop himself disappearing too.

Beyond the window the light was fading, and the sky was the same leaden grey as the Atlantic Ocean far beneath them. With infinite weariness, Tamsin looked down at the magazine on her knee and read the same paragraph for the hundredth time. 'Next season's key trend will be camouflage', it said.

How appropriate, she thought, stifling a yawn with her hand.

'You're tired.'

She jumped as Alejandro's voice broke the thick silence that had lain between them for ages now. 'Get some sleep,' he said coolly. 'You know where the bedroom is.'

He had shown her when they had first boarded the jet, and she'd been utterly taken aback by such insane luxury. She'd like nothing more than to curl up now on the large bed—which was ridiculously out of proportion with the scaled-down proportions of the plane—and go to sleep, but Alejandro's faintly scornful tone made it impossible to admit that.

Straightening her spine, she blinked rapidly. 'I'm fine. It's your bed, you have it.'

'I have reading to catch up on. Business.'

His cold superiority made invisible hackles rise on the back of her neck. 'Yep. Me too,' she said briskly, picking up her laptop and flipping it open. 'Lots to be getting on with.' The sideways glance she shot him was filled with loathing, but her voice was deliberately sweet. 'After all, the sooner I make a start on this, the sooner I can go home again, and I think we'd agree that would be best all round.'

At least there was one thing they could agree on, Alejandro thought sourly, leaning forward to lower the blind on the window and block out the reflection of her face in the glass. As the darkness had deepened outside her reflection had gradually come to life, like a Polaroid photograph developing, and he had found his eyes were constantly drawn to it, noticing the way she chewed her bottom lip when she was reading, and how her fingers stroked the hair behind her ears.

All of which was completely irrelevant to the company he was currently thinking of buying, he thought scathingly, returning his attention to the share report.

Business was a game like any other, Alejandro had discovered. You had to observe the tactics of your opponents, recognise their strengths and exploit their weaknesses. You had to know when to hold back, and when to surge forward and press your advantage home. And you had to be able to do it without emotion.

He was good at all that.

Unconsciously now he found himself turning towards Tamsin, and felt an instant dropping sensation in his chest. She was sitting perfectly straight, her legs tucked up to one side of her on the wide leather seat, the laptop balanced on her thigh. The screen was blank, and her head was bent forward slightly so her long fringe fell down over her face.

She was asleep.

In one fluid movement Alejandro got out of his seat and crossed the narrow space between them, removing the computer from her knee and putting it on the table in front of her. Then, slipping one arm behind her neck, he slid the other beneath her knees and scooped her up, holding her against his chest.

Her head fell back, rolling against his arm and giving him a perfect view of her small face with its wide cheekbones and full, generous mouth. His heart gave a painful kick as he looked down at her. For six years he had painted her in his mind as a sort of cross between Lolita and Lady Macbeth, but it was impossible to reconcile that image with the soft, fragile girl in his arms. As he watched, her lips parted slightly and she gave a small, breathy sigh of contentment, and then tucked her head into his body.

With a low curse he turned abruptly and carried her to the back of the plane, kicking the door to the bedroom open and depositing her quickly on the bed. A cashmere blanket lay folded neatly at its foot, and he shook it out and laid it over her, briskly, his hands not making any contact with her body at all.

And then he left, as swiftly and as brutally as he had come, slamming the door shut behind him.

Tamsin's eyes snapped open the moment he was out of the small room.

A few seconds ago she'd been so tired she'd felt as if her eyelids had lead weights attached to them, but now she was wide, wide awake. Her heart was thumping against her ribs like a caged animal, and every cell of her body seemed to vibrate and thrum with painfully heightened awareness. It was as if someone had just injected her with concentrated caffeine.

Being in his arms for those few moments had done that to her.

She pushed back the blanket he had laid over her so perfunctorily and sat up, running her tongue over her dry lips and looking around her in something like desperation. When she'd felt his arms around her, felt the hardness of his broad chest against her, she'd thought for a dizzy, disorientated moment that she was dreaming and had given herself up to the bliss of being close to him...

Oh, no. She'd *sighed*, hadn't she? She'd actually sort of *moaned* with pleasure.

Springing up from the bed, she paced restlessly around it. She'd known it was going to be difficult, being thrown into such close contact with him, but she hadn't even come close to realising how hard. They were only halfway there, for crying out loud, and already she'd managed to make an almighty fool of herself—not once but twice.

Panic rose within her as she thought of the hours that stretched ahead, but there was no escape, and nothing to be done except try to keep her mind off Alejandro D'Arienzo altogether. Work was the answer, but her laptop was in the cabin, and there was no way she was going back out there to get it—although if she could just find some paper and a pen she could make a start on some sketches now. Her gaze fell on a little drawer set into the sleek cabinetry beside the bed, and she ran her fingers along it, trying to locate the concealed catch.

It sprang open, immediately revealing a blank notepad. Tamsin gave a little hiss of triumph as she took it out, looking underneath to see if she could see a pen.

There was one. Right there in the bottom of the drawer, half-buried beneath a lot of small, silver packets.

With a trembling hand she reached out and scooped them up, staring at them as a sick feeling spread through the pit of her stomach and an assortment of unwelcome images filled her head: Alejandro, his skin dark against the white sheets, his hair falling over his face as he lifted his mouth from the pouting, scarlet lips of a sultry beauty and reached over to the drawer for condoms.

The door handle turned with a muffled click. Tamsin gave a gasp of horror and slammed the drawer shut, stuffing the condoms into the back pocket of her jeans and spinning around as the door opened and Alejandro appeared.

'I thought I heard something. So, you're awake.'

'Of course,' she said as casually as possible, holding up the pad. 'As I said before, I've got work to do. I haven't got time to sleep.' She ran her shaking hands through her hair in the manner of someone who was perfectly relaxed and didn't have her pockets stuffed with condoms.

Alejandro advanced into the room. Apart from the fractional lift of his eyebrows his face was as expressionless as ever, but his eyes glittered with sardonic amusement. 'I see,' he said quietly. 'You were doing a pretty good impression of it before.'

'That wasn't sleep. That was a power nap.' Even to Tamsin's own ears her voice sounded ridiculously shaky, but she couldn't help it. It was the effect of being in this small space with him. This small, intimate space, with the huge bed stretching between them like a taunt, and the images conjured up by her own pitifully overactive brain refusing to go quietly. She turned away, hoping that it would help her keep her composure. 'I won't need proper sleep for ages now,' she said airily.

'Oh, you won't? That's good news.'

His voice was soft, hypnotising. Unwillingly, she felt herself turning back to face him. Unsmiling, he was looking at her steadily as he took hold of the bottom of his dark cashmere jumper and pulled it over his head. Tamsin's heart-rate doubled instantly and her mouth went dry.

'Why?' It came out as a hoarse croak. The pressurised air seemed to be filled with the sound of her throbbing heart.

His mocking smile was like icy water in her face.

'Because I assume that means you won't mind me having the bed.' He held open the door for her. 'Don't work too hard.'

The sky was pale pink by the time Tamsin set aside her laptop and rubbed her hands wearily across her face. Her eyes felt gritty and her head and neck ached with exhaustion, but she had a good basis for four different designs to show Alejandro and the board of Los Pumas. Letting her head fall back against the seat, she closed her stinging eyes and allowed herself a moment of triumph as she took a couple of deep breaths in, savouring the smell of fresh coffee that was coming from Alberto's galley kitchen, and the faint, skin-tingling scent of lime that was coming from…

Her eyes flew open. Alejandro was standing over her, smiling wryly. His hair was slicked back and damp from the shower, and in the golden morning sunlight he looked like something from an advert for men's expensive grooming products—relaxed, tanned, fresh, and gut-wrenchingly gorgeous.

'Good morning,' he said. 'I take it you slept well?'

Tamsin sat bolt upright and pushed her hair back from her face. 'No, I didn't, I—' she spluttered in protest. 'I wasn't asleep. I've been working! That was just—'

'Another power nap?' he said, with mocking gravity. 'Of course. Anyway, you'll be pleased to know that we'll be landing in a few minutes.'

She would have liked nothing more than a shower and a change of clothes, but there was no time, so had to content herself with brushing her teeth and splashing her face with water in the tiny but opulent shower room, emerging just in time to fasten her seatbelt as the plane came in to land.

It touched down with a bump and came to a standstill on the tarmac. Tamsin felt desperately impatient to be out of the confined space, and she watched as the ground crew placed the steps alongside. Alejandro didn't seem to be in any hurry, hardly glancing up from his coffee as the door was thrown open.

Tamsin gave a small gasp.

Two uniformed men appeared at the top of the steps and came into the body of the plane. In the sunlight from the open door, she caught the dull gleam of guns at their belts as they spoke in low, rapid Spanish to Alberto.

'Alejandro!' she croaked, instinctively moving towards him and reaching out to touch his arm. Her heart was hammering and her skin felt suddenly clammy. There seemed to be an iron band around her chest, making it difficult to breathe. Beside her Alejandro felt very strong and very safe. 'Alejandro—look.'

'Hmm? Is something wrong?'

'They have guns.'

Slowly Alejandro raised his head. His expression of total

impassivity didn't flicker as he looked across at the men, but surreptitiously he reached to unfasten his seatbelt.

'Don't make any sudden moves, and do exactly as I say,' he said very quietly.

Swallowing hard, Tamsin nodded, desperately trying to resist the urge to throw herself into the safety of his arms. He leaned closer to her to whisper into her ear, and she closed her eyes, focusing on his voice, knowing absolutely that if anyone could protect her, it would be him.

'You can start by getting out your passport,' he breathed.

Her eyes flew open, and her gasp of fury and outrage was lost as the two uniformed men spotted Alejandro and came forward with jovial cries of welcome, uttered in exuberant Spanish. While they greeted each other in a flurry of handshaking and back-slapping, Tamsin gritted her teeth and waited for the burning in her cheeks to subside as it dawned on her that these were customs officials.

This was no ordinary plane, and Alejandro D'Arienzo was clearly no ordinary passenger here. There was no queuing to get through customs for him. Here the mountain came to Mohammed.

As Alejandro spoke to the men in rapid Spanish, Tamsin listened in fascination to the rise and fall of his low, musical voice. This was the language he had been born to speak, she thought distractedly. It was like suddenly seeing a beautiful piece of art in its proper setting. He had always spoken perfect English, so that anyone hearing him would never guess that he had neither heard nor uttered a word of the language for the first five years of his life, but there was a slight stiffness in his speech. A formality that contributed to his aura of distance.

Not so now when he spoke Spanish. He came alive. His voice flowed across her like a caress. A promise. An invitation. She felt her stomach tighten and heat spread downwards through her as her imagination supplied fanciful meaning to the delicious-sounding words she couldn't understand.

And then suddenly she realised that they were all looking at her, and that one of the men, the swarthy, bearded one, was coming towards her. She stiffened, throwing back her head and looking questioningly at Alejandro as the man gave her a courteous nod of his head and made a gesture she didn't understand.

'What do they want?' she said warily.

'Relax. It's just a formality. They're from customs. They just want to give you a quick search.'

Tamsin felt her eyes widen in shock and fear as the bearded man advanced on her, and she found herself automatically moving towards Alejandro. 'Oh, for goodness' sake,' she hissed. 'What do I have to do?'

'This.'

He stood in front of her and lifted her arms. Then, keeping his face perfectly still, his hands came to rest lightly on her waist and he murmured, 'Good. Now, stand with your legs apart.'

A wave of liquid heat crashed through her. She looked up to find his eyes on hers, filled with smouldering amusement. The bearded customs official moved round so that he was standing behind her, and began skimming his hands over her.

His touch was completely professional, totally impersonal, but pinned beneath Alejandro's shimmering, golden gaze Tamsin felt like she was naked. She kept her chin held high, biting her lip to stop her breath from escaping her in ragged gasps of fury and humiliation as Alejandro looked at her, and kept on looking.

'Is this really necessary?' she said through clenched teeth, aware that nerves had made her voice take on a cut-glass haughtiness that was wholly unnatural. 'I'm hardly a drug-smuggling criminal.'

Alejandro's eyes darkened to the colour of rich honey, and she watched as his mouth curved into a smile of pure, mocking pleasure at her discomfiture as the customs officer's hands moved down her body, lightly touching her ribs beneath her breasts, grazing her waist, her hips. 'Unfortunately, they don't know that. Your title means nothing here, Lady Calthorpe. Nothing good, anyway,' he drawled, the husky gentleness of his tone belying the cruelty of his words. Tamsin's insides melted as her eyes blazed with defiance.

The customs man's hands were moving upwards again, lightly patting the outsides of her legs, her hips, her bottom...

He stopped, and said something in Spanish. Alejandro gave a curt nod.

'He'd like you to empty your back pockets, please.'

Oh, God.

No.

Tamsin felt the blood rush to her face in a shaming tide of crimson as panic gripped her by the throat and squeezed. 'What? I've got nothing—why should I?'

Alejandro's voice was like velvet now. 'Your pockets.'

Setting her chin and lifting her head, Tamsin moved her hand to the back pocket of her jeans. Alejandro watched her with the intensity of a lion watching a deer, his eyes glittering with an emotion Tamsin couldn't and didn't want to interpret.

At that moment she didn't want to do anything except vanish in a puff of smoke. Or be kidnapped by aliens.

Her fingers fumbled for the back pocket of her jeans.

About now would be good—*just before she had to pull out a handful of condoms in front of Argentine customs officials and Alejandro D'Arienzo.*

She held her hand out, and then looking defiantly at the customs man, uncurled her fist. Frowning, the man looked uncertainly at the foil packets lying on the palm of her upturned hand. Time seemed to hang suspended for a moment while he picked one up and looked at it.

His shout of laughter echoed through the body of the small plane. Clutching his sides with mirth, he turned round and showed the other guard, who joined in the hilarity.

Smoothing back her hair, composing her face into an expression of haughty resignation, Tamsin's gaze flickered across to Alejandro's face as she steeled herself against the blistering mockery she expected to see there too.

Her heart stopped and her throat tightened as she saw that it was as cold and hard as marble.

## CHAPTER EIGHT

AND THAT WAS WHAT YOU called being caught red-handed.

Red-handed and red-cheeked, Alejandro thought contemptuously as he recalled the colour that had risen into her upturned, defiant face as she'd stood there with her outstretched hand full of condoms before shoving them back into the pocket she'd taken them from. She'd said nothing, probably because she was intelligent enough to realise that even she, Tamsin Calthorpe, who always managed to flirt and charm her way out of any awkward situation, had backed herself right into a corner this time. It was exactly that habit of seducing herself out of trouble that had just been exposed.

Because it was embarrassingly obvious that that was exactly what she'd intended to do. She'd clearly planned on using every trick in the book so that by the time they landed in Argentina he would be eating out of her hand, and the whole inconvenient business of the job she was supposed to be doing would be forgotten.

Her confidence in her own powers of seduction was quite breathtaking. Alejandro wondered how many men had fallen for it.

Tapping one finger irritably against the walnut inlay of the car door, he stared unseeingly out of the window at the familiar, flat landscape of the Argentine pampas. Usually his heart lifted whenever he travelled this stretch of road towards San Silvana, which was the only place that had ever felt like home, the only place he could ever relax. But now, with Tamsin Calthorpe sitting beside him, the possibility of being able to relax seemed as remote as walking on the moon.

The chauffeur swung the car smoothly between the tall gateposts of San Silvana, and Alejandro caught his first glimpse of the house in the distance through the avenue of eucalyptus trees. At least, unlike the close confinement of the plane, San Silvana was big enough so that they wouldn't be on top of each other.

*Unfortunate turn of phrase.*

'That's where you live?'

Her voice interrupted his thoughts, and he turned to look at her. She was leaning forward, craning her head to see the building that was still tantalisingly screened by the canopy of the trees, and for a moment he was caught offguard by the sweetness of her profile, with its small, slightly upturned nose and her softly bowed lips.

He gave a brusque nod. 'Welcome to San Silvana.'

'It's pretty impressive.' She was trying to sound nonchalant, but Alejandro picked up the hint of irritation behind the words. He felt a momentary spark of satisfaction. What had she expected—some primitive shack with a corrugated-iron roof and a tin bath?

'Civilisation has spread to this far-flung corner of the globe, you know,' he said dryly. 'Did you think that gracious living didn't extend beyond English shores?'

'Of course not,' she snapped. 'I'm just intrigued, that's all.'

'By how I came to own it?' he demanded.

'Well...' Once again, a rose-pink blush was creeping up into her cheeks. 'You did say that you'd come from nothing, and that you'd worked for everything you have,' she said crossly. 'So what exactly do you *do* for a living?'

'I'm in business.'

They rounded the last corner of the sweeping drive, and Tamsin lowered the window and leaned her head out, both to get a better look at the house and escape his maddening scrutiny. The heat closed around her like a blanket as up ahead the house came properly into view. Built at the end of the nineteenth century in Spanish style, San Silvana rose up from the flat plains of the Argentine pampas like an ornate wedding cake.

When Alejandro had told her that he lived on an *estancia* she had imagined something rustic and low key, a comfortable old farmhouse or something. This fairy-tale palace was just one more shock to deal with.

She wasn't sure that her very hasty packing was going to be adequate.

'What business?' she muttered. 'International arms dealing? Opium farming?'

'I buy companies. Businesses that are struggling or facing liquidation. If they're worth saving, I invest in them and get them back on their feet. If they're not, I strip them down and sell off the assets.'

He spoke with a clinical detachment that sent a shiver down Tamsin's spine and brought back the cold feeling inside her chest, like she was choking on an ice cube. She thought of the pile of bills at home that she hadn't been able to face opening.

'Nice,' she said bleakly.

'Not always. But life in the real world isn't always *nice*.'

He didn't bother to keep the stinging disdain from his voice. The car came to a standstill in front of the house, and Tamsin fumbled with her seatbelt, keeping her head bent so he couldn't see her face. He obviously assumed a girl like her would know nothing about the harsh realities of business.

If only.

'I know that, thank you very much,' she said with admirable calm as the driver opened her door and stood back. 'But it doesn't make it any easier if you're the one whose assets are being stripped down and sold off. Of course, I don't suppose any of that matters to you.' She got out of the car and looked pointedly up at the majestic white frontage of the house. 'Profit is obviously what counts.'

He didn't reply. *Couldn't* reply, she thought smugly, crossing her arms. He clearly couldn't think of any smart way of ducking out of that one, when the evidence was right in front of them both. Keen to press home her advantage, she carried on.

'Of course, I don't suppose it would occur to you that behind every business failure there's a whole lot of heartache. Broken dreams can't have a price slapped onto them and be sold on, you know.'

Still no answer, eh? She'd really got him there. Turning round with a superior smile, she prepared herself to face the hostility that would tell her he knew she was right.

But he wasn't there. The driver was unloading their baggage from the back of the car, but there was no sign of Alejandro at all. Giving a gasp of outrage, she looked around, and saw his broad, retreating back just about to disappear around the other side of the house.

'Alejandro!'

Stamping her foot in frustration, she watched him stop and turn round, shading his eyes against the sun as he looked back at her.

'Yes?'

His voice was totally flat, utterly indifferent to the fact that he'd just brought her halfway around the globe and abandoned her on the doorstep. She opened her mouth, but, at the sight of him standing in his faded jeans and soft white T-shirt, with the sun turning his skin to burnished bronze, she felt the words die in her dry throat. Suddenly she wasn't angry any more. She was just tired. And lonely. And unsure.

'What do I do now?' she croaked.

He didn't hear. Dropping his hand, he was already starting to turn and carry on in the direction he'd been taking. 'Just go in,' he called over his shoulder. 'Giselle will show you to your room.'

'Giselle?'

'My PA. She's on her way.'

He was almost at the corner of the house now. 'Where are you going?' Tamsin shouted, wincing at the blatant neediness in her voice.

'It's the polo season,' he said simply. 'I'm going to the stables.'

The stables.

OK, well that was one place he was quite safe, because there was no way Tamsin was going near any horses. Which left her little choice but to do as he'd said.

Wearily she climbed the stone steps to the front of the house. Ahead of her the double doors were thrown open against the sticky heat of the day, and the interior of the house looked cool and dim. She peered into the gloom for this Giselle, preparing herself to confront some glossy super-model type with melting brown eyes and hair like oiled mahogany. Tentatively she pulled an iron bell-pull, wincing slightly as she heard its ring echoing through the silent house in the distance, but almost immediately a door opened and rapid footsteps clattered across the polished wooden floor towards her.

'*Hola!* Forgive me, Señorita Calthorpe, how terrible that you are left to find your own way in. Come in, come in!'

Tamsin smiled as relief crashed through her. The woman who came bustling towards her was in her sixties at least, short and comfortably rounded with a faded rose-patterned apron covering her ample bosom, and her grey hair swept up into a magnificent arrangement on the top of her head. 'Oh, please, don't worry. You must be Giselle?'

The woman gave a snort of disdain and rolled her eyes. She opened her mouth to speak but was at that moment interrupted by a cool, husky voice from the doorway behind them.

'Thank you, Rosa, I'll look after Lady Calthorpe now.'

Tamsin's heart sank as the sultry Latin beauty from her tortured fantasy stepped elegantly out of her imagination and into real life, swaying seductively across the faded silk-rug on impossibly sexy four-inch heels. She held out a slender, scarlet-tipped hand as her lips spread into a smile that didn't reach her eyes.

'Lady Calthorpe. I'm Giselle, Alejandro's personal assistant.'

Whatever her other talents—and Tamsin could quite easily imagine—it became clear as Giselle led her through the spacious rooms and wide, high-ceilinged corridors of the beautiful house that Alejandro hadn't hired his PA for her skill in making small talk or putting people at ease. Even walking three paces ahead of Tamsin at all times, and speaking only when absolutely necessary, she still managed to emit signals of unmistakable unwelcome. At least with Giselle on his staff he wouldn't need a guard dog, Tamsin thought sourly.

Finally they came to a suite of offices at the back of the house. She followed Giselle into a room that was long and sunny, with glorious views out onto the kind of lush garden that people back in England paid to visit. The room was furnished in a simple, modern style, which contrasted with the heavy grandeur of the rest of the house, and at one end a large, square fabric-cutting table had been set up, alongside a desk complete with state-of-the art computer equipment and a sewing machine.

'This is where you will work,' Giselle said, flicking her curtain of dark hair over her shoulder. Looking around, Tamsin gave a slow nod of approval. It certainly compared pretty favourably with her scruffy studio above the tattoo parlour in Soho where the England strip had been created. But then she spotted the other desk. The one in front of the heavy mahogany door to an adjoining room.

'And this desk?'

'Is mine.' Giselle gave Tamsin a smile that reminded her of an alligator—languid, but dangerous.

'How cosy,' said Tamsin, with only the barest hint of sarcasm. Obviously Alejandro had instructed Giselle to keep an eye on her, and make sure that she wasn't going to import a busload of 'proper' designers the moment his back was turned. 'Where is Alejandro's office?'

In a gesture that managed to be both indolent but distinctly proprietorial, Giselle waved her manicured hand in the direction of the door behind her desk. 'There. If you'd like to see him, just ask,' she said loftily.

'Thank you,' said Tamsin, smiling through gritted teeth.

It would be a cold day in hell before that happened.

'So, it sounds like you've got the kit design in hand, but how's it going otherwise? D'Arienzo's place is supposed to be quite something.'

Tamsin hesitated and looked out over the rolling sweep of emerald lawn to the wide, open plain of the pampas beyond. Steve Phillips was the production manager of the sportswear company who'd manufactured the England kit, and she'd got to know him pretty well in the months that they'd worked together. The Great Shirt Disaster had certainly been a very bonding experience, but, even so, she didn't know him well enough to answer his question honestly.

'It is,' she said bravely. 'The weather's gorgeous, and I've spent the last couple of days working on my laptop in the garden under a massive tree. It sure beats being in a stuffy old studio any day.'

At the other end of the line she could hear groans of envy as Steve relayed her message to the rest of the office. Imagining them all amidst the chaos of fabric samples and coffee mugs, with the traffic roaring past on the rainy Archway Road outside, sent a wave of homesickness crashing through her.

If only they knew, she thought bleakly as she said goodbye

and hung up. San Silvana might be heaven on earth, but even paradise could get pretty lonely when the only other people in it hated your guts.

It was a relief that in the three days since they'd arrived she hadn't seen Alejandro at all, but what bothered her was the sour, churning certainty that Giselle was seeing him all the time.

She'd managed just one tense morning in their shared office before it had all got too much. Giselle's blank hostility was bad enough, but Tamsin could deal with that. No, it was the sudden warmth and animation she showed when she was on the phone to Alejandro that had really got on Tamsin's nerves. Watching for the third time as Giselle had rotated languidly on her leather office-chair, swinging one long, slim leg and curling a strand of dark hair around her finger as she'd spoken into the receiver in low, husky Spanish, Tamsin had realised that she would never finish the commission if she stayed working there. Mainly because she would end up throwing her laptop at Giselle's head.

Taking her things and venturing outside, she'd found this shady spot under a huge, spreading cedar tree and had set up a makeshift office. From here, for the last two days she'd been liaising with the manufacturers in London, as well as cleaning up and finalising the four designs she'd come up with on the plane, until they were all at a stage she was happy with.

But despite the fact the work was going smoothly she felt miserable and on edge. The feeling reminded her of when she was a child, after she'd had the accident. She remembered being terribly anxious for a while, secretly and shamefully afraid of hurting herself again, quietly trying to avoid situations that seemed even remotely unsafe. That was how she felt again now, only it wasn't her elbow she was trying to protect. It was her heart.

Suddenly she became aware of a sound in the distance that made the hairs stand up on the back of her neck and hot needles of fear prickle all over her scalp. For a moment she thought she was imagining it, that thinking about the accident had brought it all back, but the unmistakable sound of hoofbeats grew louder and closer. Desperately she scrambled to her feet and moved around to the other side of the tree as a refuge.

The horse appeared from behind a thicket of shrubs about twenty metres away. Relief burst inside her as she saw that there was a rider on its back—someone who would be able to make it stop or keep it well away from her. Leaning against the rough trunk of the massive cedar tree for support, she waited for it to pass.

It was galloping, but there was something almost leisurely about its pace, giving the impression of plenty more power waiting to be unleashed from its glossy, muscular quarters. And then her heart seemed to stop altogether as she realised with a jolt of agony and deep, primal recognition that the rider was Alejandro.

He was wearing knee-length boots over his jeans, but no hat. Even Tamsin, who knew nothing about these things, could see that he sat on the horse with natural grace and ease, so that the glossy, vibrant animal seemed to be almost like an extension of himself. Suddenly noticing her, he pulled the horse up so that it swung round on its hind legs like a ballerina. Tamsin felt faint with terror.

'So this is where you're hiding. I was about to send out a search party.'

'Hiding? I'm not hiding,' snapped Tamsin. And then, realising she was in fact cowering behind a tree, she stepped forward. Brushing imaginary dust off the front of her white linen shirt, she tried to keep the fear from showing on her face as she kept one wary eye on the stamping, sweating horse. The other was all too easily diverted by the sight of Alejandro's long thigh, just about level with her gaze. Mesmerised, she saw the powerful muscles flex as he held the horse steady.

'Giselle says you haven't been in the office since the day before yesterday,' he said tersely. 'She was worried.'

Tamsin gave a sugary smile. 'Oh, how *sweet* of her. Do reassure her that I'm fine.'

For a moment his eyes seemed almost iridescent with anger, and Tamsin felt a sick lurch inside her as she wondered if she'd overstepped the mark.

'Maybe you could do that yourself when you get back to your desk and get on with some work.'

Taking a step forward, she crossed her arms in front of her, determined to hide her fear. 'I *am* working.'

'Out here?' With faint incredulity he looked at the laptop on the ground, obviously switched off, and the mobile phone and bottle of suncream beside it. 'Working on your tan, maybe.'

'No. Working on your designs,' she replied hotly. 'Not that you seem to be very interested any more. I notice you're not exactly chained to your desk, either.'

The horse was twitching and dancing, tossing its head and rolling its eyes alarmingly. But none of that frightened her half as much as the lethal note in Alejandro's voice when he said, 'I don't have to answer to you, Tamsin.'

Her fingers tightened around her arms, the left hand instinctively cupping the right elbow. Her heart was pounding like a sledgehammer in her chest as she looked up at him.

'Implying that I have to answer to you?'

'Exactly.' At the lightest movement of Alejandro's legs the horse surged forward, he circled once around her. 'I think it's about time I had a look at what you've been working so hard on. I'll see you at seven o'clock tonight. At the pool house.'

# CHAPTER NINE

EXPERT hands moved slowly, firmly, over Alejandro's aching back and stiff shoulders, smoothing out the taut muscles, pressing away the tension.

Or that was the idea.

Lying on his stomach in the low, bluish light of the steam-room, he shifted restlessly, moving his head to the other side where he could see the smooth curve of Madalena's pretty behind as she leaned over him, massaging his back with long, firm strokes.

The steam closed around him, seeping into his tight muscles. He needed this, he told himself grimly. The Barbarians rugby match had cost him a lot of time away from polo, and he'd spent the last three days in the saddle, working obsessively on his technique and getting to know the new horses ahead of tomorrow's match.

'You're very tense, *señor*,' Madalena said softly.

Making a huge effort, Alejandro flexed his fisted fingers and tried to relax, tried to focus his mind on the game. The new palomino was a dream to ride, and he was looking forward to trying her out tomorrow. She had an energy and a responsiveness that told him that whatever he asked of her she would give—quicker, better, more bravely than he would ever have expected. With her gleaming golden colouring and silver-blonde mane, she was also beautiful.

*Now who did that remind him of?*

'Please, you must try to relax, *señor*.'

Madalena's fingers pressed into his tense, aching shoulders and Alejandro gritted his teeth.

*Mind on the game. Concentrate.*

Tomorrow's game was an important one. San Silvana and La Maya were old rivals, and the eight players on the field would be some of Argentina's highest ranking and most respected, himself included. *That* was why he'd been practising for twelve hours at a stretch for the last three days. Of course it was. It was to ensure that they got back the title taken from them by La Maya last year, and had nothing at all to do with trying to avoid...

'That will be enough, Madalena,' he snapped, sitting up abruptly.

The masseuse stepped backwards in surprise, her oiled hands held out in front of her. 'But, Señor D'Arienzo, I've only just begun. There's a lot of tension in your lower back and your thighs—'

'I said *enough*.'

Skilled and professional though it was, tonight her touch did nothing but set his teeth on edge. There was no way he could endure the feel of her hands working down his body, over his heated skin, while his mind refused to concentrate on tactics for tomorrow's match, and instead insisted on returning to the same dangerous territory.

Tamsin bloody Calthorpe.

Madalena slipped quietly away and he threw himself down onto a mosaic-tiled bench, breathing in the dense, pine-and-lavender-scented steam. The heat seared down inside him, scouring his throat and lungs, and he ran a hand over his sweat-slicked face.

She really was incredible. He'd thought that at least she'd

make some pretence of working on the commission, but Giselle had informed him that apart from a couple of hours on the first day she hadn't even seen Lady Calthorpe. This afternoon, seeing her sitting outside, it had become abundantly clear why. She could hardly get her London contacts to send through designs for her to pass off as her own with Giselle sitting only a few feet away, could she? No wonder she'd looked so terrified when he'd come across her. She'd even tried to hide.

He sighed, letting his head fall back onto the warm tiles, and staring into the clouds of steam that billowed and swirled in the subdued lighting. She'd be here any minute to show him what she'd supposedly been working on. Maybe then he'd be able to cut through the deception and the pretence and expose her once and for all for the fraud she was.

And after that he would deal with the other bit of unfinished business that lay between them like an unexploded bomb.

For six years he'd berated himself bitterly for letting lust overcome judgement that night. However, what was starting to bother him more was not what he'd done, but what he *hadn't* done. If he'd been carrying condoms, as he usually did, if he hadn't left her, if he'd had her then on the cool, stone bench, he wouldn't be so tortured now by what he'd missed out on.

Back then he'd been punished for a sin he hadn't even had the chance to commit, he mused darkly. And, since he'd already paid the price, wasn't it only fair that now he got to taste the fruit?

The sun was beginning to slide down a sky the colour of watermelon as Tamsin made her way down to the pool house, her laptop under her arm.

She was early by at least half an hour, but it was quite deliberate. She wanted to make sure she had the laptop set up and all the information ready to be accessed in a couple of clicks before Alejandro got there. She knew that, the moment he came within a couple of metres of her, efficiency, competence and clear-headed professionalism were likely to be the first casualties.

She couldn't afford to let that happen. Having just spent the last hour in her room trying on every single combination of all the clothes that she'd brought, her confidence was at a low enough ebb already, and it wouldn't take much to get her well and truly flustered now.

If only she'd brought her red Temperley dress. That always made her feel strong and in control. Or the little lime-green shift that she'd designed herself for Coronet, with the tiny black cardigan that slipped over her shoulders...That would be perfect for a warm evening like this. Cool and slightly sassy, but still professional.

Grimly she looked down at the pink and gold Indian-silk tunic she'd finally chosen in desperation. Usually she wore it over jeans, but she'd decided that that would send out a message that was way too casual, so she'd left her legs bare. At least they were brown from three days outside, she thought bleakly, stepping into the cool gloom beneath some eucalyptus trees. It was unfortunate that she looked like she was dressed for the beach rather than a professional presentation, but that was his fault. If he hadn't been so...so...*there* while she'd been packing she might—

Tamsin started as a woman in a short white dress, like a nurse's uniform, appeared from behind the row of trees. She walked with a languid grace, her treacle-dark gaze barely flickering in Tamsin's direction as she murmured, *'Buenas tardes,'* and passed her, going back in the direction of the house.

She might not have felt so out of place here among all these beautiful women.

Although maybe she would. Maybe she was kidding herself that clothes and fashion and this season's colours made the slightest damned bit of difference, because underneath she just wasn't sexy enough. That was why he'd walked out on her six years ago, leaving her with her dress around her ankles and her pride in bleeding ribbons.

The pool house, like the rest of San Silvana, had an atmosphere of grand European colonialism. A tall, square building, with white pillars and arched cloisters, from a distance it looked like an ancient Spanish church, but as Tamsin drew closer she could see that the old building was combined with elements of startling modernity. One wall had been completely removed and replaced with sliding-glass panels, which opened out onto an area decked in smooth, dark wooden boards.

Tamsin put her computer down on the big, square table in the centre of the deck and sat down in front of it, stubbornly refusing to be impressed by the stunning surroundings.

Cool and professional, she thought, squinting down at the screen. Cool and professional, that was how she needed to play this. Briskly she clicked open the files containing the designs, and the technical specifications and rough costings for each, and checked that all the information was there. And then she checked again. And then she sat back, chewing on her lip and glancing at her watch.

Still twenty minutes to go before he arrived. Her stomach gave a nervous lurch that was neither cool nor professional and yet again her gaze flicked towards the house, looking for him. Maybe it had been a mistake to be so early after all. She'd be a nervous wreck by the time he finally showed up.

Pushing back her chair with a harsh, scraping sound, she stood up. Now that the rosy sun had slipped down below the trees it was much cooler, and, rubbing her arms through the thin silk of her dress, she strode crossly into the pool house. The cold; that was what it was. The sudden drop in temperature was responsible for the goosebumps on her skin, not nervous anticipation of his arrival.

Inside the building the swimming pool itself only took up about half of the space, with the rest of it being given over to a sunny seating area, where wicker armchairs arranged beside an old wooden bar-area gave an impression of colonial elegance. There was also a smaller spa-pool, and a wet area, where water cascaded down from a lion's head shower, and in the wall at the far end were two frosted-glass doors. Tamsin found herself walking towards them, as curiosity fought with cynical indifference, and won.

The first door opened into a changing room. Two huge antique-looking porcelain basins stood side by side beneath a big-carved wooden mirror, and a kingfisher-blue wrap hung on a hook on the wall beside them. Hesitantly she walked over and ran a hand down its slippery folds. It was made of exquisitely fine silk, which shimmered and changed colour beneath her reverential fingers as she held it, at one moment appearing blue, the next changing to dark, shiny green.

It was lovely.

She took a sharp step backwards, letting the fabric fall from her hand, and watching it slither back into its shiny, secretive folds. Oh yes, it was certainly lovely. And Giselle no doubt looked great in it. Stiffly, Tamsin turned and left the room, rubbing her hand down her thigh as if the sumptuous fabric had contaminated it.

She pulled open the second door.

Instantly she was enveloped in a warm billow of pine-scented steam that curled itself around her and drew her forward. The room in front of her was dark and cave-like, lit by tiny blue lights set into the tiled floor, and in the thick swirl of steam it felt like she was stepping into a cloud on a hot summer's night. She took a couple of steps forward, tipping her head back and inhaling deeply as the door swung shut and the warmth embraced her.

Oh, this was good.

This was more than good.

The vaguely astringent fragrance of pine and lavender soothed her frazzled nerves as the heat eased the tension from her rigid shoulders. Pushing both hands through her hair, she closed her eyes, tipped her head back and breathed in again. And out, with a low sigh of pleasure.

There was nothing to see but blue-lit whiteness, shifting and melting into the darkness beyond. Blindly, Tamsin moved backward, groping for the seats she guessed would run along the wall. Her fingers brushed something hard and warm, and for the briefest fraction of a second a frown passed across her forehead as she tried to make sense of what she was feeling. She moved the flat of her hand further downward...

She froze.

'What the...? *Oh, my*...!'

Then her heart, which seemed to have stopped for a few beats, went into painful overdrive as she felt a lazy hand caressing the back of her leg. 'No, please, don't feel you have to stop,' said the all-too-familiar drawl. 'That was just getting interesting.'

She should move. Of course she should. Away from the fingers that were tracing languourous circles of bliss on her thigh. Away from the sense of menace that was now enfolding her along with the steam. But...

'I had no idea you were here. I thought...'

She felt the back of Alejandro's hand brush her inner thigh. She heard him sigh softly and felt him lever himself upright. The movement caused the steam to eddy and whirl, enabling her to see him in the gloom.

Her breath hitched in her burning throat.

God, he was magnificent. Naked apart from a pair of dark swimming trunks, he was sitting with his head thrown back in an attitude of dangerous ease. His skin gleamed like burnished copper in the low, bluish light, and her eyes travelled automatically to the sun tattoo that blazed on his chest. The steam thickened again, like drawing a veil between them.

'If you've come for our meeting, you're early.'

Low-pitched and languid, his voice seemed to curl around her like the steam. She could still feel the sensation of his fingers on her skin, almost as if they'd left a pattern etched into her flesh, and had to force her mind back to what he was saying.

'I know. I came to prepare.'

The haze of steam made everything sound sensuous. Even her own voice, in the dark and quiet and the obliterating mist, sounded husky and intimate.

He laughed softly, and the sound was like a kiss. 'Of course. I should have guessed you would. I'm looking forward to the rest of your *presentation*. But...' Tamsin could detect a sinister edge to his honeyed voice that made her spine stiffen. 'I warn you, my expectations are high.'

'If you're trying to intimidate me, it won't work.'

'No? And yet you sound nervous.'

She heard him move, sensed him coming towards her. Her body was hot and damp, the silk of her tunic was clinging to it like a second skin, but as he got closer she felt another, secret surge of moisture inside her. Desperately hoping for nonchalance, she let her head fall back against the wall she was leaning against and raised her knee, placing her foot flat against the wall.

'Nervous?' she said carelessly, 'Not in the slightest. Why would I be—?'

She broke off with a gasp as she felt his hand slip beneath her damp dress, against her heart. Her treacherous, thundering heart.

'You tell me.'

He was close enough now for her to see his smile and the dull, triumphant gleam in his eyes. 'Ah, but I forgot,' he went on quietly, his thumb very lightly stroking the sweat-beaded valley between her breasts. 'You can't, can you?'

Her whole body seemed to harden, throbbing in time to the painful beating of her heart beneath his hand. Her nipples were tight buds of concentrated longing. She wanted to move away but a terrible, silken languor had stolen over her, brought on by the caress of his voice and his gentle, insistent touch.

'You can't,' he breathed, 'Because honesty isn't exactly your strong point, is it, Tamsin?'

The words were like sharpened spurs on tender flesh. Pain tore through her, instantly bringing her back to her senses. Viciously she knocked his hand away and made to move past him to the door. But, with the lightning reactions that made him such a success on both the rugby pitch and the polo field, Alejandro reached out and grabbed her right wrist, pulling her back so she almost fell against him.

Tamsin went very still. Everything in her was telling her to pull back from him, but his grip on her wrist was like steel, and an instinct born of years of habit warned her not to make any sudden movement. Her arm was very slightly twisted, and bitter experience had taught her that it would take only the slightest movement now for the fragile set of the bones in her elbow to shatter again.

Slowly she tipped her head and met his gaze. His eyes were shadowed, impossible to read in the gloom. 'You know nothing about me,' she hissed, as adrenalin pulsed through her in waves and her breath came in shallow gasps. She frowned, desperately tensing her body against the urge to press itself against him.

'Wishful thinking, sweetheart,' he murmured.

And then—Tamsin wasn't sure afterwards how it had happened—some slight movement or change in their position caused red-hot daggers of agony to shoot up her arm. Momentarily distracted she went completely weak, falling against him as her lips parted to let out a small cry of shock, pain and misery. He let go of her wrist, his arms closing round her to support her, his mouth coming down on hers.

And she kissed him back. She didn't want to, but she could no longer hold back the tidal wave of annihilating desire crashing through her. Raising her hands, she gripped his face, feeling the stubble rasp against her palms as she slid her fingers into his damp, tangled hair. His skin was hot and wet.

Just like her. Just like she was.

The moist heat of the steamroom was nothing compared to the liquid fire that was building inside her as he stood in front of her, hard and strong and beautiful. His hands moved down from her waist, slipping beneath the flimsy fabric of her dress and then sliding up again, over the moist skin of her midriff, her ribs, up to her breasts. The high note of yearning that came from her mouth as he pushed down the lacy cups of her bra and her hard nipples brushed his palms was lost in his kiss.

His knee came between her legs and automatically she parted them, feeling herself pushing her hips downward, forward, against the rock-hardness of his thigh. Inside her head there was nothing but darkness and space.

And heat. So much heat.

Their mouths tore at each other, tongues clashing, probing, retreating, in the same primitive rhythm as the movement of her hips. It was as old as time, and yet it was making Tamsin feel things that she'd never felt before.

Not since the first time.

The first and only time.

She jerked her head back, gasping for air as Alejandro's fingers dug into her waist.

'Alejandro...'

Darkness surged into the space behind her eyes, and before it overwhelmed her completely she made a lunge for the door, pulling it open and feeling the blissful rush of cool air wash over her feverish body. She took a couple of stumbling steps forward before she felt her knees give way and the roaring in her ears become thunderous, consuming her, sucking her down...

Alejandro caught her as she fell.

Bending to scoop her up, he gave a muffled curse. Desire still rampaged violently through him, and holding her lithe, pliant body against him was hardly helping. Her skin was hectically flushed, and her hair was dark gold with sweat, swept back from her face to show the angularity of her cheekbones.

Lust twisted painfully inside him, mixing with some other, less simple emotion.

*Concern*, he told himself scathingly. She was that English-rose type. He should have known she wouldn't be able to take the heat.

Striding over to the shower that was set into the wall, he turned it on full blast and stood beneath it, letting cold water cascade down, and taking the force of the powerful jets on his own shoulders so it ran onto her in gentle rivulets. As soon as the water touched her hot skin she stirred, opening her eyes and struggling to be released from his arms.

'Just wait,' he said harshly, his grip tightening around her.

'Let me *go*.'

He did as she said, and immediately she swayed and faltered, grabbing hold of him and coming to a standstill with her forehead against his chest. Glancing down at the back of her slender golden neck, Alejandro felt his sardonic 'I told you so' smile die on his lips as want kicked him viciously in the ribs. He just hoped she didn't look down or she'd find out exactly what havoc she was playing with his self-control.

He took her firmly by the shoulders and turned her round, so that the water was falling onto her back instead of his. And so that he was standing behind her. She made a murmur of protest.

'You overheated,' he said tonelessly. 'You need to cool down. Just stand there.'

She nodded, and he watched the water trickling down the back of her neck, making shimmering trails on her apricot skin. For long minutes he held her, until she stiffened and stood properly upright, and he released her.

'Sorry,' she mumbled, without turning round. 'I don't know what happened.'

'I do.' He turned off the shower, and as the splashing sound of the water died away the room suddenly seemed very quiet. 'You fainted in the heat. It seems that you can dish it out, Lady Calthorpe, but you just can't take it.'

She spun round, and Alejandro was surprised by the vehemence in her eyes. The pink-and-gold dress thing she was wearing was plastered to her body, so that her bra and pants were clearly visible underneath. Alejandro recognised the plain-white cotton underwear she'd thrown into her bag as she was packing, trying to make herself look so pure and virginal.

'Dish it out? Since when do I *dish it out*?'

She was shivering violently from the cold water now, and she spoke through teeth that were clenched to stop them chattering. The lips that had been so plump and reddened a moment ago had now taken on a bluish, bloodless tinge.

Without bothering to answer her, he strode over to take a towel from the pile on a rack near the shower and, throwing it over his shoulder, came back towards her.

'Take that wet thing off,' he said curtly.

With obvious effort she jerked up her head. 'Oh, I will...' she said through the castanet rattle of her teeth. 'But if you think I'm doing it here, you're horribly mistaken.'

And, grabbing the towel from over his shoulder, she stalked off into the changing room.

# CHAPTER TEN

COOL AND PROFESSIONAL?

Oh, please. What a joke.

With a low groan Tamsin looked at her reflection in the mirror above the twin basins. The pale face that stared back at her with the dark smudges of mascara beneath the eyes and her hair plastered so unbecomingly to her skull was awful enough, but much worse was the memory of the wanton creature who had writhed against Alejandro in the humid haze of the steamroom.

Oh, God, the embarrassment.

But the pleasure too. The forbidden, delicious pleasure of kissing him, of feeling his hard body against her, and of fooling herself for just a moment that everything was as simple and as right as it felt. That they were just a man and a woman drawn together by mutual attraction, and he wasn't playing cruel mind-games with her.

She closed her eyes and rested her forehead against the glass for a moment before turning on the tap and splashing her face with water, rubbing away the mascara smudges. That was what he was doing; she was certain. He had brought her here determined to prove that she was nothing but a clueless posh girl with not an ounce of talent, but maybe he was beginning to worry that he'd got it wrong. And that would never do, would it? she thought furiously, rubbing her face vigorously with a soft towel. Alejandro D'Arienzo would rather die before admitting he'd made a mistake. He'd rather *seduce* her. Even though he'd made it abundantly clear that he found her about as attractive as yesterday's breakfast, he'd still rather kiss her into a frenzy just to undermine her professionalism and give her the best chance of completely fluffing the presentation.

And he'd nearly succeeded.

Who knew how far she would have gone if she hadn't fainted?

Furiously she peeled the soaking top upwards over her head, hesitating for a second before taking her sodden underwear off too, and then towelling her body and her hair with hard, decisive strokes as anger set like cement around her bruised heart.

Finally she grabbed the kingfisher-blue robe and pulled it on. It felt like adding insult to injury to wear something that belonged to Giselle, but she hardly had a choice. It was either wear the robe or do this thing naked.

It felt like heaven against her bare, tingling skin, and in the mirror she noticed with a jolt of surprise how the colour made her green eyes seem almost aquamarine. Not that you'd notice when the rest of her looked such a mess: her hair was beginning to dry already, and without the help of a ton of styling products was as soft and floppy as a baby's. Her skin, in protest at being steamed alive then blasted with icy water, was now glowing like a nuclear disaster.

Wonderful, she thought acidly, belting the robe a little more tightly as she went to the door. She was a fashion designer about to give the presentation of her life, and she looked like a seaside landlady after a night on the gin. One day she was sure she would look back on this and laugh.

It just wouldn't be in this lifetime.

Alejandro heard the door open behind him as she came out of the changing room, but he kept on swimming, keeping his mind focused on the rhythm of his stroke. Reaching the far end of the pool, he twisted beneath the water and, breaking the surface again, saw her walking towards him.

His smooth, effortless passage through the water almost faltered.

The blue silk-robe she was wearing clung to her slight figure, and with her hair white-blonde and falling softly over her face, and her skin glowing like sun-kissed rose petals, there was a simplicity about her that sliced into some unguarded part of him.

He reached the other end of the pool and ducked beneath the water again. The silent green world beneath the surface brought sense flooding back. Clearly he hadn't been entirely immune to the temperature in the steamroom either, and was suffering from an overheated brain.

Tamsin Calthorpe, *simple*?

Yeah, right. In the same way that Cruella De Vil was a dog lover, maybe.

Out on the deck she bent over the laptop she'd left on the table, but Alejandro kept swimming, cutting through the water with clean, forceful strokes, putting off the moment when he'd have to get out and face all of this. His head, which up until now had been so preoccupied with outing her as a talentless heiress with an influential daddy, was now unwilling to actually confront the evidence he had waited so long to see.

He couldn't even begin to unravel the reasons behind that.

Hauling himself out of the pool, he reached for a towel and dried the water from his face. His jeans were lying on a teak steamer-chair in the corner and he reached for them, checking that she was out of sight before slipping out of his wet trunks and putting them on. Normally he wouldn't have bothered getting dressed again, but this wasn't normal. With the feel of her lips, her thighs, her breasts still imprinted on his body and his mind, he could hardly sit beside her—knowing that beneath that blue silk thing she was naked—in *swimming trunks*.

Taking a couple of bottles of chilled beer from the cooler in the bar, he went out onto the deck. The heat had gone, and an apricot-tinted moon now hung like a jewel low in the pink sky. Tamsin glanced up as he put the beer in front of her.

'Thanks,' she said neutrally. 'I hope Giselle won't mind me borrowing this? It was all I could find.'

Alejandro let his gaze wander over the robe. Over her body *in* the robe. 'How do you know it's Giselle's?'

She looked up again, surprised. 'Well, I just assumed...'

Alejandro took a mouthful of beer. 'You assumed wrong.'

Two small creases appeared between her fine eyebrows, and she looked at him suspiciously. 'Then who?'

He shrugged. 'I don't remember. But, since I undoubtedly paid for it, don't worry about it. Now, shall we start?'

'Yes. Yes, of course.'

*That's it; look at the screen, Tamsin. Open the file. Ye-es, that would be the one marked 'Los Pumas'...*

Scowling with concentration, Tamsin attempted to force her shaking fingers to operate the laptop's irritating touch-cursor pad, swearing softly under her breath as the tiny flashing hand flailed wildly across the screen. '*I don't remember*'? *How many women did this guy have*?

'I'll start with the design that I think works best,' she heard herself saying as she brought it up on screen, and was surprised at the steadiness of her voice. He was standing behind her chair, and even though she couldn't see him she was painfully aware of the nearness of his broad, brown chest as he bent slightly to look at the screen.

She glanced up. The rose-tinted evening light made the skin on his hard, high cheekbones gleam like polished copper. As they flickered over the image his eyes were hooded, dark and unreadable.

'OK,' he said tersely. 'Next.'

That was it. Her best design, dismissed in one curt word.

'This one is more traditional.' She was aware that the effort of keeping the tremor from her voice was making it sound cold and hard. 'The colours of the Argentine flag are—'

'I can see. Next.'

*Bastard.*

Nervousness was beginning to give way to anger. Why did he have to be so rude? The third design appeared on the screen. Tamsin took a deep breath.

'You'll notice that the front of the shirts in each design has a space left somewhere for the sponsor's name.'

'Yes. Next.'

Her finger hovered over the file, but she didn't click to open it. Had no one ever told Alejandro D'Arienzo that if you wanted something you had to ask nicely?

'Do you have any idea who the main sponsor might be yet? Only it can have a surprising impact on the rest of the design if the company name has a particular font that has to be used, or a specific colour that their brand relies on.'

'That's something that the board are still in negotiation over. We won't know for some time yet,' he said with barely concealed impatience. 'Now, can I see the rest of the designs?'

Tamsin hesitated. 'There's only one more,' she said stiffly. He was towering over her. She could smell chlorine on his skin, but beneath that the bass note of his own warm scent vibrated in her head as she let the cursor hover over the file for her fourth design. Her throat felt dry as she clicked to open it.

This was the one she had designed with him in mind.

She took a deep breath. 'The shirts are designed to fit close to the body,' she said quickly, feeling her cheeks begin to burn. Her voice was a husky croak, and she paused, clearing her throat and slicking her tongue over her lips before continuing.

'In this one I moved away from having the traditional puma on the chest, and put the sun from the Argentine flag instead.'

Her heart was beating so hard she was certain he could hear its strong, primitive throb filling the dense twilight around them like a jungle drum. He came closer still, standing so that he was almost brushing her shoulder, and she could feel his warmth and hear the faint sigh of his breathing.

'On the flag the sun appears in the centre. You've put it to one side.'

Tamsin swallowed. 'Yes,' she whispered.

'Why?'

The single word was ground out through clenched teeth. For a moment Tamsin closed her eyes, willing herself to stay strong for just a bit longer. He hated the designs. He hated her. Things couldn't get any worse, which meant they had to get better soon, after this...didn't it?

Carefully she stood up, and tucked her chair under one table neatly before looking up at him. 'I did it for you. I was thinking of you.' And with her fingertips she very lightly touched the sun tattoo on his chest.

Alejandro felt his whole body go rigid at her touch, which was as soft and fleeting as the brush of a butterfly's wings. He was aware of a swell of emotion building up inside him, and concentrated on making sure his face didn't betray a flicker of what he was feeling inside.

His face, or his body.

So it was all her own work. No corporate-design team could have come up with something so personal. For a moment he couldn't speak as he watched her gather up her things, and bend down over the computer as she closed down the files, stroking her finger over the mouse-pad in a way that sent shivers across his skin. The light from the screen illuminated her face, and he noticed that the silk robe had fallen open slightly, revealing most of one small, lush breast.

He felt like he'd just taken a kick in the stomach from a fifteen-stone forward.

She folded the screen down with a click and picked it up.

'Perhaps now you'll believe that I am responsible for coming up with the designs, if only because you hate them all,' she said with a low note of irony in her voice. 'I'm sorry if you feel you've wasted your time bringing me over here, and obviously I'll arrange my own flight home as soon as possible.'

'No.'

The word had left his lips before he could stop it. He saw her freeze. Pausing, he thrust his hand through his hair as he fought to regain control. 'I don't hate it, and I haven't wasted my time,' he said very evenly. 'On the contrary. My plan was always to extend the commission, once the rugby designs were agreed. I'd like you to stay.'

Her mouth opened, but for a second she seemed to struggle to speak. 'Extend the commission?' she stammered eventually. 'Extend it to what?'

'Polo,' he said simply. 'Shirts for the San Silvana polo team.'

The warm twilight seemed suddenly to be heavy with invisible charge, like in the moments before a big storm. Tamsin shook her head, quickly, looking away from him and out over the garden to where the moon was climbing into a sky that was still streaked with fire from the slowly setting sun.

'I can't,' she said with quiet ferocity. 'I know nothing about polo.'

He gave an impatient shrug. 'So stay and find out. You can start tomorrow. There's a big match between San Silvana and La Maya, our biggest rivals. Come and watch.'

A shivering breeze briefly stirred the evening air, lifting her silken hair back from her face for a second before all was still again. A handful of tiny stars had appeared, and even they seemed to be poised, waiting for her to answer. She had half-turned to face him, the laptop clutched against her body like a shield, and he could see the indecision on her face. Complicated emotions clashed and warred inside him.

'OK. I'll do it.'

The tension Madalena had felt earlier in Alejandro's shoulders was instantly released. Managing to resist the urge to punch the air in triumph, he gave a curt nod of approval.

'Good.'

Quickly, as if she couldn't trust herself not to change her mind, she walked across the deck back towards the house, her eyes downcast. Alejandro watched her go, feeling frustration claw at his insides like a hungry beast as her robe fluttered open, giving him a glimpse of one slim, tanned leg as she hurried past him.

'Oh, and Tamsin?'

She swung slowly round to face him. Alejandro thrust a hand through his hair and kept his tone utterly nonchalant. 'After the polo, tomorrow night, there's a party at the club. You might find that useful to attend too.'

'*Useful*,' she repeated ruefully. 'Well, thank you. That's very… considerate of you.'

He scowled. 'So you'll come?'

'If it'll help my work, how can I refuse?'

What the hell had just happened back there?

Tamsin walked quickly, holding the laptop awkwardly against the slippery silk of the robe, and simultaneously trying to keep the front from opening up to reveal too much bare flesh, although the words 'stable door' and 'horse' seemed painfully relevant there.

She brushed that particular embarrassment aside. Showing a bit of leg seemed pretty irrelevant in view of the fact that she'd just agreed to stay on at San Silvana. Stay on and design *polo shirts* next, for crying out loud.

When it came to Alejandro D'Arienzo, she seemed to have some minor issues around saying the word 'no'.

For the sake of her mental health and her poor, foolish heart she really ought to be rushing back to her room to book herself on the first flight back to London and pack her bags. He liked her designs—whoopee—which meant that just as soon as she'd met with the Pumas' board and had a decision on a final design she'd be free to go. To get back to her business and her life.

Anguish gripped her, squeezing her insides as she realised the terrible truth behind those words.

What business, and what life?

Coronet was her life, and it was sinking fast. Sally had phoned earlier full of more doom and gloom. A rip-off of one of Coronet's signature dresses from the upcoming spring collection was already in the window of a high-street retailer on Oxford Street, she'd said. She'd sounded faintly accusing, like it was all Tamsin's fault.

This polo commission was not only a financial lifeline, it was a stay of execution, postponing the time when she would have to return to London and deal with it all. And postponing the time when she would have to leave Alejandro. Because, even when he was making her feel about two inches tall, she felt more alive in his presence than she ever had before.

And that, of course, was the real reason why she'd agreed to stay.

Her thoughts rushed onwards to tomorrow and what she'd just agreed to do, and she felt sweat break out between her shoulder blades at the prospect of spending an entire day that close to horses. Her elbow ached just thinking about it. And then, she thought with a rising sense of dread, once the horse part was over there was the party he had mentioned, which she could picture with horrifying clarity. Polo was the most exclusive, the most expensive of sports. What had she let herself in for?

But, more to the point, *what the hell was she going to wear*?

## CHAPTER ELEVEN

THE PRINTER CLICKED and whirred into life, spitting out a succession of pages which Alejandro removed from its jaws without looking up.

The cup of coffee that Rosa had brought him earlier was cold and untouched at his elbow, and the only light in the room came from the glow of his computer screen and the glacial light of the moon falling through the long, uncurtained windows. Flicking the switch of the brass desk-lamp beside him, the company report on Coronet London was thrown into sharp black-and-white relief before his tired eyes.

For the last few hours he'd scoured the Internet, tapped the few business contacts in London he knew well enough to call out of hours, and looked under every stone he could think of in his pursuit of information about Tamsin Calthorpe's company.

At the beginning he'd still been pretty sceptical. OK, so she'd come up with some interesting ideas for Los Pumas. He'd been surprised, he wasn't ashamed to admit it, but, having just browsed through endless paparazzi snaps of celebrities wearing Coronet on red carpets around the world, now he was a little less quick to dismiss her. Little Lady Calthorpe had set up quite a brand.

With a spasm of desire he remembered the grey dress she had worn at the post-match party; the way the gossamer-light fabric had hugged her body, the rather dramatic effect it had had on *his* body when she'd turned round and he'd seen the back.

All right, he couldn't deny it. Her clothes were good, so why was she losing money all over the place? Turnover looked healthy enough, and share prices were—

With a sudden sound of impatient self-disgust he threw down the report and stood up.

What was he doing?

This was the woman who'd lost him his job. The only question he should be asking himself about her business was why the hell he cared.

Tamsin took a deep breath and closed her eyes, wincing painfully as she made the first cut into the king-fisher blue silk. The sound of the scissors slicing through the fabric had an ominous resonance in the silence of the shadowy house.

She opened her eyes and looked down at the slash she had just made in the beautiful silk robe. Oh well, there was no going back now, she thought, cutting quickly up the line she had marked on the silk as she'd stood in front of the mirror earlier. It wasn't as if she had any choice, anyway, since she could hardly wear any of the stuff she'd brought with her, all of which would make her look like a Sunday school teacher at an orgy.

This was her best chance.

It was a long shot though. In her student days Tamsin had frequently raided second-hand shops and vintage markets for items to customise or remodel, but now the stakes were slightly higher. If she turned up at this glamorous event tomorrow looking like she was wearing something from a thrift shop, it wasn't only her personal pride that would suffer; Coronet's fate would be sealed.

The world beyond the pool of lamplight over the table faded as she snipped and pinned, working to some vague plan that existed only in her head. It was like alchemy. On the flat surface of the cutting table the fabric looked horribly raw, but she knew that it was important to keep going, to keep faith. Actually, it felt good to be working like this again. Sally handled most of the hands-on, cut-and-stitch practical side of the business while she did the designing, and she hadn't realised how much she'd missed it. Just the feel of the silk beneath her fingers was indescribably soothing.

It was very late and the big house was dark and silent around her as she slipped off the oversized white-linen shirt she wore over her bra and pants and gingerly stepped into her new creation. It was difficult to tell what it looked like with no mirror, but it *felt* pretty damned good.

Shutting the office door to keep in the noise, Tamsin stepped out of the dress again and sat down at the sewing machine. This was her favourite part: when the pins were replaced by stitches as a finished garment flowed from beneath her fingers.

The whirr of the machine seemed deafening in the moonlit quiet. Gritting her teeth, hoping that the house was big and solid enough to muffle the noise, she kept her head down and sewed on.

She was naked.

That was his first thought, before his eyes caught the narrow strap of a pale-pink bra across her back, and matching figure-hugging pants. Standing behind her at the door of his office, watching her bent over the sewing machine in the pool of lamplight, Alejandro felt the desire that had been beating a quiet, constant rhythm in accompaniment to his heart suddenly get louder, faster and a lot more insistent.

Testosterone, he thought dryly. Such a wonderful asset on the rugby pitch and the polo field, and yet such a pain in the backside in so many other situations. Especially when this girl was around.

'Your brief was to design the shirts, not make them.'

# CHAMPAGNE SUMMER

He barely raised his voice, but she seemed to sense his presence. Twisting round on her seat, her hands flew to her cheeks and then, as she realised that she was wearing next to nothing, to cover her chest. Making a quick lunge, she grabbed the white shirt that lay discarded on the floor by her chair and hastily shrugged it on.

'What are you doing here?'

'Working. You see, I do spend some time chained to my desk, although admittedly not during conventional office hours. More to the point, what are you doing?'

She glanced down at the puddle of blue silk in front of her, which shimmered like oil on water in the light of the lamp. 'Oh. This is for the party.' Their eyes met and she gave a faint, self-deprecating smile. 'Oddly enough, I didn't pack anything suitable to wear.'

The image of her standing in her bedroom with her arms full of clothes, that defiant, combative light in her eyes, came back to him. 'Of course not,' he said gravely. 'You didn't come here to enjoy yourself.'

She turned away, but not before he'd seen the pink blush stealing over her cheekbones, and he wondered if she was thinking of the steamroom. 'No. Well, I hope it's alright to... do this.'

'Be my guest. *Can* you do it?'

The light above the table in front of her shone through the fine linen of the shirt she had slipped on, so Alejandro had a clear view of the outline of her body. 'That remains to be seen,' she sighed. 'It's been a while since I made anything that didn't have to stand up to being grabbed in a scrum.'

'Given the behaviour of most polo players, and the way that these parties tend to end up, you might be wise to apply the same principles on that,' he drawled, trying to make light of the lust that was circulating through his veins like pure alcohol.

Maybe he'd been wrong to ask her to the party. Knowing her track record with the England rugby team, putting her in a room full of predatory polo players would be like letting an excited child loose in a theme park. She wouldn't know what—or who—to go on first. Crossing the room towards her, he felt the acid burn of primitive sexual jealousy as he wondered whose bedroom floor that dress would end up on in twenty-four hours' time.

'This is what you really do, though, isn't it?' he said abruptly, fingering the fluid blue silk and attempting to turn his mind, and the conversation, back to business. Her business, and why the hell it was in such trouble.

She didn't look up, hesitating before saying in a low voice, 'Yes.' The sewing machine started up again and he watched her slender, agile fingers guide the fabric through to the end of the seam. Then she stopped, and in the sudden silence gave a small, sarcastic laugh. 'It's what I used to do, anyway. I'm not sure there'll be much opportunity left to do it any more when I get back to London.'

'Why?'

'The business isn't going well.' Her head was bent, her silken fringe falling down over her face and hiding it from his view while her fingers went on working, deft and sure, finishing off the seam she'd just made. And then, so unexpectedly that for a second he thought he'd imagined it, a tear fell, glittering in the lamplight before sinking into the silk in her hands.

Emotion ripped through Alejandro like a flash-fire, a complicated mix of surprise, lust and a primitive urge to protect her. A primitive *ironic* urge, given how she'd screwed him over in the past.

She stood up, pressing her fingers to her cheeks, rubbing the tears away. 'Oh, God. Sorry,' she said with a gust of a laugh. 'How ridiculous. I never cry. Honestly, *never*. This is *so* stupid.' She backed away from him, swiping away the tears that kept falling with the heel of one hand as she bent to collect some scraps of material from the floor and gather sheets of paper together. Her movements were clumsy and uncoordinated, and a moment later she had knocked a box of pins onto the floor.

'Oh, sod it,' she moaned, dropping to her knees and trying to pick them up with shaking fingers. 'It's supposed to be lucky when you pick up a pin, isn't it?' She laughed bitterly. 'Maybe my fortunes will change now.'

'Perhaps I could help?'

'You're lucky enough already,' she muttered. 'Anyway, I can manage.'

'I wasn't talking about the pins.' Alejandro leaned down and took hold of her elbow. 'I meant help with your business.'

She went completely still for a moment, and then let him pull her to her feet. As she stood before him he could see the silvery tear marks on her flushed cheeks. Her eyes were the intense, glittering green of the garden after a sudden downpour.

'No. No. Absolutely not. Please, you mustn't think that's why I told you. It's fine. I'll sort it out myself, one way or another. I wouldn't dream of imposing my trivial business problems on you.'

The vehemence in her voice surprised him almost as much as her distress. He had got used to thinking of Tamsin Calthorpe as a girl who had nothing more serious to worry about than which designer handbag to buy next. It was taking some time to adjust to this new perspective on her.

'You'd hardly be imposing.' And from what he'd read the problems were hardly trivial, either. 'It is how I make my living, after all.'

'Oh, yes. I forgot. You buy up failing companies.' Trying to pull away from him, she gave a shaky laugh. 'You'll be stripping my assets before long.'

His grip on her elbow tightened. 'It won't come to that.'

'No?' She sounded angry now. 'Unfortunately, I don't have your confidence.'

*Maybe not, but you do have a very rich father*, said the cynical voice in his head. It cut through the cyclone of emotions, reducing them to an uneasy whisper in the back of his mind, but the lust that had been spitting and sizzling inside him for the last week was harder to dampen. She was looking up at him now, her eyes sparkling with angry tears, her cheeks flushed. Alejandro felt dizzy with want.

'Then let me help.'

Tamsin felt her resolve weaken. His voice was rough, but his gaze held her, and it felt like lying in a pool of sunlight. Strength, capability, total self-assurance radiated from him, and she wanted nothing more than to let herself sink into his arms, to let him take over, take everything on his broad, powerful shoulders.

'I...'

Unconsciously she relaxed the arm that he was holding, dropping it closer to her body so that his fingers touched her breast.

Her lips parted and a small gasp escaped her. It was barely audible, hardly more than a breath, but it was all it took to plunge them off the edge of the abyss around which they'd been circling since earlier.

His lips came down on hers, slowly, languidly. Heat exploded inside her as his tongue met hers and they began their erotic dance. His arms went round her, drawing her in close to his body so that she could feel his warmth and strength, and the hard, exciting pressure of his arousal through his clothes. His big hands were gentle on her back, and through the boneless, melting haze of desire she felt safe.

*Safe?*

What the hell was she thinking?

Who was she trying to fool?

With all her might she pushed against his chest, breaking free of the circle of his arms and stumbling backwards. She wasn't safe with this man. She was in more danger with him than with virtually any other man on the planet.

Alejandro D'Arienzo had the capacity to hurt her like no

one else, and it would be the kind of hurt that would make the trauma of watching her business go under seem like a broken fingernail in comparison.

'Tamsin.' His low, fierce growl reached her as she ran for the door, biting down on her lip to stop herself crying out in anguish and confusion. She yanked open the door and ran into the dark corridor beyond.

In the darkness and moonlight everything was faded to ashes and pearl. Tamsin ran through the house on bare, soundless feet, thinking only of getting away from Alejandro, knowing that if she spent another second with him she'd crumble, and the silent battle that had raged between them since the moment she had faced him in the tunnel at Twickenham would be lost.

He had won anyway. All along she had maintained the struggle, but the most important victory had been his right from the start. Her heart had been his from the moment he'd first touched her six years ago. Before that, even, when she'd papered her bedroom walls with his pictures and kissed them every night before she'd gone to bed.

The game was lost. All she was fighting for now was her dignity and her pride.

From behind her in the gloom she heard a door open, and footsteps on the polished floor. Her pulse rocketed and adrenalin flooded every cell. He was coming after her. She let out a whimper of panic, looking around in desperation for somewhere to hide.

*And what was that she'd just been telling herself about pride?*

Quickly she ran across the hallway, making straight for the stairs. The moon was pouring molten silver through the high window beyond, lighting the staircase as brightly as a stage set. Tamsin's heart felt like it would burst out of her chest as she raced up the first few steps, but then she missed her footing and fell forward, knocking her shins painfully on the stair edge.

Two at a time, lithe as a panther, he was coming up the stairs towards her. With a gasping sob, Tamsin struggled to her feet, flattening herself against the wall as he approached.

'Are you alright?' His voice was like black ice.

'Yes,' she gasped.

'Good,' he said with sinister courtesy. 'Well, if you haven't got the excuse of any broken bones, perhaps you'd like to tell me what the hell you're playing at?'

'I'm not playing at anything,' she spat. 'We agreed. I'm here to work. That's as far as it goes.'

'I see. And since I've approved your designs there's no need for you to resort to any more of your seductive little business incentives?'

His words sliced into her like razor blades, cutting her so deeply that for a second she just felt numb. And then suffocating pain kicked in.

'No! You can't surely think that I would do that?'

Standing in front of her on the half-landing, with the moonlight falling on his huge, broad shoulders and silvering his dark hair, he'd turned into a statue. His physical perfection was like a taunt. 'What?' he said, and there was a hard, cruel note in his voice that she hadn't heard before. 'Use sex as a means to an end, to manipulate or betray? *Can't I?*'

'You *bastard*,' she breathed, stumbling to her feet. Her hands were balled into fists as she went towards him. Anger was closing her throat, making her feel like she was choking.

Alejandro turned round. His face was chilly and remote but his eyes glittered with malice. 'That's exactly how it looks from here, Tamsin, and, let's be honest, you do have previous form. Why else would you keep leading me on and then backing off?'

'Because I'm scared!' The words were out of her mouth before she could think, high and loud, a wail of anguish that echoed through the close night. 'I'm scared because I've never done this before with anyone except you, on the night you walked out on me!' He stood motionless before her, his face a silver mask in the moonlight. 'I'm a virgin, Alejandro. A pathetic, clueless virgin, with no more experience, no more seduction tricks or bedroom strategies to make things any less tedious than they were back then. *That's why!*'

He didn't move.

'Tamsin...' The word was a hoarse rasp. She carried on backing away, tears streaming silently down her face.

'Hilarious, isn't it? she laughed scornfully. 'Absolutely priceless. I'm so sorry for the embarrassment caused.'

And with that she pushed past him and ran up the stairs to her room.

This time he didn't try to follow her.

# CHAPTER TWELVE

'SHE'S BEAUTIFUL, ALEJANDRO. Where on earth did you find her?'

Absent mindedly fastening his leather knee-pads over his white polo-breeches, Alejandro was about to reply, 'London,' when he realised that Francisco was referring to the new palomino mare.

He smiled wearily, ruefully, at his teammate. 'Palm Beach. She's very green, no match experience, but she feels like a natural and she's a joy to handle.'

He bent his head again, hiding his face and concentrating on buckling the leather straps as a wave of emotion smashed through him. He and Francisco were friends as well as teammates, but the near-telepathy they shared on the polo field meant that Francisco would be quick to pick up on any hint that Alejandro had something on his mind, and the last thing he wanted to do was have to explain about Tamsin.

Not when he didn't understand what the hell was going on himself.

He stood up, picking up his helmet as he walked grimly towards where the ponies waited, tied up in the shade of the tall trees that ringed the ground. The palomino mare was standing slightly apart from the others—old hands who were all languidly resting a bandaged leg in the heat and dozing with their eyes closed against the flies. As he approached he could see that the little palomino was tense and alert, quivering slightly.

She reminded him of Tamsin the night he'd met her, set apart from those other girls with their practised, confident charm.

He had got her so wrong, and now, somehow, he had to try to put things right.

He hadn't seen her this morning, but had sent Rosa up with coffee and a message that he would like her to accompany him and the grooms to the match and sit with them all in the pony lines to watch the game. It was a peace offering; a considerable concession. Before a match he usually made sure distractions were kept to a minimum, and apologising to a woman and talking about feelings had to qualify as a distraction of nightmare proportions.

*No thank you*, the reply had come back. She would prefer to watch from the stands and would make her own way there with his driver. And Alejandro had realised that not being able to talk to her, not being able to explain, was going to be a far more serious distraction all day.

Francisco and the other two team members were standing together in their emerald-green shirts, the colour of which represented the lushness of the San Silvana landscape. Alejandro joined them, knowing that as the captain it was up to him to summarise their tactics for each chukka in the match and say something suitably inspiring.

But now, like last night, words failed him.

Looking across the sunny ground, his eye was drawn to a figure in the stand. Amongst the diamond-draped glitz of the polo wives and girlfriends, Tamsin's understated beauty set her apart. Dark glasses covered the eyes that would have outshone the most dazzling emerald, and she was wearing a simple, pale-grey tunic top that covered her arms.

Alejandro felt his heart twist.

With Herculean effort he dragged his attention back to the three men in front of him and managed a grim smile.

'A lot rests on today. We have everything to fight for, everything to prove.'

Tamsin had never seen so many beautiful, glamorous, groomed women in one place. Sitting in the stands, surrounded on all sides by gleaming golden flesh bedecked in designer silks and diamonds as big as billiard balls, she felt as out of place as a dandelion in a bouquet of exotic blooms.

Not that it mattered. Bleakly she recalled the look on Alejandro's face last night when she'd spilled out the truth about herself. It wasn't just surprise, or even shock. It was total horror.

He hadn't even managed to say anything. This morning's invitation, sent via Rosa, definitely came under the heading 'too little, too late'. Even if it hadn't been for her pathological fear of horses, there was no way Tamsin would have accepted his patronising offer to join him and the grooms in travelling to the match. What was she, some awkward child to be appeased with a treat?

Shrinking further down in her seat, she tucked her knees up in front of her and opened her sketchbook, glad of the sunglasses that hid her reddened eyes.

It'll be fine, she told herself severely. All she had to do was get some idea what the game was about and how the kit had to perform. There were—what?—seven other players on the field. She didn't even have to look at...

*Oh, God.*

A sudden burst of applause signalled the arrival of the teams. Tamsin's fingers tightened convulsively on the pencil in her hand, jerking it against the page so that the lead broke as her gaze went straight to Alejandro. Instantly she felt the air whoosh from her lungs and her insides melt with scorching desire.

Shadowed by his black polo-helmet and a day's stubble, his face was as hard and grey as granite. In white breeches and leather boots, and a green San Silvana shirt with a number two on the back, he looked so impossibly sexy that Tamsin's throat went dry. He was astride the golden horse she'd seen him on yesterday, sitting in the saddle with an ease and insouciance that contrasted powerfully with the grim set of his face.

The two teams rode onto the field like warriors coming into battle, their mallets held aloft against their shoulders like weapons. As they lined up in front of the stands, the atmosphere in the ground was electric, mirroring the palpable tension that crackled between the rival teams. But Tamsin was oblivious to everything and everyone but Alejandro.

The game got underway, and her aching heart felt like it had been ripped from her chest and thrown beneath the wild, thundering hooves of the horses. Never had she witnessed such violence. It was like a scene from Armageddon as the players pitched their galloping horses at each other so the animals clashed and reared, while all the time mallets sliced through the air and the ball ricocheted around like a missile. Transfixed with terror, Tamsin couldn't take her eyes off Alejandro as he streaked down the field, pursued by La Maya's number four. Despite their protective green bandages, the pale blonde legs of the San Silvana horse looked horribly delicate as she galloped for all she was worth, Alejandro bent low over her neck. Tamsin felt sick with fear as she watched the number four ride straight into his path, like a jousting knight. She felt the impact viscerally within herself as the horses clashed, throwing their heads up and wheeling round in a storm of flailing hooves.

How could the silken polo beauties around her watch this carnage so calmly? Were their smooth, impassive faces the result of genuine nonchalance or industrial quantities of Botox?

Just when she thought she couldn't take it any more, the umpire blew his whistle. It was like throwing a bucket of water over a group of fighting dogs; the two sides instantly separated, coming together at separate ends of the pitch in their own team colours. Tamsin breathed a shaky sigh of relief as her gaze followed Alejandro, unable to suppress the shiver of envy that rippled though her as she watched him stroke the pony's silken blonde neck. *Thank God,* she thought shakily. *Thank God he's alright, and thank God it's over.*

But a moment later she had to bite back a moan of dismay. The grooms were gathered at the edge of the field, each holding more ponies, and instead of dismounting Alejandro deftly slid from the back of the golden pony straight into the saddle of a mean-looking black one.

Tamsin turned to the expensively streaked blonde on her right. 'Excuse me? Is this half time?'

For a moment she thought the woman hadn't understood. Tamsin was about to repeat the question when she saw the beginnings of a smile lift the corners of her shiny red mouth. Slowly the woman slipped her diamant-encrusted designer shades down to the end of her very straight nose and looked at Tamsin curiously over the top of them.

'No. This is just the end of the first chukka.'

'Oh.' Tamsin's battered heart sank. 'And how many chukkas are there, again?'

This time the woman couldn't quite keep her amused, incredulous smile from breaking through. 'Six.'

Tamsin could have wept as she watched the players line up again for the game to restart. This time, on the black horse, Alejandro reminded her of a dark knight in some brutal medieval battle. She noticed how the other team members deferred to him, and how whenever he scored a goal the polo beauties lost their insouciance for a moment and the stands were filled with the glitter of a thousand diamonds as they raised their hands and applauded him.

Out on the pitch the sun gleamed on the muscular quarters of the ponies, now dark and shiny with sweat, as the battle raged on. Tamsin wanted to shut her eyes—behind her dark glasses no one would know—but she couldn't manage more than a couple of seconds before they flew open of their own accord again and desperately searched for Alejandro, making sure he was all right.

*Why do I care?* she asked herself in an agony of desolation.

The answer came straight into her head but did nothing to make her feel any better.

*Because I love him.*

Riding back to the pony lines at half time, Alejandro felt the black dogs of despair gathering around him like a pack of demonic foxhounds.

Against the odds he was playing well. Despite limited practice-time thanks to the Barbarians commitments, and a pretty much sleepless night last night thanks to Tamsin, he had scored eight goals.

If he could only keep his full attention on the game, he thought savagely, they might even stand a chance of winning.

But Tamsin's presence in the stands was like a thorn in his flesh. The first chukka hadn't been so bad; he'd been so blown away by the performance of the little palomino mare that he'd been mercifully oblivious to much else. But during the last two chukkas he'd been unable to shake off the awareness of her— so near, and yet so utterly unreachable. Her face was pale, half-hidden behind the dark glasses, and as he saw her drop her head into her hands it was impossible to tell whether she was caught up in the drama of the game or simply bored to death.

Hell, he needed to speak to her.

A crowd of autograph hunters waving huge photographs of him bought from the stands around the ground converged around his horse as he approached the pony lines. Alejandro was almost suffocated by the cloud of expensive perfume that engulfed him as he stopped to sign them. He gave in to one girl's request for a birthday kiss, but declined a rather emotional proposal of marriage from her friend who'd obviously over-indulged in the champagne tent at lunchtime, then quickly kicked the horse on, grateful that he had sixteen-hands-plus of rippling horseflesh between himself and the rapacious polo women.

Back in the pony lines he leapt lightly off the chestnut he was riding and, throwing the reins to a groom, went to find his mobile phone in the front of the horsebox. Shutting the door to keep the call private, he dialled Giselle.

'I need some phone numbers,' he said tersely.

The calls took longer than he'd thought, and when he emerged from the horsebox Francisco was waiting, his swarthy face creased with concern.

'Are you OK, my friend?'

'Fine.' Alejandro strode over to where the ponies were tied up, automatically going to the palomino mare first. The moment he touched her, her head jerked up. He could feel the tension in the bunched muscles beneath her satin coat; she was as taut as a bow string, but he knew that she was ready to go again, to keep giving, keep trying.

Just like—

'She's pretty special, huh?' Francisco's voice was gentle as it interrupted his thoughts.

Alejandro sighed, despair surging over him.

'Yes.'

It was only as Francisco gave the mare an affectionate slap on the neck that Alejandro realised he'd been talking about the horse.

Back on the field, the first thing he noticed was that Tamsin wasn't in her seat.

*Get a grip*, he thought furiously, galloping the mare round the perimeter boards, refusing to let himself look for her in the crowds of people coming back into the stands. But as the umpire threw the ball in for the start of the second half he couldn't help noticing her seat remained empty.

So she had been bored. So bored she didn't even stick

around to watch the second half. Well, that was a first, he reflected, taking a vicious shot at goal. He was used to women eagerly taking whatever he offered, whether it was dinner invitations, gifts, or tickets for exclusive polo-matches. Given that Tamsin had just shown her utter disdain for one of the above, it didn't bode well for the peace offering he'd just ordered on the phone.

Applause broke out in the stands, telling him the ball had gone between the posts. Impaled on unfamiliar spears of fury and self-doubt, he was playing superbly, but for once it brought him no satisfaction. Unable to concentrate in the first half because of Tamsin's presence, Alejandro found her absence in the second half even more of a distraction. He played by pure instinct, and it almost came as a shock when the umpire blew the final whistle.

San Silvana had won the game, but, as Francisco galloped over to embrace him and slap his back, Alejandro felt no euphoria. He felt nothing but a cold suspicion he'd just lost something much more important.

Dejectedly Tamsin stood in front of the mirror in her room.

Well, that served her right, for getting side-tracked in the middle of cutting a pattern.

The kingfisher-coloured silk was as delicious as ever, but somehow she'd made the dress way too tight, so that instead of a subtle, figure-hugging wrapover style, she'd ended up with something that clung to her backside and plunged almost to the point of indecency at the front.

At least, now it was transformed into an evening dress, the robe was almost unrecognisable. Which was just as well, she thought bitterly, since there was every likelihood its previous owner would be at the party. She'd seen the women that had pressed around Alejandro at half time when she'd made her way over to tell him she was leaving. She hadn't bothered in the end. How pathetic of her to think he'd even notice she was gone.

She turned around, frowning at the way the iridescent silk shimmered over her bottom, making it look at least three times the size. 'Basic error,' she muttered gloomily at her reflection. She deserved to have her couture business go down the tubes if she didn't anticipate that tight fit plus shiny fabric equalled huge bottom.

She jumped as someone knocked loudly on the bedroom door, and hurried to open it. Giselle stood there, looking tall and willowy and so self-satisfied that it was obvious she'd never spent a single second worrying about the size of her bottom. Which was completely understandable, since it was as pert and perfect as the rest of her.

'Alejandro asked me to make sure you got this,' she said coolly, her glance sliding curiously over Tamsin, and making the blue dress feel even tighter and shinier. 'He says he is...' She paused, seeming to weigh up the word. 'Sorry.'

'Thanks.' Tamsin reached out and snatched the stiff, shiny carrier bag Giselle proffered. Then, made ungracious by bottom envy, shut the door in her face.

Her heart was racing as she crossed the room to the bed, placing the sumptuous bag onto it. With shaking hands she pulled out the layers of tissue on top, finally reaching what lay beneath.

As her fingers closed around the silky fabric she felt her pulse go into overdrive. Slowly, wonderingly, she lifted it out, letting the fabric fall from her trembling hands.

It was as if the fairy godmother had just arrived and waved her wand, turning Cinderella's rags into the dress of her dreams. The emerald-green silk was as cool and fluid as water, falling in soft ruffles from the shoulders. Her professional eye traveled over it, admiring the exquisite cut, the originality of the design, while the rest of her swooned in an ecstasy of breathless delight at its sheer loveliness.

For about two seconds.

And then reality descended on her like an icy shower.

It was sleeveless.

Cinderella would be going to the ball in rags, after all.

There was a special kind of magic about the gardens of San Silvana at sunset. Usually, after a day in the office or out on the polo field, Alejandro found that going out onto the terrace with a drink in his hand, as the sun dipped down behind the fringe of trees by the pool house and cast long shadows over the lush grassland, was enough soothe the thorniest business problem or bitter match defeat.

But not tonight.

Ignoring the various comfortable chairs positioned around the paved terrace, he leaned against the stone balustrade and gazed restlessly out over the garden. He had waited for the opportunity to speak to Tamsin all day, but now his chance was almost here he was at a total loss as to what to say.

He had let her down last night; he knew that much. He should have told her straight away that her lack of experience made no difference at all. But that would have been a lie, and Alejandro D'Arienzo prided himself on always telling the truth.

The truth was, it *did* make a difference.

It changed everything.

He thought he was playing her at her own cold, ruthless game. Bedding her, on his terms this time, would be his victory.

So, yes, what she'd said changed things. He'd misjudged her, been wrong about her on every level, and now he felt he had to make appropriate amends. He had already set the ball in motion to help out with her business crisis, but the wrong he'd done her personally was less easy to put right. The dress he'd ordered was a peace offering, but it was utterly inadequate.

What he really had to give her was respect, and that meant having the courtesy to keep his hands off her from now on.

'Drinking alone?'

He turned round. Tamsin was walking towards him across the terrace, and instantly the stiffness in his shoulders from today's match, and the ache in his back where he'd been hit by a La Maya mallet, faded into insignificance beside the twist of pain somewhere deep in his chest.

She wasn't wearing the dress he'd bought. The peace offering had been rejected.

Bitterness hardened inside him as he summoned an icily polite smile. 'Celebrating, if you'd care to join me?'

'You won? Congratulations,' she said lightly. 'I left at half time, so I didn't see your victory. Perhaps that means I forfeited my right to celebrate it too?'

'Not at all. Champagne?'

'Lovely.'

Rosa had left a bottle in the ice bucket, and as he tore off the foil he had a chance to look at her properly. If he hadn't seen her making it himself, he would never have recognised the plunging evening dress she was wearing as the robe she had found in the pool house last night. The transformation was incredible. Miraculous. She seemed to have sewn it so that it completely crossed over at the front, showcasing the smooth and perfect golden skin of her cleavage, gathering slightly on one hip, and then falling in a narrow column to the floor. When she moved it parted slightly on one side, showing an occasional flash of slender leg.

Gripping the bottle, he was just prising out the cork when she turned round and leaned her elbows on the balustrade, looking out over the garden as he had just done.

Lust exploded inside him like a plume of champagne foam.

Heaven help him. How was he supposed to keep his hands off her when her backside looked that good?

'Great dress,' he commented dryly.

She turned, her gaze meeting his across the space that separated them. The evening sun gave her skin a soft rosy glow that made him want to touch it. Or maybe that was nothing to do with the sun, he thought darkly.

'I'm sorry; I should have said thank you for the one you sent. It was lovely.'

He gave an impatient shrug. 'No need to be polite. If you didn't like it, it's hardly important.'

'I assume that Giselle chose it?'

'No,' he said shortly. Giselle had supplied the name and number of the boutique, but it had been he who had described Tamsin's shape, her size, and the extraordinary green of her eyes to the assistant on the phone. 'I did.'

'Oh.' She glanced at him from under dark lashes as he handed her a glass of champagne.

'But since it's hardly likely to be a regular occurrence there's no need to tell me where I went wrong. I don't pretend that fashion is one of my strong points. It was a long shot, just in case you had nothing else.'

Tamsin felt irritation, like an electrical charge, crackling through every sensitised nerve in her body. *I don't pretend that fashion is one of my strong points.* Meaning, presumably, that she did? That she did *pretend*? Suddenly she was glad to be wearing the too-tight, cobbled-together bathrobe dress, and that his exquisite silken caress had been folded up and put back in its bag. She would rather have walked naked through a pit of rattlesnakes than give him the satisfaction of admitting he'd got it right.

'Well,' she said sardonically, turning towards him with a small, determined smile. 'Here's to you. The winner. Again.' She held her glass up to his, and as the rims touched she saw the dark, closed expression on his face. 'It must get rather predictable, being successful at everything you do.'

'No. I never take anything for granted.'

He spoke tersely, moving away from her and draining half

his glass in one mouthful. The tension between them, veiled by brittle courtesy, was like broken glass underfoot. *Why did I say yes to a drink?* Tamsin berated herself, remembering the girls who had flocked round him earlier. Here she was, delaying his arrival at the party by forcing him to make small talk, when clearly he just wanted to get away.

She took a huge gulp of champagne, turning her head away so he wouldn't see the dull blush that had spread across her cheeks. 'Sorry, I'm keeping you from the party.'

'No hurry,' he said coolly, watching her take another hefty swig of her drink. 'And, I think I'd better warn you, these parties can get a bit out of hand. Polo players are as passionate about women as they are about horses, so be careful.'

Hot adrenalin burst inside her, making her whole body fizz and sing with anger. 'Thank you for that, Alejandro,' she said through gritted teeth. 'But there's really no need for you to feel responsible for me. I might be a virgin, but I'm not a child. I have been to parties before, thank you very much. And anyway—' she tossed back the rest of her champagne '—I can't imagine I'll be in any danger of having my virtue compromised, since it's so completely offputting. Now, let's go, shall we?'

'Tamsin—'

But she was already at the door and she didn't stop.

It was obvious they had nothing to say.

# CHAPTER THIRTEEN

A RED lace thong hung from one of the strings of fairy lights that lit the polo-club garden and, looking around, Tamsin spotted the matching bra draped over an azalea bush. From behind it came the distinctive sounds of passion in progress.

Alejandro had been right again, she thought sourly. Polo parties were pretty wild.

The scene before her was beautiful, but definitely debauched. The party was being held in a series of tents, which added to the historical atmosphere Tamsin had identified earlier. The overall effect was like some extravagant medieval pageant—from a distance, at least. The reality was less romantic. Rival polo teams lined up at the bars to compete with each other at downing shots, while couples were entwined together on the dancefloor in poses she'd only previously seen depicted in the Kama Sutra.

In the midst of it all Tamsin felt unutterably lonely.

She'd spent the whole evening focusing on avoiding Alejandro. The short journey had passed in complete silence, and from the moment they'd got out of the car she had made absolutely sure that she stayed as far away from him as possible.

This hadn't been difficult, since he was permanently surrounded by a crowd of glamorous people, all clamoring for his attention. The crowd was mainly composed of terrifyingly beautiful women who draped themselves around him like expensive accessories, but there were men there, too, other polo players who wanted to bask in a little of Alejandro's reflected glory. Tamsin was determined not to cramp his style, so had ended up talking to an endless stream of people she didn't know and with whom she had nothing in common.

Politely extricating herself from a rather one-sided conversation about diets with a pipe-cleaner-thin Brazilian model, she took refuge in the nearest tent. There was a bar set up in the middle where some kind of cocktail was being made.

'Ah...the elusive Lady Calthorpe,' said a warm voice close to her ear. 'Such a pleasure to meet you at last.'

She turned. In the dimness she could see little of the man who had spoken, apart from the gleam of his eyes and the flash of very white teeth in his swarthy face.

'I am Francisco. I play on the San Silvana team, alongside Alejandro. Let me get you a drink, *querida*, and then you can tell me all about yourself.'

He was back a moment later, handing her a shallow cocktail-glass and guiding her gently, his hand in the centre of her back, out into the softly lit garden.

'Do you mind if we sit down?' he asked, steering her towards a bench set into an arbour smothered with clematis. 'Today's game was pretty vicious, and I'm aching all over.'

Tamsin smiled. 'You mean polo isn't always that violent?'

Francisco laughed. 'It's rough, yes, but between La Maya and San Silvana it's more than that. It feels like a battle.'

'It looked like that too,' said Tamsin with a shudder. 'I was worried someone was going to get killed.'

'Someone in particular?' Francisco enquired gently.

Tamsin glanced at him sharply. In the light of the paper lanterns strung above them, his eyes were kind, and she could see the laughter lines fanning out from them, giving him an air of dissipated merriment. The urge to confide in him was too strong to resist.

'Yes,' she admitted bleakly, taking a sip of her drink. It tasted delicious, like melted chocolate. 'How did you guess? It's horribly predictable, and of course completely futile.'

'Predictable, maybe; Alejandro is an attractive man. But you are a beautiful girl, *querida*, so futile? I think not.'

'You're very kind, but unfortunately, even if I was in the same league as the women he surrounds himself with, I'm afraid that wouldn't be enough. There are other…issues.' She took another mouthful of her drink, and was surprised to find that the glass was empty. 'This is gorgeous. What is it?'

'Chocolate vodka. Is good, no?' Francisco laughed. 'I think perhaps in heaven they drink it all the time, but since I'm not sure I will be good enough to go there I have to drink it while I can. Wait here, I'll get us another one, and then you can tell me all about these other issues. Who knows, maybe I can help?'

The music pounding out of the disco tent had slowed to a more languid beat as Alejandro fought his way between the dancing couples that had spilled out onto the lawn. His progress was slow, as every few paces he kept being accosted by women entwining themselves around him and asking him to dance. Some were remarkably hard to disentangle, and his efforts to do this were becoming less patient and gentle.

He had to find Tamsin.

All evening he had tried to stay near her, near enough to make sure that she was all right, but every time he came close she seemed to drift away again, so that the next time he looked she was nowhere to be seen. She had had no shortage of men hanging round her, he thought grimly, but, whereas a few days ago that would have filled him with contempt, now it made him feel fiercely protective. If any of them laid a finger on her…

'Hey, Eduardo!' Alejandro spotted the San Silvana number

four coming towards him, his arms around a dark-haired girl in a silver dress. 'Have you seen Tamsin?'

Eduardo frowned. 'Blonde girl? Blue dress? Great backside? Sure.'

Alejandro resisted the urge to flatten him. 'Where?'

'She was talking to Francisco over there, in a seat behind the vodka tent. But,' he warned jokingly, 'It looked pretty heavy, like they might not appreciate being disturbed. Hey—Alejandro! Alejandro, man! Take it easy!'

But it was too late. Pushing past him, Alejandro was already melting into the darkness, his expression murderous.

'To me, little one, the solution seems simple.' Francisco sighed theatrically. 'I cannot see why you say no.'

Tamsin picked up the hand he had placed on her thigh.

'It wouldn't work, Francisco,' she said with a regretful smile, holding his hand between both of hers. 'I know that he would find me much more attractive and exciting if I was more experienced, but the irony is that I don't want to get that experience with anyone but him.' She sighed. 'I think that's what you'd call a catch-twenty-two situation.'

Francisco stroked the back of his other hand along her cheek. 'Alejandro has always been something of an enigma. I have played polo alongside him for five years, and still I feel there are huge parts of his heart that I do not know.' In the darkness, Francisco's voice was suddenly serious. 'But never have I thought he was a fool, Tamsin. And, if he doesn't want a beautiful girl because she is not experienced, then that is exactly what he is.'

Tamsin closed her eyes for a second and took a deep breath of fragrant night air. The effect of the two chocolate vodkas was beginning to wear off now, and where half an hour ago she had felt elation she now felt only sadness. Francisco was so kind and so sympathetic; there was a tiny part of her that was telling her to do as he suggested. She could do a lot worse than being gently initiated into the art of sex by someone as sweet and experienced as he was. Someone uncomplicated, who would expect nothing she couldn't give in return.

And yet, of course, it was hopeless. The thought of sleeping with anyone but Alejandro was incomprehensible. It always had been. That was precisely why she was in her current situation.

She leaned forward, putting an arm around Francisco's shoulder and pressing a kiss on his cheek. For a long moment he held her. 'Thank you for listening,' she murmured. 'Just talking has—'

She didn't get any further. Suddenly Francisco was being yanked away from her and pulled to his feet by the open collar of his white dress-shirt. Tamsin gave a gasp of shock and terror as Alejandro towered above them in the darkness, his face a mask of rage.

Francisco wrenched himself free and for a moment the two men squared up to each other. 'What the hell do you think you're doing, feeding her vodka and feeling her up?' snarled Alejandro. 'Did you touch her? *Did* you?' His voice was a low, animal growl. Tamsin felt a cold wave of horror wash away the last lingering effects of the chocolate vodka as she saw that his hands were bunched into tight fists.

She leapt up, pushing between the two men. Adrenalin pulsed through her, icy and invigorating as she tipped her head back and faced Alejandro.

'You have no right to ask that question,' she hissed. 'I told you before that I'm perfectly capable of looking after myself. You couldn't have made it more clear that I'm nothing to you, so if Francisco—'

'Did—he—touch—you?'

Every precisely spoken word was edged with steel. His fingers bit into her shoulders, and his narrowed eyes glittered down at her from a face that was blank with fury.

Behind her Francisco spoke, his voice quiet and ironic. 'I

think this primitive display of masculinity tells you what you wanted to know, Tamsin.' Gently he leaned forward and kissed her on the side of her cheek, before throwing Alejandro a warning glance and moving away.

Alejandro closed his eyes and let his head fall back for a fraction of a second. When he spoke again the blazing anger in his voice had died down to a white-hot glow.

'Did he?'

Tamsin held her head very straight. 'No. He *listened* to me. He let me talk, and he listened to how I felt, and then he…' Her bravado faltered here, and she felt her throat constrict, making her voice crack. 'He offered to show me…to teach me… He was kind; he didn't pressure me; he just wanted to help.'

Alejandro's jaw was like iron as he put his hands to his head and shook it incredulously.

'God. My God, Tamsin… What did you say?'

She looked down. 'I said no.'

'Thank God for that,' he snarled, seizing her arm and dragging her forwards. 'Now, let's get out of here.'

'Why?' Tamsin stumbled, and he turned back to catch her, scooping her into his arms. 'Where are we going? Alejandro, what are you doing? I've told you, I'm not a child, and I'm not drunk, I'm perfectly able to—'

'Shut up,' he said in a voice like thunder, striding through the dark garden with her in his arms. 'I don't give a toss how old you are or what you're able to do. All I care about is getting you out of here and into my bed, because if anyone's going to show you anything, Tamsin, I want it to be me.' He swore quietly and succinctly. 'And, Lord, I want it to be soon.'

The moon had retreated like a shy bride behind her veils of cloud as they drove home, and the Argentine night was soft and dark. Alejandro made no move to touch her on the journey, and he was so silent and distant that Tamsin was certain that he must have changed his mind. When the moon peeped from behind the cloud, she glanced across at him and felt her insides constrict with excruciating need.

Feeling her eyes on him, he slowly turned to face her. His expression was terrifyingly bleak.

'Is this what you really want? You're sure?'

'Yes,' she whispered. 'It's all I've ever wanted.'

The hallway was completely silent. The moonlight made it look like a black-and-white photograph of itself a century ago. Time had stopped. The moment stretched and quivered as Alejandro came towards her from the shadows, his face inscrutable, unreadable.

And then he touched her, cupping her cheek with one strong, rough hand.

Her swift, indrawn breath was a whisper of transparent longing in the intimate darkness. His thumb brushed her jaw, and Tamsin felt her lips parting in blissful, hopeful anticipation of his touch on her mouth.

She was trembling, quaking, with need and want and fear and ecstasy. Hot shafts of sensation crackled and juddered up through her pelvis, until it felt like she was going to split wide open with the strength of her longing.

He raised his other hand, and for a moment he cupped her face, holding her steady.

His voice was low and gritty. 'Come upstairs.'

She whimpered as he led her through the shadows, feeling her heart clench and twist as she caught a glimpse of his blank, perfect face as they crossed a bar of moonlight. Upstairs the blackness was more intense. Alejandro melted into the darkness in his black dinner suit, but his fingers laced between hers were warm and hard and real. He led her steadily, unhurriedly, so that by the time they reached the bedroom she was almost sobbing from fear and excitement.

Very slowly he took her over to the bed.

The curtains were drawn back from the windows, but the

moon, from modesty, was round at the other side of the house and the light that came in here was a soft, smoky grey.

She heard him sigh, a lingering exhalation that touched her in deep, undreamed-of places. His fingertips skimmed her waist, her hips, the small of her back, and then he brought her very gently into his body, dropping his mouth to kiss the side of her neck

Spiked stars of pleasure exploded inside her like fireworks.

'Your dress,' he breathed against her ear. 'How do I take it off?'

Just the words were enough to drench her with creamy expectation. Her voice was little more than a moan as her fingers fumbled with the concealed button she had put where the dress gathered on one hip.

'Button. Here,' she rasped, pulling impatiently at the fabric so that she felt the stitching give.

Alejandro's hand was perfectly steady as it covered hers, his voice almost severe.

'I'll do it.'

She dropped her arms to her side as his strong fingers worked at the fastening.

'It's coming apart at the seams,' he said quietly, finally freeing the button and letting the silk fall away from one side.

*Like me*, thought Tamsin desperately as desire rampaged through her boneless, hungry body. Unravelling.

The other side was easier. Alejandro found the narrow satin ribbon and pulled it undone, so that Tamsin stood before him in her underwear. She was trembling violently. Alejandro's jaw ached with tension as he kept his teeth clenched together, biting back the moan of fierce pleasure that rose up in his throat as he looked at her. She was so perfect; he wanted nothing more than to crush her in his arms and kiss the breath from her body as he ravished her. But the effort of not rushing her, not frightening her, was monumental.

He had to take it slowly.

In a life of relentless physical challenge, this was going to be the toughest one yet.

His exhausted, battered body thrummed with urgency as, very gently, he pushed the silken robe off her shoulders so that it fell to the floor with a sound like a sigh. He sensed her tensing, and straight away saw her bow her head, her arms come up across her body, covering herself.

'You're beautiful,' he whispered, cursing himself for the note of hoarse desire that roughened the words. Resisting the urge to tear her arms away from their shield-like position in front of her, he dipped his head, barely brushing her collarbone with his lips, trailing them across the satin of her skin towards her neck, the hollow at the base of her throat, and upwards to where the pulse jumped beneath her ear.

Slowly, gradually, as his mouth finally found hers, he felt her arms slipping downwards, and the terrible trembling that shook her slender body subside. Alejandro felt dizzy with the effort of keeping his hands gentle as his head filled with the scent of her, the taste of her vanilla-ice-cream skin and chocolate kiss.

He wanted her so much. He couldn't hold out much longer.

Wrenching his mouth from hers for a moment, he pulled back the soft goosedown cover on the bed and lifted her up, laying her gently on the cool cotton sheets before shrugging off his jacket and kicking off his shoes. He didn't want to frighten or pressure her so he was going to leave the rest of his clothes on, but she rose up from the bed, and he felt her hands groping for the buttons of his shirt.

'Please. I want to see you, Alejandro.' She gave a muffled sob of longing. 'Oh, God, I want to *feel* you...'

Lust tore through him like a cyclone, shaking his noble intentions to their very foundations. He stood as still as a statue as she undid his shirt, and had to throw back his head and bite down on the insides of his cheeks to stop himself crying out a jagged shout of pure, devouring want when he felt her hands sliding across the bare skin of his chest, his shoulders, pushing the shirt off him.

The subdued glow of the moon turned her hair to silver and her skin to velvet. She was so pure and perfect, it almost felt like a violation to touch her. His hands felt too big, too coarse for such ethereal beauty, and he was grimly aware of the roughened skin of his palms. Gently he laid her back on the bed again, trailing the backs of his fingers down the length of her arms.

Tamsin stiffened, instinctively jerking her right arm away from him, but his steady, languid, expert touch didn't falter. He knelt over her, and in the soft, pearly light his face was as cool and remote as the moon, his eyes dark and secret like the unfathomable night sky. With his strong, sexy hands spanning her waist, he held her, then slowly lowered his head, and she gasped with joy and frustration as his mouth brushed one hip bone, then skimmed across the quivering hollow of her pelvis. His tongue circled round her navel, then very gently probed the dip of her belly button.

*Oh, please, please, please...*

Did she say the words aloud? Tamsin wasn't sure. Her head seemed to have been plundered, so that every thought, every naked, shameless desire, echoed through the throbbing darkness between them. She was still in her silken underwear, and Alejandro moved lower now, his hands still gripping her hips, holding her still and pulling the silk taut as his mouth closed over the place that hid the aching, pulsing core of her.

The silk of her knickers both veiled and heightened the sensation, diffusing the warmth as he breathed out against her. Tamsin was drifting on clouds of bliss, utterly deranged with desire, so that when his tongue slipped beneath the wet silk of her pants the ecstasy was indescribable. Bucking and wriggling her hips against his steadying hands, she screamed with joy and need.

Alejandro lifted his head. He had reached the limits of his

endurance. Having her, feeling her around him, was now an imperative more urgent than breathing.

He had never wanted anyone, or anything, so much.

'Show me. Show me now, Alejandro.'

Breaking away from her long enough to kick off the rest of his clothes and grab a condom, he felt like he was coming home after some long and arduous race as he gathered her into his arms and their mouths met. She had slipped out of the silk knickers now, so only the little bra remained between them. Without letting his lips leave hers, Alejandro unhooked it with one steady hand, unable to suppress the ragged moan of greed that escaped him as her breasts spilled out against his chest.

And in the end he didn't have to show her anything. Easing into her with a gentleness that stretched his flayed nerves almost to breaking point, Alejandro barely even felt her stiffen before her legs wrapped around his waist and she was gripping him, arching up, and then, astonishingly, crying out in pure, abandoned pleasure.

Alejandro let go, his desire exploding with the force of a rocket in the night sky, shaking him, shattering him, and leaving him empty.

# CHAPTER FOURTEEN

THE beat of Alejandro's heart filled her head and the Argentine sun on his chest was warm beneath her cheek as she lay there. Tamsin had never known such profound peace.

In the silvery darkness all was silent and still again. Gone was the roaring in her ears, the sound of thunderbolts and orchestras and fireworks that had echoed through her dazzled head a few moments before; gone was the scarlet whirlpool of ecstasy that had sucked her down. Now she was adrift on some warm tropical sea, rocked by gentle ripples of pleasure that still lapped through her blissed-out body.

Alejandro moved slightly, leaning away from her a little so he could look down into her face. He smoothed her hair from her forehead and held his palm against her cheek. In the half-light she could see him frowning.

'Are you alright? I didn't hurt you?'

She shook her head. The low, grave tone of his voice made her heart flip, and she didn't trust herself not to say something ridiculous, probably involving the word 'love'.

He sighed, and lay back again, pulling her against him. His hand moved downwards, lightly caressing her skin with gentle fingers. As he trailed them down her right arm she felt herself flinch automatically.

Instantly his fingers stilled. 'What's wrong?'

'Nothing,' she whispered. 'It's fine.'

He shifted position, so that he was propped up on one elbow beside her, and pulled her arm towards him. 'It's not fine. Let me see.'

'Don't.' Tamsin stiffened, trying to snatch it away, but his fingers were firm on her wrist as he straightened her arm and turned it over. Even in the dusky moonlight the mess of scars and stretched tendons was all too easy to see.

'Please, Alejandro,' she moaned. 'It's so ugly and horrible.' She had willingly opened up the most intimate part of herself to him only moments ago, but as he gazed down at her arm she felt truly naked and exposed. Her happiness ebbed away, leaving anxiety and shame.

'Of course it's not,' he said harshly, rubbing his thumb over the puckered skin. 'They're just scars. Marks of courage.'

Still holding her wrist, he moved her arm downward, tucking her against the strong wall of his body and bringing the goosedown covers up over her so that her back was against his chest, her arm cradled in his.

She sighed. 'That's one way of looking at it. To me they've always been marks of weakness. To my father, too. He can't bear to see it. I guess that's why I'm so self-conscious about it.'

Alejandro stiffened slightly. After a moment he said, 'Why? Why doesn't he like it?'

The curtains were open, and from where she lay Tamsin could see out into the moonwashed velvet sky. She felt like she was floating in space. The past seemed very distant, like she was looking at it through the wrong end of a telescope. Like it had happened to someone else.

'Well,' she said sleepily, 'because the accident was his fault, I guess.'

'What accident?'

Alejandro's mouth was close to her ear, his breath caressing her neck as he spoke. Tamsin stared out into an infinity of stars. Safe in his arms, she could speak without anguish.

'It was my birthday, my sixth birthday, and my father bought me a pony.'

Alejandro laughed shortly. 'Of course. What else?' he said in a voice that was tinged with mockery and a hint of an English upper-class accent.

'Well, one of those dolls with the hair you can style would have been my choice,' she said wryly. 'I was utterly terrified of horses.'

The fingers that were tracing delicate webs of pleasure over her hip slowed slightly. 'Why did he buy it, then?'

'He had no idea I was scared of them. To him, fear was weakness, so it was something I hid at all costs. Anyway, when this pony arrived, instead of being terribly grateful I refused to get on it.'

Her tone was rueful and ironic, but Alejandro could sense the pain that lurked deep beneath. He felt it in his own skin. Familiar hatred for Henry Calthorpe flared up, like an old wound opening.

'There was a terrible scene,' she went on quietly. 'He thought I was being rude and disobedient, and it became a matter of discipline that I had to do as I was told and get on the horse. In the end, he lifted me onto the bloody thing, and I was terrified so that I screamed and tried to get off straight away. I had my feet half out of the stirrups, and I was kicking, and he was shouting, and I guess it frightened the poor thing. It just took off. One of my feet was still caught in the stirrup, so I didn't fall off straight away.'

Holding her against him, Alejandro could feel the rapid beat of her heart beneath his forearm as the words spilled out of her in a breathless stream. Spikes of light burst behind his eyes as he pictured the scene she'd described. 'You were dragged?'

'No, not really,' she said with a half-hearted attempt at brightness. 'Well, not far, anyway.'

'You were bloody lucky it was only your arm that got broken.' His voice was like sandpaper.

'Oh, it wasn't. There were other things, but the elbow was the worst thing. The joint was completely shattered and I had to have lots of operations in the years that followed. That's why it's such a mess. And why it's not very strong.'

Tamsin's hair was soft against Alejandro's tense jaw. 'And what about your father? Did he apologise?'

'No.' It was a wistful sigh. 'He never mentioned it again. The pony must have been sent back while I was in hospital, and it was as if the whole thing never happened.'

Alejandro felt faint. 'God...'

'No; in a way it was the best thing he could have done. My mother and my sister would have wrapped me up in cotton wool—pink cotton-wool, probably—but he just carried on exactly as before. No sympathy, no allowances, no special treatment. It was good, really. I was so scared for a while, of being hurt again, but he made me hide it.'

Her words made him think of the time he'd challenged her to the game of pool. She'd played left-handed. No special treatment, she'd said. It seemed like a lifetime ago, when he'd thought she was spoiled and flaky.

'He made you hide the scars too, though.'

'Yes, that too.' Beneath the covers Alejandro felt her hand automatically go to her elbow, covering it in the way he'd seen her do so many times but hadn't understood. 'But he's right. They are hideous.'

He sat up suddenly, leaning over her in the dark. Against the pillow her face was as pale and cool as milk, her eyes shadowed and inexpressibly lovely. Alejandro spoke so fiercely it was little more than a growl. 'They're not hideous. I told you, they're a badge of honour. They show how strong you are.'

She raised her hand to his lips, the tips of her fingers lightly brushing the place where his lip had been split during the Barbarians game.

'You must have your share of them,' she said very softly.

He nodded. 'Hundreds.' For a long moment they just stared

at each other. Alejandro felt his pulse begin to quicken, his tired, sore body harden again. She moved, raising herself up a little so that the sheet fell away, exposing her perfect breasts. She was astonishing. Ethereal in the gloom, she knelt up in front of him, pushing him down against the pillows and stroking her hand up his thigh.

'Let me see how many I can find...'

When Tamsin woke up she wasn't sure whether it was the misty violet light that was making everything look so absurdly beautiful, or the joy that glowed inside her newly awoken body.

Turning her head and looking up at Alejandro's sleeping face, she felt her heart blossom and burst, and knew it was the latter. A prison cell would look like paradise if she was waking up in it with him.

It was very early. Not yet morning, but no longer night. She wasn't sure how long they'd slept, tumbling into mutually sated oblivion with Alejandro's hand on her breast and his taste on her lips.

Her nipples hardened at the memory.

Beside her Alejandro stirred, pressing his lips to her bare shoulder, simultaneously caressing her tingling breast with one hand while sleepily lifting her arm with the other, and burying his mouth in the crook of her elbow. Tamsin felt a sensation like butterflies fluttering in the pit of her stomach, but she didn't pull away.

'The dress.' Behind her his voice was a growl, sexy and sleepy. 'That's why you didn't wear the dress I bought, isn't it?'

With a little wriggle of her hips, Tamsin flipped around so she was facing him, his sun tattoo level with her mouth. She kissed it.

'Good morning, sunshine,' she whispered with a smile, and then raised her head to look into his. Her insides melted with a mixture of raw desire and dreamy adoration. 'Yes. I'm sorry.'

'Where is it now?'

'In my room.'

In one fluid movement he got up and she watched him cross the room, too busy admiring his lean, brown back to wonder what he was doing. Grabbing a small towel from the *en-suite* bathroom, he slung it around his hips before pulling open the door and leaving the room.

He was back a moment later, the carrier bag in his hand.

Tamsin sat up, clutching the sheet to her chest and sweeping her hair back from her face. He stood at the foot of the bed, his eyes dark and hooded. Unshaven, he looked like a pirate. 'Come here.'

He took the dress out of the bag, letting it slip through his fingers like something living. Tamsin walked towards him, naked in the melting half-light, her head bowed, her eyes on his. He caught her hand, pulling her forward and positioning her in front of him as he stood in front of the big cheval glass.

For a second she was lost for words as she gazed at their reflection. He stood behind her, above her, his skin dark against hers, his powerful, muscular shoulders making her seem tiny by comparison. His hand held her waist, his fingers lightly spanning her ribs. They looked perfect together. Not just beautiful, but *right*.

And for the first time she could remember since the accident, her gaze didn't automatically go to her damaged arm.

His face was inscrutable as her eyes met his in the mirror. Slowly he picked up the dress, gathering it in his hands.

'Lift your arms.'

She did as she was told, like a person in a trance. The fabric felt luscious against her naked skin, and when she looked again she gave a little sighing gasp of surprise.

'Can you see how beautiful you are?' he said roughly.

'It's a beautiful dress,' she admitted.

'No. *You're* beautiful.' His fingers closed around her wrist, straightening her arm, exposing the scarred skin. 'Every inch of you. Can you see that?'

She looked. Maybe it wasn't so bad. He had looked at it and touched it and kissed it, after all. She smiled shyly, meeting his gaze in the mirror.

'I don't know. Perhaps.'

He turned away abruptly and went over to the damask-covered sofa at the foot of the huge bed. From the heap of clothes thrown down on it, he picked up a pair of polo breeches and pulled them on.

Tamsin felt a tiny dart of disappointment. 'Where are you going?'

He zipped up his boots and took her hand. 'You'll see,' he said curtly. 'You're coming with me.'

They stepped outside into a world of milky purity. The air was still cool, but with that damp, blue, hazy quality that holds the promise of heat later. Trailing across the glittering, dew-soaked grass, their fingers loosely entwined, neither of them spoke. With every step Tamsin's newly awakened body tingled and sang, and every time her shoulder brushed the bare skin of his arm tingles of bliss shimmered through her, like a meteor shower.

At the edge of the garden, where manicured formality gave way to untamed lushness, Alejandro let his fingers slide from hers.

'Wait here.'

He vaulted easily over the fence and walked away from her through the long grass of the field. He was wearing nothing but his polo breeches and knee-length boots, and she could see the muscles moving beneath the butterscotch skin of his back. Watching him melt into the blue mist, Tamsin felt weightless and dizzy with longing.

Everything was unreal, too perfect to be true. Leaning against the fence, she tipped her head back and closed her eyes, breathing in air that was as cool and clear as sparkling water. There was some small cynical voice in the darkest part of her heart that wanted to puncture this new-found bliss, and perversely she found herself thinking of Coronet, Sally, and the mountain of problems that awaited her in London. But in that moment, standing there in the opalescent dawn, she felt oddly at peace with it all.

As she heard the rumble of hoofbeats she opened her eyes and straightened up. Cantering towards her through the veils of mist on the pale-gold horse, Alejandro looked like some heroic prince from a story book, riding out into the world to seek his fortune or claim his bride. The frisson of familiar fear she felt as the horse came closer was dampened by the deafening beat of desire that instantly started up inside her as she looked up at him.

He slowed the horse to a walk, and it picked its way on delicate hooves through the long, wet grass. Sensing her uncertainty, Alejandro slid down from the saddle and came towards her.

'Alejandro...' Her tone hovered somewhere between an apology and a reproach.

'Shh.' He reached out and took her by the shoulders, stroking his thumb across her lips. 'There's nothing to be afraid of. I won't let anything bad happen. Here.' He drew her forward very gently. 'I wanted you to meet her.'

'I don't know, Alejandro.' But Tamsin knew that the frantic thud of her heart was nothing to do with being so close to the horse and everything to do with being close to Alejandro's broad, hard chest. The long grass was soaking the hem of her dress. His warm scent enveloped her, familiar and delicious as, taking her hand in his, he placed it on the horse's nose.

She jumped slightly as the horse lowered her head and blew down through her nostrils. Her nose felt like velvet, and her eyes were gentle, almost as gentle as Alejandro's fingers on her nape. As Tamsin ran her hand through the horse's silvery mane, Alejandro dropped his mouth to her shoulder, trailing a path of shivering kisses up the delicate skin of her neck, while his hand moulded one breast, teasing the nipple to hardness beneath the thin silk.

Clutching a handful of mane, Tamsin moaned.

'Do I take it you've got over your fear of horses?' he murmured into the side of her jaw.

'Mmm...I think it's what's called aversion therapy. You provide a distraction from the fear with—with another, stronger emotion.'

'In this case...?'

'In this case, the overwhelming desire to have sex with you in a field.'

He bent his head, and she watched the lines fan out at the corners of his eyes as he smiled a smile that sent another rush of liquid need pulsing down through her.

'Not here. We'll frighten the horses,' he said, putting his foot in the stirrup and swinging effortlessly up into the saddle.

'That would be a refreshing inversion of the norm,' Tamsin muttered, her hand instinctively going to her elbow as she took a step back. Left alone on the ground, her uncertainty returned.

'Come on.'

Alejandro was looking down at her, holding out his arms.

'No, I—' she protested, but he looked so strong, so solid, and so gorgeous, that she was lifting her arms even as she said it.

In a flurry of emerald silk he had lifted her up beside him, and his voice was low and warm in her ear. 'Good girl. I've got you. You're safe.'

His arm was tight around her waist. The movement of the horse beneath her was an undulating sway, and Tamsin gave a gasp of surprise and delight. 'Oh, Alejandro, it's amazing! I'm doing it—I'm riding!'

'If you take to this as naturally as you've taken to your other new-found skill, I'd better sign you up for the San Silvana team,' he murmured, and desire rippled through Tamsin's body like the wind through her hair. The pressure of the saddle against her bare flesh was a reminder of past ecstasy and a promise of pleasure to come. She swung her legs and felt her hips undulating in time to the movement of the horse.

'Faster.'

It was a low, breathless plea.

Alejandro pulled her closer to him. She could feel the pressure of his arousal against the small of her back, and the hard muscles of his thighs flexing as he urged the horse forward into a languid canter.

Tamsin gave a high cry of pleasure.

It was like flying.

The sun was just beginning to come up, leaving only a veil of mist lying low over the grass, so it felt like riding over the clouds. The fluid silk of her dress billowed up around her bare legs and her hair blew back from her face. Ahead of them San Silvana languished in the golden morning light like an enchanted palace.

The horse's hooves clattered on the gravel as Alejandro gently eased its pace, bringing her to a halt in front of the steps. Dropping the reins, letting go of Tamsin's waist, he placed his hands on her knees and brought them slowly up her thighs beneath the silk dress. Tamsin lifted her arms above her head, anchoring them around his strong neck as she arched her back and tilted her hips forward.

The horse shifted beneath them, and Alejandro's thumbs met the slippery wetness at the top of Tamsin's legs.

His low moan of longing was muffled in her hair, and then he jumped lightly down and held up his arms to her. The expression of blazing lust on his face turned her insides to water.

'You have precisely fifteen seconds before I combust with desire,' she said softly as he took her into his arms. 'Do you think we can make it upstairs in time?'

## CHAPTER FIFTEEN

'THAT WAS COMPLETELY DELICIOUS.'

With a sigh of total contentment, Tamsin collapsed back against the pillows. Alejandro laughed softly, removing the tray of croissants and coffee and placing it on the table beside the bed.

'Are you referring to breakfast, or what came directly before it?'

'Well, I was thinking about breakfast, actually, but now you come to mention it the starter was particularly lovely too.' Closing her eyes, she slid one bare foot up his leg and ran her tongue lasciviously over her lips. 'I think, Mr D'Arienzo, I may have to have you tested for performance enhancing drugs. But first I may just have to test your performance one more time...'

Alejandro felt the blood rush into his groin again, and it took all of his considerable self-control to kiss her lightly on one peachy shoulder and get out of bed.

'Not now. There's some business I have to see to.' He crossed the room to the huge, old mahogany chest of drawers and began pulling out clothes. If he didn't get dressed and get out of the room soon, the sight of her naked body in the tangle of sheets would prove too much, and the rest of the day would be lost in sensual oblivion.

The thought of which was tempting. In fact, irresistible, but he had to make these calls. For her sake.

'Get some sleep,' he said huskily as he opened the door and looked back at her. With her white-blonde hair tousled and her lips reddened and swollen from his kisses, she looked sweet and wanton and gorgeous. 'You'll need it for what I've got planned for you later.'

Her eyes widened and her mouth curved into a smile of pure wicked invitation, and he had to force himself to leave. As he strode along the corridor, desire zig-zagged through him like forked lightning, and he hoped this share buy-up was going to be straightforward. Then tonight they could celebrate Coronet's salvation in style.

In bed.

Tamsin's first thought when she woke up was that she'd dreamed it all. It had happened so many times: her night of deep and secret passion in the arms of Alejandro D'Arienzo, shattered by the shrill of the bell, and she would open her eyes and find herself back in the freezing dorm at school on another grey morning.

Fat slabs of buttery sunlight fell across the bed, and the green-silk dress and Alejandro's polo breeches lay abandoned on the floor. Stretching out between the rumpled sheets, she breathed in the musky scent of their love-making, and was pierced through with a shaft of pleasure so pure it made her gasp.

Not a dream. Real. But almost too perfect to be believed.

Looking at her watch, Tamsin was amazed to find that it was early afternoon. She scrambled out of bed and grabbed a towel from the bathroom to wrap around herself while she went back to her own room.

Everything was as she'd left it last night when she'd changed for the party and her heart had been as heavy as lead. As she moved around the room, picking up clothes and tidying away make-up, happiness bubbled up inside her. So much had changed since then; it felt like thick, heavy curtains had been drawn back and her life lay in front of her, glittering with promise.

Absently she picked up her mobile, lying as it was amid the chaos on the dressing table, and checked the calls. Serena had tried to ring, several times, and her father too. Her heart gave a tiny lurch of apprehension as she imagined how he'd react if he knew how she'd spent the last twelve hours. In time she'd tell him, but right now she just wanted to talk to someone who would share her joy.

But just as she was about to dial Serena the phone came to life in her hands, ringing and vibrating simultaneously, and making her jump out of her skin. Laughing, she held it to her ear, making a serious effort to control her amusement as she heard the dry, precise voice of Jim Atkinson, her accountant.

'Tamsin, we have a problem,' he said without preamble.

Tamsin felt the smile die on her lips. Twisting the silver ring around her thumb, she felt a cold sensation creep up from her stomach.

'What's the matter, Jim?'

'We're not entirely sure.' He gave a nervous laugh. 'It's all highly unusual—unprecedented, in fact—for such dramatic activity to take place over such a short period of time. We're still trying to make sense of how this could have happened, but I felt I had to let you know as soon as possible.'

Somewhere in the back of Tamsin's mind an alarm bell was ringing. She gave her head an abrupt shake. 'Sorry, Jim, let me know *what,* exactly?'

'There's been a lot of activity involving the company's shares on the stock market today. All of the shares available on the open market were sold at the start of trading this morning.'

Tamsin's grip on the phone relaxed a little. 'Well, that's OK, isn't it? I mean, there can't have been that many shares available, so even if they've been bought by one individual it's not a major threat to the company. The majority are owned by me and Sally.'

There was a pause, and seven-thousand miles away in London Jim Atkinson cleared his throat. 'It appears that that may no longer be the case,' he said in a subdued voice. 'About two hours ago another large number of shares were sold, which as far as we can tell could only have come from one of you. I'm assuming you haven't released any yourself?'

'No.' Tamsin's voice was hoarse. 'But Sally wouldn't...'

The words petered out. 'Well,' Jim said gravely, 'as I said, it's most irregular. We're still trying to make sense of the limited information available, but I'm afraid it appears that we're looking at a hostile-takeover bid.'

'But who would do that? And *why*?' she moaned.

'I just don't know. I'll get back to you the minute I can tell you anything.' He paused, and Tamsin waited for him to tell her not to worry, as he had done so many times in the past, that it was a simple enough matter to sort out.

'Tamsin, I'm sorry,' he said quietly.

For a moment after the line went dead she held the phone in her hand, staring down at it as her head swam sickeningly. In the sunny, serene room it was almost possible to believe she'd just imagined that whole conversation.

Almost possible and, oh, so tempting.

Outside, the day that had started so magically was now heavy and golden. Her body still throbbed with repletion, and downstairs in his office Alejandro was working, maybe even distracted by the same memories of last night that flickered tantalisingly through her head. Jim was overreacting, she thought with a surge of optimism. He was obsessively cautious—that was what made him so good at his job, after all. He'd phone in a little while and tell her it was all sorted and there was nothing to worry about.

She gave a little cry as, right on cue, the phone in her hand began to ring.

'Jim!'

'Darling, you've obviously been away too long.' The familiar voice was clipped and sardonic. 'You've forgotten your own father. Hardly surprising, since you haven't called home in almost a week.'

'Sorry, Daddy. I was expecting a call from Jim Atkinson.'

'Oh? Problems?'

'I don't know. Something about a lot of shares being bought very quickly. He was muttering about hostile takeovers, but he's probably over-dramatising. I can't think why anyone would want to take over Coronet. Anyway, other than that, everything's fine. Apart from sponsors, the Pumas strip is well underway, and Alejandro has asked me to stay on and design shirts for his polo team.'

She felt herself blushing as she said his name, and was glad that Henry couldn't see. Nervousness was making her talk too much, and she had to stop before she found herself blurting out more than would be wise at this stage. But she needn't have worried. There was a long silence on the other end of the phone, and when Henry spoke again his voice was stiff and distant, almost as if he hadn't been listening.

'Does Atkinson know who's bought the shares?'

'No, not at the moment. He thinks that Sally might have sold hers, but that's impossible. She'd never do anything like that without telling me first.'

'Unless someone told her to keep it from you until it was too late.'

Tamsin gave an uncertain laugh. 'You sound like Jim. Who would do that?'

Henry sighed heavily. 'Someone who knows you're out of the country. Someone who wants to hurt you.'

Tamsin's heartbeat quickened painfully as anger warmed her blood. 'Oh, I see where this is going,' she said quietly. 'You're trying to say it's Alejandro. You just can't get past the fact that you *don't like* him, can you, Daddy? You think that just because he didn't fit in with the rest of your respectable English public-school boys—'

'No.' Henry's voice was heavy with regret as he cut her off. 'It's not that. It's because he has good reason to want to hurt you, Tamsin. Look, I really didn't want to have to say all this, but I suppose I should have talked to you before you left.' He hesitated, then said bleakly, 'About the circumstances under which he left.'

'What do you mean?'

'It was because of what happened that night at Harcourt. Because of you.'

The room seemed to sway slightly. The sunlight coming through the tall windows was suddenly hard and dazzling. Tamsin put a hand up to her head. 'What do you mean?' she said faintly. 'You said you didn't trust him.'

'With you. I didn't trust him with *you*.' Henry spoke as if he were in pain. 'I knew how infatuated with him you were—all those pictures in your room, the sudden interest in rugby. I knew he'd only hurt you, and then that night at Harcourt when I caught him coming out of the orangery I—'

'You sacked him because of that?'

'Yes.'

Tamsin's voice was a cracked whisper. 'That's so *unfair*!'

'Tamsin, I'm sorry. I was trying to protect you. I handled it badly, I know that now.'

Mindlessly Tamsin rubbed her elbow as her mind staggered to get a hold of reality. 'So, you think he's doing this to get back at me?' she murmured through bloodless lips. 'He lost his job because of me, and now he's trying to take my company from me?'

'I could be wrong.' Henry's tone was brisk now. 'It might not be him. I'm just warning you…'

Letting the phone drop to her side, Tamsin very quietly cut the call while he was still speaking and sank down onto the bed. She felt sick. There was a sharp, stabbing pain somewhere inside her, radiating out from her chest. For a long time she just sat numbly, waiting for something, without quite knowing what it was.

And then the phone rang again, and Jim Atkinson's voice spoke to her from half a world away, and the pain intensified into a searing blaze of agonising fury.

'I've discovered the name of the buyer for Sally's shares,' he said soberly. 'It's a company based in Buenos Aires. They're called San Silvana Holdings.'

'I need to speak to Alejandro.'

Giselle was out of her seat in a flash, placing herself in front of the door to Alejandro's office and crossing her arms. She reminded Tamsin of some sleek, pedigree cat; in spite of the casual pose, Tamsin just knew that if she had a tail she would be lashing it now.

'I'm afraid he's busy,' she purred. 'But I'll tell him that you wished to see him.'

'It's urgent.'

Giselle shrugged elegantly. 'Sorry.' Malice glinted in her eyes. 'It's very important business, and he specifically asked that you should not be admitted.'

*Of course*, thought Tamsin in horror. *She's in on all this. I knew from the start that she hated me, and now I know why. She's been involved all along.*

Adrenalin burned through her veins like acid. She was shaking with fury, and hurt. 'How thorough of him. Maybe he didn't realise that I'd find out exactly what kind of "very important business" it is through my own channels.' She raised her head and met Giselle's hostile gaze. 'I was prepared to do him the courtesy of giving him the chance to explain, but I'm afraid I'm not going to wait around while he finishes taking everything I have. Tell him I said goodbye.'

'Certainly.' She had just reached the door when Giselle

added in the same cool, superior tone, 'Is there anything else I can help with?'

Tamsin hesitated. 'Yes. You can arrange a car to take me to the airport. I'm sure that'll give you great satisfaction.'

By the time Alejandro put the phone down his head ached and his shoulders were rigid with tension. He dragged a hand over his unshaven jaw and leaned back in his chair.

What a day.

It was just past five. He hadn't stopped since he'd left Tamsin after breakfast this morning, and he suddenly realised how hungry he was. Hungry and tired, meaning that dinner in the same place where they'd shared breakfast would be good. Preferably with the same hors d'oeuvres, and plenty of champagne to toast Coronet's new beginning without its second director.

The answer had been lurking at the back of his mind all the time, but it had all fallen into place this morning when he'd looked back over the file of cuttings and company information he'd compiled the other night. A single phone call to Sally at the Coronet office, pretending to be a buyer from Dubai interested in placing some fake Coronet designs in his shop, had yielded instant results.

Sally could hardly have denied any of the accusations he'd levelled at her after that. Neither had she been in any position to refuse to hand over her shares, all of which were now registered safely under the name of a couple of his companies, awaiting transfer back to Tamsin.

*Tamsin...*

He stretched, his mind drifting back to this morning—riding through the dawn mist with her in front of him, the feel of her hot, wet body as he'd pulled her down into his arms, the excitement that had shone from her lovely eyes.

Instantly he was as hard as hell. Closing down his computer, he got up, suddenly impatient to see her for reasons that had nothing whatsoever to do with shares.

By the time Tamsin had arrived at Ezeiza airport the last remaining flight to London was fully booked. Unable to bear the thought of waiting in the airport overnight, she had simply enquired which flights did have seats available, and had booked herself onto the next plane to Barcelona.

Numbness had descended on her like some inbuilt opiate as she eased herself into the cramped seat, dulling the terrible pain in her heart until it was a generalised ache that spread through her whole body.

The plane seemed to wait an eternity to take off. Around her, other passengers were getting restless, and the stewardesses fluttered between them, smoothing frayed nerves and shooting each other uncertain glances. Eventually there was a commotion at the door, and everyone tensed as a uniformed man appeared at the front of the plane with one of the stewardesses.

He was looking in Tamsin's direction, and suddenly she recognised him as the customs official who had searched her on Alejandro's plane.

'Lady Calthorpe. Come with me, please.'

Leaden with shock, Tamsin did as she was told, oblivious to the curious glances of the other passengers as she climbed clumsily over the long legs of the backpacker next to her. Her heart was thudding so hard it felt like it might break out of her chest, but it missed a beat as she came to the front of the plane and saw Alejandro standing in the small space at the top of the steps.

His massive shoulders filled the doorway, blocking out the light beyond, his back towards her. Her throat constricted around a twisted knot of emotion, and tears prickled her eyes. She put her hand up to her mouth as he turned round. The expression on his face was chilling.

'Don't tell me, you suddenly had an overwhelming urge to see the sights of Barcelona?' His voice as always was perfectly controlled, but it was as taut as razor wire.

Tamsin lifted her chin, leaning against the wall of the cabin and trying to stop herself from shaking.

'Hardly,' she said with stinging bitterness. 'I had a sudden overwhelming urge to get home and try to salvage what's left of my business.' She gave a short, scathing laugh, gesturing around the cramped interior of the plane. 'Of course, I should have known that it wouldn't be that simple. Corruption is second nature to you, isn't it, Alejandro? Bribing customs officials and holding up a plane is nothing to a man who's prepared to *sleep* with someone while he's planning to strip them of everything they own.'

The noise level in the cabin behind her was rising as the other passengers were getting increasingly impatient, but Tamsin was aware only of Alejandro. His eyes had darkened from gold to dull bronze, and a muscle was flickering in his stubble-darkened jaw. His face bore the same expression of dangerous calm she had seen on the polo field.

'Don't judge people by your own standards, Tamsin,' he said very quietly. 'I'm trying to *help* you.'

A stewardess appeared, looking extremely agitated. 'If I could ask you to hurry, please...' she began sharply, then, seeing the expression on Alejandro's dark, beautiful face, backed off.

'Trying to help?' Tamsin hissed. 'What, by staging a hostile takeover of my company? I've got to hand it to you, my accountant had never seen anything like it. We didn't stand a chance, but then I suppose that's hardly surprising. You're as ruthless as you are cold and unscrupulous.'

'I'm touched that you think so highly of me,' he said with biting sarcasm. 'I should have realised you only accept help when it's offered in such a way as to make it appear you've done the work yourself. My mistake.'

Tamsin gasped. 'What are you talking about?'

'The RFU commission; what was it you said, you got it on merit? You had to compete?' Alejandro laughed softly. 'I don't think so. Yours was the only proposal that was passed to the board.'

She felt like she'd swallowed a hot coal. Vehemently she shook her head. 'No! That's not true...'

The captain appeared, laying an apologetic hand on Alejandro's shoulder. 'Alejandro, my friend, please.' He made a helpless gesture to the body of the plane, in which the atmosphere was growing more restless.

Alejandro nodded tersely, his eyes burning into Tamsin's. For a long moment they looked at each other. Tamsin felt like she was falling, falling, and that somewhere there was a cord that would open a parachute, but she didn't know how to find it. Alejandro's face was ashen, with lines of fatigue etched around eyes that blazed with emotion. And then, with a look that was almost like despair, he turned and walked down the steps.

Tamsin's breath caught in her throat as iron bands gripped her chest. She wanted to speak, to cry out and make him turn round, but she was suffocating, gasping, and then the gentle hands of the stewardess took her shoulders and guided her back into the cabin, towards her seat.

A grim cheer of satisfaction went up from the passengers as, seven minutes late, the plane left the runway and surged upwards. But as it climbed higher and higher into the faded blue evening the falling sensation Tamsin had felt earlier intensified. It was peaceful and unreal, but she closed her eyes tightly and waited helplessly for the agonising moment when she hit the ground.

# CHAPTER SIXTEEN

*Four months later.*

TWICKENHAM on match day always had a carnival atmosphere, and today, with the crowds basking in unexpectedly warm spring sunshine, the mood was particularly celebratory. The Six Nations tournament had finished, and in the stands there was a laid back, end-of-term sense of excitement about the prospect of a friendly match. Los Pumas were formidable opponents, and the game promised to be hugely entertaining.

In the luxurious comfort of the members' lounge, Tamsin felt cut off from the good-humoured crowd in every way possible.

Beside her Serena leaned back in her chair and rested her empty plate on the huge mountain of her stomach. 'I wonder if the team medics have experience of delivering babies,' she said dreamily. Tamsin glanced at her in alarm.

'You don't think that you might... What, now? Here?'

'No, I shouldn't think so,' Serena sighed. 'I don't actually think this baby's ever going to be born. I'm just going to go on getting fatter and fatter until I can't move at all. Talking of which, would you mind awfully getting me another of those lovely anchovy things?'

Tamsin stood up quickly and took the plate from Serena's

bump, glad of the excuse to do something, however trivial. She felt restless to the point of panic. The long room with its balcony over the pitch was filled with rugby dignitaries from both England and Argentina, making the most of the lavish hospitality. Tamsin was haunted by the thought that the tanned, elegant Pumas contingent must all be colleagues of Alejandro's, and found herself desperately eavesdropping on their conversations in the hope of hearing his name.

She was that pitiful.

'Just the anchovy thing, or would you like some kiwi fruit and mayonnaise with that?' she asked with a wan smile. 'In fact, you don't even have to answer. I like to think I'm something of an expert on your insane cravings now. Leave it to me.'

'You can laugh,' Serena called after her. 'But you just wait! One day it'll be your bottom that's the size of Denmark, and your fridge that's full of mayonnaise, and my teasing will be merciless.'

Reaching across the table where the buffet was laid out, Tamsin felt her smile die as knives of anguish sliced into her. It was utterly inconceivable that the air of voluptuous, milky contentment that cocooned Serena in the final weeks of her pregnancy would ever be hers. Barren survival was about as much as she could hope for, and that was in her more positive moments. She had smashed her own fragile chance of happiness when she had so brutally misjudged the man who'd held it in his hands.

'Tamsin.'

She jumped, jerking the plate upwards and sending anchovies and kiwi fruit flying. 'Please, darling,' Henry Calthorpe said gently. 'Don't run away. I just wanted to say how glad I am that you came today. How proud I am of you.'

Tamsin ducked her head and struggled to pick up a slice of kiwi fruit between shaking fingers. It kept sliding out of her grasp. 'At least the Pumas commission is one that I really did get on my own merit,' she muttered bitterly.

'*Touché*,' Henry said dryly, sliding more fruit onto Serena's plate. 'I deserve that.' He hesitated for a moment before continuing in an awkward undertone. 'Look, darling, I know this is hardly the time or the place, but I've been wanting to talk to you since the day you got home. I know you were angry then and you wouldn't listen, but I just want to say I'm sorry. I've handled everything so badly; I know that. Your mother always says that I have to let you go and watch you fall. But...' He faltered. 'I did that once and I've never been able to forgive myself.'

Tamsin sighed and shook her head sadly as she put the plate down. 'It all comes back to the accident, doesn't it?'

Henry nodded. 'I was responsible, and I felt so guilty. But it also brought home to me how fragile you are underneath that tough exterior, and how much I love you. I knew it was important not to wrap you up in cotton wool after that, but I couldn't bear to watch you struggle. I just wanted you to be safe.'

'You can't rearrange the world like that, Daddy.'

'Why not?' A look of anger passed across Henry's patrician face. 'It's a natural instinct. I can't bear the thought of anyone hurting you.'

'Yes, well, *you* hurt me,' Tamsin said in a low voice. 'You diminished me. You made it clear that you think I'm not capable of achieving things myself, or...or being loved for who I am, scars and all.'

Her throat burned with the effort of holding in the huge sob that was building inside her. Every word took her back to Alejandro, and lying curled up against him as the day broke, letting him touch and kiss the shameful, damaged part of her.

It took her breath away to think now about how monstrously she'd misjudged him. He'd been so tender, so perfect, and in the space of one magical night had taught her so much.

*So much.*

But even so, when faced with uncertainty she had instantly assumed the worst about him. She'd realised exactly how wrong she'd been when she'd arrived back in England and found all the shares in her name, and Sally gone. Alejandro had seen what had been right in front of her all the time; had seen it and dealt with it. It was Sally who had betrayed her.

Not him.

'So, will you accept my apology?' prompted Henry gently. Around them the excitement was mounting, and a blast of spring air hit them as the doors onto the balcony opened and people went outside. Tamsin looked up at Henry and gave a swift, painful smile. 'It's not your fault,' she admitted. 'Not entirely, anyway, though you have to promise me that you won't—'

She broke off as Serena appeared beside them—or, rather, the huge mound of Serena's stomach appeared, with Serena some distance behind. 'I'm fading away from hunger over there,' she grumbled before stopping abruptly. 'Oh, God, sorry, I'm interrupting something important, aren't I?'

Tamsin shook her head. 'No, it's fine. I was just warning Dad that if he ever interferes in my life again I shall change my name and move to the other side of the world.'

Henry and Serena exchanged a meaningful look.

'OK, well the game will be starting soon,' said Serena in an oddly bright voice, hustling Tamsin towards the door. 'I really think we should go and find Simon. He'll be in the company box knocking back corporate champagne, but I don't want him to miss the moment when your brilliant shirts first appear, Tam. Are you excited about seeing them?'

Letting Serena drag her out into the corridor, Tamsin felt her stomach lurch.

The shirts she'd never seen and had had no control over, since Alejandro hadn't returned her phone calls. The shirts she'd designed with his body in mind. The shirts that in a few short minutes were going to be mocking her fifteen times over with memories that burned into her head like acid.

'Excited' was hardly the word. She felt like a driver looking into the twisted wreckage of the car that had nearly killed her.

Fascinated, maybe. But not in a good way.

Alejandro tipped his head back and closed his eyes, listening to the roaring chant of the crowd echoing around the stadium, counting the passing seconds by the painful thud of his heart.

The last few moments before the start of a game were always the worst, but never before had he felt tension like this. Sitting alone in semi-darkness in a VIP-hospitality-box, he almost wished he was down there in the dressing room preparing to go out onto the pitch, but at the same time he recognised that the competitive buzz that had always driven him was suddenly utterly absent. In a few moments Argentina would be taking on England out there, and Alejandro couldn't care less who won.

It was a game. Nothing more.

In his hands he held a single sheet of thick, pale-blue notepaper, covered on both sides in spiky black handwriting. Henry Calthorpe's letter had reached him via the offices of the Argentine Rugby Union, and he had received it when he'd arrived for the board meeting where the sponsors for the new kit were to be decided.

It had rocked him to the core, which accounted for the rather rash offer he now felt so uncertain about.

He expelled a long, shaky breath and dropped his head into his hands. What the hell had Tamsin Calthorpe done to him? Control had always been paramount to him. Control and focus and drive, and yet she had turned him into a man who held up aeroplanes, who could focus on nothing but the remembered feel of her skin against his, and the scent of her hair, who caused a stir in board meetings by making hugely inflated, last-minute sponsorship offers.

He shook his head helplessly as he remembered the look of astonishment on the faces of the board members around the table as he'd made his offer. It was one way of livening up a board meeting, he thought acidly. And every one of those present had found room in their diaries to make the trip to Twickenham for this game.

Abruptly he got up and went to stand at the window, his whole body rigid. In his career Alejandro had coped with agony and injury. He was used to physical pain. He could deal with it, understand it, work around it.

But this mental agony was different. It tortured him, so that in his blacker moments he knew that he would do anything to be free of it.

Kill or cure.

That was why he was here. That was why he was about to lay his pride and his reputation bare before a watching world. Because if Tamsin didn't want him, if she didn't come, he was ruined anyway.

'It must be pregnancy hormones,' moaned Serena, slowing down and leaning against the wall of the plush corridor inside the west stand for a moment. 'I can't remember where he said the box was. Have you tried that door there?'

'There's no name on the door, so it's probably not in use,' said Tamsin patiently. 'Look, don't worry; he's probably back in the members' lounge by now. Let's go back and—'

'No! Just try the door, please, Tamsin.'

Even in the insulated comfort of the VIP corridor they were both aware that the atmosphere in the ground had changed. The noise of the shouting and singing had cranked up a level, and from far below they could hear the sound of a band playing.

'Please, Tam,' said Serena, and there was a note of desperation in her voice that made it impossible not to obey. 'Hurry. We're going to miss the start.'

'OK.' Exasperated, Tamsin opened the door. Instantly the noise from the stadium reached them more loudly, but the room itself was quiet and unlit. She took a step forward. 'See, there's no-one here—'

She gasped and her heart leapt into her throat as she caught sight of the figure silhouetted against the glass wall of the box. For a moment those broad, powerful shoulders, the narrow hips, had reminded her of...

'No one? I was hoping you'd stopped seeing me in those terms.'

The familiar low, ironic drawl sent tidal waves of emotion smashing through her. In an instant her frozen body was brought back to life. She could feel the colour flood into her cheeks, the heat surge through her pelvis, just at the sound of his voice.

And then he came towards her in the dim light, and she saw him properly.

The world stopped.

His remote, warrior face was pale, the shadows around his eyes almost as dark as the bruise he'd had when she'd seen him at Twickenham that last time. For a moment she could do nothing but gaze at him, unable to take in that he was really there. Then, aware that she was staring, she dropped her head, a blush of confusion and shame deepening in her cheeks.

'Sorry. I thought—I meant—I didn't think there was anyone in here.' She gave a nervous start as behind her the heavy door swung shut with a muffled bang. 'I didn't think *you* were here at all,' she whispered. 'I'm sorry. I wouldn't have come if I'd known.'

She made to turn round again and open the door, but he held his arm across it to bar her way. Tamsin took an abrupt step back to avoid touching him.

'Which would have meant I'd travelled seven-thousand miles for nothing.'

His voice was like gravel. Tamsin couldn't bear to look up into his face.

'You've come to see the game,' she muttered, looking distractedly out at the huge expanse of sunlit pitch beyond the glass. It seemed unreal.

'No. I've come to see you.'

She gave a short laugh, which seemed to hitch in her throat. 'You could have just phoned me back.'

Both of them were being very careful to stand a little distance apart from each other, but now he reached out and took her shoulders in his hands, looking down into her face. He was frowning. 'Phoned you back—you rang me?'

Tamsin nodded. 'I left a message with Giselle.'

Rolling his eyes, he let her go, and thrust his hands into his pockets. 'That must have been a while ago. I sacked her a few days after you left.' He walked over to the huge wall of glass that looked out over the pitch. 'What was the message?'

Tamsin stayed where she was, by the door.

'Sorry,' she said quietly. 'Sorry for being so quick to jump to conclusions. Sorry for not trusting you.'

'Obviously all that was too complicated for Giselle to grasp,' he said with heavy sarcasm. 'Was there anything else?'

Behind him the pre-match display was coming to an end, but it was as if the electric atmosphere out there in the massive arena had been captured and crammed into the small space where they stood facing each other.

'Yes,' Tamsin said, and took a few hesitant steps towards him. 'I told her to say thank you for what you did for Coronet. I was so stupid, not guessing what Sally was doing, and without you I would have lost everything—' She faltered, absently rubbing her elbow as the irony of those words hit her.

She *was* without him, and she had lost everything.

'Was that all?'

'Yes,' she said dully, keeping her eyes fixed to the floor. There was a long pause. 'No,' she added in a whisper. 'There was more, but... Oh, it doesn't matter...'

She made the mistake of looking up then. His face was shuttered and barred, a mask of indifference, but his eyes burned into hers with an intensity that made her heart falter.

'What?' he said mockingly. 'That you're madly in love with me and you can't live without me?'

Pain tore through her with the ferocity of a blow torch. 'Don't laugh! That's exactly what it was. But don't worry; I know it's completely unreasonable, and that's why I didn't say it! I know how badly I've treated you, how much suffering I've brought to you—'

'I don't think you do,' he moaned, thrusting his hand through his hair. As he pushed it back from his forehead, Tamsin could see the lines of anguish there.

'I'm sorry,' she said hopelessly as a fat tear slid down her cheek, closely followed by another. 'What I did was unforgivable; I know that. It's my fault. I blew it, and now too much has happened and there are too many things between us for it to be possible that we could ever be...'

Her voice cracked. Through a haze of tears she was aware of the tormented tenderness on his face as he took her hand and pulled her to him, opening the door onto the private balcony of the box.

'Oh dear.' He spoke so softly his voice was barely audible above the noise of the crowd. 'In that case I'm about to be humiliated very, very publicly...'

Out on the field the teams were coming out. Very gently he drew her forward to the railing at the front of the balcony, keeping his eyes fixed on her face as the Pumas players filed out.

Tamsin gave a whimper of disbelief, and the crowd erupted into a tumult of screaming and applause. One by one the players turned so they were facing the box where she stood in front of Alejandro, his hands resting on her waist.

In the place she had intended the sponsor's name to appear each shirt bore a different word. As the fifteenth player, whose shirt showed only a question mark, joined the line, the sentence was complete:

## TAMSIN CALTHORPE I LOVE YOU SO VERY MUCH PLEASE PLEASE WILL YOU MARRY ME?

The players stood, impassive, heroic, blazing their message of love while the spellbound crowd stilled expectantly. Tamsin turned round to face him, her eyes wide and shining with tears, her mouth opening wordlessly as she struggled to take it in.

He caught her face between his hands. 'You have no idea how much it stretched my creative powers to convey that message in exactly fifteen words,' he moaned softly against her cheek, before finding her lips with his in a kiss that was filled with desperate, hopeful tenderness.

A minute later he pulled gently away, and looked at her with eyes that were opaque with anguish and love.

'I really hate to break this off, because I have wanted to kiss the living daylights out of you every minute of every day for the past four months—but do you realise that I, and eighty-thousand other people, am waiting for your answer?'

'Yes,' she breathed. 'My answer is yes. Now, will you please kiss me again?'

And he did. Pulling her roughly against him, he cupped the back of her head with one hand, and the thumbs-up sign he did with the other was picked up by the zoom lens of the cameraman below and beamed onto the big screens.

As a roar of delight went round the crowd, the Pumas players leapt up, punching the air and embracing each other in celebration. On the balcony of the members' lounge some distance away more champagne was opened, spraying the crowd below with plumes of foam as grinning Argentine officials shook hands with tearful Calthorpes.

Without letting his mouth leave hers, Alejandro scooped

Tamsin up and carried her back inside, closing the door as the band started playing.

'It's completely disrespectful,' he murmured hoarsely, setting her down and sliding his hands underneath her top as they both sank to the floor. 'But I'm sure that just this once it won't matter if we don't stand up for the national anthems…'

# EPILOGUE

A DRIFT of confetti fluttered from Tamsin's hair as Alejandro dropped her onto the bed in the jet's small cabin. He kicked the door shut, and then turned back to her with a smile that made her wriggle with ecstatic anticipation.

'Did I tell you how beautiful you look today?' he said huskily, dropping a kiss onto her collarbone as she rose up onto her knees and wrapped her arms around his neck.

'Only about a hundred times.' She smiled. 'But it's a long flight. You have time to mention it quite a bit more before we get to San Silvana.'

Alejandro reached over and lifted a bottle of champagne out of the ice box where Alberto had left it for them. Tamsin felt weak with longing as she watched his strong, practised fingers tear the foil off. 'Sorry,' he said nonchalantly, handing her a glass of golden bubbles. 'I intend to get that delicious slip of a dress off you in the next couple of minutes, and then conversation isn't really on my agenda for the next fifteen hours. So I'll say it one more time.' He bent to kiss her lingeringly, his warm hand moving over her back to the zip of the dress as he murmured gravely against her mouth, 'Tamsin D'Arienzo, you are the most incredibly, unreasonably, excruciatingly lovely bride ever.'

In one lithe movement Tamsin stood up and let the dress

fall to the floor in a papery rustle of silk. Alejandro gave a moan of naked longing as she stood before him in her ivory silk stockings and the briefest, sheerest pair of silk pants with 'just married' embroidered across them.

'Come here,' he said thickly.

Tamsin was a mass of quivering, wanton longing in his arms by the time he finally dragged his mouth from hers and leaned over to open the drawer of the bedside cabinet.

She gave a gasp of realisation as he rummaged with increasing exasperation through the contents of the drawer. Pulling him back down onto the bed, she bit her lip to suppress the wicked, delicious smile that was building inside her.

'Darling,' she breathed, taking his face in her hands and brushing her lips against his cheek. 'What would you say to the idea of a honeymoon baby...?'

\* \* \* \* \*

*Sarah*

For Debbie and Alyson,
without whose wit, wisdom and daily conferences
in the school car park
this book would have been written much more quickly
(but at further risk to my sanity).

# CHAPTER ONE

*ELIGIBLE* bachelor.

Sarah came to a standstill in the middle of the car park, her fist tightening around the envelope in her hand.

She had to find an *eligible bachelor*. As an item in a scavenger hunt.

Since she'd conspicuously failed to find one of those in real life, her chances of success tonight seemed slim.

Beyond the rows of shiny Mercedes and BMWs parked outside Oxfordshire's trendiest dining pub, the fields and streams and woodland coppices she had grown up amongst lay golden and peaceful in the low summer sun. She gazed out across them, the envelope still clutched in her hand as adrenaline fizzed through her bloodstream and her mind raced.

She didn't have to go in there; didn't have to take part in this stupid scavenger hunt for her sister's hen weekend; didn't have to be the butt of everyone's jokes all the time—Sarah, nearly thirty and on the shelf. No, she knew these fields like the back of her hand, and could remember loads of good hiding places.

Thrusting a hand through her tangled curls, she sighed. Hiding up a tree might be considerably more appealing than going into a pub and having to find an eligible bachelor, but at the age of twenty-nine it was slightly less socially acceptable. And she couldn't really spend the rest of her life hiding.

Everyone said she had to get back out there and face it all again, for Lottie's sake. Children needed two parents, didn't they? Girls needed fathers. Sooner or later she should at least try to find someone to fill the rather sudden vacancy left by Rupert.

The prospect made her feel cold inside.

Later. Definitely later, rather than sooner. Right now she was going to—

The doors to the bar opened and a group of city types spilled out, laughing and slapping each other on the back in an excess of beery camaraderie. They barely glanced at her as they walked past, but almost as an afterthought the last one dutifully held the door open for her.

Hell. There was no way she could not go in now. They'd think she was some kind of weirdo whose idea of a good night out was hanging around in a pub car park. Stammering her thanks, she slipped into the dim interior of the bar, shoving the envelope into the back pocket of her jeans with a shaking hand.

In the years since she'd moved away from Oxfordshire The Rose and Crown had transformed itself from a tiny rural pub with swirly-patterned carpets and faded hunting prints on the nicotine-stained walls to a temple of good taste, with reclaimed-oak floors, exposed brickwork and a background soundtrack of achingly trendy 'mood music' obviously intended to help the clientele of stockbrokers and barristers feel instantly 'chilled out'.

It made Sarah feel instantly on edge. And about ninety years old.

She was about to turn round and walk straight out again when some latent sense of pride stopped her. It was ridiculous, she thought impatiently; she was used to doing things on her own. She put up shelves on her own. She did her income-tax form without help. She brought up her daughter completely singlehandedly. She could surely walk into a bar and get herself a drink.

Murmuring apologies, she slipped through the press of bodies into a space by the bar and glanced nervously around. The doors were open onto the terrace and she could see Angelica and her friends gathered round a big table in the centre. It would have been impossible to miss them. Even in this place, theirs was easily the noisiest, most glamorous group and was clearly attracting the attention of every single male within eyeing-up distance. They were all wearing T-shirts provided by Angelica's chief bridesmaid, a gazelle-like girl called Fenella, who worked in PR and who was also responsible for the scavenger-hunt idea. The T-shirts had 'Angelica's final fling' emblazoned across the front in pink letters, and Fenella had only had them made in a size 'small'.

Sarah tugged at hers surreptitiously, desperately trying to make it cover the strip of bare flesh above the waistband of her too-tight jeans. Perhaps if she'd actually stuck to her New Year diet she'd be out there now, laughing, tossing back cocktails and shiny hair and collecting eligible bachelors with the best of them. Hell, if she was a stone lighter perhaps she wouldn't even need an eligible bachelor because maybe then Rupert wouldn't have felt the need to get engaged to a glacial blonde Systems Analyst called Julia. But too many nights spent on the sofa while Lottie was asleep, with nothing but a bottle of cheap wine and the biscuit tin for company, had meant she'd failed to lose even a couple of pounds.

She'd definitely try extra-hard between now and the wedding, she vowed silently, trying to make her way to the bar. It was taking place in the ruined farmhouse Angelica and Hugh had bought in Tuscany and were currently having lavishly done up, and Sarah had a sudden mental image of Angelica's friends floating around the newly landscaped garden in their delicious little silken dresses, while she lurked in the kitchen, covering her bulk with an apron.

Fenella passed her now, on the way back from the bar with a handful of multicoloured drinks sprouting umbrellas and cherries. She eyed Sarah with cool amusement. 'There you are! We'd almost given up on you. What are you drinking?'

'Oh—er—I'm just going to have a dry white wine,' said Sarah. She should really opt for a slimline tonic, but hell, she needed something to get her through the rest of the evening.

Fenella laughed—throwing her head back and producing a rich, throaty sound that had every man in the vicinity craning round to look. 'Nice try, but I don't think so. Look in your envelope—it's the next challenge,' she smirked, sliding through the crowd towards the door.

With her heart sinking faster than the *Titanic,* Sarah slid the envelope from her pocket and pulled out the next instruction.

She gave a moan of dismay.

The beautiful, lithe youth behind the bar flickered a glance in her direction and gave a barely perceptible jerk of his head, which she took as a grudging invitation to order. Her heart was hammering uncomfortably against her ribs and she could feel the heat begin to rise to her cheeks as she opened her mouth.

'I'd like a Screaming Orgasm, please.'

The voice that came from her dry throat was low and cracked, but sadly not in a good way. The youth lifted a scornful eyebrow.

'A what?'

'A Screaming Orgasm,' Sarah repeated miserably. She could feel the press of bodies behind her as other people jostled for a place at the bar. Her cheeks were burning now, and there was an uncomfortable prickling sensation rippling down the back of her neck, as if she was being watched. Which, of course, she was, she thought despairingly. Every one of Angelica's friends had temporarily suspended their own professional flirtation operations and was peering in through the open doors, suppressing their collective mirth.

Well, at least *they* were finding this amusing. The youth flicked back his blond fringe and regarded her with dead eyes. 'What's one of those?' he said tonelessly.

'I don't know.' Sarah raised her chin and smiled sweetly, masking her growing desperation. 'I've never had one.'

'Never had a Screaming Orgasm? Then please, allow me...'

The voice came from just behind her, close to her ear, and was a million miles from the hearty, public-school bray of The Rose and Crown's usual clientele. As deep and rich as oak-aged cognac, it was infused with an accent Sarah couldn't immediately place, and the slightest tang of dry amusement.

Her head whipped round. In the crush at the bar it was impossible to get a proper look at the man who had spoken. He was standing close behind her and was so tall that her eyes were on a level with the open neck of his shirt, the triangle of olive skin at his throat.

She felt an unfamiliar lurch in the pit of her stomach as he leaned forward in one fluid movement, towering over her as he spoke to the youth behind the bar.

'One shot each of vodka, Kahlua, Amaretto...'

His voice really was something else. Italian. She could tell by the way he said 'Amaretto', as if it were an intimate promise. Her nipples sprang to life beneath the tiny T-shirt.

God, what was she doing? Sarah Halliday didn't let strange men buy her cocktails in pubs. She was a grown woman with a five-year-old daughter and the stretch marks to prove it. She'd been madly in love with the same man for nearly seven years. Lusting after strangers in bars wasn't her style.

'Thanks for your help,' she mumbled, 'but I can get this myself.'

She glanced up at him again and felt her chest tighten. The evening sun was coming from behind him but Sarah had an impression of dark hair, angular features, a strong jaw shadowed with several days of stubble. The exact opposite of Rupert's English, golden-boy good looks, she thought with a shiver. Compelling rather than handsome.

And then he turned and looked back at her.

It felt as if he'd reached out and pulled her into the warmth of his body. His narrowed eyes were so dark that even this close she couldn't see where the irises ended and the pupils began, and they travelled over her face lazily for a second before slipping downwards.

'I'd like to get it for you.'

He said it simply, emotionlessly, as a statement of fact, but there was something about his voice that made the blood throb in her ears, her chest, her too-tight jeans.

'No, really, I can...'

With shaking hands she opened her purse and peered inside, but the chemical reaction that had just taken place in the region of her knickers was making it difficult to see clearly or think straight.

Apart from a handful of small change her purse was virtually empty, and with a rush of dismay she remembered handing over her last five-pound note to Lottie for the swear box. Lottie's policy on swearing was draconian and—since she'd introduced a system of fines—extremely lucrative. Clearly her killer business instinct had come from Rupert. The frustrations of the scavenger hunt this afternoon had cost Sarah dearly.

Now she looked up in panic and met the deadpan stare of the barman.

'Nine pounds fifty,' he said flatly.

*Nine pounds fifty?* She'd ordered a drink, not a three-course meal—she and Lottie could live for a week on that. Faint with horror, she looked down into her purse again while her numb brain raced. When she raised her head again it was to see the stranger hand a note over to the blond youth and pick up the ridiculous drink.

He moved away from the bar, and the crowd through which she'd had to fight a passage fell away for him, like the Red Sea before Moses. Unthinkingly she found herself following him, and couldn't help her gaze from lingering on the breadth of his shoulders beneath the faded blue shirt he wore. He seemed to dwarf every other man in the packed room.

He stopped in the doorway to the terrace and held out the drink to her. It was white and frothy, like a milkshake. A very expensive milkshake.

'Your first Screaming Orgasm. I hope you enjoy it.'

His face was expressionless, his tone dutifully courteous, but as she took the glass from him their fingers touched and Sarah felt electricity crackle up her arm.

She snatched her hand away so sharply that some of the cocktail splashed onto her wrist. 'I doubt it,' she snapped.

The stranger's dark eyebrows rose in sardonic enquiry.

'Oh, God, I'm so sorry,' Sarah said, horrified by her own crassness. 'That sounds so ungrateful after you paid for it. It's just that it's not a drink I'd usually choose, but I'm sure it'll be delicious.' And account for about three days' calorie allowance, she thought, taking a large gulp and forcing herself to look appreciative. 'Mmm...lovely.'

His eyes held her, dark and steady. 'Why did you ask for it if it's not your kind of thing?'

Sarah gave a half-hearted smile. 'I have nothing against screaming orgasms in theory, but,' she held up the envelope, 'it's a scavenger hunt. You have to collect different items on a list. It's my sister's hen weekend, you see...'

*Half-sister. She probably should have explained. Right now he was no doubt wondering which one of the beautiful thoroughbred babes out there she could possibly share a full set of genes with.*

'So I gathered.' He glanced down at her T-shirt and then out into the warm evening, where Angelica and Fenella and their friends had collected a veritable crowd of eligible bachelors and were cavorting conspicuously with them. 'You don't seem to be enjoying it quite as much as the others.'

'Oh, no, I'm having a great time.' Sarah made a big effort to sound convincing. One of Angelica's friends was a holistic counsellor and had told her at lunchtime that she had a 'negative aura'. She took another mouthful of the disgusting cocktail and tried not to gag.

Gently he took the glass from her and put it on the table behind them. 'You are one of the worst actresses that I've come across in a long time.'

'Thanks,' she mumbled. 'There goes my promising career as a Hollywood screen goddess.'

'Believe me, it was a compliment.'

She looked up quickly, wondering if he was teasing her, but his expression was utterly serious. For a moment their eyes locked. The bolt of pure, stinging desire that shot through her took her completely by surprise and she felt the blood surge up to her face.

'So what else is on your list of things to find?' he asked.

'I don't know yet.' She tore her gaze away from his and looked down at the envelope in her hand. 'It's all in here. As you get each item you open up the next envelope.'

'How many have you got so far?'

'One.'

His long, downturned mouth quirked into half a smile, but Sarah noticed that it didn't chase the shadows from his eyes. 'The drink was the first?'

'Actually it was the second. But I gave up on the first.'

'Which was?'

She shook her head, deliberately letting her hair fall over her face. 'It's not important.'

His fingers closed around the envelope in her hand and gently he took it from her. For a second she tried to snatch it back but he was too strong for her and she looked away in embarrassment as he unfolded the paper and read what was written there.

She looked past him into the blue summer evening. Out on the terrace, Fenella was watching her, and Sarah saw her nudge Angelica and smirk as she nodded in Sarah's direction.

'*Dio mio*,' said the man beside her, his husky Italian voice tinged with distaste. 'You have to "collect" an eligible bachelor?'

'Yes. Not exactly my forte.' Angrily Sarah turned away from the curious glances from the terrace and gave a short, bitter laugh. 'I don't suppose you're one, are you?'

The moment she'd spoken she felt her face freeze with embarrassment as she realised how it had sounded. As if she was desperate. And as if she was coming on to him. 'Sorry,' she muttered. 'Let's just pretend that I never asked that—'

'No,' he said tersely.

'Please...' she ducked her head, staring down at the fashionably worn wooden floorboards '...forget it. You don't have to answer.'

'I just did. The answer's no. I am neither a bachelor nor remotely eligible,' he said gravely, reaching out and lifting her chin with his finger, so that she was left with no choice but to look up into his face. His eyes were black and impossible to read. 'But *they* don't know that,' he murmured as he moved his lips to hers.

As ideas went, it probably wasn't his most sensible, Lorenzo thought as he tilted her face up. He saw her dark eyes widen in shock as he brought his mouth down to hers.

But he was bored. Bored and disillusioned and frustrated, and this was as good a way as any of escaping those feelings for a while. Her lips were as soft and sweet as he'd imagined they would be, and as he kissed her with deliberate gentleness he breathed in the clean, artless smell of soap and washing powder.

She was shaking. Her body was rigid with tension, her mouth stayed tightly closed beneath his. Anger at the women on the terrace, who had obviously given her a hard time, churned inside him, adding to the sour disappointment of the day. Instinctively he raised one hand to cradle her face while the other slid beneath the warm tumble of her silken hair and cupped the back of her head.

Patience was one of the things that made him good at his job. The ability to make women relax and release their inhibitions was another. He held her with infinite care, close enough to make her feel cherished, but not so tightly she felt threatened. Gently his fingers caressed the nape of her neck, the secret dip at the base of her skull as his mouth very languidly explored hers.

Triumph shot through him as a soft moan escaped her and felt the stiffness leave her body. Her plump lips parted, her spine arched towards him and then she was kissing him back, with a tentative passion that was surprisingly exciting.

Lorenzo found he was smiling. For the first time in days… *Dio,* months, he was actually smiling, smiling against her mouth at the sheer unexpected sweetness of kissing this woman with the glorious auburn curls and the spectacular breasts and the sad, sad eyes.

He had come to Oxfordshire on a sort of desperate pilgrimage; a search for places that had long existed in his head thanks to a tattered paperback by a little-known author, picked up by chance years ago. The landscape described so lucidly in Francis Tate's beautiful, lyrical novel had haunted him for years, and he had come here in the hope that it might rekindle some spark of the creativity that had died alongside the rest of his emotional life. But the reality of the place was disappointing; a far cry from the gentle, rural paradise Tate depicted in *The Oak and the Cypress.* Lorenzo had discovered a parody of picture-postcard England, bland and soulless.

This woman was the most real, genuine thing he'd come across since he'd arrived here, and probably long before. Emotions played across her face like shadows on a summer day. She didn't conceal anything. Couldn't pretend.

After Tia's prolonged, sophisticated deception he found that profoundly attractive.

And she was actually as sexy as hell. Beneath that self-deprecating insecurity, this girl had depths of heat and passion. He'd kissed her because he felt sorry for her; because she looked sad; because it would cost nothing and mean nothing...

He hadn't expected to enjoy it as much as this.

Lorenzo felt his smile widen as his hands moved down to her curvaceous waist and pulled her against him, desire spiralling down through the pit of his stomach as his fingers met the warm, soft flesh beneath the T-shirt...

She froze. Her eyes flew open, and then suddenly she was pushing him away; stumbling backwards. Her mouth was reddened and bee-stung from his kiss, and above it her dark eyes welled with hurt as they darted wildly in the direction of the whooping, clapping girls on the terrace before coming back to him.

For a second she just stared at him, her face stricken, and then she turned and pushed her way through the crush of bodies towards the door.

It was a joke, of course. That was what hen parties were all about. Jokes. Fun. Flirting. It was just part of all of that.

Pushing through a gap in the hedge at the back of the car park, Sarah felt the thorns scrape at her bare arms and angrily scrubbed the tears from her face with the back of her hand. *Ouch*. It hurt. That was why she was crying. Not because she couldn't take a joke.

Even one as hurtful and humiliating as being kissed in a pub by a complete stranger who couldn't even keep a straight face while he was doing it. God, no. She wouldn't get upset about a silly, harmless thing like that.

Hell, she thought, striding angrily through the waist-high wheat, she was the woman who only a week ago had done the catering for an engagement party and dropped the cake—complete with lighted sparklers—in front of all the guests and the happy couple. One half of which just happened to have been her lover of seven years and the father of her child. Embarrassment and abject shame were old friends of hers. The small matter of being set up to provide hilarious entertainment for her sister's hen party was nothing to Sarah Halliday: the original poster child for humiliation.

The sun was low, dipping down to the horizon, dazzling her through her tears and turning the field into a shimmering sea of gold. Sarah swiped furiously at the wheat in her path, giving vent to the fury and resentment that buzzed through veins that a few moments ago had been thrumming with desire.

That was the worst bit, she thought despairingly. Not that she'd been set up, but that it had felt so wonderful. She was so lonely and desperate that the empty kiss of a stranger had actually made her feel cherished and special and desirable and *good*...

Right up to the moment she'd realised he was laughing at her.

Reaching the brow of the hill, she tipped back her head and took a big, steadying breath. High up in the faded blue sky the pale ghost of the moon hovered, waiting for the sun to finish its flamboyant exit. It made her think of Lottie, and she found that she was smiling as she started walking again, quickening her pace as she descended the hill towards home.

Lorenzo bent to pick up the envelope that she'd dropped in her hurry to get away from him.

Funny, he thought acidly, in all the versions of the story he'd ever read it was a shoe Cinderella left behind when she fled from the ball. He turned it over. Ah. So her name wasn't Cinderella...

It was Sarah.

Sarah. It sounded honest and simple and wholesome, he reflected as he pushed through the crowd towards the door. It suited her.

He strode quickly out into the middle of the dusty lane that ran in front of The Rose and Crown and looked around. To the right, the car park was packed bumper-to-bumper and he half expected to see one of the gleaming BMWs shoot backwards out of its space and accelerate out into the narrow road. But no engine noise shattered the still evening.

There was no sign of her.

Intrigued, he shaded his eyes against the low, flaming sun and turned slowly around, scanning the fields of wheat and hedgerows that unfolded on every side. The air was thick, dusty, hazy with heat and, apart from the distant sound of voices and laughter from the terrace, all was quiet. It seemed she had completely vanished.

He was about to turn and go back inside when a movement in the distance caught his eye. Someone was walking through the field beyond the pub, wading through the rippling wheat with fluid, undulating strides. Unmistakably female, she had her back to him, and the sinking sun lit her riot of curls, giving her an aura of pure gold that would have won any lighting technician an Oscar.

It was her. Sarah.

He felt the deep, almost physical jolt in his gut that he got when he was working and instantly his fingers itched for a camera. This was what he had come here looking for. Here, in front of him, was the essence of Francis Tate's England, the heart and soul of the book Lorenzo had loved for so long, encapsulated by this timeless, sensual image of a girl with the sun in her hair, waist-high in wheat.

On the brow of the hill she paused, tipping back her head and looking up at the pale smudge of moon, so that her hair cascaded down her back. Then, after a moment, she carried on down the slope and disappeared from view.

He let out a long, harsh lungful of air, realising for the first time that he'd been holding his breath as he watched her. He didn't know who this Sarah was or what had made her run out like that, but actually he didn't care. He was just very grateful that she had, because in doing so she'd unwittingly given him back something he thought he'd lost for ever. His hunger to work again. His creative vision.

Which, he thought grimly as he walked back across the road, just left the slightly more prosaic matter of copyright permission.

## CHAPTER TWO

*Three* weeks later.

Sarah's head throbbed and tiredness dragged at her body, but as she closed her eyes and took a deep inhalation of warm night air she felt her battered spirits lift a little.

*Tuscany.*

You could smell it; a resiny, slightly astringent combination of rosemary and cedar and the tang of sun-baked earth that was a million miles from the diesel smog that hung over London's airless streets at the moment. Britain had been having an extended spell of hot weather that had made the headlines night after night for weeks, but here the heat felt different. It had an elemental quality that stole into your bones and almost forced you to relax.

'You look shattered, darling.'

Across the table her mother's eyes met hers over her glass of Chianti. Sarah smothered a yawn and smiled quickly.

'It's the travelling. I'm not used to it. But it's great to be here.'

She was surprised, as she said the words, to realise how true they were. She'd got so used to dreading Angelica's wedding with all its leaden implications of her own conspicuous failure in so many departments—most notably the 'finding a lifelong partner' one—that she had neglected to take into account how wonderful it would be to come to Italy. The fulfilment of a lifelong dream, from way back when she could afford to have dreams.

'It's great that you're here.' Martha's eyes narrowed shrewdly. 'I think you needed to get away from things because frankly, my darling, you're not looking in great shape.'

'I know, I know...' Aware of her straining waistband, Sarah squirmed uncomfortably. The bonus of having a broken heart was supposed to be that you lost your appetite and the weight fell off, but she was still waiting for that phase to kick in. At the moment she was stuck in the 'bitterness-and-comfort-eating' stage. 'I *am* on a diet, but it's been tough, what with Rupert and work and worrying about money and everything—'

'I didn't mean it like that,' Martha said gently. 'I meant mentally. But if money is difficult, darling, you know Guy and I will help.'

'No!' Sarah's response was instant. 'Really, it's fine. Something will come up.' Her thoughts strayed to the letter she'd had a couple of weeks ago from her father's publishers, the latest in a long line of requests she'd received for film options on *The Oak and the Cypress* in the eleven years since she'd inherited the rights. In the beginning she'd actually taken several of these offers seriously, until bitter experience had taught her that Francis Tate seemed to attract penniless film students with a tendency to bizarre, obsessive psychological disorders. Now, for the sake of her sanity and her burdensome sense of responsibility to her father's memory, she simply refused permission outright.

'How's Lottie doing?' Martha asked now.

Sarah glanced uneasily across at Lottie, who was sitting on Angelica's knee. 'Fine,' she said, hating the defensive note that crept into her voice. 'She hasn't even noticed that Rupert isn't around any more, which makes me realise just what a terrible father he's been. I can't remember the last time he spent time with her.' Latterly most of Rupert's visits to the flat in

Shepherd's Bush had been for hasty and singularly unsatisfactory sex in his lunch hour when Lottie was at school. Sarah shuddered now when she thought of his clumsy, careless touch, and his easy excuses about problems at the office and the pressure of work for the evenings and weekends he no longer spent with her. She wondered how long he would have carried on the deceit if she hadn't found him out so spectacularly.

'You're better off without him,' Martha said, as if she'd read Sarah's thoughts. Sarah sincerely hoped she hadn't.

'I know.' She sighed and got to her feet, starting to gather up the plates. 'Really. I know. I don't need a man.'

'That's not what I said.' Martha stood up too, reaching across for the wine, holding the bottle up to the light of the candle and squinting at it to see if there was any left. 'I said without *him,* not without a man in general.'

'I'm happy on my own,' Sarah said stubbornly. It wasn't exactly a lie; she was happy enough. But she only had to think back to the dark, compelling Italian who had kissed her at Angelica's hen party to know that she was also only half-alive. Briskly she moved around the table, stacking crockery, keeping her hands busy. 'You're just missing Guy. You always get ridiculously sentimental when he's not here.'

Guy and Hugh and all his friends weren't arriving until tomorrow, so tonight it was just 'the girls', as Angelica called them. Martha shrugged. 'Perhaps. I'm just an old romantic. But I don't want you to miss your chance at love because you're determined to look the other way, that's all.'

*Fat chance of that,* thought Sarah, carrying the plates back to the kitchen. Her love life was a vast, deserted plain. If anything ever did chance to appear on the horizon she'd be certain to see it. Whether it would stop or not was another matter altogether.

Looming ahead of her through the Tuscan night, the farmhouse was a jumble of uneven buildings and gently sloping roofs. The kitchen was at one end, a low-ceilinged single-storey addition that Angelica said had once been a dairy. Sarah went in and switched the light on, tiredly setting down the pile of plates on the un-rustic shiny marble countertop. Despite being utterly uninterested in cooking, Angelica and Hugh had spared no expense in the creation of the kitchen, and Sarah couldn't quite stamp out a hot little flare of envy as she looked around, mentally comparing it with the tiny, grim galley kitchen in her flat in London.

Crossly she turned on the cold tap and let the water run over her wrists. Heat, tiredness and a glass of Chianti had lowered her defences tonight, making it harder than usual to hold back all kinds of forbidden thoughts. She turned off the tap and went back out into the humid evening, pressing her cool, damp hands against her hot neck, beneath her hair. As she returned to the table Angelica was running through the catalogue of disasters that had beset the renovations.

'...it seems he's absolutely fanatical about having everything as natural and authentic as possible. He confronted our architect with this obscure bit of Tuscan planning law that meant we weren't allowed to put a glass roof on the kitchen, but had to reuse the old tiles. Something to do with maintaining the original character of the building.'

Fenella rolled her eyes. 'That's all very well for him to say, since he lives in a sixteenth-century *palazzo*. Does he expect you to live like peasants just because you bought a farmhouse?'

Martha looked up with a smile as Sarah sat down again. 'Hugh and Angelica have fallen foul of the local aristocracy,' she explained. 'From Palazzo Castellaccio, further up the lane.'

'Aristocracy?' Angelica snorted. 'I wouldn't mind if he was, but he's definitely new money. A film director. Lorenzo Cavalleri, he's called. He's married to that stunning Italian actress, Tia de Luca.'

Fenella was visibly excited. Dropping a celebrity name in front of her had roughly the same effect as dropping a biscuit in front of a dog. 'Tia de Luca? Not any more apparently.' She sat up straighter, practically pricking up her ears and panting. 'There's an interview with her in that magazine I bought at the airport yesterday. *Apparently* she left her husband for Ricardo Marcello, *and* she's pregnant.'

'Ooh, how exciting,' said Angelica avidly. 'Ricardo Marcello's *gorgeous*. Is the baby his, then?'

You'd think they were talking about intimate acquaintances, thought Sarah, stifling another yawn. She knew who Tia de Luca was, of course—everyone did—but couldn't get excited about the complicated love life of someone she would never meet and with whom she had nothing in common. Fenella was clearly untroubled by such details.

'Not sure—from what she said, I think the baby might be the husband's, you know, Lorenzo Whatshisname.' She lowered her voice. 'Have you met him?'

Across the table, Lottie was lolling on her grandmother's knee, her thumb in her mouth. She was obviously exhausted, and Sarah's own eyelids felt as if they had lead weights attached to them; leaning back in her chair, she tipped up her head and allowed herself the momentary luxury of closing them while the conversation ebbed around her.

'No,' Angelica said. 'Hugh has. Says he's difficult. Typical Italian alpha male, all arrogant and stand-offish and superior. We have to keep on the right side of him though, because the church where we're getting married is actually on part of his land.'

'Mmm...' Fenella's voice was warm and throaty. 'He sounds delish. I wouldn't mind getting on the right side of an Italian alpha male...'

Sarah opened her eyes, dragging herself ruthlessly back from the edge of that tempting abyss.

'Come on, Lottie. It's time you were in bed.'

At the mention of her name Lottie struggled sleepily upright, reluctant as ever to leave a party. 'I'm not, Mummy,' she protested. 'Really...'

'Uh-uh.' Lottie had the persuasive powers of a politician, and usually Sarah's resistance in the face of her killer combination of sweetness and logic was pitifully low. But not tonight. A mixture of exhaustion and an odd, restless feeling of dissatisfaction sharpened her tone. 'Bed. Now.'

Lottie blinked up at the sky over Sarah's shoulder. Her forehead was creased up with worry. 'There's no moon,' she whispered. 'Don't they have the moon in Italy?'

In an instant Sarah's edgy frustration melted away. The moon was Lottie's touchstone, her security blanket. 'Yes, they do,' she said softly, 'but tonight it must be tucked up safely behind all the clouds. Look, there are no stars either.'

Lottie's frown eased a little. 'If there are clouds, does that mean it's going to rain?'

'Oh, gosh, don't say that,' laughed Angelica, getting up and coming over to give Lottie a goodnight kiss. 'It better not. The whole point of having the wedding here was the weather. It *never* rains in Tuscany!'

It was going to rain.

Standing at the open window of the study, Lorenzo breathed in the scent of dry earth and looked up into a sky of starless black. Down here the night was hot and heavy, but a sudden breeze stirred the tops of the cypress trees along the drive, making them shiver and whisper that a change was on the way.

*Grazie a Dio.* The dry spell had lasted for months now, and the ground was cracking and turning to dust. In the garden Alfredo had almost used up his barrels of hoarded rainwater, laboriously filling watering cans to douse the plants wilting in the *limonaia,* and in daylight the view of the hillside below Palazzo Castellaccio was as uniformally brown as a faded sepia print.

Suddenly from behind him in the room there came a low gasp of sensual pleasure, and Lorenzo turned round just in time to see his ex-wife's lover bend over her naked body, circling her rosy nipple with his tongue.

Expertly done, he thought acidly as the huge plasma screen above the fireplace was filled with a close shot of Tia's parted lips. Ricardo Marcello was about as good at acting as your average plank of wood but he certainly came to life in the sex scenes, with the result that the completed film—a big-budget blockbuster about the early life of the sixteenth-century Italian scientist Galileo—contained rather more of them than Lorenzo had originally planned. Audiences across the world were likely to leave the cinema with little notion of Galileo as the father of modern science but with a lingering impression of him as a three-times-a-night man who was prodigiously gifted in a Kama Sutra of sexual positions.

With an exhalation of disgust Lorenzo reached for the remote control and hit 'pause' just as the camera was making yet another of its epic journeys over the honeyed contours of Tia's flatteringly lit, cosmetically enhanced body. *Circling the Sun* was guaranteed box-office gold, but it marked the moment of total creative bankruptcy in his own career; the point at which he had officially sold out, traded in his integrity and his vision for money he didn't need and fame he didn't want.

He'd done it for Tia. Because she'd begged him to. Because he *could*. And because he had wanted, somehow, to try to make up for what he couldn't give her.

He had ended up losing everything, he thought bitterly.

As if sensing his mood the dog that had been sleeping curled up in one corner of the leather sofa lifted his head and jumped down, coming over and pressing his long nose into Lorenzo's hand. Lupo was part-lurcher, part-wolfhound, part-mystery, but though his pedigree was dubious his loyalty to Lorenzo wasn't. Stroking the dog's silky ears, Lorenzo felt his anger dissolve again. That film might have cost him his wife, his self-respect and very nearly his creative vision, but it was also the brick wall he had needed to hit in order to turn his life around.

Francis Tate's book lay on the desk beside him and he picked it up, stroking the cover with the palm of his hand. It was soft and worn with age, creased to fit the contours of his body from many years of being carried in his pocket and read on planes and during breaks on film sets. He'd found it by chance in a secondhand bookshop in Bloomsbury on his first trip to England. He had been nineteen, working as a lowly runner on a film job in London. Broke and homesick, and the word *Cypress* on the creased spine of the book had called to him like a warm, thyme-scented whisper from home.

Idly now he flicked through the yellow-edged pages, his eyes skimming over familiar passages and filling his head with images that hadn't lost their freshness in the twenty years since he'd first read them. For a second he felt almost light-headed with longing. It might not be commercial, it might just end up costing him more than it earned but, *Dio,* he wanted to make this film.

Involuntarily, his mind replayed the image of the girl from The Rose and Crown—Sarah—walking through the field of wheat; the light on her bare brown arms, her treacle-coloured hair. It had become a sort of beacon in his head, that image; the essence of the film he wanted to create. Something subtle and quiet and honest.

He wanted it more than anything he had wanted for a long time.

A piece of paper slipped out from beneath the cover of the book and fluttered to the floor. It was the letter from Tate's publisher:

*Thank you for your interest, but Ms Halliday's position on the film option for her father's book* The Oak and the Cypress *is unchanged at present. We will, of course, inform you should Ms Halliday reconsider her decision in the future.*

Grimly he tossed the book down onto the clutter on the low coffee table and went back over to the open window. He could feel a faint breeze now, just enough to lift the corners of the papers on the desk and make the planets in the mechanical model of the solar system on the windowsill rotate a little on their brass axes.

Change was definitely in the air.

He just hoped that, whoever and wherever this Ms Halliday was, she felt it too.

# CHAPTER THREE

SARAH woke with a start and sat up, her heart hammering.

Over the last few weeks she had got quite familiar with the sensation of waking up to a pillow wet with tears, but this was more than that. The duvet that she had kicked off was soaked and the cotton shirt she was sleeping in—one of the striped city shirts that Rupert had left at her flat—was damp against her skin. It was dark. Too dark. The glow of light from the landing had gone out and, blinking into the blackness, Sarah heard the sound of cascading water. It was raining.

Hard.

Inside.

A fat drop of water landed on her shoulder and ran down the front of her shirt. Jumping up from the low camp-bed, she groped for the light switch and flicked it. Nothing happened. It was too dark to see anything but instinctively she tilted her face up to try to look at the ceiling, and another drop of water hit her squarely between the eyes. She swore quietly and succinctly.

'Mummy,' Lottie murmured from the bed. 'I heard that. That's ten pence for the swear box.' Sarah heard the rustle of bedclothes as Lottie sat up, and then said in a small, uncertain voice, 'Mummy, everything is wet.'

Sarah made an effort to keep her own tone casual, as if

water cascading through the ceiling in the middle of the night was something tedious but perfectly normal. 'The roof seems to be leaking. Come on. Let's find you some dry pyjamas and go and see what's happening.'

Holding Lottie's hand, Sarah felt her way out onto the landing and felt her way gingerly along the wall in what she hoped she was remembering correctly as the direction of the stairs.

'Please can we switch the light on?' Lottie's whisper had a distinct wobble. 'It's so dark. I don't like it.'

'The water must have made the lights go out. Don't worry, darling, it's nothing to be afraid of. I'm sure—'

At that moment loud shrieks from the direction of Angelica's room made it clear that she had just become aware of the crisis. Then the door burst open and there was a sudden and dramatic increase in the volume of her wailing. 'Oh, God—wake up, everyone! There's water *pouring* through the roof!'

Lottie's grip tightened on Sarah's hand as she picked up on the hysteria in her aunt's voice. 'We know,' said Sarah struggling to keep her irritation at bay. 'Let's just keep calm while we find out what's going on.'

But Angelica only did calm if it came expensively packaged in the context of a luxury spa. Fenella appeared beside her, ghostly in the gloom, and the two of them clung together, sobbing.

'Darlings, what on earth has happened?' As she joined them Martha's drawl was faintly indignant. 'I thought I'd fallen asleep in the bath by mistake. Everything's soaking.'

'Must be a problem with the roof,' Sarah said wearily. 'Mum, you look after Lottie. Angelica, where would I find a torch?'

'How should *I* know?' Angelica wailed. 'That's Hugh's department, not mine. Oh, God, why isn't he here? Or Daddy. They'd know what to do.'

'*I* know what to do,' said Sarah through gritted teeth as she made her way towards the stairs. Because that was what happened when you didn't have a man around to do everything for you; you developed something called *independence*. 'I'm going to find a torch and then I'm going to go out and see what's wrong with the roof.'

'Don't be silly—you can't possibly go climbing up onto the roof in this weather,' snapped Angelica.

'Darling, she's right,' said Martha. 'It's really not a good idea.'

'Well, let me know the minute you have a better one,' Sarah called back grimly. The dark house was filled with the ominous sound of trickling water and her feet splashed through puddles on the tiled floor of the kitchen as she searched for Hugh's expensive and unused collection of tools.

Amongst them was a small torch. Flicking it on, Sarah let its thin beam wander around the walls and felt her heart sink. Water was dripping from the ceiling and running down the walls in rivulets, just like the ones streaming down the window panes outside. The patio doors shed squares of opaque grey light over the wet floor. She opened them and stepped outside.

It was like walking into the shower fully clothed. Or maybe not quite *fully* clothed, she thought, glancing down at Rupert's striped shirt. Within seconds it was soaked and clinging to her, which at least meant that she couldn't get any wetter. Shaking her hair back from her face, blinking against the teeming rain, she sucked in a breath and forced herself to walk further out into the downpour, holding the torch up and pointing it in the direction of the roof.

The low pitch of the single-storey roof was easy to see, but the torch's weak light showed up nothing that would explain the disaster unfolding inside.

'Sarah—you're soaked! Darling, come in.' Her mother had appeared in the doorway, a raincoat over her elegant La Perla nightdress, an umbrella shielding her from the rain. 'We're way out of our depth here. Angelica and Fenella have taken Lottie with them to get help from the yummy man next door.'

Sarah directed the torchlight higher to the spine of the roof, squinting against the rain. 'But it's the middle of the night. You can't just appear on someone's doorstep at this hour.'

'Darling, we're damsels very much in distress,' Martha yelled above the noise of the rain, collapsing the umbrella as she retreated indoors. 'This is an emergency. We can hardly wait until morning—we need to be rescued now.'

'Speak for yourself,' muttered Sarah disgustedly under her breath, dragging over one of the patio chairs so she could stand on it. Clamping the torch between her teeth, she used the drainpipe to hoist herself onto the low roof.

The tiles were rough beneath her bare knees, but they felt firm enough. Cautiously, shaking dripping hair from her eyes, she stood up, freeing her hands to hold the torch again. The roof sloped gently upwards to the main part of the house, and she carefully climbed higher, the dim beam of light wobbling erratically over the glistening terracotta tiles in front of her. They were uneven and bumpy but none seemed to be missing. Sarah directed the torch to the highest point, where the kitchen roof joined the wall. There seemed to be a gap...

At that moment she heard voices below and the wet blackness was suddenly flooded with blinding white light. Sarah gave a gasp of shock and, lifting her hands to shield her eyes from the glare, she accidentally let the torch slip from her grasp. She heard it clattering down the roof as she struggled to keep her balance on the slippery tiles.

'Bloody hell!'

'Stay there. Don't move.'

The light was shining right up at her, making it impossible to see anything beyond the silver streams of rain in its dazzling arc. Staggering backwards, she squinted into its beam, instinctively trying to see the owner of the deep, gravelly Italian voice while simultaneously peeling the soaking shirt from her wet thighs and bending her knees in an attempt to make it cover as much of her as possible.

'I said, keep still. Unless, of course, you want to kill yourself.'

'Right now I'm tempted,' Sarah muttered grimly, 'given that I'm half-naked and you're shining a spotlight on me. Could you possibly just turn that light off?'

'And if I do that, how are you going to see to get down from there?' He didn't have to raise his voice above the noise of the rain. It was rich and deep enough to need no projection.

'I was managing all right until you came.'

'Meaning you hadn't broken your neck yet. What the hell did you think you were doing, going up there in this weather?'

Sarah gave a snort of exasperation. 'God, you sound just like my mother. Can I just point out that I wouldn't be up here in any other kind of weather, since I'm trying to find out where the water's coming in. Up there I think I can see a—'

'On second thoughts, I don't really want to know,' he interrupted, and Sarah clearly heard the exasperation in his tone. 'I just want you to come very slowly towards the edge of the roof.'

'Are you mad?' She pushed dripping tendrils of hair back from her wet face. 'Why?'

'Because I know there'll be a joist there that will support your weight.'

'Oh, thanks a lot! Would this be a special steel-reinforced—?'

'Sarah, just do it.'

Hearing him say her name detonated a tiny explosion of shock in her abdomen that stopped her dead for a moment. Her mouth opened, though it was a couple of seconds before she was actually able to speak.

'How do I know I can trust you?' she said sulkily, squinting into the dazzling light, wishing she could see him. 'You could be anyone.'

'You don't, and I could, but now's not really the time for lengthy introductions. Let's just say that my name is Lorenzo, and right now I'm all that's standing between you and a very nasty fall.'

His voice was doing things to her. Inconvenient things, given her position. Irritation fizzed inside her. 'I don't mean to be rude when we've only just met, Lorenzo, but you're building your part up just a little bit. I'm not stupid, you know—I did check before I got up here that it was safe. The roof hardly slopes at all and the tiles are fixed down properly—'

Sarah took a step towards the edge and as she did so felt the tile beneath her foot crack and give way suddenly. She let out a sharp cry of anguish, her arms windmilling madly as she tried to keep her balance.

Suddenly she was afraid.

'It's OK. You're all right.'

'That's easy for you to say,' she gasped with a slightly wild laugh. 'You're not the one who's about to crash through the roof and end up on the kitchen table.' She closed her eyes for a second, waiting for the adrenaline that was pumping through her and making her feel shaky and unsteady to subside.

'That's not going to happen.'

'How do you know?'

'Because I'm not going to let it.' The beam of light swung away from her and she shivered in the sudden darkness. But a moment later he spoke again, and his voice was closer now.

'I can't do this and hold the torch, so you're going to have to listen very carefully and do what I say. OK?'

'OK.' Her voice sounded small and quiet. But perhaps it was just because her heart was suddenly beating very loudly, making the blood pound in her ears. The torch was on the ground far below, its powerful beam cutting through the indigo darkness and turning the rain on Angelica and Hugh's limestone patio into pools of mercury. Up here it seemed very dark.

'Come carefully towards the edge of the roof and stop when I tell you.'

Sarah did as he said, letting out another whimper of fear as she felt another tile crack. Rain was running down her face, making her eyes sting. She closed them.

'That's it. Stop there,' he ordered, and although his voice was harsh there was a peculiar intimacy to it. 'Now, reach out your arms. I'm going to lift you down.'

'No! You can't! I'm too heavy, I'll...'

But the rest of her protest was lost as she felt one arm circle her waist, and then she was being pulled against his body. Through the thin layer of their wet clothes she could feel the warmth of his skin, his hard-muscled chest. Instinctively her hands found his shoulders, and even through her shock and fear she was aware of their power. Heat suddenly erupted inside her, tingling through her chilled body.

'Thank you,' she muttered, trying to pull quickly away from him as her feet made contact with something solid. Instantly the world tilted and her stomach gave a sickening lurch as she felt herself falling and realised she had just stepped off the edge of the table they were standing on. He grabbed her again, pulling her back into the safety of his arms.

'I'm beginning to think you have a death wish,' he said grimly, sweeping her legs from under her and holding her against him as he climbed down from the table in one fluid movement.

'If I did I could think of more elegant ways to end it all than falling off a roof while wearing nothing but my nightie. Now, *please,* put me *down.*'

'The gravel is sharp and you've got no shoes on.'

'I'm fine. I can manage. Please...' she said, miserably aware that by now his back was probably groaning with bearing the weight of her. Although he certainly showed no sign of noticing that she was heavier than your average feather pillow. Against her ear his breathing was perfectly slow and steady, and his pace easy. It didn't slow at all at her words either, she noticed with a thud of alarm and helpless excitement as they rounded the corner of the house and he made straight for the hulking shape of a large 4x4 that loomed out of the darkness.

'Where are you taking me, anyway?'

'Home.'

'Look, stop, please. And let me go!'

He sighed. 'If that's really what you want...'

Unreasonable disappointment shafted through her as he set her down on the wet gravel and stood back. She wobbled slightly as the sharp stones cut into her feet. Out of the warmth of his arms, she realised how cold she was.

'It is,' she said and hoped that the sudden feeling of uncertainty about that wasn't evident in her voice. 'Look, it's very kind of you to help, but we'll be fine here until morning. We've never even met before and there are five of us here, so—'

'Actually, you're wrong.'

'What do you mean?'

'Well, for a start, your family are already there, at Castellaccio.'

'What? But they can't...we can't...possibly descend on you. It's out of the question—we'll manage fine here.'

'Funny. That wasn't what your sister said. Or her friend—Fenella, was it?'

Bloody Fenella. Her words from earlier echoed mockingly around Sarah's head. *He sounds delish. I wouldn't mind getting on the right side of him...* Of course, never in a million years would she pass up the opportunity to get a foot in the door of a film director's luxury *palazzo*. Limping as quickly as she could after Lorenzo Cavalleri, it wasn't just the sharp gravel beneath Sarah's bare feet that made her wince.

He reached the car and pulled open the door. A small light inside went on and she felt her heart stop, and then start again with a painful thump as she caught a fleeting glimpse of hard cheekbone and sharp jawline darkened with stubble before he melted back into the darkness and went around to the other side of the car.

For a moment he had reminded her of the man in the pub

that night. The man who had kissed her. But of course that was ridiculous; he was Italian, and male—that was where the coincidence ended. Getting into the car, she quickly did up her seat belt and, as he got into the driver's seat beside her, deliberately turned her head and looked out into the wet night.

She could hardly remember what he looked like anyway, she told herself crossly. Because it was unimportant. *He* was unimportant.

'First thing tomorrow I'll get a decent local builder to come and have a look at the roof and then hopefully we can get it sorted out,' she said stiffly as he started the engine.

'You know many decent local builders?'

'No, but I'm guessing that any local builder would be better than the idiots that Hugh and Angelica brought over from London. God knows what they've done.'

'My guess is they've put the tiles on upside down. Tuscan roof tiles curve slightly, and it appears they've laid them so that the water flows right down between the gaps. If I'm right the whole roof will need redoing.'

Sarah groaned. 'Oh, God, but the wedding's the day after tomorrow. I'll have to think of something.'

There was a slight pause, and then he said quietly, 'Why is it your responsibility?'

Sarah stared through the silvery lines of rain on the window. 'You've met Angelica and my mother. They're each as hopeless as the other, and we can't wait until Hugh and Guy get here if it's going to be sorted out before the wedding.'

'Hugh I've met, but who's Guy?'

The windscreen wipers beat a steady tattoo, like a heartbeat in the womb-like interior of the car, and warm air from the heater curled around her, making her chilled skin tingle. She felt suddenly very, very tired and leaned her head back against the soft leather seat, closing her eyes. 'Guy's my stepfather. Angelica's father. He's the kind of person who makes things happen and gets things done—especially for Angelica, but I suspect that re-roofing an entire house in under twenty-four hours is beyond even his capability.'

'You don't get on with him?'

'Oh, I do. You couldn't not. He's charming, witty, extremely generous...'

'But?'

She was dimly aware that the car had come to a standstill, but he didn't turn the engine off. Below the throb of the engine she could hear the rain pattering on the roof, and it made her feel oddly safe and protected. Or maybe it was this man that made her feel like that—this stranger, Lorenzo Cavalleri. For a moment she thought back to how it had felt to be in his arms when he had rescued her from the roof. The strength that she had sensed in him, that was more than just a matter of hard muscle...

She sat up abruptly and opened her eyes, feeling for the door handle.

*Rescued her.*

Uh-uh. She didn't need to be rescued. She didn't ask for it and she didn't want it. She could cope perfectly well without a man, and she wasn't going to make the mistake of letting her hormones rule her head again. Not after Rupert. Not after the man in The Rose and Crown that night. Perhaps she should ring Italian Accents Anonymous.

'He's not *my* father, that's all,' she said abruptly, pushing the door open and getting out of the car. The shock of the cold rain on her newly warmed skin was almost a relief.

Small world, thought Lorenzo, getting out of the car and walking round to where she waited by the *palazzo*'s double front doors. He felt a smile touch his mouth as he looked at her. She was standing perfectly still, perfectly straight, almost as if she was oblivious to the rain that was plastering her hair to her head and running down her face. Most women he knew would be horrified at the idea of being so thoroughly drenched—like her sister, for example, who had insisted on an umbrella being found before she would even make a dash for the car back at the farmhouse.

'The door's not locked. Please, go in.'

She didn't move. 'Look, I'm sorry about this,' she said as Lorenzo moved past her, pushing open the door. 'Really. It doesn't seem right. We don't even know you. Maybe we should just go and—'

The light from the hallway spilled out into the wet night. Standing back to let her go ahead of him, he saw her blink in the sudden brightness, and then watched her eyes widen, her lips part in silent shock as realisation hit her.

Her hand flew to her mouth, colour blooming in her rain-shiny cheeks as she took a couple of steps backwards into the darkness. Lorenzo reached out and grabbed her wrist, pulling her into the hallway.

'You're not going anywhere,' he said softly. 'Not this time.'

# CHAPTER FOUR

'This time.'

Pressing herself back against the closed door, oblivious to the grandeur of the enormous room in which she found herself, for a moment the only words Sarah's shocked brain could come up with were a numb echo of his. '*This time?* So you *knew?* All this time I've been out there making a complete and utter spectacle of myself, you knew it was me.' Horror crept over her as her mind replayed the events of the past hour in this new, humiliating light. 'You could have *said*.'

'And if I had?'

'I would have stayed up on the roof.'

She closed her eyes, hot shame flooding her as she thought about what she must have looked like from below in her skimpy shirt. How she must have *felt* when he'd lifted her down.

*Oh, God.*

Having to surrender your scantily clad self—all too-many stones of it—to the arms of a stranger was bad enough, but discovering that he wasn't entirely a stranger was infinitely worse. The man who had been shining a torch up her soaked-to-transparency shirt, the man who had lifted her considerable weight down from the roof, was the same man who had kissed her as a joke on her sister's hen night. It was almost more than she could bear.

'Exactly,' he said gravely.

At that moment they were interrupted by a familiar voice from the doorway. 'Oh, there you are, darling! Honestly, talk about drowned rat!' Sarah felt the colour deepen in her glowing cheeks as her mother advanced towards them, still in her nightdress and coat but now with a large drink in one hand, as if she were at a slightly bohemian cocktail party. 'Come through and get a towel, darling—we're all drying out in front of a lovely fire and warming up with some of Signor Cavalleri's excellent brandy.' She batted her eyelashes in Lorenzo's direction. 'He's been so kind, I can't tell you.'

Sarah gritted her teeth, feeling the way she had when she was at school and Martha and Guy used to turn up at her sports day in the open-topped Rolls-Royce, and loudly uncork bottles of vintage champagne while everyone else was opening flasks of tea. 'Mum, please,' she hissed, following her across the inlaid-marble floor and through a doorway on the right. 'I really don't think we can...'

She stopped. The room she found herself in had the same majestic proportions, the same ornate plaster panelling as the hall, but here the stately impact was lessened by the fact that it was incredibly untidy. Papers covered every surface, from the vast antique desk that stood between the windows, to the low table in front of the fire and the deep leather chesterfield sofa. Or the bits of it that weren't taken up with Angelica, Fenella, Lottie and a large grey dog.

'Lottie's fast asleep already, bless her,' Martha continued, peering down at her small pyjama-clad form. 'Isn't she sweet? Signor Cavalleri, I really must thank you for taking pity on us in our hour of need. Now we're all here, please let's introduce ourselves properly.'

Standing shivering in her wet shirt, Sarah gave a short, humourless laugh. 'I don't think there's any need for that. I believe that Angelica and Signor Cavalleri already know each other.'

Angelica blinked and shook back her silky blonde hair.

'Oh, no, I don't think so, but I believe you've met my fiancé, Hugh? You were kind enough to come and offer your advice on—'

Beside her Fenella nudged her and murmured something inaudible, glancing at Sarah. Angelica's blue eyes widened. 'Oh, my goodness, yes! You were in the pub that night, weren't you? The Rose and Crown, on my hen night.'

Sarah felt as if there were something wrapped tightly around her neck as Lorenzo gave a curt nod.

'Oh, gosh—I don't believe it! What an *amazing* coincidence, isn't it, Fenella?'

'Amazing,' smirked Fenella, unfolding herself from the sofa in one elegant movement and letting the long cashmere cardigan she was wearing fall open to reveal little shorts and a vest top beneath it. 'Of course, if we'd had the chance to talk we might have discovered the coincidence sooner but, as I recall, Sarah rather naughtily monopolised you. You both disappeared rather suddenly too.'

Sarah snatched up a towel and began vigorously rubbing her hair, which was the only way she could stop herself from taking Fenella's elegant neck in her hands and wringing it. It also provided her with a diversion as she struggled to fit this new and unexpected information into the mental slot marked 'Bastard' she had created for the Screaming Orgasm man.

If Angelica and Fenella hadn't set him up that night, then why the hell had he kissed her?

From behind the towel she watched as he briefly shook the hand Fenella held out. 'As *I* recall,' he said casually, turning away, 'you were monopolising the rest of the males in the vicinity, so I'm sure it was no loss.'

'Well, how astonishing that you should find yourself in our very sleepy corner of darkest Oxfordshire,' Martha interjected hastily. 'I'm Martha, by the way. Martha Halliday.'

Lorenzo stopped, tensing into complete stillness for a second. Then he turned round again, his narrow eyes very dark.

'Not so sleepy, Signora *Halliday*.' Sarah noticed the slight emphasis he placed on her mother's surname. 'Certainly not on the night I was there. Have you lived there for long?'

'Since I was nineteen and I fell in love for the first time. You're right—it's nothing like it used to be,' Clearly eager to steer the conversation back into harmless waters, Martha was at her most chatty and expansive. 'I grew up in suburbia and it was like being dropped into the middle of a Thomas Hardy novel. Wildly romantic in theory, but the reality was harsh. In those days The Rose and Crown was a tiny little country inn where regulars used to help themselves from behind the bar and put the money in a box. Francis—that was my first husband—spent more of our married life in there than at home. He used to sit at a table in the corner by the inglenook and write. Said it was the only place he could keep warm enough to think in winter.'

'Write?'

'Yes. Poetry, mainly, but—'

'Mum,' Sarah hissed, 'it's three o'clock in the morning. I hardly think this is the time to be discussing literature.'

Especially not the singularly unsuccessful literary efforts of her father. Sarah just knew what Martha had been about to say next—that as well as endless volumes of strenuous, angry poems describing the industrialisation of the rural landscape, the late Francis Tate's canon also included a book, set in Oxfordshire and Tuscany. The fact that it too had been a complete commercial flop never stopped Martha from talking about it as if it were some work of staggering, underrated genius, much to Sarah's embarrassment.

'Sorry. Of course, darling, you're right,' Martha laughed, putting down her empty brandy glass. 'We've caused you quite enough disruption already, Signor Cavalleri. It's not too inconvenient to put us up for the night, I hope?'

'Not at all,' Lorenzo said tersely. 'Although I can't promise five-star service, I'm afraid. I should explain that I'm here alone at the moment. My housekeeper left a while ago and I haven't got round to finding a replacement yet, so you'll have to look after yourselves. You found the rooms all right?'

'Oh, yes, thank you.' Martha beamed. 'You have such a beautiful home, and perhaps tomorrow we can see it properly, but now, girls, I think it's time we took ourselves out of Signor Cavalleri's way.'

The dog lifted its head mournfully as Angelica and Fenella got up from the sofa and said their goodnights, but it didn't move. Sarah eyed it warily as she looked down at Lottie, wondering how best to pick her up without waking her. In the warm glow of the firelight she was curled up tightly, her hands tucked neatly beneath one rosy cheek, like a child in an old-fashioned picture book.

She jumped as a low voice broke the silence. 'So, you have a daughter.'

Her sudden indrawn breath made a little hiss in the quiet room. Lorenzo was standing on the other side of the sofa, watching her expressionlessly.

'Yes.' She wasn't as good as he was at keeping the emotion from her voice, and the short word bristled with defensiveness.

This was the point at which most men would say something bright and howlingly insincere about how sweet Lottie was, how adorable, whilst mentally calculating the quickest method of exit, but Lorenzo Cavalleri simply nodded. His eyes never left hers. It was as if he was looking right inside her. Sarah felt her stomach tighten with reluctant excitement as heat zigzagged down to her pelvis. And then she remembered that she was wearing nothing but a wet shirt, and that she'd towel-dried her hair so vigorously that she was probably doing a very good impression of Neanderthal woman. Quickly she bent over Lottie, hoping he wouldn't see that she was blushing.

'I'll help you get her to bed,' Lorenzo said flatly, and she was aware of him moving round the sofa to where she stood.

'No. It's fine. I can manage.'

'How did I know you were going to say that?' he said, his voice laced with sardonic mockery. 'Do you ever accept help?'

'I'm used to doing things myself, that's all,' Sarah muttered, wondering how she was going to bend down enough to gather Lottie up without completely exposing herself. Again. She wasn't sure if the fact he'd pretty much seen it all already made it worse or better. 'Lottie's father wasn't exactly the hands-on type.'

'Where is he now?'

'In bed with his ice-blonde, beautiful fiancée, I imagine,' she said bitterly.

Lorenzo nodded slowly. 'I see.'

She gave a harsh gust of laughter. 'I doubt it,' she snapped, sitting down abruptly on the sofa beside Lottie, bending forward to gather her into her arms from there.

They both jumped as the huge plasma screen above the fireplace flickered into life, displaying a close-up image of a woman's bare midriff—as smooth and brown and endless as a stretch of desert sand. The camera travelled upwards, lingering lovingly on the hollow between her incredibly firm, neat breasts, the ridges of her collarbones and the sharp jut of her jaw as she stretched her head back and opened her mouth in a breathless cry of pleasure...

Sarah's mouth dropped open too, although it was a look she couldn't carry off half as sexily as Tia de Luca.

Because there was no mistaking that was who it was. No mistaking those slanting eyes, as cool and green as apples, or the famous pillow-plump lips, which were now quivering with anticipation as the hero's mouth moved up the column of her throat towards them...

Sarah's sharp, high gasp matched Tia de Luca's as Lorenzo's

hand slid beneath her thigh. The next moment the screen was black and empty again.

Whipping her head round, she looked at him. He was standing perfectly still, the remote control held in his hand. For a second Sarah glimpsed a blaze of some unidentifiable emotion in his eyes, but then it was gone; replaced once more by an expressionless mask.

He threw the remote control down onto the low table in front of the fire.

'You sat on it,' he said shortly.

Sarah stumbled to her feet. 'Oh, God, I'm so sorry.'

Lorenzo shrugged impatiently. 'No problem.'

She shook her head. 'No, not for sitting on the stupid remote. For saying that before, about you not knowing what it's like. To be left. I was forgetting. I mean, I don't know anything about it, but Angelica and Fenella were talking earlier about your wife and—'

'I'm sure you're tired,' he interrupted coldly. 'Perhaps I could show you to your room now.'

Sarah ducked her head, pushing back the trailing sleeves of her shirt as she prepared to pick Lottie up. 'Of course. Yes. Sorry.'

'Here. Let me take her. You're soaking.'

'So are you.'

'Yes, but I can take this off.' He was already undoing the buttons of his shirt, impatiently, with a kind of resignation that told her that he just wanted to get rid of her, with as little fuss as possible. And, of course, she didn't blame him. He must have been watching the film when Angelica interrupted him, asking for help. That explained why he was still awake, still dressed in the small hours of the morning...

It also explained the sadness she had sensed behind the mask. And probably it accounted for why he'd kissed her that night too, she thought with a wrenching sensation in her chest.

When your heart was broken you'd do anything, use anyone to blot out the hurt and loneliness for a while.

Lorenzo didn't bother undoing all the buttons, pulling the shirt quickly over his head and throwing it hastily on top of the pile of books and papers on the table in front of the sofa.

'This way.'

Following him across the hallway and up the wide, sweeping staircase, she kept her eyes fixed determinedly on Lottie's head, resting against his upper arm. It was important not to allow herself to look at the wide shoulders or the way the muscles rippled beneath his olive skin, because then she might start making disloyal comparisons with Rupert's English pallor; his square, stocky frame that was showing the beginnings of a paunch.

There wasn't an ounce of spare flesh on Lorenzo Cavalleri. Sarah could see shadows between the ridges of his ribs, and his hip bones jutted above the top of his jeans. For all his strength, he was too thin, she thought with a twist of unexpected compassion.

'This is it.'

He stopped so suddenly in front of a closed door that Sarah, lost in forbidden thought, walked straight into him. Muttering apologies, she instantly leapt away. He opened the door and went into the room, but she stayed where she was in the dimly lit corridor, pressing herself against the wall and waiting for her breathing to steady. Looking around her, back along the corridor through which they'd just come, she realised guiltily that she hadn't taken in a single detail of her surroundings as she'd followed him through the *palazzo,* which was amazing considering that, from the little she could see now, it was pretty damned impressive.

Just not as impressive as Lorenzo Cavalleri's body.

She closed her eyes, tipping her head back against the panelling and trying to bring her wayward thoughts under control. Or her wayward hormones. It had been a long time since she and Rupert had—

'She's all yours.'

She opened her eyes, which was a bit of a mistake. He was standing in front of her, the low light from further along the passageway gleaming on the bare skin of his collarbone, the curve of his shoulder.

'Thanks,' she croaked ducking her head and sliding along the wall towards the bedroom doorway. 'For everything. And sorry.'

As she went into the bedroom she heard him say something in reply, but was so busy cursing her own gaucheness that she didn't catch what it was. Too late; through the half-open door she could hear his footsteps already dying away on the landing outside, and anyway a moment later all thoughts dissolved in her head as she turned to look around at the room.

It was as if she'd stepped into the pages of a book of fairy tales. The soft glow of the bedside lamp gleamed on the polished parquet floor and made the pale green silk curtains on the four-poster bed shimmer like waterfalls. Lottie lay against a froth of old white linen and lace like a miniature Sleeping Beauty, and Sarah gave a quiet sigh of delight as she imagined what her reaction would be when she woke and found herself in the midst of such storybook perfection.

The bed looked unbearably inviting, and all at once she realised that she was bone-tired and aching in every limb. She shivered, suddenly aware of the chill of the wet shirt against her skin, and longing to be between the soft, dry sheets. Quickly she lifted the shirt over her head and was just pulling the heavy covers back when there was a soft knock at the door behind her.

Her heart practically jumped right out of her chest. Gasping, 'Wait a second!' she dived beneath the covers and pulled them right up to her chin, the second before the door opened wider and Lorenzo's shape appeared in it.

He advanced towards the bed. The lamplight cast inky shadows in the hollows of his cheeks and accentuated the deep lines etched around his mouth and between his brows, making him look very, very tired. And sad. For a second an image of the woman on the screen flickered into Sarah's mind.

'I thought you might want this, but I can see you're managing perfectly well without.'

Tentatively Sarah inched herself upwards in the bed, clutching the sheets against her as she cautiously extended an arm to take what he held out to her. It was a T-shirt. A grey T-shirt, soft and faded.

'Thanks,' she said, not meeting his eye.

She expected him to turn and leave straight away, but he didn't. The room was very quiet, very still. The only sound was the distant rattle of rain on the windows and the gentle sigh of Lottie's breathing.

'So...' he said gruffly, lifting one hand and pushing his hair back from his forehead and then letting it fall again. 'You still haven't introduced yourself properly.'

'I don't need to. You already know my name.'

'Do I?'

Something about the way he said it made her heart lurch and her gaze fly up to meet his. 'Sarah,' she said, almost warily. 'My name is Sarah. You said it when I was on the roof.'

He nodded slowly, his eyes still boring into hers with an intensity that made her shiver and burn. '*Si*. But that doesn't mean I know who you are.'

'Then we're equal,' she said ruefully, looking down. The T-shirt he'd just given her was twisted into a knot between her hands. 'Apart from the fact that I'm nobody, and apparently you're some world-famous film director.'

'I'm hardly world-famous,' he said dismissively. 'And you're not nobody.'

'Yes I am.' She laughed uneasily, and beside her in the bed Lottie stirred and sighed, turning over so that she was lying on her back, her chestnut curls falling over her face, until she pushed them impatiently away with one plump hand. For a few long moments neither of them spoke or moved as they waited for her to settle again. Watching her face, the little frown that flickered across it for a second, the way her rosebud mouth pursed and then relaxed into a dimpled smile, Sarah found that she was smiling too. When she spoke her voice was very soft.

'I'm a mother. That's it. That's all that matters, anyway.'

She looked up, and the smile died on her lips when she saw the shuttered, cold expression on Lorenzo Cavalleri's face. He turned away, walking across the miles of gleaming parquet to the door.

'It's very late. I'm keeping you up.'

'Many would argue that it was the other way round,' Sarah said hastily. 'Look, I'm really sorry for the intrusion. My family is a full-on nightmare. You'll seriously regret your kindness, believe me.'

He stopped at the door and turned back to look at her for a second with a brief smile of distant courtesy. 'Not at all,' he said tonelessly. And then he was gone, shutting the door very quietly behind him.

*Not at all.*

Sarah Halliday couldn't begin to know how wrong she was. As Lorenzo walked away down the corridor he felt edgy with adrenaline, almost unable to take it in.

Oh, yes, it was a small world, and it was being managed by a very benevolent God. Lorenzo sent up a silent prayer of thanks to Him for delivering Francis Tate's stubborn and elusive daughter right into his hands.

It was more than he could ever have hoped for. Now the rest was up to him.

# CHAPTER FIVE

SARAH propped the broom up against the wall and looked round despondently. Almost an hour of hard labour in the waterlogged wreck of the farmhouse kitchen had resulted in minimal improvement. She'd been able to sweep out the worst of the water and make a start on wiping down the surfaces, but there was nothing at all she could do about the plaster coming away from the walls or the ominously sagging ceiling.

An hour of hard labour hadn't quite succeeded in shifting the restless, jumpy feeling she had somewhere deep down inside of her either. It had been there all night, and had made sleep elusive and unrefreshing, filled with uneasy dreams in which Lorenzo Cavalleri had held her against his bare chest and carried her along endless dark corridors...

With a sigh of exasperation she seized a cloth from the sink and began to scrub vigorously at the grimy marble worktops, as if by doing so she could also scour the unwelcome feelings from her mind and her body. It was because she was missing Rupert, she told herself fiercely. He might not have been great at a lot of things, like taking Lottie to the park, and mentioning that he was intending to marry someone else, but he'd certainly found the time to call round regularly for swift, no-nonsense sex.

She was ashamed to admit how much she missed it.

Sexual frustration, that was what all this was about, she thought, scrubbing hard. What she was feeling was a normal, healthy part of the process of letting go. She'd been with Rupert a long time, so it was inevitable that she would go through lots of stages of grieving. Fantasising about other men was obviously one of them. Breathing hard with exertion, she paused to peel a soggy copy of a celebrity magazine from the countertop where Angelica had left it. She was just about to deposit it into the bin when a headline on the cover caught her eye:

'BITTERSWEET BABY JOY FOR TIA DE LUCA.'

Sarah stopped dead, the magazine dangling between her fingers, suspended above the bin. Then, glancing guiltily around, she dropped it back down onto the bit of worktop she'd just cleaned and began to flick through. The pages were damp and stuck together, but she eventually located the full-page picture of Tia de Luca languishing on a pile of fuchsia-pink silk cushions wearing a chiffon kaftan-type thing that managed to make her look simultaneously demure and maternal without compromising her high-octane sex appeal. Propping her elbows on the worktop, Sarah began to read.

'Oh, yuk...' she muttered, skimming increasingly quickly over the interviewer's gushing inventory of Tia's finer points.

*'Miss de Luca's legendary beauty has a delicate, luminescent quality that is even more powerful in the flesh than it is on the big screen. Her figure is impossibly slender...'* Sarah gave a grimace of irritation *'...showing only the barest hint of the pregnancy she announced last week. At the mention of this her extraordinary eyes cloud for a moment. "I've wanted a child for so long, and I thought my husband felt the same way," she whispers, referring, of course, to acclaimed director Lorenzo Cavalleri, whom she has just divorced after five years of marriage. "He found it impossible to adjust to the idea of a child in his life, but I'm so lucky that Ricardo shares the joy I feel about this blessed miracle..."'*

'Hard at work, I see,' said a mocking voice behind her.

Sarah whirled around. Grabbing the magazine, she clasped it behind her back with shaking hands as she looked into Lorenzo Cavalleri's coal-black eyes. He was unshaven, and the sparklingly bright morning light highlighted streaks of grey in his hair that she hadn't noticed before. Her heart gave an uneven kick.

'I was... I mean, I am... I'm just...'

He shrugged, a tiny smile lifting the corners of his sad mouth. 'I'm teasing. When I left your sister was having a leisurely breakfast, so I shouldn't feel too guilty about taking a break from clearing up her house.'

'Was Lottie there?' Sarah asked automatically, then instantly wished she hadn't. From what Tia de Luca had said, this man didn't even want his own child around, never mind someone else's. Behind her, the magazine seemed to be burning her fingers.

'Very much so,' he said drily. 'She seems to approve of Castellaccio.'

Sarah winced. 'Oh, dear. I'm sorry. Where we live there's barely enough room to swing a hamster, and she's already wildly overexcited about the wedding and being a bridesmaid and everything.' Hurriedly she turned and dropped the magazine into the bin before picking up the cloth and scrubbing at the worktop with great focus. 'I'll just finish cleaning up in here and then I'll...'

She stopped. He had come to stand right beside her, and now reached out to cover her hand with his, stilling it. 'What? Clean the rest of the house and retile the roof before lunch?'

She froze. Common sense told her to pull her hand from beneath his and put as much distance between them as possible so he didn't notice that she was blushing like a schoolgirl and breathing like an asthmatic who'd just run a marathon. But she didn't want to. It felt too good. 'Well, maybe not quite,' she said in a low voice, 'but at least I can make it look a bit better for the wedding.'

He made a little sound of contemptuous disbelief, and moved his hand, stepping back and pushing it through his hair. '*Dio,* Sarah...'

She started cleaning again, covering the worktop in sweeping strokes that she hoped would make her look brisk and efficient. 'I know it's still a mess in here, but Angelica doesn't even have a mop. Once I get the right equipment it'll all be much easier, and then I can—'

'I didn't mean that,' he said curtly. 'Why is this your problem? It's your sister's house. Your sister's wedding.'

'Ah, yes, but, since I'm doing the catering, it's pretty much my problem, because until I can get this place cleared up I can't even make a start, and I'm going to be cutting it pretty fine as it is.'

Lorenzo shook his head in disbelief. 'Wait a minute. You're doing what?'

'The food.'

His face darkened. 'For the whole wedding? *Dio.* How many people are coming?'

'Only thirty.' He didn't have to be so appalled at the idea of her being in charge of the food, she thought sulkily, going over to the sink and holding the cloth under the tap. 'It's just a small, simple ceremony for close friends and family. They're having a big party in London next month.'

'Couldn't they get professional caterers?'

She turned off the tap and squeezed the cloth. Hard. 'I *am* a professional caterer. I worked for a company doing business lunches in the city.'

Those dark, narrow eyes didn't miss a thing. 'Worked? You don't any more?'

She looked around for more worktop to clean. 'No. No. I—er—left after an incident involving a cake at an engagement party.' She laughed uncertainly. 'Some girls wear engagement rings. I wear engagement cakes. It wasn't pretty. Anyway,' she said hurriedly, 'money's been a bit tight since then, so instead of buying a wedding present I offered to do the food. I really must get a move on—I still have to shop for ingredients.'

'Get some shoes on,' he said grimly. 'You're coming with me.'

She shook her head. 'Oh, no, I can't. I couldn't put you to any more trouble, and besides, there's no point in shopping for food until I've cleaned up here. There's nowhere to put anything.'

'We're not going shopping—yet—and you're not cleaning up here. I'm taking you back to Castellaccio.'

She opened her mouth to argue, as he knew she would, but he didn't wait to hear what she was going to say. Levering himself upright, he stalked across the kitchen to the door, saying, 'The kitchen there isn't perfect, but at least it's unlikely to give thirty of your sister's closest family and friends serious food poisoning.'

Direct hit, he thought with satisfaction, hearing her footsteps following him across the gravel a moment later. He barely knew her, but instinct told him that, though she'd fight like a cat to maintain her own spiky independence, she had an inbuilt selflessness that wouldn't allow her to put her principles before other people's well-being.

'OK. You win. Again. I'll come back with you. But first, can I go and get a change of clothes for me and Lottie? I won't be a minute.'

She was standing in the sunlight, and with her hair scraped back in some sort of pink, glittery band, wearing denim shorts and the too-big T-shirt he'd lent her, she looked oddly vulnerable.

'Of course. I'll wait in the car.'

He'd expected to be waiting for ages, but it seemed that she'd hardly gone before she was back again. She'd swapped the grey T-shirt for a coral-pink linen shirt that brought a glow to her clear skin. Skin that was, he noticed wryly as she opened the car door and got into the passenger seat, still completely bare of any trace of make-up.

'Sorry to keep you waiting,' she said breathlessly, throwing a battered straw basket stuffed with clothes into the space by her feet. In her hand she carried a pair of child's red canvas pumps which she laid on her knee, and in that second Lorenzo was pierced by an image, as clear as if he'd shot it himself on 35 mm film, of Lottie's small bare feet as he'd slid her into bed and folded the covers over her last night.

He averted his eyes.

'You didn't.' His voice sounded colder and harder than he'd intended. 'In my experience when a woman goes to change it involves at least five outfits and takes about an hour.'

'I don't have five outfits, which I suppose makes things a lot simpler.' The 4x4 bounced over a pothole in the road and she steadied herself, shifting her position at the same time as he moved down a gear so that his hand brushed her warm bare thigh. She jerked away again as sharply as if she'd touched a live wire.

For a moment neither of them spoke, then she said in a brave, bright voice, 'Anyway, this is really kind of you. At least if I can prepare the food in your kitchen, then tomorrow morning I'll come and get it and—'

'Don't you ever stop fighting?' he said grimly, turning into the driveway and accelerating slightly up the avenue of trees. Palazzo Castellaccio stood at the end; square, uncompromising and unadorned, its only concession to any kind of ornament being the *limonaia* on the side.

'Fighting what?'

He stopped the car in the shade at the side of the house and turned off the engine. The sudden silence seemed to crackle with tension.

'Logic. Reason. Common sense,' he said quietly. 'The farmhouse is a mess, and not even you can put it right in time for tomorrow. I didn't just mean that you could cook here—I meant that the wedding would be held here too.'

She laughed shakily, pulling at a trailing bit of straw that was unravelling from her basket. 'No. No way. It's impossible. Please, don't even think about mentioning that to Angelica because before you know it your house will be completely overrun with the whole bridal steamroller and you'll wish you'd never set eyes on any of us.'

He couldn't help smiling at that. 'I don't think so.'

'Y-you're sure?' Hesitantly she looked up. Straight into his eyes. And he knew that he had her exactly where he wanted her. Sarah Halliday was a girl with an outsized sense of responsibility, and he knew that after he'd done her family a favour on this scale she'd find it hard to say no to anything.

Including film rights to her father's book.

# CHAPTER SIX

'Mummeeeeee!'

Sarah was making lists at the table at one end of the cavernous kitchen when Lottie came hurtling in through the open doors to the courtyard. Sarah put her pencil down and caught the wriggling little body that hurled itself at her.

'There you are, sweetheart. I was wondering where you'd got to. Auntie Angelica said that you and Granny had gone exploring.'

'Yes—we found the church where Auntie Angelica's getting married, and met the gardener—he's called Alfredo—and there's a temple thing with steps up to it. And we saw a statue of a man with no clothes on and you can see his—'

'Good old Granny,' Sarah interrupted firmly, kissing the top of Lottie's head and setting her down again. 'Trust her to give you the full, x-rated, unabridged tour.'

'You must come and see it. Granny said you should. And Granny said it's not rude because it's *culture*.'

'I see, so Granny thinks I don't have enough culture in my life, does she?' Sarah said crossly.

'No,' said Martha drily, coming in from the bright sunlight outside. 'Granny thinks you don't have enough naked men in your life. Mind you, you could probably do better than that one. *Not* very impressive. I'm sure you wouldn't have to look very far to find a much more virile specimen, if you haven't already...' Her blue eyes twinkled wickedly. 'Ah, hello, Signor Cavalleri! We were just talking about you—weren't we, Sarah?'

'Were we?' Sarah snapped, feeling heat explode in her cheeks as she frowned down at her list with what she hoped was an air of total preoccupation. God, why did her mother have to be so embarrassing? Lorenzo Cavalleri had been married to someone widely acknowledged as the most beautiful woman in the world. As if he was going to be interested in flirting with her.

'No, you weren't, Granny,' Lottie protested. 'You were talking about the statue we saw in the garden of the man with no clothes on. You said that he had—'

Martha laughed, completely uncontrite. 'OK, my darling, I think you've got me into quite enough trouble already!' She turned her dazzling smile on Lorenzo. 'I was just about to say how very, very kind you are to be doing this for us. Really. It's so much more than anyone could have expected, and I can't begin to tell you how grateful we are—now, that *is* true, isn't it, Lottie?'

'Yes.' Lottie nodded vigorously, her eyes widening with sincerity. 'We think this might actually be the most beautiful place in the whole world. Auntie Angelica is very lucky to have her wedding here, and I'm very lucky to be a bridesmaid here, but you're luckiest of all because you live here.'

Lorenzo nodded. 'I'll remember that.'

Lottie looked at him thoughtfully for a moment. 'Do you live here by yourself?'

A faint smile touched the corners of his mouth. 'Yes.'

'It's very big for one person.' Lottie's voice held a slight air of disapproval and Sarah noticed anxiously that she was looking at Lorenzo with that beady, appraising look that suggested more devastatingly to-the-point questions and observations might follow.

Lorenzo met her gaze unflinchingly. 'It is,' he said gravely. 'Far too big. It has sixteen bedrooms.'

Lottie's eyes were as round as saucers. '*Sixteen?*' she echoed. 'But that's—'

'Enough,' Sarah interrupted firmly, and then, seeing Lottie was about to protest, added, 'And don't argue.' She softened her words with a swift kiss on the head, then picked up her list. 'Right, I'd better get going. Do you want to come with me, sweetheart?'

Lottie frowned. 'Where are you going?'

'Shopping.' Looking round, Sarah picked up her straw basket and busied herself checking that her purse was in it. 'To buy food for Auntie Angelica's wedding.'

'I'd rather stay here, with Granny.' Lottie hesitated, then added kindly, 'But I don't mind coming with you if you'll be lonely on your own.'

'How about if I go?' Lorenzo was looking at Lottie, his expression completely neutral. Giving a happy little jump, Lottie clapped her hands and cried 'Yes!' at exactly the same moment as Sarah said an emphatic

'No.'

'You might get lost,' said Lottie pityingly. She smiled at Lorenzo. 'I think you should definitely go too. Mummy's always saying she needs a nice man to take her out.'

After yesterday's rain it seemed hotter than ever, the sky a hard, glittering arc of polished lapis lazuli.

Lorenzo had dropped her off in a little street that ran down to the main square, and stepping out of the climate-controlled interior of the car had felt like walking into an oven. But in many ways it felt easier to breathe in the scorching heat than it had done when she was near him in the air-conditioned car.

The market was set out in the piazza, the brightly coloured awnings of the stalls contrasting vividly with the stinging yellow and rich, earthy reds of the buildings all around the square. The sun was relentless, but it seemed a shame to dim the astonishing colours behind dark glasses, so Sarah slid them up onto her head and enjoyed the vibrant glare. Wandering through the crowds of people, her list clasped in her hand, she had quickly become completely absorbed in her task, pausing beside stalls piled high with produce to pick up a tomato and test the firmness of its flesh, or hold a melon to her nose, inhaling its cool green perfume.

The colours, the scents and textures dazed her. She was in Italy. *Italy.* All around her she could hear the most beautiful language on earth rising and falling in musical cadences, the occasional isolated word resonating in her head and striking chords of half-forgotten meaning. She was here. Far, far away from London and traffic jams and office blocks, in the spiritual home of good food, great art and hot sex.

The thought took her by surprise and made her heart perform a little acrobatic flip.

Her Italian was basic, but the stallholders were so friendly that she soon found that much could be achieved with a smile and a gesture. Slivers of velvety prosciutto were pressed on her—salty-sharp and melt-in-the-mouth; smoky Provolone cheese; olives that tasted of sunshine and Italy. She bought bags of peppery fresh rocket, courgettes with the flowers still attached, lemons as big as tennis balls and heads of fragrant garlic from a stout, smiling man in a striped apron, whose eyes twinkled above his bristling moustache as he heaped her purchases into her basket and pressed a ripe peach into her hand once she'd paid.

*'Grazie, signor.'*

He dismissed her thanks with a wave of his plump hand and, dark eyes snapping, answered with a stream of rapid Italian that went completely over her head. Biting into the peach, Sarah shrugged helplessly and laughed. 'I don't understand!'

'He's saying that it's a pleasure to serve such a beautiful

girl who clearly understands good food,' said a low voice behind her.

Sarah didn't turn, but felt the laughter fade on her lips. Her mouth was filled with the exquisite sweetness of the peach and her stomach tightened.

The stallholder's smile widened into a beam of delighted recognition when he saw Lorenzo, and he broke into a flood of excited conversation that involved much arm-waving and laughter. Taking another bite of the peach, Sarah stepped to one side, so that she wasn't caught in the middle of all the exuberant back-slapping as the man greeted him as an old friend. The stallholder's infectious bonhomie was in direct contrast with Lorenzo's habitual aloofness, but somehow that only served to emphasise the gorgeous richness of Lorenzo's deep, grave voice. Eating her peach in the sunshine, she listened to him with a pleasure that was almost physical.

*Actually, there was no almost about it.*

Suddenly she gave a start, as she realised that both men were looking at her, as well as a fair number of passers-by, who had temporarily stopped passing by and were lingering, feigning interest in piles of oranges while stealing curious glances at her and at Lorenzo. Oh, God, did she have peach juice running down her chin? Hastily she wiped her mouth on the back of her hand. Lorenzo was smiling at something the man had said, shaking his head, but his eyes met hers and she felt a bolt of electricity shoot through her, like the lightning before a sudden summer storm.

'An old friend?' she asked when they eventually made their escape in a flurry of handshaking and *ciao*s.

They were walking across the square, away from the market. Lorenzo was carrying a box containing the courgettes, on top of which a handful of dark, bulbous truffles had mysteriously been added.

'No. But having a job that gets your picture in the papers makes people feel that they know you.'

Sarah looked down at her feet in their battered flip-flops. Her toes bore the chipped remains of some pale green nail varnish Lottie had got in a party bag ages ago. 'What did he say?'

Lorenzo shot her a speculative, sideways glance. 'He asked if you were the new woman in my life.'

Sarah took her glasses from the top of her head and pushed them on again, so she didn't have to meet his eye. 'Oh, God. How embarrassing for you. I'm so sorry.'

'Don't be. When I said no, he asked why not.' He began to weave through the busy tables of a little restaurant in a sunny corner of the square.

Surprised, she asked, 'Where are we going?'

'For lunch.'

She stopped dead, feeling deeply foolish. 'Oh. Right. OK, then...you should have said. I'll just look round the shops and I'll meet you when you're finished—'

Shifting the box of courgettes to under one arm, he put his other hand in the small of her back and drew her gently, firmly forwards into the dim interior of the restaurant.

'No, you won't. You'll have lunch with me. After all, you have to eat.'

Inside the restaurant was empty, cave-dark, the colour of its walls impossible to make out behind the forest of framed photographs, newspaper cuttings, old menus and napkins scrawled with the indecipherable signatures that covered them. Lorenzo led her to a table in the farthest corner and pulled out a chair for her.

'Not really. I'm hardly going to fade away, am I?' she muttered, picking up the menu and holding it in front of her face so he couldn't see her flaming cheeks. 'As the man said, I clearly know all about good food.'

Gently he removed the menu from her hands and put it down on the table. And then he reached across and pulled off her sunglasses.

'It was a compliment,' he said, very quietly.

His dark gaze enveloped her. It was like standing outside on the warmest summer night, and feeling perfectly safe in the blackness. For a moment she just looked back at him, not thinking, not wanting to think. Only wanting to feel that indefinable, inexplicable sense of being protected...

She blinked, and looked away with a quick, self-deprecating smile.

'Of course, this is Italy. I'd forgotten how different it is from buttoned-up, poker-faced England,' she said soberly, pushing her chair back and getting to her feet. 'Excuse me a moment.'

In the tiny ladies' cloakroom out the back, with the scent of garlic wafting in from the kitchen, Sarah looked dismally at her reflection in the mirror. Her face was shiny and the sun had already brought out the freckles across her nose, but that was nothing compared to the disaster that was her hair. With a groan of dismay she tugged it free from the Disney princess band that had been the first thing that came to hand this morning and frantically tried to pull her fingers through the wild curls that last night's soaking followed by enthusiastic towel-drying had turned into a tangled mane.

She exhaled heavily so that one curl fluttered upwards for a moment before bouncing back onto her nose. So, the question was, which was worst? The pink, glittery hairband with its picture of Cinderella's disembodied head, or the mad hippy look? Grimly, she turned on the tap and ran her hands beneath the blissfully cool water before smoothing them over her hair in an attempt to flatten it into some semblance of normality. At least with it down she would have something to hide behind.

Back at the table, Lorenzo poured dark red wine into two glasses and watched her make her way through the tables towards him. That was something at least, he thought wryly. It wouldn't have surprised him if she'd made a run for it through the kitchens.

He was used to women clinging. Fawning. Playing complicated games that were calculated to catch his attention and keep him interested, which he suspected was exactly what Tia's last fling had started out as. But this girl, he thought, looking at her as she smoothed a hand over the curls she'd just let down, this girl would obviously rather be pretty much anywhere else, and she couldn't hide it if her life depended on it.

That was one of the first things he'd noticed about her, back in England. Her emotions were written all over her sweet, open face, which should make it a hell of a lot easier for him to find out more about her father, he thought idly. He just had to get her to relax enough to open up a bit.

He pushed a glass towards her as she sat down again, and was rewarded with a quick smile that brought out the dimples in her smooth cheeks and made her look about sixteen.

'Oh, God, I really shouldn't. I've got to cook this afternoon, and I haven't even decided on the menu yet. Lunchtime drinking is a really bad idea.'

'You haven't decided on the menu? *Bene,* in that case we can call this research.'

She looked at him warily, but he was absurdly pleased when she took a large mouthful of wine. 'Research?'

He nodded to the swarthy man nonchalantly polishing glasses in the shadows behind the bar. Gennaro was far too discreet to approach them without invitation, but he came forward now with a wide smile.

'Sarah, I'd like you to meet Gennaro, owner of this place, and consummate menu-planner.'

She smiled—a warm, genuine smile—half rising from her chair as she held out her hand. Gennaro took it, but leaned forward and kissed her on both cheeks too, and when he turned back to Lorenzo his dark eyes gleamed with approval.

'*Delizioso,*' he said in rapid, local Italian. 'Your taste in women is definitely improving.'

Lorenzo pulled out a chair and motioned for him to sit down. '*Non e come cio,*' he said curtly. It's not like that.

'*Che?*' Sitting down, Gennaro threw his hands up in mock

despair, replying in impenetrable dialect, 'This is the first woman you bring here in seventeen years who doesn't look like she's going to order an undressed chef's salad and spend the whole time picking out the pancetta, and you tell me *it's not like that?*' He shook his head hopelessly.

Very deliberately Lorenzo switched back to English. 'Sarah's a cook,' he said, hoping that Gennaro would pick up the warning note in his voice. 'It's your advice about *food* I'm after, *grazie mille.*'

Gennaro laughed. 'Of course. My pleasure. It is my second favourite subject. How can I help?'

'You can start by bringing us some of your bresaola, and then whatever you're recommending today to follow.'

'Ah—you came on the right day, my friend. Today we have porcetta slow-roasted with herbs. *Fantastico.* Leave it to me. I bring you the best food in Tuscany, Sarah.'

'Bresaola,' Sarah repeated as Gennaro disappeared in the direction of the kitchen. She took another mouthful of wine and Lorenzo noticed that her expressive dark eyes were shining with a light he hadn't seen in them before. 'That's beef, right?'

He nodded. 'Air-dried and salted, like prosciutto, but forget any preconceptions you have about what it's like until you've tried Gennaro's. It comes from a local farmer, whose identity Gennaro keeps top secret. However,' he drawled with a lazy smile, 'I'm absolutely certain that *you* could charm him into spilling the information.'

She laughed awkwardly, looking down and realigning her knife and fork on the scarred pine table top. 'Is there a shortage of women around here or something?'

'No. What makes you say that?'

'It's just that I don't usually have men falling over themselves to do things for me.'

'Maybe that's because you usually give the impression that you'd rather die than accept help. Or kill anyone who offers it.'

'I would not,' she protested hotly, 'I—'

She stopped as Gennaro reappeared with several plates. Sensing the atmosphere, he slid them quickly onto the table with a murmured 'Buono appetito' and melted away again.

Her eyes were troubled as they briefly met his across the table. 'Sorry. You're right. I'm not good at accepting help, but I hope you don't think it's because I'm ungrateful.'

'I don't.' He picked up a piece of warm bread and dipped it into the shallow dish of oil, then tore off a strip of the dark, silken bresaola and held it out to her. 'But I'd like to know what it is.'

She took the bread from him and, slightly self-consciously, took a bite. He watched, fascinated, as her expression changed, a slight frown of concentration appearing on her smooth forehead.

Frustration mixed with amusement as he realised she was totally focused on the food and his question was now forgotten.

'Good?'

She nodded vigorously, so that her curls bounced. She swept them back with an impatient hand. 'Better than good. Unbelievable.' She tore off another ribbon, crumbling some delicate shavings of parmesan over it with quick, light fingers. 'And it would be perfect as a starter for the wedding—beautifully simple to prepare, although the cost might mean it's out of the question.' She'd almost been talking to herself, he realised, but then suddenly she glanced up at him and smiled guiltily. 'What a fabulous place. D'you come here a lot?'

He hesitated a fraction too long before answering. 'Not as much as before.'

Not now he was alone, he meant. Tia had liked to eat out, although eating really didn't come into it. She'd liked to be seen and photographed, and she particularly liked to be seen and photographed looking as if it were the last thing she'd expected. Gennaro's, with its atmosphere of unpretentious authenticity, made her look grounded and low-maintenance, which was laughably far from the truth.

Sarah nodded, looking away quickly as she understood his meaning. 'Oh, look,' she said in surprise. 'That's you, isn't it? In the picture?'

Wiping her hands on her shorts, she got up from the table and went to look more closely at the photograph, which hung on the wall just to his right, amongst all Gennaro's other bits of memorabilia and souvenirs left by previous guests. He glanced quickly to see which picture she had noticed, and saw that it was of him and Tia at one of the tables outside, a bottle of Prosecco in an ice bucket between them. It had been during a break from filming, and Tia was spilling out of a low-cut lace-up bodice. Aware of the camera on her, she was throwing her head back and laughing while he looked at her, unsmiling.

'Gosh.' Sarah's husky voice was wistful. 'She's so beautiful.'

'Yes.' He sounded unnaturally harsh, and he realised it must seem as if it bothered him to be reminded of her. He dragged a hand through his hair and tried to make up for it by adding, 'It was taken last summer when we did some location work here for a film. That's why she's wearing that dress.'

'Oh, yes. I didn't even notice.' Sarah gave a breathy little laugh as she came to sit down again. 'That's how cool I am—for all I know film stars dress like that all the time. What film was it?'

'It's called *Circling the Sun*.'

'Should I have seen it? I can never get a babysitter, so I'm terribly behind everyone else when it comes to cinema.'

He poured more wine into both their glasses. 'It's not out yet. It'll be premiered at the Venice Film Festival at the end of the month.'

'And your...Tia...is the female lead?'

'Yes.' He picked up his glass and took a mouthful of wine. 'Alongside her new partner, who played the title role.'

His tone was bland, completely without bitterness, but even so, Sarah felt her throat tighten with compassion. What she'd felt that day in the boardroom of Lawson Blake as she watched Rupert holding hands with the blonde in the business suit paled into insignificance next to how it must have been for Lorenzo, directing their love scenes, watching reality overlap fantasy, life obliterate art.

Squashing the last few crumbs of bread beneath the ball of her thumb, she desperately cast around for a subtle way to divert the subject on to safer ground. 'What's the film about?'

His wide, down-turned mouth twitched into a momentary grimace. 'Galileo, supposedly.'

'He invented the telescope, didn't he?' She leaned back, flashing a quick smile of appreciation up at Gennaro, who appeared to take their empty plates and melted away again with a wink.

'Amongst other things.' Lorenzo dragged a hand over his face. In the dim light of the restaurant he looked much older than the man in the photograph watching his laughing wife. He leaned forward, resting his arm on the table, his dark gaze steady on hers. 'Galileo was a fascinating man, who challenged everything that people had previously believed about the universe. He was also a devout Roman Catholic who had a passionate relationship with a woman called Maria Gamba and fathered three illegitimate children with her.' He gave an ironic smile. 'It's that aspect of his life that the American backers wanted to emphasise, rather than his revolutionary theories on the solar system.'

Gennaro was weaving through the tables towards them, a huge white plate in each hand from which fragrant clouds of steam were rising. Part of the skill of the successful restaurateur lay in knowing when to talk to your guests and when to leave them alone, and Gennaro was a very successful restaurateur. Putting the succulent porcetta before them on the table, he silently left again without breaking the fragile spell of intimacy that had come to rest over the small table.

'Lottie won't approve,' Sarah said, breathing in the aroma

of herb-spiked porcetta and suppressing a moan of greed as she picked up her fork. 'She's obsessed with the solar system, but not so much with passionate relationships.'

'She's a bright little girl.'

'Yes.' Sarah finished her delicious mouthful and took a sip of wine before adding, 'I think she must get that from her father. And the lack of interest in relationships.'

'What's he like?'

'Clever...analytical,' she said thoughtfully. 'Focused, ambitious, driven...' She laughed. 'When I say all that it makes me realise how amazing it is that we ever got together in the first place.'

'How did you meet?'

He wasn't eating much, she noticed, instantly feeling embarrassed that her own plate was already half-empty. She laid down her fork and played idly with a rocket leaf, twirling it between her fingers. 'He worked for an investment bank in the city. I often did business lunches for them, and I guess that maybe at that stage he thought I'd make a good corporate wife.'

'Love at first sight?' His voice was gently ironic, but his steady gaze held no trace of amusement. Sarah felt herself squirm a little beneath such scrutiny, aware of the warmth that was stealing up through her. Helpless to stop it.

'Pregnancy on first night,' she said in a low, self-mocking voice, trailing her finger through the rich juice on her plate and sucking it. 'Poor Rupert. He must have felt the noose tightening around his neck. It was all such a far cry from what he wanted, but—'

Lorenzo gave a little snort of disdain. 'What *he* wanted? What about what you wanted?'

'Oh, I just want Lottie to be happy,' she said quickly, with what she hoped was an air of finality. She was talking too much about herself. To a top film director whose address book was no doubt stuffed with the names of fascinating, beautiful people. She was bound to have a certain novelty value for him, but she didn't want to push it too far. 'To have a good life, and grow up well-adjusted and able to look after herself. She already does a pretty good job of looking after me, so I probably shouldn't worry.'

Smiling, she leaned back and pushed her plate away in a gesture that was supposed to stop herself from eating every remaining scrap and probably picking the plate up and licking it too, and also give him a chance to change the subject. But his dark, focused gaze didn't falter.

'What about before that,' he said quietly. 'Before you were a mother. What about *you?*'

She paused. 'Funnily enough, I wanted to come to Italy. To live here, and learn all about Italian food. But anyway, it's irrelevant now. I *am* a mother.' She laughed, trying to lighten the atmosphere a little. 'Not a very good one, admittedly.'

And suddenly, unaccountably she felt the needle-sharp sting of tears at the backs of her eyes. Biting her lip, she looked away, towards the door of the restaurant and the bright, sunlit square beyond, blinking as everything in her fought desperately not to humiliate herself again by crying in public for no good reason whatsoever.

She'd shredded the rocket leaf now, so that only the stalk remained. Very gently he took it from between her fingers and Sarah gave a sharp little inward breath as he took her hand in his.

'Why do you do that?'

'What?' she whispered.

'Put yourself down all the time.'

She sniffed and gave a watery smile, not meeting his eye. 'Sorry.'

'And apologise for everything.' He sighed wearily. 'I work in an industry where everyone devotes their whole lives to making themselves look significantly better than they really are—in every way—and yet you do the opposite. Why is that?'

The warmth and strength of his hand on hers was doing

strange things to her ability to think clearly. Her throat still prickled with unshed tears, but stronger than that was the sudden insistent pull of desire low down in her pelvis.

She closed her eyes for a second, shaking her head. Fighting it. 'I don't know. Guilt, probably.'

'What do you have to feel guilty about?'

Her laugh was edged with despair. 'Where do I start? For not giving Lottie holidays in Disneyworld or Mauritius. For not having those pink shiny nails with the white tips that other mothers have. For not being able to make her father love me enough to stay around for her, for not giving her brothers and sisters...'

For the briefest second his hand tightened reflexively on hers. 'She wants brothers and sisters?' he said flatly.

'She's never said that, but I know the rest of my family think she's missing out. And I do think that she should spend more time with children and less with adults. She's such a funny little thing, an old head on young shoulders...'

Sarah stopped mid-sentence. Across the table their hands were still entwined, but his face wore an oddly blank expression, and she suddenly realised that it was she who was holding his hand now, squeezing it hard as she spoke about worries she was used to keeping locked safely inside. Flaming embarrassment swept through her as she realised how tedious this must be for him. Held hostage by an emotionally unstable single mother intent on using him as a therapist.

Swallowing hard, she carried on in a rush, disentangling her fingers from his as she made an attempt at laughter. 'Which can't be my influence because I have the head of a particularly gormless teenager on the shoulders of a middle-aged housewife.'

He didn't smile. When he spoke his voice was stiff and rusty. 'What about you? Do you want more children?'

She shook her head, the laughter dying on her lips. 'I love her so much. And it's not that I don't think I'd love another child, because I'm sure that kind of mother-love is infinite, but...'

'Go on.' He might not still be holding her hand, but his gaze was so intense that it felt almost as if he were. It enfolded her, drawing out the truth that she hadn't dared to admit to anyone before.

'It hurts too,' she whispered. 'The worry, about whether I'm doing the right thing for her, the anxiety about whether she's happy or not. The...*responsibility.* I couldn't do it again. I don't want to. Does that make me an awful person?'

He smiled now, and it was filled with a mixture of compassion and pain and strength that made her feel shivery inside. 'No,' he said gently. 'Not at all.'

# CHAPTER SEVEN

As THE car bumped up the track back to the *palazzo* Lorenzo cast a surreptitious glance at Sarah in the passenger seat beside him. Her face was turned away as she stared out of the window, so all he could see was the afternoon sunlight glinting on the coppery highlights in her hair, her hands clasped round a bag of groceries on her lap.

Her knuckles were white.

He wasn't sure what had happened back there in the restaurant. He'd been making progress, getting her to open up, so why the hell had he allowed himself to get sidetracked by asking her about children, for pity's sake? He was supposed to be focusing on her father, on *her,* not himself.

And it was going to be hard enough getting to know her without complicating matters with his own issues. He felt the ghost of a smile touch his lips as he remembered the way her face had lit up as she ate, the passion she clearly felt for food which she was at such pains to hide. Gradually, millimetre by cautious millimetre, she had relaxed a little, allowed herself to talk. But it seemed that every time he got close to her she pulled back. Clammed up.

He suppressed a sigh of frustration.

She reminded him of Lupo. Lorenzo had come across him in the backstreets of Pisa when he'd been filming there, and the dog had been so badly beaten that, even though he was starving, he was too mistrustful of humans to come and take food from him. They'd been on location for three weeks, and it had taken Lorenzo almost that long to get close enough to touch him.

He still remembered the sense of achievement it had given him.

As they passed through the arched gateway to the *palazzo* she turned back towards him and gave him a small, shy smile.

'Thanks for today,' she said softly. 'For helping me get all the food, and for organising Gennaro's mystery farmer to deliver the other stuff. I don't know what I would have done without you.' She paused, her lips twitching into one of her swift, wicked smiles. 'Frozen pizza, probably.'

'Your sister and her friend don't look like they eat much,' he remarked drily. 'You might have got away with it.'

She laughed—and it was so unexpected and so good that it made him smile too. He pulled the car around the side of the house, and in the distance they could see people sitting on the lawn, and Lottie running across the grass, Lupo lolloping at her heels.

'Oh. Hugh's arrived. And Guy,' said Sarah, and her voice was suddenly flat and cold.

'Darling, that was marvellous, as always. A triumph. How can tomorrow's food beat that?'

'Oh, Guy, you're very kind.' Sarah leaned across her stepfather to take his empty plate. 'It was only a very simple risotto. I hope tomorrow's food is a little bit more memorable.'

'How's the kitchen? D'you have everything you need?'

She shrugged slightly, the cheap polyester lining of her dress rustling as she moved around the table in the candlelight. 'It's amazing. Gorgeous, just like the rest of this place.'

They were eating at a long table in the *limonaia,* the candles in their ornate wrought-iron candelabra reflected in the rows of windows now that the summer night had deepened to indigo. Leaning back in his chair, Hugh smiled fondly across at his wife-to-be. 'I must admit it's all worked out rather well. When you rang and told me about the roof my heart sank, but you've done jolly well to sort all this out. Well done, darling.'

Gritting her teeth, Sarah kept piling up the plates.

'Oh, it was nothing really,' Angelica said airily. 'From what you'd said about Signor Cavalleri—Lorenzo—I thought he might be difficult, but in fact he couldn't have been kinder. Although there aren't many men who can resist Fen when she's in persuasive mode.'

Fenella smirked. 'I did ask him to join us for dinner, but he said he had work to do. Shame.'

Sarah picked up the salad bowl and balanced it awkwardly on top of the teetering pile of crockery. She didn't blame Lorenzo for shutting himself away in his study instead of joining them for dinner. She would have given just about anything to do the same, or to go up and join Lottie in between the cool linen sheets of the fairy-tale bed, but she still had a lot of preparation to do for tomorrow, so that luxury was a long way off. Crossing the courtyard on her way back to the kitchen, she took a deep breath of warm, herb-scented night air and consciously tried to loosen the iron band of tension that seemed to be gripping her head.

Why did her family always do this to her? It was bad enough when it was just her mother and Angelica, but their scatty helplessness was simply irritating. Guy and Hugh were another thing altogether. They'd only been there a few hours and already they'd taken over, striding through Lorenzo's home with an arrogant complacency that suggested that they'd planned the whole thing. As always, Sarah instantly felt like the hired help.

What must Lorenzo feel like? she wondered with a stab of anguish. This was his home. It seemed profoundly wrong that he should be forced to retreat to his study while her loud, insensitive family took breathtaking advantage of his courtesy. His kindness.

And he was kind, she thought with a stab of surprise, setting down the pile of dishes on the mammoth butcher's block in the centre of the kitchen. A sudden shiver shimmered through her whole body as she thought back to lunch in the little restaurant, the way he'd made her feel as if he was interested in her. As if she was important.

*Desirable, almost...*

Which was ridiculous. He'd been married to Tia de Luca, for pity's sake. He was a world expert on *desirable,* and she didn't even make it into the qualifying round.

Sighing, she dried her hands and pushed back her tangled curls. It was important not to make the mistake of mixing up courtesy with genuine interest. He had an inherent integrity and a natural honour that clearly dictated that he look out for people. Especially people like her.

She wondered who looked out for him, now his wife had gone. He seemed so strong, so in control, but from the emotion she had glimpsed in his eyes, the lines etched into his angular face, the ridges of his ribs on his powerful, too-thin body, she suspected this was an illusion.

She expelled a shaky breath. Better not to think about his body.

Her eyes fell on the huge pan of risotto standing on the stove, and she levered herself away from the sink with a renewed sense of purpose, grabbing a clean bowl. He'd been so sweet to her today, the least she could do was try to repay that a little.

The hallway was in half-darkness as she walked through it on bare feet, a tray in her hands, but she could hear the faint strains of music coming from behind the closed door of Lorenzo's study, floating languidly through the warm violet night. She caught a glimpse of herself in an ornate Venetian mirror as she passed; the steam of the kitchen and the humidity of the evening had made her hair wilder than ever, and her eyes in the half-light were shadowed with exhaustion. She hesitated for a fraction of a second, wondering whether to abandon the tray with the pasta and the wine and rush upstairs to hastily slap on some make-up, but quickly dismissed the idea, smiling a little at her own foolishness.

It would take more than a bit of under-eye concealer to put her in the same league as Angelica and Fenella and Tia de Luca. Major cosmetic surgery and liposuction wouldn't even do it.

She paused at the study door, listening. It was a dreamy orchestral piece, an arrangement of soaring strings, melancholy and beautiful, and, leaning against the doorframe in the majesty of the shadowy *palazzo,* she felt her throat tighten with an unexpected rush of emotion. Oh, dear, she had to pull herself together. With the tray in her hands she couldn't even blow her nose. Or knock, she realised, making a clumsy attempt at it with one elbow.

The door flew open and the wine sloshed over the rim of the glass as she staggered forward into the room.

Lorenzo was sitting amid the chaos at his desk, papers spread out all around him. He looked up as she made her undignified entrance, and for a second she saw surprise and then anger flash across his face, before it resumed its deadpan expression.

'Sorry, I just thought—'

With a swift, savage jab of a remote control he silenced the music, and Sarah's voice sounded loud and unnatural in the sudden silence.

'—you should eat.' She hesitated, moderating her tone so she wasn't shouting like a madwoman. 'I tried to knock, but I couldn't,' she added lamely, holding up the tray by way of explanation.

But he wasn't even looking at her. There was a sinister, focused energy to his movements as he gathered up the papers around him, shoving them into an open drawer and shutting the book that lay open before him as she approached the desk.

'You didn't have to do this,' he said tersely, and his tone told her what he was too courteous to say in words. That he wished she hadn't.

'It was no trouble. Obviously. I mean, I'd cooked for *them*, anyway, so...' She put the tray down on the edge of the desk. The dog pushed against her knees, looking up at her longingly as he caught the scent of food. At least someone appreciated the gesture, she thought miserably. 'Sorry about the wine. I'll get some more in a—'

'No.'

The word was like a gunshot in the quiet room. There was a small, shocked silence, before Sarah turned and all but ran to the door. She had just reached it when Lorenzo spoke again, making a deliberate and very obvious effort to soften his tone. 'Thank you for this.' He gestured to the bowl of cooling risotto. 'It looks superb.'

Muttering a meaningless reply, Sarah closed the door and fled back to the kitchen.

*Cazzo.*

Lorenzo dropped his head into his hands and exhaled heavily, cursing again in the sudden, thick silence. He couldn't have handled that more appallingly if he'd tried.

Lupo, alarmed by the swearing, slunk off and lay down in front of the empty fireplace. Lorenzo reached over and switched on the music again, more quietly this time, then opened the desk drawer where he had hastily shoved the location photographs and Francis Tate's book.

Instead of hiding them, maybe he should just have told her. Asked her. Whatever. Come clean, anyway.

But it was too soon, and he was scared of frightening her off. He wasn't sure why she'd refused permission before, but he understood that if he was to have any chance of making this film he was going to have to win Sarah Halliday's trust, and that meant getting to know her. Trying to understand her and what made her tick. From what he knew of her already he realised that could be a very long, very delicate process.

Especially if he behaved like that.

Picking up the half-full glass of wine from the tray, he slumped back in the chair. No, it was too soon to say anything to her yet. Not only did he need to understand what it was that made her refuse his first offer, but he also wanted to make sure that when he asked her again he could present her with a proposal that would do justice to his vision, and to her father's work. A proposal that she couldn't turn down.

He'd do whatever it took.

And he'd better start with an apology.

*Don't think about it. Just concentrate on making the custard. At least that's something you can do right...*

The thoughts circling Sarah's head kept time with the rhythm of her spoon as she stirred the pale-primrose mixture of egg yolks and cream in the pan. Consciously she made an effort to slow the rhythm, which had increased from steady and soothing to fast and furious as her thoughts strayed again to what had just happened.

The look on his face; a mixture of anger and impatience that he hadn't been able to hide fast enough.

*Don't think about it. Keep stirring. Slow. Calm.*

She gave a sigh of despair, blowing the damp hair off her forehead as she did so. Over the years her love of cooking may have had a very detrimental effect on her hip measurement, but it had certainly saved her sanity on several occasions, and this was definitely one of them.

God, it was hot. Everyone else had gone to bed long ago, extinguishing the candles in the *limonaia* so that the open doors of the brightly lit kitchen had been a lone beacon of welcome for every moth and mosquito in the area. They had launched bombing raids on the light above the table, dropping, stunned, into the vinaigrette dressing she had made to accompany the bresaola and the cream she had whipped for the cake, until eventually it seemed simpler to just close the doors and swelter.

And swelter she did. During the day the castle-thick walls of the *palazzo*'s amazing kitchen kept the space cool, but now, with the oven on and not a breath of air from outside, the heat gathered and swelled within them. Sarah's hair was damp with sweat as she kept her stove-top vigil over the custard, and beneath her apron the nylon lining of her dress stuck to her body like a polythene bag.

Another boiling surge of shame rose inside her as she remembered the way Lorenzo had looked at her when she had walked into his study, with that mixture of irritation and alarm. With a groan she pulled desperately at the apron strings knotted around her waist. Yanking the apron over her head, she wiped her damp face with it, making sure that her stirring didn't falter. It was cooler without it, but not much. Her dress was clinging to her like bindweed, so that it was impossible to breathe. She couldn't bear it any longer. Undoing the small pearl button at the neck, she dropped the spoon long enough to pull the dress down over her shoulders and let it fall to the floor.

The relief was blissful.

Instantly she felt calmer, more in control. She picked up the apron and looped it back over her head, loving the feel of the sweat cooling on her back as she tied it round her again. If anyone came in she would still look perfectly respectable from the front, but the likelihood of that happening was remote. It was almost two o'clock in the morning; everyone was asleep. Silence lay over Castellaccio's lovely rooms like a sepia shroud, a brief spell of peace before the frantic activity of the wedding tomorrow.

The wedding. She felt overwhelmed with weariness at the thought.

Earlier she'd heard Lorenzo pointing Guy in the direction of the cellars, where the tables that had been used at his own wedding were stored, and her heart ached for him as she realised how awful it must be to have all this taking place around him. No wonder he had looked at her with such annoyance. She wondered if he'd been thinking about Tia; if that beautiful, poignant music held some special significance for them both.

The mixture in the pan was thickening now, approaching that magical point where its transformation to the rich, unctuous crème patisserie that was needed for traditional Italian wedding cake would be complete. Sarah kept stirring, not taking her eyes off it for fear of missing the crucial moment when it would go too far and curdle; not wanting to lose her nerve and take it off the heat too soon.

The door opened.

Stupidly, for a second all she felt was a distant irritation at being disturbed at such a critical time. And then, of course, she looked up and saw it was Lorenzo, bringing back the tray, and remembered at that exact moment that she had taken her dress off.

Horror drenched her; a suffocating wave.

She half turned, so that she was standing at an awkward angle beside the cooker, facing him stiffly. The huge butcher's block stood between them, affording her a measure of protection.

'Just leave the tray on there,' she said quickly.

He put it down.

'*Grazie*. It was delicious.'

His tone was distant and formal, and she replied with the same stiffness. 'No problem. As I said, it was no trouble, but I'm sorry to have disturbed you.'

He hesitated for a moment, then sighed. 'No, I came to apologise to you. For being so rude. I'm very antisocial when I'm working.'

Sarah glanced down and let out a yelp of dismay, yanking

the pan off the heat as she realised—too late—that the glossy, silken crème of a moment ago was now separating into a disastrous grainy mess.

'What's the matter?'

'The custard's curdled,' she moaned, gritting her teeth against the tide of vitriolic curses that would virtually bankrupt her if Lottie had been in earshot. Lorenzo was by her side in an instant, silencing her anguished protests as he removed the heavy pan from her hands, leaving her free to rush to the sink and turn on the cold tap.

Water cascaded down so forcefully that it sprayed all over her, but she hardly noticed. Spinning round to get the pan, she almost collided with him bringing it over to her, and for a split second they hesitated, staring helplessly at each other. Suddenly the heavy air seemed to pulse with meaning. His eyes burned into her as she reached out to take the pan from him, her hands closing over his on the handle.

He let go immediately, standing back as she plunged the pan into the cold water, then as she bent over the sink and started to whisk for all she was worth he leaned over and held it steady for her, his eyes never leaving hers.

Except when they moved downwards, to where her breasts were virtually falling out of her bra beneath the apron.

She gave a low moan, trying to focus her attention on what she was doing. What she was *actually* doing, not what she wanted to do, and what every atom and fibre of her being was screaming at her to do. *Like twist her body round so that she was standing in front of him, lift her arms and wrap them around his strong, tanned neck, tilt her face up and press her lips against his hard, set mouth...*

Oh, God, it was no good. The custard was disintegrating, and so was she. Falling apart. Desperately she redoubled her efforts, whimpering with the effort of not giving up. Or giving in.

'Sarah...stop.'

Lorenzo barely recognised that guttural rasp as his own voice. Letting go of the pan, he took hold of her upper arms, wrenching her round. He could feel the heat coming off her damp, voluptuous body and as he touched her she gave a shivery gasp, jerking beneath his cold, wet hands.

That was what did it, what tore through his iron self-control. That shiver of sensual awareness seemed to reverberate through his own body and galvanise him into actions he couldn't control. Suddenly he was pulling her against him as their mouths met and their lips parted and he was running his slippery hands over her bare back, beneath her hot, vanilla-scented hair and dripping cold water on her burning skin.

The kiss was hungry, devouring, urgent. She moved round so that she was leaning with her back against the sink, her fingers grasping his shoulders as their teeth clashed. Lorenzo could feel the jut of her hip bones against his, rising, pressing against his thudding body. His arousal was so sudden, so intense it was almost painful. He fumbled for the bow at the back of her apron, stretched to breaking point as his fingers moved across her bare, satin-smooth back. He wanted to have her, now, standing up against the sink...

As if she'd read his mind she shifted slightly, tearing her lips from his for a moment as she hoisted herself upwards so that she was half sitting on the edge of the worktop. The movement made a little space between them, and without the bewitching ecstasy of her mouth on his, her hot body pressed against him, Lorenzo was pierced through with sudden, chilling awareness.

*What the hell was he doing?*

He took a step backwards, thrusting both hands into his hair, balling his fists and pressing them against his temples.

'No,' he rasped. '*No.* This is wrong.'

He'd come in here to apologise, *per l'amore Dio*. He was supposed to be winning her trust, not stripping her of her self-respect. And that was exactly what he'd do to her if he took her now, like this, for a few moments of snatched pleasure.

He turned away, not wanting to see the expression on her flushed, lovely face change from wanton arousal to disbelief and then aching hurt. Wanting to give her that bit of dignity at least. And wanting to explain that he was doing it for her own good, because he knew that she was too sweet, too giving and generous, too vulnerable to use like that.

But he didn't.

'Forgive me,' he said harshly, and he left the room without looking back.

## CHAPTER EIGHT

'MUMMY. Wake up. It's *today*.'

Lottie's loud stage whisper in Sarah's ear and the feel of her soft palm against her cheek broke into Sarah's dreamless sleep. She half opened her eyes with a moan.

It felt as if she'd only just got to sleep. When she'd eventually slipped beneath the single linen sheet beside Lottie last night she'd lain there for hours, staring into the hot darkness as regret and self-recrimination buzzed around her head and thwarted desire pulsed through her tense body. It was amazing that she'd slept at all.

She rolled over, pulling the pillow over her head and squeezing her eyes shut against the bright slice of sunlight falling through a gap in the curtains. However, Lottie was not to be diverted.

'Did you make a new cake? Does it have little people on the top that look like Auntie Angelica and Uncle Hugh? Can I put on my bridesmaid dress now?'

'Lottie, you're like an alarm clock,' Sarah groaned from under the pillow. The cake was the last thing she wanted to discuss, so in an effort to distract her she groped for Lottie's nose. 'Do you not have an "off" button?'

Lottie laughed delightedly. 'I do, but you're not allowed

to use it because you have to get up. The big hand is on the twelve, and the little hand is on the *nine*.'

Instantly Sarah sat bolt-upright, throwing the pillow down and clutching her head as Lottie handed her her watch. 'See?' she said helpfully. 'Nine is definitely past get-up time, isn't it? So can I put on my bridesmaid dress now?'

Panic joined the misery and self-pity weighing down Sarah's heart. The wedding was at eleven.

'No. You can very quickly have breakfast in your pyjamas and put your dress on afterwards,' she muttered, staggering out of bed and clumsily pulling on yesterday's denim shorts and coral-coloured shirt, which were lying on the floor where she'd dropped them, before her life had taken another unerring swerve towards disaster.

Downstairs, the kitchen that she had cleaned up in a trance-like frenzy last night before she'd finally fallen into bed now looked as though Genghis Khan and five hundred of his hungry marauders had just passed through it. Sarah followed the sound of voices from the courtyard and found an impromptu breakfast party in full swing, complete with champagne and a whole lot of people she'd never laid eyes on before. Hugh's old school friends and city colleagues, she guessed, judging by their confident, drawling voices and the casual arrogance with which they'd taken over the place.

'Mummy, why didn't you let me put my dress on?' Lottie hissed, tugging urgently at her hand. 'Everyone else is dressed properly. It's *embarrassing*.'

She was right. There was no sign of Angelica, of course, but Hugh was already in his morning-suit trousers and white shirt, his very English complexion still slightly pink from the shower. She was nearly knocked sideways by the cloud of expensive aftershave that hung around him as he came over to press a glass of champagne into her hand.

She took it numbly.

'We were wondering when you were going to surface, old

thing,' he said heartily. 'Had to dig around to find breakfast ourselves, but not to worry, we managed OK in the end.'

Sarah forced a smile of sorts. 'What a relief. You are clever.'

The irony in her tone was completely lost on him. Taking a hefty slug of champagne, he pulled over one of the newcomers, another city type who was already perspiring in his morning suit. 'Jeremy, this is Sarah, Angelica's sister, who I was telling you about.' A tiny flicker of surprise and pleasure briefly illuminated the frozen darkness inside Sarah's head, but it instantly died again when Hugh continued, 'Remember? She's the one in charge of the food, so it's her you have to sweet-talk about your wedding present.' He winked mischievously at Sarah.

Her heart sank even further. Jeremy beamed, rocking back on his heels and looking very pleased with himself.

'Oysters,' he boomed. 'A hundred and twenty of the blighters, fresh from the good old English Channel. Angelica's favourite—a big surprise for her. Thought they'd make a super starter for the wedding breakfast.'

Hugh clapped him on the back fondly. 'You sly old devil, that's damned fantastic. Isn't it, Sarah?'

Frankly, 'damned fantastic' was not exactly how Sarah would have described the careless havoc wreaked on her menu. She was still grappling for a more appropriate choice of words for Jeremy and his unexpected wedding gift as she looked despairingly down into the crate of oysters an hour later. Still dressed in yesterday's clothes, her hair still uncombed and her teeth unbrushed, she had spent the morning clearing up the kitchen—again—as well as charging round overseeing some of Hugh's more biddable friends setting up tables in the *limonaia* and positioning the vast arrangements of stephanotis and white roses delivered by the florist. And there was still the small problem of the cake to sort out.

Sucking in what was meant to be a calming breath, she was

assaulted by an eye-watering smell of seaweed from inside the crate and instead felt another surge of fury, resentment and despair. Dropping the lid hastily back on the box and its unpromising-looking contents, she swore with satisfying unrepentance. Twice.

'What's it worth not to tell the swearing police?'

She stiffened instantly as she glanced up and saw that Lorenzo was standing in the doorway to the courtyard.

'How long have you been there?' she said, wishing she could sound as cool and nonchalant as he did.

'Long enough to know you're not having a good day.' He didn't move. 'Shouldn't you be getting ready for the wedding?'

'It looks like I won't make it down to the church.' She turned away, picking up a pile of side plates and moving them pointlessly to a different place on the worktop.

'Why not?'

She nodded to the crates. 'Oysters,' she said, unable to entirely keep the bitterness from creeping into her tone. 'A surprise addition to today's menu from Hugh's best man. Unfortunately I haven't the faintest idea what to do with them, but I imagine whatever it is will take a couple of hours at least.'

He came forward then, slowly. Sarah's skin tingled all over with embarrassment and wicked, shameful longing as her body recalled last night. She couldn't bring herself to look at him, but his voice was as devoid of emotion as ever. 'What about the cake?'

She couldn't breathe. When she tried to speak it sounded as if she was being strangled.

'Disaster.' Which pretty much summed up everything else too. 'The custard was too far gone and—'

He cut her off, cold and decisive. '*Tutto bene*. Leave it to me. I'll arrange a replacement from Gennaro. No one need ever know.'

'No,' she said unhappily. No one needed ever know what

had happened, or why. Not that they'd believe it anyway. 'Thanks.'

He nodded, and for a second he seemed to hesitate, as if he wanted to say something and wasn't sure where to start. Then he sighed. 'Where's Lottie?'

'Upstairs. My mother's getting her ready.' Sarah's voice cracked, and blindly she picked up the side plates again. Suddenly that, on top of everything else, was almost more than she could bear. Totally unused to expensive clothes and smart shoes, Lottie had been beyond excited about the pale gold silk dress with its froth of tulle petticoats that had hung, shrouded in crackling plastic, on the back of Sarah's bedroom door for the last couple of months. She'd been counting the days until she'd be wearing it for real, and the thought that right now she was upstairs, squirming with excitement as somebody else buttoned her into it was so…

Unfair.

*Hell-o?* She sneered silently at herself. *Since when had life been fair?*

'Go up and find her,' Lorenzo said curtly, taking the plates from her. His fingers brushed hers and she jumped back, shaking her head with unnecessary vehemence.

'No. It's fine. My mother will have it covered, I'm sure.'

'Then go up and get yourself ready.'

'No, really, I can't.' She glanced at her watch and gave a suicidal smile. 'They'll be leaving for the church in half an hour, and even if you take care of the cake I really do have to work out what to do with the sodding oysters. Open them for a start, I suppose.'

'No.' Firmly, he took hold of her shoulders and turned her round so that she was facing the door. Sarah felt her insides leap with treacherous joy, and she had to tense herself against it, holding herself very, very straight and stiff as he propelled her gently forward and opened the door for her. His voice in her ear was husky and grave. 'Leave it to me. Oysters should never be opened until they're ready to be eaten. Unless you want to give everybody food poisoning.'

She knew when she was beaten.

'Not quite *everybody*,' she muttered darkly, ducking her head and hurrying towards the stairs.

*'Ciao, Gennaro. E grazie mille...'*

Lorenzo put down the phone and sighed heavily, rubbing his hands over his face. Problem solved: thanks to Gennaro, he'd secured a suitably impressive wedding cake and arranged to borrow a kitchen assistant and two of his waiting staff. They would be arriving at the *palazzo* within the hour.

It would cost him, of course. But at twice—no, ten times the price it would only be a fraction of what he deserved to pay.

Of course, her stepfather should be paying too, he thought bitterly, getting up and walking stiffly to the window. Hugh and his friends were out there, adjusting their ties, posing for photographs around a shiny red Ferrari that had appeared in front of the house, white ribbons fluttering across its bonnet. Anger hardened in Lorenzo's chest. Vulgar cars like that didn't come cheap, but then money clearly wasn't a problem for either Guy Halliday or Hugh Soames.

They were the ones who should be reaching into their Savile Row pockets to pay for cakes and catering staff, but of course there was no chance that was going to happen while they had Sarah to do everything for them for nothing. The sunlit morning blackened in front of his eyes as he thought of last night, when she had still been slaving away while everyone else was asleep—relaxed with wine and replete after the dinner she had cooked for them earlier. It had been almost two in the morning when he had come across her in the kitchen: pink-cheeked, exhausted, shiny with sweat. He recalled the heat and the panic he had felt coming from her body...

He slammed his fist down on the windowsill with such force that Lupo yelped and cowered. Guilt instantly assailed him.

More guilt. To add to the burden of remorse that, after last night's incident in the kitchen, lay across his shoulders like a mantle of lead.

To her idle, selfish family Sarah was nothing more than a pair of hands to cook them excellent meals and to clear away afterwards, invisibly and efficiently. He had watched them. He had watched *her, per l'amore di Dio.* No one concerned themselves with her as a person—how she felt, what she wanted. And the awful thing was that he had almost done the same.

Treated her as a warm, voluptuous body. A ripe pair of lips...

Self-disgust hardened inside him. He barely knew Sarah Halliday, but he'd spent enough time with her to understand that the last thing she needed was empty, meaningless sex. No matter how fleetingly pleasurable. Her self-esteem was low enough already without being used in that way.

No. If he wanted to gain her trust and get her to open up to him, it wouldn't be by seducing her.

Unfortunately.

The roar of the Ferrari's engine outside and whoops and cheers from the bridegroom's party cut through his thoughts. Which was probably just as well. He sighed, and was just about to sit down at his desk again when he heard voices in the hallway.

Angelica must be coming down. He glanced at his watch. It was barely twenty minutes since he'd sent Sarah upstairs to have a shower and get ready; surely she couldn't have managed it in that time? Which meant she'd be missing out on seeing Lottie in her finery.

Grabbing the small camera he kept for location research, Lorenzo crossed quickly to the door and opened it a little. Angelica was coming slowly down the stairs, the sunlight shimmering on her papery silk pearl-white dress, the gossamer-light froth of her veil. She was smiling for the photographer who was waiting below, his shutter clicking like a machine gun. There was something almost triumphant in her bearing, and the expression on her face was one of utter serenity and self-assurance.

Behind her Fenella was wearing a dress of dull gold that clung to her body; no doubt chosen to show how thin she was. He ignored her, focusing his camera on the little girl who bobbed in their wake, her eyes wide with solemnity and awe beneath her crown of ivory roses.

His chest constricted suddenly. He should have been ready for it by now, but the pain still took him by surprise sometimes, closing around his throat so tightly it felt as if he were being strangled.

He zoomed in on Lottie's face, keeping his eyes fixed on the viewfinder. The camera was his shield. It distanced him from life and all its complications and difficulties. Like Galileo's telescope, it enabled him to see things that he couldn't bear to examine without its impassive filter. On the small screen he watched Lottie let go of her posy of roses with one hand and push a stray curl back from her face. As she did so her dark eyes flickered upwards and she gave a smile which lit up her face and carved deep dimples in her plump cheeks.

Now, who did that remind him of? he thought sardonically.

He followed her gaze and felt a peculiar fizzing sensation, like pins and needles in his head, as he saw Sarah. Wrapped in a towel, her hair still wet from the shower, she was leaning against the banister on the landing above. As she caught Lottie's eye her face broke into an answering smile.

The camera caught it all. The joy and pride that shone from her face, the shimmer of tears in her eyes, her lips as they mouthed the words 'you're beautiful' at her little daughter and pressed a kiss to her fingertips, which she blew down to her.

'Could we have the little bridesmaid down at the front, please?' said the photographer briskly and, with a last glance up at her mother, Lottie was hustled into position for the shot by Fenella. Lorenzo kept his lens trained on Sarah, trying to resist the temptation to zoom in on her glorious cleavage as she leaned over the banister, looking down.

The light had left her, and suddenly she just looked unbearably sad. Stricken almost.

A sudden burst of laughter echoed round the walls as the photographer said something to make the bridal party relax their stiff poses. Lorenzo's focus didn't waver, and as the others collapsed with laughter he caught the single tear that fell from above, glinting as brightly as the diamonds in the bride's tiara for a second before shattering on the floor.

When he looked up again Sarah had gone.

Quietly, carefully, Sarah shut the door to her room and leaned against it for a moment, her palms pressed to her cheeks as she struggled to suppress the sudden swell of emotion that had caught her offguard.

She never cried.

Crying got you nowhere, unless you were Angelica and could do it cleanly and gracefully and use it to gain advantage in all kinds of situations. For Sarah, whose face instantly took on a blotched and swollen appearance that lasted for hours, it was undignified and definitely best avoided.

But back there, just for a second she'd been absolutely flattened by a wave of annihilating emotion. For Lottie, who was so sweet and good that sometimes she literally took Sarah's breath away; but also for the perfection of the morning and the sense of anticipation of the day ahead; the whole champagne and cake and silk and roses celebration of love and togetherness. Beneath the expensive designer trappings there was something primitive about it; something deeply profound and momentous, and all of a sudden Sarah had felt as if she was standing at the gates to paradise, looking in through the bars and knowing they were locked to her forever.

Anyway, self-pity was yet another indulgence she just didn't have time for right now, along with putting conditioner on her hair and shaving her legs. She'd showered and washed her hair in record time, even for her, so it would be stupid to waste valuable minutes bemoaning the fact that she was almost thirty and undoubtedly facing a future of spinsterish celibacy.

Hardly surprising, she thought bleakly, struggling into the most hideously unglamorous knickers on the planet. They were flesh-coloured and designed to 'smooth away all those lumps and bumps for a slender silhouette', but utterly kill any possibility of a passionate encounter. Mind you, she thought sadly, she seemed to do a pretty good job of that on her own if last night was anything to go by.

Averting her gaze from the mirror, she grabbed her dress and quickly shrugged it on. It was a lilac silk shift dress she'd bought in the sales a couple of years ago when Rupert had promised to take her to the polo at Windsor. Those were the days when she'd been on a constant diet, convinced that if she was thin enough and smart enough Rupert would be miraculously shaken out of his overwhelming apathy and realise he was deeply in love with her.

Predictably, neither the trip to the polo nor the dazzling epiphany about how desirable she was had ever happened.

She was standing in front of the mirror, smoothing the dress over her rigid new 'slender silhouette', when a knock at the door made her jump.

'Come in.'

The door opened and Lorenzo appeared. He was holding a glass of champagne.

'For you.'

'Oh…gosh, thanks,' Sarah stammered, taking it from him awkwardly. 'But you didn't have to—'

'I just came to tell you that you don't need to worry about the cake and the oysters.'

'Really?' Her blotched face brightened. 'But how?'

'I called Gennaro. He'll bring a cake up here while everyone is in church.'

'And the oysters?'

'He wouldn't spare his staff for just anyone, but you made quite an impression yesterday. Alfredo's wife, Paola, will come over too, as long as she can bring her little boy. It's hardly an army, but it should help.' He hesitated, then reached out and lightly brushed her swollen upper lip with his thumb. 'With the work at least. I'm not sure about everything else.'

'No.' She sat down suddenly on the stool in front of the dressing table. 'For that I'd need a make-up artist and a miracle. But in the absence of either I'm grateful for the champagne. Thank you for bringing it up.'

Walking to the door, he shrugged. *'Figurati.'* Walking to the door he smiled wryly. 'I'm just relieved that this time you're dressed.'

'Yes. But let's face it, it would hardly have mattered if I wasn't,' she said sadly. 'There's not really much of me that's left to the imagination now, is there?'

'Don't you believe it,' he said drily. 'Come down when you're ready. I'll give you a lift to the church.'

## CHAPTER NINE

IT WAS a beautiful wedding.

Everyone said so. They whispered it to each other in the church, with the honeyed sunlight pouring down through the high-up windows and scattering dancing rainbow points of light from the diamonds in Angelica's heirloom tiara across the worn stone floor. They said it afterwards, as they spilled out into the fierce heat and were introduced to people they hadn't yet met from the other family. And later, when generous quantities of the excellent champagne bought by Guy had made everyone sentimental, they looked around the flower-decked *limonaia* and said it again.

Sarah came out of the kitchen carrying a tray laden with coffee in tiny gold-rimmed cups. The ordeal of lunch was over and had passed blessedly smoothly, thanks to Gennaro's menu advice, his cake and also his hulking, taciturn kitchen assistant. Sarah had been so busy overseeing everything that she hadn't actually had time to sit down and eat, but from the empty plates Alfredo's pretty wife, Paola, was bringing back into the kitchen she could tell that the food had been a success.

Now the hard, enamel-blue sky had lost some of its glare and was beginning to soften to the shade of forget-me-nots, but it was still horribly hot. The *limonaia* looked like Titania's bower, and the scent of orange blossom and lilies and jasmine was enough to knock you out. Some people had moved outside, abandoning empty glasses and coffee cups for Sarah to find all around the courtyard and the top part of the garden, while others moved away from the places they'd been allocated at lunch and regrouped around the tables.

'Thank you, you're a saint,' sighed one of Hugh's aunts as Sarah put a coffee cup down in front of her. *St Knickerless,* thought Sarah wearily. It was so hot in the kitchen that she'd admitted defeat and put comfort before vanity, nipping upstairs an hour ago and taking off the punishing magic knickers.

'Beautiful wedding,' said the aunt.

'Yes.' Dutifully Sarah rested the tray on the edge of the table and surreptitiously leant her knee on the chair, taking the weight off one aching foot for a moment. 'It was so terrible to have to rearrange everything at the last minute, but—'

'Typical of Hugh and Angelica to turn a disaster round and make it into something positive,' said the aunt warmly, taking a sip of her coffee. 'They're so clever at that sort of thing. Angelica has a knack of doing everything brilliantly, and making it look so effortless, doesn't she?'

'Well, y-yes...I suppose so.' Sarah looked across at Angelica, who was holding court to three of Hugh's best-looking friends at the top table. 'Effortless is certainly the word.'

'And how do you know her?' said the aunt politely.

'I'm her sister.'

With an inward sigh Sarah waited for the inevitable, unflattering surprise. It came as expected.

'*Really?* Good lord, you don't look a bit alike. Her *sister?*'

'Well, half-sister,' Sarah explained dully. 'Different fathers.'

That was an understatement. Francis Tate and Guy Halliday were so different they were basically unrecognisable as the same species. No one could accuse Martha of falling for the same type.

At that moment a flash of white through the open doors of the *limonaia* caught her eye. Lottie, running across the lawn beyond the courtyard, her silk dress billowing out around her. Another small figure darted after her—a little dark-haired boy. Sarah seized her chance of escape and straightened up.

'If you'll excuse me, I'll just go and see if my daughter—'

But, unwilling to be left stranded at the table with no one to talk to, the aunt wasn't ready to relinquish her yet. 'Ah, she's yours, is she, the little bridesmaid?' she said warmly. 'Isn't she adorable? Is your husband here?'

Sarah had seen that coming, like a ten-ton lorry lumbering towards her that she was powerless to avoid. She opened her mouth to reply—

'There you are, *tesoro*. I was looking for you.'

A warm hand came to rest on her shoulder, the thumb caressing her neck.

'Oh!' It was little more than a breathless gasp. She turned her head, vaguely noticing the expression on Hugh's aunt's face, which was one of respectful incredulity. But as she turned to face Lorenzo she forgot everything in the intensity of his dark eyes as they locked with hers, the very slight smile that touched the corners of his mouth.

She felt weak.

'Will you excuse us, *signora?*' Lorenzo murmured.

How, Sarah thought breathlessly, did he manage to sound so polite and at the same time so bloody sexy? His hand was firm on her elbow as he steered her towards the door. She arranged her face into what she hoped was an extremely nonchalant smile and said, without moving her lips, 'Why did you do that? She'll think you're my husband now.'

Lorenzo's voice was low, husky. 'I heard what she said. I thought that you needed rescuing.'

It was cooler outside. Sarah's heart was thudding hard and she was conscious of his closeness, of the height and strength of his body beside hers, the warmth of his hand on her bare arm. Too conscious. Although it went against just about every instinct in her tired being, she stopped walking and gently pulled her arm away.

'Look,' she said awkwardly, her voice low, 'you don't have to do that all the time, you know.'

They were standing in the shade of the kitchen wall. From inside she could hear water splashing in the sink and crashing pans, and from the other direction, from the *limonaia,* the sound of voices and laughter and glasses clinking. But here, in the middle, with the gardens rolling away in front of them, it was very quiet.

'Do what?'

'Rescue me.' She looked out across the lawn, watching Lottie and her mysterious new friend play beneath the trailing fronds of a weeping willow in the distance. 'I can look after myself.'

He gave a harsh, abrupt laugh. 'I don't think so.'

She froze. For a second it was all she could do to keep upright as anger and hurt exploded inside her, momentarily filling her head with blinding white light. Stepping backwards, staggering slightly, she put her hand against the wall for support.

'Well, I can. I always have, and tomorrow when this is all over I'll leave here and get on with doing just that again.'

Pushing past him, she headed back to the familiar safety of the kitchen.

Lorenzo slammed his fist against the wall, cursing viciously and eliciting a look of great alarm from a passing wedding guest.

What was it about Sarah Halliday that made him screw up *so* spectacularly every time he spoke to her?

*Dio,* he was used to dealing with demanding producers, bolshy film crews and Hollywood A-list actresses, who were surely some of the most volatile, egocentric, emotionally unstable people on the planet, and he was renowned in the business for his ability to get them to do what he wanted. But put him in front of this girl—this ordinary, unassuming, self-deprecating girl—and suddenly his responses were all over the place.

He hadn't meant it to sound like that. He hadn't meant to put her down—she had her family for that, *per l'amore de Dio,* and he'd seen how she not only looked after her child, but the whole useless, lazy lot of them too. He'd simply meant that she put herself last. Always.

And that he didn't like it.

He shook his head, suddenly noticing the throbbing in his knuckles where they'd hit the stone. God, what a fool, he thought bleakly as he gingerly flexed his aching fingers. What a bloody stupid thing to have done.

Although actually, when you looked at it in context of the greater scheme of things, punching a wall wasn't so bad. After all, he actually had the girl who owned the rights to the film he'd been wanting to make for the last fifteen years right there in his house. Right there in his arms, at one memorable point. And he hadn't even got around to mentioning it yet.

That was even more stupid.

He inhaled, deeply and rapidly, and leaned back against the wall. Most stupid of all was the fact that with everything he said to her, everything he did, he seemed to be making it more and more difficult to bring the subject up, and more and more likely that if he did she would tell him exactly what he could do with his film. And now time was running out. Tomorrow, as she said, she would be leaving.

Shouts of children's laughter drifted through the drowsy afternoon. It was a sound not previously heard in the elegant formality of Castellaccio's gardens. Not by him, anyway, although the *palazzo* itself had been here for five hundred years, so countless children must have run across its lawns and shrieked with excitement as they played hide-and-seek in the trees. Through a dappling of leaves at the end of the lawn he could see the pale glimmer of Lottie's dress as she ran, chased by Alfredo's little boy, and before he had time to think about what he was doing he found himself walking across the lawn towards them, a plan half forming in his mind.

Not so much a plan as an impulse, actually. Like a plan, but less sensible. Less logical. And with a lot more potential for disaster.

'Mummy, this is Dino. He's my new friend.'

Sarah put down the dripping roasting pan she was about to dry and pushed one limp curl back from her forehead as she turned to face Lottie. Lottie, and a dark-haired little boy with eyes like molten chocolate. She gave him a tired smile.

'Hello, Dino. It's very nice to meet you.'

Dino smiled back, but shot a sideways glance at Lottie, who explained, 'Dino doesn't speak English, but he's teaching me Italian. I already know the words for hello and moon. Moon is *luna*.'

Sarah rolled her eyes and grinned. 'Trust you to find that one out first.'

'New moon is *luna nuova*. Did you know there's one tonight? We've told Auntie Angelica to make a wish on it, and I've wished for a telescope and a new teacher next year who's nicer than mean old Mrs Pritchard.' Lottie took hold of Sarah's soapy hand and tugged it. 'It's your turn now. Will you come and wish on it?'

'Wait!' Sarah protested. 'I've got all these horrible pans to wash. Couldn't you two do it for me? I'd like you to wish for...' she hesitated, ruthlessly suppressing the little voice inside her head that was whispering wicked things about Lorenzo Cavalleri. She laughed uneasily '...gosh, I don't know...world peace, and a big tub of chocolate fudge-brownie ice cream?'

'It won't work if we do it,' Lottie said stubbornly. There was a glint in her eye that Sarah recognised with a sinking heart as meaning she was Up To Something. 'You have to come and do it yourself. Maybe you could wish for the pans to wash themselves, and when you get back they'll all be done. Come on, Mummy.'

Lottie gave another pull on her hand, and as she followed reluctantly after her and Dino Sarah was torn between amusement and irritation. There was no stopping Lottie once she got an idea into her head, but tonight Sarah really wasn't in the mood. She was tired and hot and...hungry, she realised with a jolt of surprise. She couldn't remember the last time she'd eaten.

But more than all of that she was sad. Lorenzo had been so good to all of them, and she had thanked him by losing her temper like some spoiled schoolgirl, taking out on him her anger at herself. And tomorrow she would be leaving, and would never see him again.

The thought drove icicles into her heart.

She was surprised to find that it was almost dark outside. She must have been in the kitchen for longer than she'd thought, during which time the jazz quartet that Hugh had booked had arrived. As Lottie led her across the courtyard 'The Way You Look Tonight' was drifting out of the *limonaia,* where the candles had been lit on the tables. The purple evening was filled with the lovely, languid music, the muted sound of conversation and the scent of orange blossom.

Little Dino raced ahead of them, his white shirt the only part of him that was visible in the velvety gloom. Sarah stumbled after them, Lottie's hand warm and soft in hers.

*'Li e! La luna! Esprimi un desiderio!'*

Dino's voice broke into her thoughts and she looked up to where he was pointing. The delicate curve of a new moon was hanging in the sky, at the melting point where it changed from dark indigo to paler violet. A single star was placed with tasteful understatement, just to the right of it.

'You have to close your eyes,' said Lottie firmly, 'and I'm going to turn you round three times and then you have to make your wish, OK?'

The children's laughter bubbled up around her as the world darkened and spun. The ground seemed to rise and fall beneath her feet as she pirouetted.

'Now, wish!' Lottie trilled. 'Open your eyes and wish!'

Sarah opened her eyes, but instead of seeing the silvery new moon in the sky she found that she was facing the other way. Ahead of her, across the grass and encircled by the dark shapes of trees, stood the temple Lottie had told her about yesterday. The rest of the garden was shrouded in shadows, layers of inky blue and grey and mauve, but golden light spilled from between the four columns that supported its ornate portico.

Confused, she turned her head. The moon was behind her, its single star seeming to wink at her conspiratorially. And then she looked back, towards the temple, and saw a dark shape detach itself from one of the pillars and step forward into the flickering light.

Lorenzo.

# CHAPTER TEN

HER heart lurched and blood thundered in her ears, so that for a moment the music floating across the lawn was drowned out by a swishing, pounding beat. Lottie slipped her hand into Sarah's, and whispered, 'Did you wish, Mummy?'

'I—I don't know. Perhaps.'

Lottie was pulling her forward again, towards the temple, Dino following at their heels. 'We made a surprise for you.'

He straightened up as they approached. Sarah felt her pulse quicken and her mouth go dry as she stared through the gloom, taking in the long legs and broad shoulders silhouetted against the golden light.

'Lottie, what's all this about? I hope you haven't been bothering Lorenzo with—'

'They haven't. It was my idea.'

He was standing at the top of the flight of wide stone steps that led up to the columned portico. His face was unsmiling, reserved, but she thought she heard a subdued note of contrition in his voice.

'What was?'

He came down the steps towards her, his hand outstretched. Sarah's stomach disappeared and her breath caught in her throat as it closed around hers.

'Dinner.'

Gently he drew her forward. The stone steps were cool under her feet, and as she reached the top she gave a gasp of astonishment.

There was a stone bench seat running along the back wall of the small square building, and at each end of it stood an elaborate candelabra holding out armfuls of flickering white candles. In the middle was a champagne bottle in an ice bucket and, on the floor beside it, an old-fashioned picnic hamper.

Her eyes flew to his face. He was watching her with his dark, hooded, unfathomable eyes. Her hand was still held in his, and it felt as if a low-level current of electricity was buzzing through their loosely entwined fingers. She pulled away, wrapping her arms around her body.

'I don't know what to say,' she whispered.

'Say you love it!' Lottie squealed, clapping her hands. 'It's like a fairy grotto!' She and Dino had crept up the steps after them and were standing side by side, looking at them both with dark eyes that shone with reflected light.

'I love it,' Sarah whispered. 'I do. But I don't know why you—'

He cut her off, turning to the children and taking something out of his pocket to give to them. '*Grazie mille, bambini.* Now, both of you, remember what we agreed? Lottie, you go straight to your grandmother. *Dino, trova il tuo madre, si?*'

'*Si!*' they chorused, clutching the coins that he had given them and turning to hurry down the steps. The sound of their voices carried across the darkening garden as they ran back towards the house, Lottie's dress melting, moth-like, into the gloom.

Sarah watched them until they were out of sight. And then slowly, inexorably she felt her gaze being pulled back to Lorenzo. He was still looking at her, and there was something almost sad in his expression that turned Sarah's heart over.

'I don't understand,' she said slowly.

'I wanted to apologise. I didn't mean what I said before.' He sighed. 'Or I did mean it, but not in the way it sounded. Not in the way you thought. I don't think for one minute you're incapable of looking after yourself, just that you don't put your own needs first.'

She shook her head dismissively. 'It doesn't matter. I'm fine.'

'Have you eaten today?'

'N-no, but—'

*'Essattamente.'* He stooped to open the lid of the basket. 'You look after everyone else. You feed them.' Sitting down, he took out a box and put it beside him on the stone seat. 'You clear up after them. You organise things for them. You even risk your neck doing property maintenance for them. But what I want to know is...' he opened the box and took out an oyster and a short, heavy-handled knife '...who looks after you?'

His voice was very quiet, very gentle. Mesmerised, she watched the movements of his strong, slender hands.

'I told you. I don't need looking after. Really, I don't. I've always been independent. I'd hate to have someone bossing me around and telling me what to do.'

'Sit down.'

She came over and, without thinking, sat. His lips quirked into a fleeting smile, and she laughed.

'OK, most of the time I'd hate it. Tonight I'm too tired to argue.'

Lorenzo slid the champagne bottle out of the bucket of iced water and tore the foil from the top. Sarah watched the icy drops of water run down over his fingers as he poured the clear, golden liquid into two glasses.

'That's a relief,' he said drily, handing one to her, 'but hardly a surprise. You've run today entirely single-handedly, from what I've seen. It can't be easy taking responsibility for everything on your own.'

'I'm used to it. As I said, Lottie's father was never around much.'

'I know. But I get the impression you've been shouldering responsibility for a lot longer than that,' he said quietly.

The darkness that was gathering outside seemed to swoop in on her suddenly, crowding into her heart, dragging it down with that familiar, crushing weight. The terrible weight of responsibility.

How had he seen that?

She took a large gulp of champagne. She didn't want to look at him. She was frightened of what else he might see.

He was holding an oyster, cupping it in his big, sensitive hands as he slipped the knife in and turned it swiftly, prising the two halves of the shell apart. Sarah watched as the oyster split open. He held it out to her.

She hesitated. 'I'm not sure... It sounds ridiculous, but I've never tried one before.'

'Your life has been far too sheltered, Miss Halliday,' he said solemnly. 'First Screaming Orgasms and now oysters. There are huge gaps in your education.'

They were sitting side by side on the long stone bench, but Sarah found that she had subconsciously turned towards him, her knee hitched up on the seat. He hardly had to reach at all to offer the oyster to her lips. Instinctively, tentatively she felt them part. Her eyes met his and locked there and she felt herself melting into their velvet depths.

'You take it into your mouth,' he said softly, 'and hold it there. Don't chew. Crush it on your tongue.'

Her eyes never left his as she did as he said. Taste exploded in her mouth as it was filled with the cool, slippery, salty flesh and an answering explosion of lust rocked through her pelvis, partly at the undeniably erotic flavour of the oyster, partly at the flare of warmth she saw in the depths of his eyes. All of a sudden the heat of the evening seemed to be concentrated in the apex of her thighs.

'Now swallow,' he said huskily.

*Oh, God. Oh, help.*

'You liked that?'

'Yes,' she breathed. 'Oh, yes...'

He picked up another one, turning it over in his hand before plunging the knife in. 'So, Sarah Halliday, what is it that gave you such a big sense of responsibility?'

Taking a long, dizzying mouthful of champagne, she was caught off guard by his unexpected question. As the bubbles prickled and died on her tongue, she put her glass down, twisting its slender stem between her fingers.

'I don't know. My father...'

She stopped abruptly, a little thud of shock spreading through her as those two words brought her back to her senses. She was tired, both physically and mentally, after the stresses of Angelica's wedding day, and there was something about the combination of the champagne, the candles, the heat of the evening and of his steady, intense gaze that was making her feel raw. If she wasn't careful she'd be spilling out the whole unedifying story of her life and boring him senseless.

Beside her, Lorenzo tipped the oyster into his mouth and let its feral, female flavour seep onto his tongue while he waited for her to continue. *Dio,* he'd known this would be difficult, but he'd failed to take into account the oysters. Eating them while looking into her dark, dilated eyes was like torment.

But this was it. He'd got her to the place he needed to be.

'What about your father?' he said, with what he hoped was almost indifference. 'Tell me about him.'

She shook her head with a swift vehemence that was both intriguing and frustrating. 'It's a long story. A long, not very interesting story.'

'Can I be the judge of that?'

Trying not to betray his interest, Lorenzo selected an oyster from the pile and looked at it, assessing where to put the tip of the knife in. People said oysters were difficult to open, but in his experience it was just a matter of knowing where to start. He found a gap and gently eased the blade in.

'Take my word for it.' Sarah spoke lightly, but her words were edged with weariness and despair. 'Other people's family dramas are always tedious. They're all just variations on the same old themes, aren't they?'

'And what themes are those?' He gave the knife a little twist and felt a beat of satisfaction as the shell gave. He was in.

'Guilt, regret, loss...'

Her words trailed off as he held the oyster up to her mouth. Her pink lips parted, and he watched her face, an arrow of lust skewering him at the expression of focused, private pleasure that flickered across it for a moment as she held the flesh in her mouth, and then let it slide down her throat.

'You loved him?' His voice was a hoarse rasp.

Outside the evening had deepened softly into night. The hopeful sliver of the new moon was too high for them to see it from beneath the canopy of the temple, too small to shed any light over the sleeping garden. It was as if the rest of the world had vanished, and it was just the two of them.

Sarah's eyes met his, and behind the shimmering candlelight reflected in them lay a continent of hurt.

'Yes, I loved him,' she said quietly.

Lorenzo swept the oyster shells back into the box and poured more champagne. The bottle rattled slightly against the rim of Sarah's glass, and he realised that his hands were shaking. He had to get a grip. Stay focused. This was his chance

'So where do guilt and regret fit in?' he said neutrally, picking up his glass and leaning back. *Don't pressure her. Don't make her feel threatened.*

'I obviously didn't show him enough. I should have done more.'

Lorenzo made himself take a long sip of champagne. 'How old were you when he died?'

She was sitting very still, her head bent. One heavy chestnut curl fell in front of her face. The candlelight made it shine like polished copper. 'I was five.'

'Like Lottie.' Lorenzo's heart clenched unexpectedly.

'Yes,' she whispered.

Carefully he set his glass down and leaned forward, stroking the curl gently to the side, tucking it behind her ear. 'That's a big burden for a little girl to carry. What makes you think you should have done more?'

'He killed himself.'

*'Ah, piccolino.'* The words escaped Lorenzo's lips stealthily on an outward breath, and his fingers tingled with the sudden urge to take her face between his hands and kiss away the frown between her delicately traced brows, the shadows beneath her eyes. He held back. He had to keep her talking, to get to a point where he could bring up the subject of the book…

Her head remained bent, her arms tightly folded, almost as if she was making herself as small and as still as possible. 'If I had been more…' she went on very hesitantly, 'I don't know… *more*…then maybe he wouldn't have done it. He wrote this book, you see, and it was kind of his life's work. He dedicated it to me, and the dedication says something about how I made his whole life worthwhile…' She stopped and gave a bitter laugh. 'At some point shortly after that he must have changed his mind, or maybe I just stopped making his life worthwhile.'

Lorenzo felt as if he'd been turned to stone. *I know,* he should be saying, *I know about the book*, but suddenly, in the face of her misery and despair, and her dreadful, unjustified guilt, it simply didn't seem important. What mattered was her.

He shook his head, slowly, emphatically. 'You can't blame yourself,' he said softly. 'He was a grown man, with all kinds of reasons that we might never know or understand to be unhappy. When things get that bad it's impossible to think clearly, or to grasp the consequences of your actions. He wasn't in any position to understand what he was doing.'

She hesitated, then slowly raised her head and looked at him.

'I wish I could believe that.'

Her voice was oddly flat, but her eyes were pools of anguish and as he looked into them Lorenzo realised he was staring into the dark and secret heart of her. Somewhere here lay the key to who she was, and why, and he wanted very much to find it.

His heart was thudding against his ribs and he said, very gently, 'It's OK to be angry, Sarah.'

The instant flare of emotion there told him he was right. She moved, leaning back against the stone wall, tucking her legs up against her body and wrapping her arms around them as she looked out into the darkness beyond their circle of gold.

'It's not,' she said hollowly. 'I have so little of him. I had so little time with him and now I have so little to remember him by that it's not OK to spoil that by being angry. It's awful.'

'No, it's *natural*. Completely natural. That's what the guilt is about too, isn't it? Not because you blame yourself, but because you blame him?'

She nodded, and he saw her stiff shoulders sag a little. 'A bit. Afterwards, when my mother married Guy, I used to wish he was my real father. He was what a proper father should be. Always laughing and pulling wads of money out of his pockets and calling Angelica "princess". But I do blame myself too. I wasn't sunny and golden and gorgeous like Angelica. I was this painfully shy, awkward child.'

'You were *his* child. He would have loved you for what you were.'

She looked at him, frowning, and for a breathless, agonising moment he thought she'd heard the wistfulness he'd tried to hide behind the words. But then she smiled, a brief, twisted echo of her familiar swift smile.

'I wasn't enough,' she said with heavy irony.

Lorenzo sighed, leaning over and taking a plate with a generous wedge of wedding cake from the basket on the floor. 'Children can't be responsible for the happiness of their parents. You know that. Is it Lottie's fault that her father didn't stay around?'

'No. No, that's my fault too.' She made a brave attempt at

a laugh. 'Oh, God, listen to me. I'm hardly the world's most scintillating dinner companion at the best of times, but I'm not usually this dull. Let's have some of Gennaro's cake and talk about something else.'

As she spoke, a single, shining tear ran down her cheek. Before he knew what he was doing Lorenzo had closed the gap between them and was cupping her warm face, rubbing away the glistening salt-trail with his thumb.

'We are going to have some cake,' he said softly, 'but we're not changing the subject until we've got a few things straight.' He could feel her trembling beneath his palm. 'One—it's not your fault that Lottie's father didn't stay. It's not even his fault. It's his *loss*.'

Her eyelids closed for a second, an expression of pain flickering over her face. He waited for her to argue, but the seconds ticked by and she said nothing, and he felt an almost visceral pull of satisfaction.

Maybe he was starting to reach her. Maybe she was listening.

He took a spoonful of cake and held it up to her lips. Her head was tipped back against the wall, her luxuriant hair fanning out like a mantle behind her, and she watched him with dark, unreadable eyes as she opened her mouth.

His whole body was thrumming with adrenaline and desire and the effort of not kissing her. 'And two,' he went on, his voice little more than a husky whisper now, 'you're not dull. You're one of the most complicated, interesting people I've met in a long time.'

He shifted his position slightly, wedging his shoulder against the wall right beside her and turning his body towards hers. He sank the spoon into the creamy cake and gave her another mouthful, which she took as pliantly as a child. Her eyes were on his, smudged and shadowed with exhaustion. Tentatively trusting.

In the distance he could hear music, reaching them faintly

from the wedding. Darkness lay in veils of purple and blue over the garden and a tentative enchantment lay over their golden temple, where the candles cast flickering shadows on the worn stone and enfolded them both. Beside him he could hear the soft sigh of Sarah's breathing, and was aware of the slow rise and fall of her chest.

Ruthlessly, gritting his teeth, he turned his thoughts away from her chest.

'*Sarah...*' he said softly, thoughtfully, as if he were turning the word over in his hands and examining it. 'Pretty name.'

She gave a tiny, sad smile. 'Not as pretty as Angelica.'

'Very different. Was it your father's choice?'

A tiny shake of her head made her rich hair glitter with a thousand golden lights. 'My mother's,' she said sleepily. 'And Angelica was too. She loves ang—' She stopped, sighed, slowly looked up at him, with huge troubled eyes. 'Angels,' she whispered. 'She loves angels.'

Lorenzo had the strangest sensation of his heart being squeezed as realisation dawned. 'Seraphina,' he said very softly.

Her eyes closed. She gave the barest nod, the shadows emphasising the dimple in her cheek as that fleeting smile touched her lips. 'It doesn't suit me. I can't live up to it. I'm much more of a Sarah.'

He put the spoon down, and moved a little so that her head was on his shoulder. She gave a tremulous, shuddering sigh, but didn't resist, and lay very still against him as he stroked her hair.

Minutes passed, stretching into longer, measureless spaces of time. The candles dipped and guttered in the little breeze, the music stopped and the darkness was opaque and silent. There was just her breathing, her soft hair, her generous, pliant body that smelled of soap and sweetness. Still he kept stroking, slow and rhythmical. It didn't matter that she was asleep. He wanted to do it anyway. For her.

# CHAPTER ELEVEN

LORENZO sat at his desk, idly toying with the orrery.

It was a mechanical model of the solar system, showing everything in its relative position. There was something soothing about watching how the moons and planets followed their own unwavering path, each one taking its own specific place in a dance so intricate it was almost beyond human comprehension. Galileo had understood it, even though it went against everything he'd been brought up to believe.

The courage of that, the audacious brilliance never failed to impress Lorenzo. Galileo had had a vision, and he had been unswerving in his pursuit of it. But even he, with his towering intellect, had never fully got to grips with the complexities of women.

With a flick of his finger Lorenzo made the earth spin on its axis, and then slowed it right down again as he thought back to last night. That was how it had felt in the temple, in the candlelight and the silence. As if he had slowed down time. Stopped the world, for a little while.

From outside the study door the sound of the grandfather clock chiming the half-hour was a stark reminder of the foolishness of that illusion. His battered copy of *The Oak and the*

*Cypress* lay on the desk in front of him and he picked it up now, frowning as he leafed through the first few pages to find the dedication.

*To Seraphina,*
*who gives me hope, joy and a reason for being.*

Lorenzo threw the book back down onto the desk and stood up with a sigh. Looking at those words now, he could understand how they could make her feel that she had failed somehow. That she was unworthy of unconditional love. That she had to earn everything.

Moving towards the window, he saw Lottie sitting on the grass that edged the gravel drive with Dino beside her. Lupo was lying a little way off, watching them as they half-heartedly threw bits of gravel at an empty juice carton they'd put beneath the study window. There was a downwards, dejected stoop to both small sets of shoulders, and as he looked more closely Lorenzo could see that Lottie had been crying. Her face was blotched with tears, and streaked with grime where she'd brushed them away with grubby hands.

As he watched she picked up another stone and threw it at the carton, but angrily this time; harder, so that it bounced up and hit the glass. She clapped a hand to her mouth, her eyes wide with horror, while beside her Dino scrambled to his feet and then pulled her up after him. A moment later they'd both scampered off.

Lorenzo turned away with a small smile. Switching on the music to break the oppressive silence, he returned to his desk, and the sunlit room filled with the swooping sound of strings and flute.

Antonio Agostino was a composer of Oscar-winning film scores. He had also been one of the first people Lorenzo had told about his plan to film Tate's book. After lending him a copy, this was one of the pieces Antonio had come up with for the film, and Lorenzo only had to close his eyes and he was back in Oxfordshire on that hot July evening, watching Sarah stride across the field of wheat as the last rays of the sun turned it to molten gold...

There was a knock on the door, and he opened his eyes with a start.

'*Entrare,*' he barked, much more harshly than he intended. For a moment nothing happened, and then very slowly, very hesitantly the door opened. After a couple more seconds Lottie and Dino shuffled in, their hands tightly clasped, their eyes downcast. Lupo skulked at their heels, his tale rammed between his legs.

'Sorry for throwing the stone,' said Lottie quietly. '*Mi dispace.*' Her chin wobbled as if she was holding back the tears by massive force of will. Lorenzo knew exactly where she got that strength from.

'*Non importa.* Nothing is broken,' he said roughly, suddenly finding that his throat felt tight. 'Your Italian is coming along very well. Has Dino been teaching you?'

She nodded, but at the same time her face crumpled and the tears welling in her eyes dripped down her cheeks.

Lorenzo frowned, feeling utterly helpless in the face of the little girl's misery. He knew nothing about children—had neither needed to nor wanted to before.

Self-defence. How stupid and cowardly that seemed now.

'What's the matter?' he said softly as he watched Dino put his arm protectively round her shaking shoulders. Perhaps he should take lessons from him, Lorenzo thought wearily. Dino's natural, empathetic manner seemed to be going down a lot better than his recent attempts at offering comfort to females in distress.

'I don't want to go,' Lottie sobbed. 'I hate London, and I hate the mean girls in my class. All they ever do is play with dolls with horrid, make-uppy faces and say nasty things about each other. I asked Mummy when we could come back here and she said we might not, and Dino is my *best friend* but I don't know if I'll see him again ever because we live thousands and thousands of miles away...'

'Shh...' Lorenzo said, painfully aware of how inadequate that was, but temporarily unable to think of anything more useful. Then he looked at the orrery.

'Come and look at this,' he said gravely, moving back slightly so that they both had a clear view of the complex arrangement of spheres and dials. Lottie looked wary, but she sniffed and came closer.

'What is it? Is that the moon?'

'That big golden orb in the middle is the sun,' Lorenzo explained. 'The smaller one here is the moon and next to it, with the funny shapes all over it, is the earth.'

'Ohhh...'

Lottie let out a breath of awe. Tears still shimmered in her eyes, but her face now wore an expression of total absorption. At her shoulder Dino's smooth, olive face was serious too.

Lorenzo turned the tiny globe around. 'Look—here's Italia, and we're there, on this side, in Tuscany. And there...' he moved his finger upwards and to the left a fraction '...there is London. See? It isn't as far as you think. Not compared to all of this...' With a swift movement he set the globe spinning and leaned back, studying the look of wonder on the children's faces as they took in the blur of sea and land, spinning on its axis as the planets and their moons kept their silent course around it.

'Lottie?'

Lorenzo looked up. Sarah stood in the doorway. Her hair was tied back, and she was wearing a faded green T-shirt and a little denim skirt that showed off her long brown legs.

Lottie didn't turn around. 'What?' she said, with as much sullenness as she dared.

'You have to come and wash your face and hands now,' Sarah said gently.

Lottie stayed where she was and cast one more covetous

glance at the orrery. 'Thank you for showing it to me,' she said, looking solemnly at Lorenzo before turning and walking very stiffly past her mother. Dino followed like a shadow at her heels, and even Lupo looked uncertain whether to stay or go.

Sarah hesitated in the doorway. 'Lorenzo, about last night...' she said with painful awkwardness. 'I'm so sorry. For boring you senseless and falling asleep on you. I don't know what came over me.'

'Extreme tiredness, I assume,' he said drily. 'You'd been working flat out all day. There's absolutely no need to apologise.'

Her head was bent and she was rubbing the brass doorknob with the tip of her finger. Her hair fell partly over her face, but he could still see that she was blushing fiercely. 'But you must have carried me to bed when I was asleep and...'

'*Si.*' He kept his voice deliberately nonchalant. 'It was a huge relief to be able to do something for you without you arguing.'

'Thank you,' she murmured in an agony of discomfort. Then, clearly at a loss for what to say next, she added, 'I hope the children haven't disturbed you too much.'

'No.' Why hadn't he noticed before what great legs she had? All of a sudden it seemed impossible to notice anything else.

'That's good.'

Sarah sighed. In the polished brass doorknob she could see the reflection of her face, looking very small and far away. 'Lottie's pretty angry with me at the moment.'

'Because you told her that she wouldn't be coming back to see Dino.'

Stung by the faintly accusing note in his voice, she let go of the door and straightened up. 'Yes, well, I don't believe in getting children's hopes up. And to be quite honest, I think it's unlikely. Angelica's love affair with the farmhouse seems to have come to an abrupt end. It's going to take so much work to put the roof right, so who knows if they'll keep it? And even if they do, air fares are expensive, especially in school holidays. Guy paid for us to come out here for the wedding, but a day trip to Brighton beach is about all we usually manage, so, all in all, I can't make any promises.'

Lorenzo looked thoughtful. 'She doesn't like school much, does she?'

The observation caught her off guard. There had been a part of her that wanted him to argue with her, to tell her that it wouldn't be so out of the question for her to return. Maybe even to make her feel as if he wanted her to.

'How do you know?'

He shrugged. 'Just something she said. She doesn't want to go back.'

'She doesn't have a choice, I'm afraid,' Sarah said bleakly. 'It's difficult for her, I know that, but I'd rather she was upset now and dealt with it instead of wasting time wishing and hoping for something that's not going to happen. It's best to be realistic.'

She wondered if he understood that she was talking about herself as much as Lottie.

Sitting at his desk, he listened with his head slightly bent, his gaze fixed straight in front of him. He waited until after she'd finished, and then after a little pause said, 'I want to offer you a choice.'

Time seemed to falter, as if the unseen hand that turned the cogs and made the planets move had slowed for a moment. Sarah felt the air catch in her throat, disrupting the rhythm of her breathing, forcing her to do an odd little gasp before she said, 'What do you mean?'

'I mean,' he said slowly, getting up and turning to face her properly, 'I want to ask you to stay. You need a job and I need—'

'*No,*' she said, instantly on the defensive. 'No, you can't do that.'

His eyebrows rose. 'Do what?'

'Rescue me again. I know that you're trying to help, but—'

'You seem to think I'm far more honourable than I really am,' he said, a faintly ironic smile touching his mouth. 'In this situation I'm the one who needs help. You know that I can't run this place on my own; that much has been obvious since the moment you arrived. I need someone to look after the house; you could do with the money, you love Italy and Lottie seems to like it here. What I'm suggesting is purely a business arrangement, for as long as you want—until the end of the summer when Lottie needs to go back to school, or longer.'

His tone was eminently, hypnotically reasonable, and after he finished speaking the room was very quiet. Dust motes swirled languidly in the streams of pale sunlight pouring through the elegant windows. Sarah watched them, trying to keep track of the same tiny individual speck as it drifted and spiralled on invisible currents of air.

It was impossible, of course. Just as it was impossible to take in what Lorenzo was saying. Up until a moment ago she had been preparing to leave, torn between wanting to imprint every detail of his face on her mind, memorise every movement and mannerism, and wanting to shut him out, walk away without looking back and try to forget.

And now this. This other *choice*.

'There's a project that I'm trying to get off the ground,' he began again, and a faint note of rare uncertainty in his voice snapped her attention right back to where he was standing by the desk, turning over a tattered and plainly bound book in his hands. 'It's at a delicate stage, but I want to make it happen. Very much.' He looked up at her and seemed to hesitate for a moment. Then he put the book down and went on more certainly, 'I'm going to be having meetings with producers and accountants and studios and backers, so I want to have someone around who can make a decent cup of coffee.'

'I don't know what to say.' Even to Sarah's own ears her voice sounded strange and distant. 'It's a bit unexpected.'

He nodded. 'Of course. Think about it. Talk to Lottie.'

'You think I'd get a balanced argument from her?' Sarah laughed shakily. 'She'd bite your hand off.'

'Then what's stopping you?'

He was looking at her. She could hear her own heartbeat; feel it, all over her body.

He turned away, gathering up a drift of papers from the desk and frowning slightly as he rustled them into a neat pile. 'You'll be completely free to do as you like. I'm going to be totally taken up with working on a script, so we probably won't even see that much of each other.'

His meaning was loud and clear. He was telling her that this was work. That there would be no more kissing in the kitchen or whispered confessions by candlelight. This was, as he said, a business arrangement. It was time to get back to reality.

Reality was London, and Rupert and Julia. It was the depressing flat with the nasty orange carpet she couldn't afford to replace and the tiny little yard that never got any sun. Reality was having to look for a job and explain about why she left the last one, and then worrying about who would look after Lottie in the holidays when she was working and how she was going to pay them.

Reality was a place where she had a lot of problems to deal with, and just the thought of it made her feel exhausted and depressed. Lorenzo had just offered her the solution to all of those problems in a single stroke. The only thing that was standing in the way was her own pride and, since she could barely even afford to buy her daughter a pair of shoes, pride was looking like a luxury that was well out of her league.

She took a step away from the door, digging her nails into her palms as she forced herself to raise her head and look at him squarely. But she couldn't manage a smile.

'Thank you,' she said solemnly, sounding slightly breathless with the effort of keeping all the doubts and misgivings and other messy, inconvenient, unbusinesslike emotions in check. 'Yes, please. If you're sure you don't mind? I'd like to stay.'

# CHAPTER TWELVE

AT FIRST Sarah had felt awkward and uneasy being at Castellaccio after the rest of her family had left. Through the long, hot days the house was very still and quiet, almost seeming to hold its breath as she passed through the elegant rooms, as if it was wondering who she was, what she was doing there.

Sarah wondered that herself sometimes, but, while it took her a bit of time to adjust, Lottie took to her new surroundings like the proverbial duck. In the days following the departure of the whole Halliday family circus Sarah wistfully watched the solemn, solitary little girl she had known in London blossom into a wild little wood-nymph with sparkling eyes and cheeks as smooth and brown as conkers.

The crowning joy in Lottie's happiness was the bedroom Lorenzo had shown her to, just after Guy and Martha had left. Picking up the bag of her things that Sarah had packed in preparation for their own departure, Lorenzo had carried it upstairs and along the corridor to a small room right at the end; a small white cell with a long uncurtained window and a domed, blue-painted ceiling picked out with tiny, faded stars and a silver crescent moon.

Lottie and Dino spent every day together, mostly in the gardens of the *palazzo,* under the watchful eye of Alfredo, as he mowed and snipped and tidied. From the kitchen Sarah could hear the children's shrieks of laughter drifting across the lawn as they chased each other through the jet of the hosepipe. Sometimes she took them both down into the village to get supplies for dinner and bought them ice cream, which they ate in rare, reverent silence as they sat in the square, or sometimes she would leave them with Dino's gentle, patient mother, Paola, whom Lottie quickly came to adore.

By contrast Sarah felt as if she was existing in a state of suspended animation. Where Lottie had come vibrantly alive, Sarah drifted, ghostlike, through each day, barely thinking beyond the moment, and certainly no further than the next meal. It was, she recognised, a self-defence mechanism, and part of the magic of Castellaccio. The peace of the place, the beauty and tranquillity were so far removed from all the problems she had left behind in London that it was as if she were looking at them through the wrong end of a telescope.

Ironically, this diminished scale on her old life gave her a much clearer perspective on it. As the days stretched into weeks she thought of Rupert less and less often, and when she did it was with increasing anger and contempt, and she wondered how she had ever thought she loved him. He had given her Lottie, and for that inadvertent blessing she was profoundly, dizzyingly grateful, but, looking back, she found it astonishing to realise how little else he had given her; how little she had asked or expected from him. Not materially; she didn't care that he had never bought her jewellery or presents, but now, in the evenings as she cooked for Lorenzo and as they sat together in the warm dusk, she understood for the first time how much she had missed having someone to talk to. Another adult with whom to discuss little details of the day, to share the latest funny development in the hybrid Anglo-Italian language Lottie and Dino seemed to be inventing, to appreciate her cooking.

By some tacit agreement their conversation was always general and impersonal. He didn't talk much about himself, and there was no repeat of the night in the temple when she had bared her soul to his tender, merciless scrutiny. But still, every day Sarah found herself looking forward to the evening, after Dino had gone home and Lottie was bathed and sweetly asleep beneath her dome of painted stars, when Lorenzo would emerge from his study and they would eat together and drink cool, sharp wine as the evening darkened around them.

Sometimes he didn't finish working until late and, heart hammering, she would knock on the door to his study to tell him that dinner was ready. Often he was on the phone when she went in, or so absorbed in whatever it was he was working on that he hadn't noticed the time, and then he would scowl and lean back in his chair, stretching his powerful, rangy body like a panther, and her heart would flip as she noticed the lines of exhaustion carved into his face, the shadows beneath his eyes. In those unguarded moments she would glimpse whirlpools of emotion in their dark depths. But then the shutters would come down and he would pour wine and talk and be himself—interesting, incisive, amusing, and she would ache helplessly for him and the loneliness he wouldn't share.

It was only natural that she should care about him, she told herself firmly as she lay awake on the hot nights when sleep eluded her. They were friends. He had done so much for both her and Lottie, more than she could ever thank him for. He had helped her to get over her broken heart—or at least helped her to realise that it wasn't really broken at all—so it was perfectly reasonable that she should want to help him in return. But staring into the velvety summer darkness, listening to the faint strains of music drifting out from his study, she would twist between the burning sheets, wracked with terrible longing that had nothing to do with friendship.

One evening as she came downstairs from putting Lottie to bed she heard the phone ringing in the kitchen. This wasn't uncommon, and usually she left it for Lorenzo to pick up in his study, but as she crossed the hallway she heard the low rumble of his voice through the study door and realised he must be on the other line. Breaking into a run, she reached it and picked up, only realising as she gasped 'hello' that if the voice on the other end was Italian she was going to be no use whatsoever as a message-answering service.

'Hello. Who's that?'

Clearly Italian, but speaking English. Thank goodness. 'Oh, um...it's Sarah. I'm Signor Cavalleri's...housekeeper.'

Relief added to Sarah's breathlessness, made her doubly incoherent. In sharp contrast to the husky, beautifully modulated voice on the other end of the line.

'*Bene*. I'm very glad to hear it, Sarah. Thank goodness he's seen sense and got someone in to look after the place. And him. Would it be possible to speak with him?'

Sarah found she was gripping the phone tightly and her palms were sticky as she recognised that sexy, slow voice with its American-accented English. It wasn't every day you had a conversation with a Hollywood legend after all. 'I'm afraid he's on the other line at the moment. Is that Signora Cavalleri? I can ask him to call you back when he's...'

She stopped. Lorenzo was standing in the doorway, his face an expressionless mask. 'Oh! Wait a moment...'

He scowled, shaking his head, but it was too late. The words had already left her mouth. 'He's just here. Hold on.

'Oh, God, I'm sorry,' she murmured as he came towards her and took the phone. His expression was still perfectly blank, but a muscle flickered in his cheek.

'*Ciao*,' he said tonelessly, turning his back on Sarah.

She stumbled outside into the hazy twilight. The days were still scorchingly hot and dry, but in the three weeks since she'd been here the evenings seemed to be falling earlier and bringing with them a breath of cool air that heralded the distant approach of autumn. August was nearly over, she thought with a shiver. Soon she would have to rouse herself from the comforting torpor that had got her through the last few weeks and make some decisions about the future.

She didn't want to go home, she admitted to herself with a thud of painful resignation. She had felt more at peace here in the last three weeks than she had in the last three years in London. She was content, and Lottie was properly happy. There really wasn't a decision to be made.

She bent down, running a head of lavender through her fingers and inhaling its evocative scent as she tried not to listen to the rise and fall of Lorenzo's beautiful voice in the kitchen. Not that she could understand a word of what he was saying, but just standing in the warm dusk, closing her eyes and listening to the ribbons of husky Italian thread themselves around her was so deliciously sensual that it felt illicit.

It's because he's talking to Tia, she reminded herself crossly, opening her eyes again. No wonder he sounds sensual—he's still crazy about her, along with half the male population of the planet. There was one word she did recognise, actually, and he kept saying it. *Venezia.* Maybe they were talking about giving things another go and planning a romantic reunion in Venice?

Barbs of anguish snagged at her and she wrapped her arms around herself and strode quickly out across the grass, not slowing her pace until she got out of hearing range of the house. The grass was soft and springy beneath her feet, and she looked down at her toes, still with the same lettuce-green nail varnish on them, sinking into the mossy ground. Noticing the nail varnish suddenly transported her back to that day in the square when Lorenzo had taken her out to lunch and talked to her.

Really talked, as though he was interested in her and Lottie and her father...

What would happen if Tia de Luca came back now? she thought miserably. There was no way she'd want a couple of strays taken in by her husband around the place, so perhaps Sarah and Lottie would be heading back to London after all.

Of course, she would be glad for Lorenzo, she thought fiercely. If Tia came back maybe his eyes would finally lose that empty look, and he wouldn't need to work fourteen hours a day to blot out the loneliness. God, she more than anyone understood about loneliness. She wouldn't wish it on anyone, and Lorenzo deserved so much to be happy. Yes. She cared for him, as a friend, and she wanted him to be happy...

She stopped walking suddenly, giving a whimper of distress as she realised where she was. In front of her, the last rays of the sinking sun painting it a glowing shade of apricot-pink, stood the temple.

Slowly she went up the stone steps, and stood between the pillars. The floor was worn and uneven, and some of the flagstones were cracked. She hadn't been down here since that night when Lorenzo had fed her and held her and she'd fallen asleep in his arms.

She hadn't allowed herself to think about it much either. It took her down shadowy, twisting, forbidden pathways that led a long way from the straight and narrow road marked 'business arrangement', but now she felt a gentle blush spread over her skin as she let herself remember. Remember the bliss of finally relaxing; of surrendering the burden and letting someone else carry it for her. Lorenzo was fathomlessly wise and incredibly strong, and he had listened and understood. And afterwards he had fed her gently and stroked her hair.

But it was what she didn't remember that bothered her. The bit where he must have picked her up and carried her through the darkness to the house...

The blush intensified to a deep, searing glow that radiated heat through her whole body, and she wrapped her arms round a cool stone pillar. She had woken in her own bed the next morning. He must have taken her dress off, but she still wore her underwear...

Her bra, anyway. Of course, she'd taken the ugly knickers

off earlier. She was miserably undecided about whether that was a good thing or not.

'There you are.'

Letting go of the pillar quickly, she looked round. Lorenzo was walking across the lawn towards her, a bottle of wine held in one hand, two glasses loosely clasped in the other. As he approached she scanned his face. He looked distracted and tired, and not particularly like a man who had just arranged a romantic reunion with his ex-wife. But, of course, they had a lot of stuff to sort out. Maybe he wasn't allowing himself to get too hopeful.

'I need to talk to you,' he said, coming up the steps.

A chill went through her. 'Right.' Irrationally she found herself wishing she'd washed her hair and that she wasn't wearing the same coral-pink shirt again. The clothes she had packed for her four-day stay at the farmhouse were doing sterling service, but she was getting heartily sick of them. She had a sudden fleeting image of Tia de Luca in her silken tunic in the magazine—exotic, sophisticated, edgy.

Lorenzo set the glasses down on the stone bench in almost the same place as last time. Sarah found herself reluctant to sit down. Instead she stayed leaning up against the pillar, her arms folded protectively across her body.

His hair was longer now, and as he bent his head to pour the wine it fell forward and she could see the streaks of grey at his temples. She felt a wrenching sensation in her chest.

'Is Lottie asleep?' he asked, coming forward and handing her a glass of pale wine.

'Yes, finally.' She took the glass from him, talking quickly to cover up her awkwardness. 'She was full of all these elaborate plans that she and Dino have been hatching together for a sleepover, in a tent. Apparently Alfredo has said that he'll stay out with them and they'll have a midnight feast of ice cream and cook sausages for breakfast. It's all very exhausting.'

Lorenzo raised an eyebrow. 'But well thought-out. Have you agreed?'

'I said I'd ask you. Sorry—I forgot to mention that they want to do all this here, in your garden. Lupo's very much a part of the guest list, and they've spent all day staking out suitable locations. But of course,' she added hastily, 'I told them not to get excited until I'd spoken to you.'

He gave that oddly formal half-smile that turned her inside out. 'I think I could be persuaded,' he said drily, 'but I have an ulterior motive. There's something I need to ask you in return.'

*Oh, God,* she thought in a panic. *This is where he tells me he needs me to leave at the end of the week.* Her heart seemed to have lodged somewhere in the back of her throat.

'OK,' she said slightly breathlessly, 'but do you think we could go back up to the house? It's just that I don't really like leaving Lottie. I mean, I know she's asleep and we're not far away, but I just want to know that if she did wake up…'

And that if Sarah felt as though she was going to burst into tears she could make an excuse about getting dinner on or fetching a cardigan. And the temple, with its beautiful memories, would remain intact in her mind as the place where she'd known a few moments of perfect peace.

They walked back across the lawn. He was the one person who could make her feel delicate, she thought sadly; because he was so tall, and his shoulders so broad, but also because she felt protected by him. The evening sun turned the *palazzo* into an image from an ancient fresco, a vision of some earthly paradise, unchanged for five hundred years. It could not have brought home to her more forcefully what she was losing.

She gave a soft, wistful laugh. 'Lottie was right when she said it's the loveliest place on earth.'

'She was also right when she said it was far too big for one person.'

They had reached the courtyard now. Lorenzo put the glasses down on the antique table with its peeling paint and

Sarah went inside to check on Lottie. Before going downstairs again she slipped into her bedroom and checked her reflection in the mirror, resisting the ridiculous urge to slap some make-up on her pink cheeks.

For what, exactly?

Lorenzo was sitting on the bench in the courtyard, staring moodily out over the garden. 'Everything all right?' he said as she came out again.

'Fine. She's asleep,' Sarah said, sitting down.

They might have been any couple discussing their child, Lorenzo thought with a wrenching sensation in the pit of his stomach. *'Bene,'* he said gruffly. 'Now, I've got something to ask you, but you must promise to say no if you want to.'

Fleetingly his mind flickered to the other question he had to ask her. About the film. Things were coming together so well that it alternately excited and terrified him. Very soon he could tell her all about it, but first he had to get this out of the way.

'That was Tia on the phone before,' he began carefully, turning his wine glass round in his fingers.

'I know.'

She was picking at the peeling paint on the table, but Lorenzo was too preoccupied to notice the note of misery in her voice. 'She was ringing to remind me about Venice. I hadn't forgotten, but I had managed to push it to the back of my mind—these things are to be endured rather than enjoyed at the best of times.'

'What things?'

'It's the film festival. *Circling the Sun* is being premiered, and she was making sure that I'd be there to witness her triumph.'

A patch of dirty grey paint was gradually being revealed beneath her nervous fingers. 'Triumph?'

He sighed. 'It's a media scrum. Obviously all the media interest will be firmly focused on her and Ricardo and my reaction to seeing them together, so the film itself will hardly get a mention. One-nil to Tia.'

'Are they still together?' she asked dully.

'Yes.' Aware of the savagery in his tone, Lorenzo took a mouthful of wine, as if that could wash it away. 'There's not much I can do to put the focus back on the film rather than the off-screen drama, but there's no doubt that much of the voyeuristic *frisson* will be taken out of the story if I don't turn up alone.' He set his wineglass down and thrust a hand through his hair. '*Dio*, Sarah, I'm not exactly selling this to you, am I?'

There was a pause. 'You're asking me to go with you?'

'*Si*. I know your track record when it comes to saying no, and the last thing I want to do is take advantage of you. I'll make it as brief and painless as poss—'

Relief made her too eager. 'OK. I mean, no, you don't have to do that. I'd be happy to come with you.'

'That was easier than I thought,' he said drily.

She took a large gulp of wine and nearly choked. 'Well, you're not the only one with an ex to score points from,' she said when she could speak again. 'It's not going to do any harm for Rupert to see me on the red carpet at the Venice Film Festival on the arm of a...top Italian film director, is it?' She was blushing more than ever now, partly because she always blushed when she lied, and saying Rupert was her reason for agreeing to this with such enthusiasm was a whopper. But mainly because she'd almost said 'sexy'. On the arm of a sexy Italian film director. 'He probably thinks I'm still sitting on the sofa in a grim flat in Shepherd's Bush, working my way steadily through boxes of tissues and packets of biscuits as I pine for him.'

'Well, he'll be in for a surprise,' Lorenzo said almost coldly. 'And there's no doubt that he will see you—the Press scrutiny is pretty harsh. You're ready for that? You don't need more time to think about this?'

She shook her head, but his words had sent a chill of uncertainty stealing down inside her. It wrapped its clammy fingers around her heart as she imagined banks of photographers lined up and pointing their long lenses at her like weapons.

'Do you? I mean, I'm not exactly red-carpet material.'

'You are,' he sighed. 'Don't worry about any of that.'

Warmth tingled inside her, deep inside her, as his unsmiling gaze moved lazily over her face, her cleavage in the unbuttoned V of her shirt. She gave him a weak smile. 'OK. Why would I? By the end of this, fashion editors across the world will be hailing "housekeeper chic" as the new look, and journalists will be clamouring to discover the secret of my unique style and how I achieve my enviable "just got out of bed" hair.'

He laughed, but his eyes were serious. 'You're probably right. Rupert won't be able to get the ring off that poor woman's finger fast enough.'

# CHAPTER THIRTEEN

'I DON'T BELIEVE IT. Why didn't you tell me you had a private plane?'

Sarah stopped just inside the doorway of the small Citation jet and turned to face him, her eyes round with amazement. Lorenzo smiled.

'I don't. It's only hired. I did promise I'd make this trip as quick and painless as possible. My excuse is that this is certainly the quickest way to do it.'

'And the most painless,' she laughed as a steward appeared with a bottle of champagne in an ice bucket.

'Would you like to take a seat, *signorina?*' said the steward. 'We will be ready for take-off in a few moments.'

'Can I have a look around first? Would you mind? I've never been on a private plane before. In fact, I've only ever been on a public one a few times, so all this is completely new. Oh, look—there's a little fridge, and a television. What does this button do?'

'It's a satellite communications system, *signorina.*'

Lorenzo watched, unable to quite suppress a smile at her excitement. God knew, he wouldn't have much to smile about over the next twenty-four hours, which promised to be about as much fun as root-canal work, but Sarah's sweetness and enthusiasm were like a shaft of sunlight in a darkened room.

Tia would have been having a diva tantrum about the champagne not being the right kind, or the air-conditioning drying out her skin or something.

Sarah turned to him, her eyes shining with delight.

'Gosh—Lottie and Dino would love this.'

'You want to phone home?'

She hesitated and for a fraction of a second her face clouded. Then she flashed that quick, brave smile again and shook her head. 'And interrupt the camping fun? I don't think so. She probably hasn't even noticed I'm gone yet.'

'Are you OK?'

'Yes. Yes, of course.' She sat down on one of the squashy seats and stroked a hand over the gleaming beige leather. 'It's weird, that's all; I mean, I've hardly ever left her overnight before. But it's good. Really good that she's made a friend and got the chance to be a bit more independent. It's what I wanted and there just weren't the opportunities in London.'

Lorenzo sat down opposite her and took the champagne bottle from the bucket of ice. 'So, in spite of having to do this, you're not regretting your decision to stay?'

'No,' she laughed, taking the glass of champagne he handed her. 'And it's not much hardship to be doing this either.'

'Yet,' he said grimly. 'This is the easy part. Wait until later when you're standing in front of the bloodthirsty Press pack.'

The laughter faded from her lips and she looked at him seriously. 'Will it be that bad?'

'I'll make sure you're protected from the worst of it.'

His fingers tightened on his glass and for the hundredth time he wondered if he was making a huge mistake. A huge, selfish mistake.

He looked at her now, leaning forward to gaze out of the window as the plane started to move along the runway. Her plump lower lip was caught between her teeth, and the sun streaming through the window highlighted the freckles on her nose, and made gold and copper lights dance in her hair. After a month at Castellaccio she had lost her haunted look and her exceptional, clear skin was tanned to the colour of the froth on the top of a cappuccino. There was still that same nervous, self-effacing edge to her that he'd noticed the moment she'd walked into The Rose and Crown that night, but it was less pronounced now, so that the first thing you noticed about her was her air of quiet, almost slumberous sensuality.

That was the first thing *he* noticed about her, anyway, he thought acidly, draining half a glass of champagne in one mouthful.

The irony was that was exactly what he'd hoped for when he'd asked her to stay on at the *palazzo*. He'd wanted to take the ghosts from her eyes, and the anxious frown from beneath her brows. He'd wanted to make her see herself as attractive and special. But in order to do that, to make her stay, he'd promised to keep his distance.

If he'd known then how hard it would be, would he ever have been honourable enough to ask?

They were airborne now, the clouds spread below them in billowing layers of gossamer like Angelica's wedding veil, the sky above them an endless expanse of cerulean blue. Looking out of the window, Sarah was aware of him looking at her and hoped he wasn't already doubting the wisdom of bringing her. She wouldn't blame him. Was she the only person who had ever travelled by private jet wearing a faded old T-shirt that had shrunk in the wash and still bore the orange stain of a particularly good ragu sauce she'd made last week?

Not that it mattered much what clothes she travelled in, but the issue of what to wear tonight was much more problematic. She'd brought the lilac dress she'd worn to Angelica's wedding because it was the only possible option, but it was hardly the stuff of red-carpet glamour. She hoped she wouldn't let Lorenzo down. She'd thought about telling him that she had nothing to wear, but suspected that he'd then feel compelled to offer to buy her something, which would be horribly embarrassing.

He'd given her so much already.

Sarah had thought the plane was impressive, but nothing could have prepared her for the hotel.

Briefly taking her hand as she stepped from the vaporetto, Lorenzo said, 'Most people going to the festival stay down in the Lido, but I prefer to be removed from the media circus as much as possible. This place is much more discreet.'

Inside the reception hallway it was cool and dim. Discreet probably wasn't the first word that would have occurred to her to describe such breathtaking grandeur, but she looked around at the vast, dark oil paintings in gilded frames a foot thick and impossibly ornate chandeliers as Lorenzo spoke to the concierge behind the desk and decided it was fitting. Everything wore a patina of age and there was nothing glossy or sleek or remotely high-tech about it, so that it felt a little like stepping out of the twenty-first century and through some secret doorway to the past...

'Ready?'

Lorenzo raised an enquiring eyebrow at her as he moved away from the desk. She hurried after him, her shamefully shabby flip-flops slapping on the marble floor.

'What time is the screening?' she asked as the lift doors slid shut, enclosing them together in dark-panelled intimacy. It was important to keep the conversation going, to drown out the thudding of her heart.

'Seven tonight,' he said curtly.

'Oh, but that's ages.' Surprised, she checked her watch. 'It's only just midday now. That means I've got loads of time to look around the city.'

He glanced at her with an expression of rueful amusement as the lift shuddered to a halt and the doors opened. 'I'm afraid not,' he said, striding along a corridor lined with marble statues of women in various stages of undress.

She frowned. 'Oh. Is there something we have to do first?'

He stopped in front of a set of huge double doors, and swiped the key card down the reader at the side. 'Not "we",' he said gently. 'You. Welcome to the world of the A-list celebrity.'

The doors opened, and Sarah felt her jaw drop. She was standing on the threshold of a huge square room with a wall of floor-to-ceiling windows overlooking the Grand Canal. After the gloom of the corridor the light shining on the polished marble floor and glinting on mirrors was almost dazzling, but it wasn't that that made her gape in astonishment, but the three portable metal clothes rails that stood in the centre of the room, shimmering with a rainbow of silks and satins.

Two effortlessly elegant women were standing by the window, their gazelle-like figures framed gorgeously by the view, so that they looked like a carefully posed photograph from Italian *Vogue*. Breaking off their conversation, they came forward, their catlike eyes flickering over Sarah appraisingly.

'Sarah, this is Natalia and Cristina. They're stylists. The dresses here have been donated by designers, and they'll help you to choose something that you like for tonight.'

Sarah looked anxiously at the rails of clothes and thought of the lilac dress in her bag. She could feel a scarlet tide of embarrassment creep up her neck. Tonight was obviously a bigger deal than she'd thought.

'O-OK,' she stammered, shaking one cool, elegant hand after the other. 'That's g-great, I think. When is everyone else getting here?'

'Well, the beautician will be arriving in the next couple of hours, when you've had time to decide what to wear. And the hair and make-up girls will come some time this afternoon.'

Sarah's mouth fell open in astonishment. 'But all these clothes can't be for me?' she said faintly. 'How will I ever choose?'

'That's what Natalia and Cristina are here for. Don't worry, everything is on loan, and they're under strict instructions not to pressure you into anything you hate. Don't let them bully you.'

Natalia and Cristina laughed politely as Lorenzo turned and walked back to the door. They were still looking at Sarah in a way that was making her nervous, as if, like the Siamese cats from one of Lottie's favourite Disney films, they were about to pounce on her and eat her up the minute Lorenzo left.

'Where are you going?' she said, trying to keep the panic from her voice.

'I have meetings lined up this afternoon. Sorry, but it's too good an opportunity to miss while everyone is in town. I'll be back to collect you about six.'

And with that he was gone.

Why, thought Sarah three hours later as she lay on the bed with a pillow stuffed in her mouth, did perfectly sensible women put themselves through this voluntarily?

She gave a muffled cry of pain as the beautician yanked another wax strip from her right shin with brutal relish. Stripping down to her awful chewing-gum-coloured underwear in front of Natalia and Cristina had been bad enough, but the day had taken on a sinister Marquis de Sade-type aspect since the arrival of the beauty team. Her face had already been steamed and scrubbed and her eyebrows agonisingly tweezered until a surreptitious glance in the mirror confirmed she looked every bit as battered and bruised as she felt.

And some women thought this was fun?

To Sarah it felt like the last stage of psychological endurance training for some dangerous job as a top-level spy. Next they'd probably be thrusting her head down the loo and demanding that she give them names.

'Legs all done,' purred the beautician girl, delicately rubbing wax from her fingers. 'Next I do your bikini line.'

'No!' squeaked Sarah, sitting bolt upright and clutching her hotel bathrobe around her. The beautician looked disapproving, as if Sarah had just announced she didn't believe in brushing her teeth.

'OK,' she sniffed. 'Nails?'

But in the end Sarah did have to admit that there was some truth in the old saying that you had to suffer to be beautiful. When it was eventually time to shrug off the bathrobe and put on the underwear Natalia and Cristina had chosen for her, she was able to do it without a fraction of the self-consciousness she'd felt earlier, and for once she didn't avoid catching her own reflection in the mirror.

Not that it would have been possible anyway, since the room was virtually all mirrors, but the smooth, bronzed, gleaming body that she saw in them was barely recognisable as her own. With ceremonial reverence Natalia and Cristina stood on either side of her, helping her into the dress they'd all agreed on the moment Sarah had tried it on. It was made of heavy duchesse satin, the colour of raspberries crushed with a little cream, and its gloriously simple empire style was the perfect showcase for Sarah's cleavage, which they declared was '*magnifico*'. Although definitely not the kind of person to swoon over a pair of shoes, even Sarah had to admit that the cerise high-heeled sandals they had chosen to go with it, with ribbons that tied all the way up her legs, were extraordinary lovely.

But the source of her most profound joy was the magic wrought by the two hairdressers, who washed and massaged and anointed her disobedient curls with expensive-smelling serums before smoothing them between straightening irons with patient ruthlessness. Now her hair fell down past her shoulders like a curtain of heavy shot silk.

'*Bella. Se Bella,*' Natalia sighed in complete satisfaction as she stood back and surveyed the finished result, and murmurs of reverential agreement went around the rest of the assembled party. Looking in the mirror, Sarah felt an inner glow of happiness, which somehow seemed to radiate outwards. She might never be beautiful, but tonight was the closest she was ever going to get to it, and with that she was content.

The knock at the door broke the enchantment and suddenly the room was filled with a crackle of electricity. Natalia and Cristina went into a flurry of last-minute tweaks, smoothing a seam here, adjusting a strap there, before melting away with the rest of the girls into the suite's adjoining bedroom.

And then the door opened and he was there.

Sarah forgot to breathe.

He was dressed impeccably, but with just a touch of disdain in a plain black suit and black shirt open at the collar. He was cleanly shaven, his hair still damp from the shower. He looked arrogant, remote and faintly menacing as his dark gaze travelled over her.

And she saw it. A momentary flash of disappointment. She felt the split second's hesitation like the lash of a whip.

'You look beautiful,' he said gruffly, forcing a smile as his eyes met hers. 'Really. Very lovely.'

She picked up her little silver clutch bag. 'Shall we go?' Miraculously, she managed to produce a smile, determined that he shouldn't see that inside she had died a little.

Beautiful for her, maybe. But just not beautiful enough.

# CHAPTER FOURTEEN

LORENZO followed her along the corridor, unable to take his eyes off her perfect, rounded behind encased in raspberry-pink satin.

At least that was one thing about her that hadn't changed, he thought wearily.

He'd been telling the absolute truth. With her designer dress, her high heels, her lipgloss and mascara she looked absolutely sensational. But completely unfamiliar. It was the difference between a glorious, full-blown cottage-garden rose, exploding with scent, and the rigid, waxen, death-like perfection of the roses that came from expensive florists, presented in layers of cellophane.

He preferred the first, and he loathed himself for his own hypocrisy. He had done this to her—she hadn't asked for any of it, and he loathed himself for that even more.

They had reached the lift again. She got in ahead of him and pressed the button for the ground floor.

'Your nails,' he said softly. 'You have the nails you always wanted.'

They were a pale, glossy pink with delicate crescents of white at the tips, just as she'd described that time in Gennaro's.

She spread her hands out and looked down at them wistfully. 'I know. At last I'm a proper woman. If only Lottie were here to see it.'

*A proper woman. Dio santo.* He had a sudden image of her in the kitchen, her hair tumbling messily around her face, her breasts straining against the faded green T-shirt as she bent to put something in the dishwasher, making her short denim skirt rise at the back to show more of her delicious legs... She was a proper woman through and through. A real woman. Not one of those dolls Lottie had described with such disdain.

The water taxi he had ordered was waiting at the hotel landing stage and he helped her in, catching a fleeting breath of her warm scent as he lowered himself in beside her.

'You smell nice.'

'Really?' Her neatly arched eyebrows rose in surprise. 'They tried to spray me with perfume but I said no. It must be the hair products or something.'

It wasn't. It was *her*.

The sun was setting over the water, and it was that hour when the city underwent its nightly transformation from crowded, noisy tourist magnet to subtle, secret city of lovers. The buildings along the Grand Canal were bathed in the dying light of the day, which flattered their faded beauty to perfection. The breeze made Sarah's straight, heavy hair fan out like the silken Venetian flags that topped so many buildings, rippling in the setting sun.

'Oh. I almost forgot. I picked this up on my way back.'

He took a flat box from his pocket and handed it to her, watching her face as she lifted the lid. Her mouth opened and her eyes widened, and despite the lipgloss and the mascara and shimmering eyeshadow she was herself again, her emotions still as clearly on display as ever as she lifted out the delicate web of silver wires and diamond stars.

'Lorenzo—it's incredible! It's the most beautiful thing I've ever seen. Are you sure it's OK for me to wear it?'

'I deliberately didn't give it to you in front of the style police back at the hotel in case they disapproved. But if you like it, wear it.'

'I do. I love it. Natalia said that they hadn't had time to organise the loan of any jewellery—insurance or something—so did you sort all that out when you borrowed it? Apparently it's a bit of a legal nightmare.'

'Don't worry,' he said drily. 'It's all under control.' Because he hadn't borrowed it, he'd bought it, amongst other things, in a fit of temporary madness on the way back from his meeting with the very up-and-coming English actor whom he had asked to play the lead in the film of Francis Tate's book. Damian King had got a cult TV-drama series under his belt and was just finishing a very successful season at the RSC when his agent had given him a copy of *The Oak and the Cypress*. This afternoon he had been perfectly upfront and unstinting in his enthusiasm.

Buoyed up by champagne and elation, Lorenzo had gone into a discreet jewellery shop in a quiet *calle* and bought the necklace with its constellations of stars and the single moon hanging in the centre. There was a smaller version, for Lottie, and...

'Please can you put it on?'

Her sleek, heavy hair glinted gold and copper in the tangerine light of the sinking sun. A tremor of pure, powerful desire shook him as he swept it to one side, exposing the nape of her neck.

It was getting more difficult to ignore, this jagged, insistent wanting, he thought darkly. And it was now no longer possible to dismiss it as being motivated by some worthy intention to protect her and look after her best interests, or even the matter of the film rights. That was how it had started, admittedly, but at some point in between the kitchen and the temple, the oysters and the cake, it had gone beyond that into something far more debilitating and difficult to shake off.

'There.' He pulled his hands away as quickly as possible,

clenching his fists against the urge to tangle his fingers in her hair and pull her head round so he could kiss off all that shiny pink lipgloss.

'Oh, Lorenzo, it's exquisite. You're so clever—I'd never have picked anything as perfect as this. Gosh, wouldn't Lottie love it? I won't mind having my photograph taken so much now, because at least it'll mean she'll get to see it. Thank you.'

'No problem,' he said flatly, turning his head away and looking out into the lagoon as it opened up in front of them. Any excuse to avert his gaze from the stars glittering against her satiny skin, the little crescent moon nestling in the honey-coloured hollow between her glorious breasts. Otherwise the photographers would get some very incriminating photographs when he got out of the boat. 'Look, we're nearly there.'

Ahead, the glare of spotlights and the glitter of camera flashes lit up the gently fading evening. As they drew closer it was possible to see the great white wall of the screening venue, the rows of flags catching the gentle breeze above it, and hear the clamour of the crowd.

'There's the car waiting at the dock to collect us.'

She looked confused. 'Oh, yes. Is it far? I thought we were only going over there…'

'We are,' he said drily. 'But celebrities don't walk anywhere.'

The boat stopped and he stood up, holding out his hand to her. In spite of the unfamiliar make-up, the veneer of sophistication, her eyes wore that wide, wary look he had seen as soon as she'd walked into The Rose and Crown, and the lust of a second ago was almost obliterated by a wave of guilt.

He was about to throw her to the lions.

It was too late to turn back now. He'd just have to do what he could to make sure they savaged him first.

It was like one of those dreams where nothing made sense, and the most extravagantly bizarre things happened in the guise of normality. Sarah found herself getting into the car and perching on the shiny, slippery seat as beyond the darkened glass the night sparkled with thousands of camera flashes. And, like in a dream, she found it was the details that she noticed. The tiny letters on the window of the car that said '*bulletproof glass*', the driver's white gloves, the muscle that was pulsing beneath Lorenzo's tense jaw.

Of course. In a few short moments he'd be coming face to face with the woman he loved, arm in arm with another man. No wonder he looked as if he was being silently tortured.

She longed to cover his hand with hers, and tell him she understood, but then the car was stopping in front of a wide building with a huge white frontage lit up with so many spotlights that it must surely be visible from the moon.

For a moment nothing happened, and then the door on Lorenzo's side was pulled smoothly open by unseen hands. In the half-second before he got out he looked at her with an expression of great weariness and said simply, 'I'm sorry.'

The noise hit her like a wall as she slid out of the car onto shaking legs. People shouting. Shouting his name—*Lorenzo*—but louder, more insistent, more fanatically, *'Tia! Ricardo!'* Camera flashes dazzled her, so brightly that she wanted to hide her head in her hands and run through them, like a sudden hail storm on the way to the Tube in Shepherd's Bush. But then Lorenzo took her arm and she ducked her head against the shelter of his massive shoulders.

'Look,' he murmured, bending his head and speaking close to her ear. 'Up there. In the sky.'

Cautiously she lifted her head and looked up, to where the pale ghost of the moon hung above them, gazing down on all the madness with her cool, impassive grace. Around them the clamour intensified. Very deliberately Lorenzo kept his eyes fixed on hers. 'The moon is looking down on Lottie too,' he said softly, so only she could hear. 'She's going to tell her how beautiful you are.' He smiled fleetingly. 'Especially your nails.'

Sarah laughed, and suddenly all the camera flashes and the spotlights put together were nothing to the light inside her. Keeping her head up, her fingers tightly laced through his, she let him guide her up the scarlet expanse towards the door of the theatre. He was very still, very upright, seemingly completely unmoved by the cheering crowd behind them, the banks of journalists to the right who shouted out his name in the hope of getting them to stop and pose for a shot or say a few words into one of the many microphones that were thrust forward. Glancing up at him, Sarah saw his face in the strobe-like flash of the cameras, and felt the glow of her happiness splutter and fade, as if the bulb she had swallowed had just gone out.

It was cold and bleak.

They were inside the mouth of the theatre entrance now, and the roar of the crowd echoed off the walls as Tia and Ricardo posed for more pictures. The sea of people who had pressed around Lorenzo and Sarah as they entered the enclosed space drew back, and suddenly there was no one between them and the other couple.

Nothing—not the airbrushed double-page spreads in lifestyle magazines, not the nude photoshoot that had caused such a stir, not the close-up camera angles in numerous films— could have prepared Sarah for how stunning Tia de Luca was in the flesh, and in that moment Sarah knew that all the make-up, the most expensive designer dresses and shoes in the world couldn't make her a millionth as lovely as the woman standing in front of her. In the glare of the spotlights her skin had a creamy luminosity, and her famous catlike eyes sparkled more intensely than the emeralds she wore at her throat and ears. She was, quite simply, very beautiful.

And very pregnant.

Oh, God, somehow, astonishingly, Sarah had forgotten that little detail. Lorenzo's fingers tightened convulsively around hers, and for a second she was distantly aware of the pain. But it was followed a moment later by a more acute hurt when he dropped her hand altogether.

'*Ciao,* Lorenzo.'

Her voice was like butter melting over crumpets: unctuous, slow, lascivious.

Lorenzo nodded. 'Tia. Ricardo.'

God, he was cool. Polite to the point of being almost insolent. Sarah was aware that every camera lens in the area was trained on them, and consciously tried to keep her misery from showing on her face. It was harder than it looked, this being-a-celebrity game, but Lorenzo and Tia and Ricardo were all masters.

'Aren't you going to introduce us?' Tia said, turning her megawatt smile from Lorenzo to Sarah.

'Sarah, this is Tia, my ex-wife, and Ricardo Marcello.'

Ricardo Marcello's handsome face was ridiculously familiar, but Sarah was completely unmoved by the legendary good looks. There was something bland and plastic about his bronzed skin and clichéd sculpted jaw, something anonymous about the straight nose and blue eyes that could make him be the face of any hero. Not like Lorenzo, who was all himself and infinitely more compelling.

'Sarah?' Tia cut through her thoughts. 'But surely we've spoken on the telephone, Sarah? You're Lorenzo's housekeeper?' The smile got wider, brighter, if that was possible. 'Oh, how lovely! You look so pretty—are you having a nice time? It's quite exciting, all this, isn't it?'

Tia turned, sweeping an elegant hand, flashing diamonds around at the Press and the crowd and the cameras. Sarah felt about two inches tall.

'Unreal is more how I'd describe it,' she said quietly.

Tia laughed, throwing back her head like in the photo in Gennaro's, and all around them the camera flashes glittered like fireworks.

'I'm afraid to us it's all *too* real, although Lorenzo has never enjoyed it, have you, *mio caro?* Ah, I think they want us over there for some photographs. I'm sure they won't mind if you come too, Sarah.'

As they stood in front of the ranks of photographers Sarah felt as if her lipglossed smile was superglued to her face. Lorenzo's arm was loosely around her, his hand warm on her bare shoulder, but in every other way it felt as though he was a million miles away.

'Are you coming to the Press conference tomorrow?' Tia asked as they moved away again, and into the screening room.

'No,' Lorenzo said tersely, and Tia looked put out.

'Really, Lorenzo, you have to face the Press at some point, you know. I know there are bound to be difficult questions,' she dropped her voice to a perfectly pitched husky murmur, 'but if we—'

'It has nothing to do with you, Tia,' Lorenzo said coldly. 'Sarah has a small daughter and we need to get back to her.'

They had come to a standstill in front of the row of VIP seats with their name cards on. All of a sudden the atmosphere seemed to change. For a second Tia went very still, and then quietly, venomously she said something in Italian that Sarah didn't understand.

*'Ipocrita.'*

As she said it her beautiful face was almost ugly.

The lights had gone up but the applause went on. And on. And on. Far longer than the film deserved. Lorenzo gritted his teeth in impatience as people in the rows behind leaned forward and slapped his back in congratulation, while Tia turned misty-eyed and waved to the cheering theatre.

Beside him, he was acutely aware of Sarah as she stretched slightly, blinking in the light and stifling a yawn. But then he'd been acutely aware of Sarah for the last two hours. It was funny, he thought. All those weeks of living under the same roof, and he'd managed to keep his distance and preserve the illusion that he was really not that attracted to her, but two hours sitting in the dark beside her, close enough to hear her breathing and to smell the warmth of her skin, to be aware of every tiny movement as she crossed her ankles, or smoothed back her hair, and he was like a lust-skewered teenager on a first date.

The film had passed him by completely, *grazie a Dio*.

The applause began to peter out and, desperate to seize the chance for escape, Lorenzo grabbed Sarah's hand.

'Come on. Let's get out of here.'

Before she could reply, Tia interrupted, 'You are coming to the party at the Excelsior, aren't you?'

'Absolutely not,' he said grimly, pulling Sarah after him as he made for the exit. 'Right,' he muttered as they reached the foyer, where the Press pack waited to engulf them again, 'hold your head up, smile like you've just had the best two hours of your life and walk quickly. The car will be waiting for us at the bottom of the steps. Everyone will assume we have somewhere very important to go.'

'And do we?'

'Yes.' He looked down at her briefly, desire churning inside him again. 'Away from here.'

They were the first out, and as they emerged the night was lit up with flashes again as a great shout went up from the gathered Press and public. Holding her hand very tightly, Lorenzo felt Sarah shiver as the cool air hit them, and he drew her quickly forward as PR girls and security men with headsets ran agitatedly up and down the cordons at the side of the red carpet.

After a moment he saw the reason for their sudden activity, and swore under his breath.

'The car's not there yet.'

Sarah's eyes widened as she looked up at him. The crowd were shouting his name. Journalists close by were calling out questions.

'What do we do?' she whispered.

'Stall. It'll be here in a moment.'

But from the crowd another shout came, clearly audible above the rest. *'Sarah! Over here, Sarah!'*

So it had taken the tabloid sharks just two hours to find out her name, Lorenzo thought with a surge of bitter fury. She was about to turn, instinctively ready to answer to her name and unwittingly surrender all her privacy, but he caught her, pulling her back and bringing his mouth down on hers.

A roar went up from the crowd and flashbulbs exploded like a meteor shower around them. Out of some inherent instinct to protect her, Lorenzo found himself taking her face between his hands, shielding it, preventing the cameras from getting a proper view of her like that.

Kissing him. Tenderly, hesitantly, tremulously, and with a quiet ferocity that left him breathless and reeling.

With mammoth effort of will he pulled away after a long, blissful moment, looking over her shoulder through a haze of debilitating desire to where the car was just pulling up in front of the steps.

'Let's go.'

## CHAPTER FIFTEEN

His face was like thunder as he slammed the car door and shut out the clamour of the crowd.

'Sorry. I shouldn't have done that.'

The chill in his voice made her wince. Shrinking back against the cold leather, she pressed her fingers to lips that still tingled from his kiss. 'Don't,' she said in anguish. 'Please. It's fine.'

He leaned back in his seat, his jaw set, his hands balled into fists. 'I didn't want them to put you on the spot. I never thought they'd find out so quickly who you are, and the last thing I wanted was for you to be put under the microscope. At least they won't be able to create too much of a story without any quotes to work with.' He stopped, rubbing a hand over his eyes for a second before continuing, 'I should never have exposed you to any of this.'

The car pulled up at the end of its short journey, but neither of them moved, and after all the frenetic noise the silence felt as soft and rich as fur. Sarah looked down into her lap, fiddling with the clasp of her handbag.

'I've told you,' she said quietly, 'I don't need protecting.'

Lorenzo was about to speak but the door opened, and they got out to walk the few steps down to the waiting water taxi. Darkness had fallen properly and the lights of the city made rippling trails of gold on the water. Behind them the disembodied screaming of the crowd rose into the night and echoed across the water and, looking back, Sarah could see a glowing arc of white light bleaching the skyline around the theatre. Ahead of them the moon was full and high, and it seemed to sail in front of them, leading them across the lagoon and back to…

*What?*

Sarah shivered.

'It's colder now,' Lorenzo said gruffly. 'Here,' and he slipped his jacket over her shoulders. Automatically, she demurred. 'No, honestly. I'm fine. I don't…'

'*Sarah, per piacere,* will you just let me do something for you for *once?*'

She stopped, her hands on the lapels of the jacket as the ragged despair in his voice tore through her. 'Sorry,' she whispered, pulling it closer around her, enfolding herself in the blissful borrowed warmth of his body. 'Sorry.'

Other boats passed them, dark shapes sliding past, bringing snatches of other people's conversation, other people's laughter. There was something spectral about the buildings on either side of the Grand Canal, floodlit from below so that their upper storeys faded into the night sky. Venice lay around them, its mysterious, ancient alleyways cloaked in darkness and silvered with moonlight, but after two hours in the cinema her head was still full of the dazzling colours and brilliant sunshine of Tuscany; a rich, sensual panorama of texture and detail that made her feel she could almost taste the wine from Galileo's cup, and smell the clean, earthy scent of cedar and lime in the air.

Lorenzo's smell, she thought with a sickening lurch of anguished yearning. He was in her, all around her, whether she liked it or not. She leaned on the side of the boat, letting the motion of the water rock through her as she gave herself up to reliving the moment when he'd kissed her. Oh, God, the ecstasy of having his hands on her face, his body pressed against hers. He'd probably been thinking of Tia, she thought despairingly. That would explain the sense of fierce, restrained passion she'd sensed in him, as if he was fighting with everything in him to keep control. He was fired up and torn apart by watching her on the screen.

The steps to the hotel landing stage loomed in front of them. Although she braced herself for the jolt when the boat hit the dock she still stumbled a little on the impossible heels, and instantly his arm was around her.

*'Bene?'*

'Yes,' she said breathlessly, forcing herself to step away from him immediately and take the hand of the hotel porter on the steps.

The hotel's reception area was softly lit and welcoming as they walked through it, Sarah's heels echoing on the marble floor. As they waited for the lift she slipped Lorenzo's jacket off her shoulders and handed it back to him.

'Thank you for lending it to me.' She gave a soft, breathy laugh. 'I feel like Cinderella—now I have to return all my borrowed finery and turn back into a kitchen maid.'

Lorenzo didn't smile. The lift doors shut behind them.

'The film was spectacular,' she said quickly, to try and break the sudden tension. 'Sorry, I should have said before. The moon sequences especially—Lottie would adore those—but all of it was brilliant. I loved it.'

Everything about him was as cold and upright and emotionless as the marble pillars they had just walked past in the reception area. 'At least that makes one of us then,' he said acidly. 'I hated every second.'

Sarah felt her insides constrict with compassion and longing. 'That's understandable,' she whispered. 'It must be very difficult to watch.'

'It's bloody excruciating,' he said through gritted teeth.

The lift stopped. Sarah nodded, biting her lip in anguish as she waited for the doors to open so she could step away from him and hopefully lessen the screaming urge to put her arms around his rigid shoulders. She pushed through the doors before they were even properly open, hurrying back along the corridor towards her room.

She didn't have the key, and stood at the huge double doors waiting for him, keeping her head down because she knew that if she watched him come towards her she would be completely undone.

The card was in his hand, but he didn't put it into the reader straight away. Sparks erupted inside Sarah's stomach as he gently took her chin in her hands and raised her face so she was looking up at him.

'Not because of Tia,' he said gruffly, 'in case that's what you think. I don't give a damn about her at all. That's not why I hate the film.'

For a second she couldn't breathe. The world blurred and stars danced in her head. 'Then why?'

He laughed softly. 'Because it's cliché-ridden, predictable, plastic Hollywood rubbish, that's why. And I *never* want to sell out by making a film like that again.'

He didn't let her go. He was frowning, almost as if he was in pain as his eyes burned into hers with that peculiar intensity that made her feel as if he was looking into her head, almost willing her to understand something.

'But I thought...' She swallowed. 'Tia—you're still in love with her?'

He laughed hollowly, shaking his head. 'No. *Dio santo,* no. I couldn't get the divorce through fast enough.'

Along the corridor the lift doors opened again and the sound of voices made them both jump. Lorenzo let her go, turning and sliding the key into the slot quickly. Sarah pushed the doors open, saying shakily over her shoulder, 'Would you like to come in for coffee or something?'

'No.'

Disappointment lacerated her at the thought of him going back to his own room, but was quickly followed by relief as he shut the door behind him and headed for an ornate, inlaid cabinet. 'I need a proper drink.'

The rails of dresses and mountains of shoe boxes had all been removed, and the huge suite was intimidatingly immaculate again. The lights had been left on in the bedroom, and through the open door Sarah could see the sheets had been turned down on the enormous bed with its carved gold headboard. Suddenly light-headed with want, she went over to the window seat and sat down, raising up her skirt to untie the ribbons on her shoes and ease her aching feet out of them.

Thoughts seemed to be whirling around in her brain, but too fast to allow her to make any sense of them, so that it was like trying to look at the scenery through the window of a speeding train. When she looked up again Lorenzo was standing in front of her, holding a bottle of brandy and two glasses, his dark eyes hooded and opaque.

She took a glass from him, holding it against her chest as if it could warm her. The only thing she could focus on with any clarity was what Lorenzo had said about Tia. About not loving Tia. But how this was possible and what it meant was part of the blur.

'She said something to you, just before the film started. What was it?'

He took a mouthful of brandy. She watched his bronzed throat move as he swallowed.

'She called me a hypocrite.'

Sarah frowned. 'Why?'

'Doesn't matter,' he said, but the steel in his tone confirmed what she already suspected.

'It was something to do with me. Me and Lottie, wasn't it? I don't need protecting, Lorenzo. I'd like to know what she meant.'

He sighed, moving across so that he was standing in front

of the window. In profile his face was harsh, uncompromising, arrogant. 'Obviously she assumed we're together. A couple.'

'And why would that make you a hypocrite?' Sarah's heart was thudding, a sensation of nameless dread creeping around her, as if ghostly faces with hostile eyes were peering at them through the blank, dark windows. 'You're divorced. You've both moved on.'

'Because you have a daughter.' He swirled the brandy around in his glass. 'And I left her because I wasn't prepared to be a father to Ricardo Marcello's child.'

Cautiously she took a sip of brandy. She didn't usually like it, but now she welcomed the burn at the back of her throat, which sharpened her senses a little, made her more able to think, and focus.

'But I thought she left you, for Ricardo,' Sarah's whirling mind swung dizzily back to the morning after the flood and the magazine in Angelica's kitchen, 'and that the baby was yours…'

His smile was chillingly bleak. 'Tia's very clever. As far as I know she hasn't said directly that the baby's mine but she's very carefully left her options open. It was me who asked for the divorce, but now she wants to come back. I think she's realising how much she liked being married to a director—it gave her a certain amount of status in the industry, and there's no room for two egos the size of hers and Ricardo's in one relationship.'

'Would you take her back?' Sarah forced the words through numb lips. 'If the baby was yours?'

'It isn't.'

Something in the way he said it made her put down her glass and get to her feet. Standing behind him, she could see his face reflected imperfectly in the glass of the window. His eyes were dark whirlpools.

'How? How do you know?'

The question came from her almost involuntarily. Part of

her didn't want to know; wanted to retreat respectfully from the wound that she sensed lay beneath the terrifyingly controlled façade. But the other part of her knew she didn't have a choice—that, whatever it was and whatever had caused it, she had to share his suffering.

He took a mouthful of brandy, draining the glass.

'Because I can't have children. I'm infertile. Completely and irrevocably. So, you see, it would be a miracle if the baby was mine.'

The ormolu clock on the mantelpiece ticked on, as the aching bitterness of his words died in the quiet room.

Sarah said nothing. There wasn't anything she could say that wouldn't seem to diminish his hurt, so instead she slid her hands across his rigid shoulders, laying her cheek against them and pulling him close as a spasm of irrational loss and longing gripped her. This was the beating heart at the centre of his pain, she thought. Not being without Tia, but without children.

For a moment he didn't move, and then she felt his hand close around hers.

They stood like that for a long moment, and then gently, almost reluctantly, he pulled her round so that she was standing in front of him. Sarah sensed him hesitate, still caged by his own demons, and the realisation touched her unbearably and gave her strength. She couldn't take his pain away, but she could show him that she wasn't afraid of it. Reaching up, she took his face between her hands and raised herself up on tiptoe so she could kiss his mouth.

It was iron-hard with tension, and as her lips very gently moved across his she remembered the night in The Rose and Crown when he'd first kissed her and she'd been too shocked, too scared, too inhibited and insecure to respond. She remembered his tenderness, his patience...his smile, that in her paranoia and self-doubt she'd thought meant he was laughing at her. But now she understood that maybe, just maybe he'd been feeling a fraction of the helpless *rightness* she was feeling now.

Her fingers slid into his silken hair, and she pressed soft kisses to the corner of his mouth and along the line of his jaw, until she felt the tautness leave it and heard him give a low moan.

'Sarah... *Dio,* I've tried to resist this for so long, but I don't think I can hold back any more.'

'Thank God for that.' She'd reached his ear, and broke off kissing to take the lobe in her mouth. 'If you did I think I'd die.'

A shudder of desire went through him and he wrenched his head round to capture her mouth with his. And suddenly everything was different. The kisses that they'd shared before—those tentative, desperate, forbidden kisses—had been like the disjointed strains of a solo violin, compared to the full orchestral symphony of this one. Sarah's body was on fire from inside, flames licking through her, spreading heat to her limbs and melting her so that she was dripping with longing and anticipation.

And she gave herself up to the blaze; arching herself against him as he held her and kissed so deeply it was as if he was looking for her soul. Her hands fumbled blindly at the buttons of his shirt, desire making her clumsy and uncoordinated. Unlike Lorenzo. Taking hold of her dress, he yanked up the heavy satin skirt in one swift tug, hitching it up and freeing her legs so that he could pick her up. Instinctively wrapping her legs around his waist, Sarah's fingers clenched and flexed and the first tremors of helpless ecstasy quivered through her as he pulled her hard against him and carried her into the bedroom.

He lowered her down onto the bed, but she kept her legs tightly clasped around him, pulling him down with her. As she grappled with his belt and the button of his trousers her mouth never left his. He tasted cleanly of brandy, and she drank him in with a desperate, urgent thirst, until at last his impatient fingers tangled with hers, swiftly, expertly tearing open his trousers, and Sarah tipped back her head and gave a triumphant cry of joy as she felt his erection against her parted thighs.

Time slowed, their breathing caught and faltered as he slid

her silken knickers down and she looked up into his face with eyes that were unfocused with desire. She felt disorientated with need...and the finger he languidly stroked through her swollen folds pushed her closer to the edge. Helplessly she writhed against his hand, her mouth opening in a breathless gasp as paradise opened up before her.

With faultless timing, Lorenzo grasped her hips and thrust into her, his teeth clenched with the effort of not erupting inside her as her slippery heat gripped him and her hips rose up to meet him. But, gazing down at her face, her cheeks flushed, her eyes black and glittering with passion, he felt his control crack, and, as her muscles tightened convulsively around him and her crimson lips parted in a cry of pure joy, it shattered completely.

Dazed, exhausted, breathless, he lay in the ruins of his self-restraint and she in the wreckage of a three-thousand-pound, borrowed dress of raspberry satin. But as he gathered her into his arms in a ridiculously ornate bed Lorenzo Cavalleri felt almost at peace.

'Oh, God, Lorenzo.'

He lifted his head, the note of anxiety in her voice making his heart crash against his ribs and jerking him from his semi-somnolent state of bliss.

'What?' He looked down into her face, brushing a damp strand of hair from her cheek. 'Sarah, what's wrong?'

'The dress,' she whispered, rolling away from him and standing up unsteadily. 'How could I have forgotten about the dress? It cost a f—'

In a flash he was behind her, taking her in his arms, rocking her gently as he pressed kisses against the warm, bare skin of her shoulders. 'Shh—'

'But it's got to go back to the designer first thing tomorrow. Oh, God, I'm so stupid, I don't deserve such beautiful things.'

'You do, *assolutemente*. The dress isn't going anywhere,

and neither is the necklace, although I have to agree it would be a lot better if we took them off now...'

'Lorenzo, no!' she said, horrified. 'I couldn't keep them. No way. Don't even *think* about it.'

'Well, I don't think the designer is going to want this back now,' he said slowly sliding down the zip of the dress and turning her around to face him as he pushed it from her shoulders, 'and the necklace was always yours to keep, so there's no point in arguing.'

The dress fell to the floor with a sigh. She wasn't wearing a bra and Lorenzo felt his head rock back as he took in the full impact of her beautiful naked body.

*'Seraphina...'*

She bent her head, letting her hair fall over her face as she crossed her arms across her breasts. Her spectacular, generous, gorgeous breasts with their blush-pink nipples, and the diamond stars and moon glittering against her velvet skin. Very gently, he took her hands and pulled them away from her body.

He sensed her resistance. 'Don't, please...'

He took her face in his hands, stroking her cheeks with his thumbs. 'Sarah, you're exquisite,' he said gravely. '*Dio,* I knew you would be, but you're lovely beyond even my wildest, most X-rated dreams.'

'I'm not. I'm—'

She squealed as he swept her into his arms and hitched her against his chest, carrying her effortlessly into the bathroom, where he turned the shower on.

'You are, which accounts for my complete lack of finesse back there. You're impossibly beautiful—although I have to admit I much prefer you without make-up and with your glorious hair how it's supposed to be.' She gasped again as he set her down under the steaming jet of water and stepped in beside her, stopping any further chance of argument with his mouth on hers as the mascara ran down her cheeks.

Her face was clean of every last trace of make-up and her

hair plastered to her head when he finally turned off the water and reached for a towel to wrap around her.

'Not Seraphina any more,' she said with a sad, shy smile. 'I'm Sarah again now.'

'You're always Seraphina,' Lorenzo growled, gently wiping the water from her face with the edge of the towel. 'You're beautiful through and through.'

The idea of taking her standing up in the shower held considerable appeal, but he had something altogether slower and more considered in mind as he led her back to the bedroom.

He had all night to show her how beautiful she was. Slowly, worshipping her goddess-like body inch by inch, with the reverence it deserved this time. He wanted to make her feel as good as she'd made him feel. Slay her demons as she'd slain his, with her understanding and her compassion and her generous, intuitive acceptance of his secret flaw.

He didn't intend to waste a moment.

# CHAPTER SIXTEEN

WAKING from a brief, disorientatingly deep sleep with the feel of Lorenzo's arm lying along her thigh, his legs tangled with hers, Sarah thought she was still dreaming. But then her eyes fluttered open and the opulent room took shape around her in the tentative grey light of early dawn, the room-service meal they'd shared at some time in the small hours, the empty bottle of champagne, and she smiled because she knew that every spine-tingling, blush-making detail was true.

Lorenzo's hand slid lazily up her thigh and he raised his head to kiss her mouth.

*'Buongiorno, bella.'*

His voice was husky and intimate with sleep and his black hair was tousled. In the half-light with the sheet barely covering him he looked absurdly young somehow, and as she leaned over and kissed him back Sarah realised it was because all the tension had left his face. She propped herself on one elbow, looking down on his body, taking deep pleasure from letting her gaze wander over his broad, powerful chest as it slowly rose and fell with each breath. His olive skin looked dark against the white sheets, and she trailed a finger down over the bumps of his ribs, remembering the first time she'd seen him without his shirt on, when he'd carried Lottie to bed that night. He'd been too thin then, but now the angles of his bones were less sharp, and she felt a deep-down, visceral sense of satisfaction that it was because of her. Her cooking, her care.

His lips twitched as her finger moved lower, and his gaze locked with hers. Sitting up, Sarah bit down on her lower lip, trying to suppress a wicked, delicious smile as she climbed on top of him and watched the darkness in his eyes deepen.

'I think I owe you a Screaming Orgasm,' she murmured as she bent her head and slid downwards.

The sky in the east was faintly tinged with pink, but the city still slept around them, its towers and domes wreathed in pearly grey mist. They were sitting on the balcony overlooking the canal, drowsy and replete, the doors behind them open and the magnificent bed in total disarray. Sarah was loosely wrapped in the satin coverlet from the bed, the diamonds glittering at her throat, her hair tumbling down about her naked shoulders and her legs tucked up in front of her as she sipped tea from a delicate china cup.

'You look like some wanton eighteenth-century duchess after a night of passion with Casanova,' Lorenzo said huskily.

She smiled at him over the rim of her cup, the steam wreathing her face. 'I feel like one. But Casanova would have been very put out to find he had a rival for the title of world's greatest lover. He probably would have challenged you to a duel on the Rialto or something.'

'The way I feel at the moment I would have taken him on,' he said drily. Tia had always made him feel as if his infertility was a weakness. It was her unspoken justification for flirting with other men, kissing them, sleeping with them, as if she was punishing him for being less of a man.

Tentative fingers of light stretched over the lagoon, and gradually the smudged silhouettes of buildings emerged from the shadows and were washed with pink and gold. Like Sarah, Lorenzo thought, coming forward into the light. In the new light her clear, clean skin was the pale rose-gold of the inside of a seashell. *Dio,* how could he ever make her see how incredible she was?

Last night he had made a start, but there was so much he still wanted to do…

He had almost said something about the film last night, when they had talked about *Circling the Sun*. He had so nearly told her about the kind of film he longed to make, but the atmosphere between them had been so highly charged that he hadn't been able to think straight. Hadn't wanted to break that sensual spell.

Hadn't wanted to risk her retreating from him again.

But he would do it soon. He had set up a meeting with distributors and studio bosses in London later in the week, but yesterday's coup with securing the lead actor made it almost just a formality. He didn't need financial backing…

All he needed now were the options rights. From Sarah.

But he didn't just want to ask her outright. This was about more than just the film now. This was about Sarah, and he wasn't just selling her the film, he was selling her Francis Tate. He was presenting to her a perspective on the past that might just change the way she saw the brilliant, troubled poet that Lorenzo had admired for so long, but who had left such scars on his own small daughter. And then she might just change the way she saw herself.

He had to make sure he handled it properly.

'Come along, Duchess.'

Getting to his feet, he held out his hand to her and gently pulled her up. The satin coverlet slid to the floor, so that she was standing naked in front of him, the new sun bathing her in apricot light.

'Where are we going?'

'The most attractive answer to that would be "back to bed",' he said ruefully. 'But there isn't time. You want to get back to Lottie, and I want to show you some of Venice before we go, and if I took you back to bed I might have to keep you there for the rest of the day.'

'Hmm...that sounds good.' Her voice was wistful, almost pleading. She placed the palms of her hands on his bare chest, and Lorenzo felt an instant, debilitating leap of desire. 'I'm sure Lottie's having the time of her life; we don't need to rush back...'

Gently he removed her hands and, taking hold of her shoulders, he drew her to him. 'We'll still have this when we get back to the *palazzo,* you know,' he said gruffly, kissing the top of her head, briefly breathing in the scent of her warm hair. 'I have to go to London on Wednesday, but when I get back we have all the time in the world.'

Sarah pulled away, hating herself for the sudden desolation she felt at the thought of leaving this enchantment and getting back to reality. Of him going away.

'You're going to London?' She said it slightly incredulously, as if she was surprised to hear that London still existed.

*'Si.'* He bent to pick up the satin coverlet and wrapped it around her, holding it tightly under her chin. 'For a day or two, that's all. I'll be back in time for Lottie's birthday on Sunday.'

Sarah laughed, torn between amusement and huge embarrassment. 'Oh, dear, she told you about that?'

'Only about fifty times. I've promised her a special treat.'

'Lorenzo, no!' she said quickly. 'You don't have to—'

'I *want* to,' he interrupted her calmly. 'Anyway, it's too late. It's all organised now, so there's no point in arguing. You'll be all right on your own at Castellaccio for a couple of days?'

'I'm used to being on my own, remember?' She ducked her head, pulling the satin wrap more tightly around herself, mumbling, 'But I'll miss you.'

'I wish I didn't have to go, but I do.' He sighed, and there was an odd note in his voice that was somewhere between wistfulness and determination. 'It's about the film project I'm trying to get off the ground.'

She raised her head. In the pale golden morning his haughty, high-cheekboned face was strangely vulnerable. Her heart clenched. 'It's important to you, this film, isn't it?'

He gave a painful smile. 'It's the most important thing I've ever done.'

The alleyways and squares were still echoing and empty as they walked through them wrapped in each other's arms. In that deserted dawn the city was so breathtaking that Sarah couldn't regret forgoing more basic pleasures for this one.

The plump pink sun turned the opaque greenish water of the canals into rivers of rosy gold and the bells of the many churches echoed out at intervals over the quiet, shimmering city. They passed a baker's, not yet open, but from which the scent of almonds and warm bread drifted enticingly, and which was happy to sell them hot croissants and fat, pale green cookies studded with pistachios to take home to Lottie and Dino.

Emerging again into the damp, cool morning, they walked back through St Mark's Square, empty but for a couple of waiters sweeping up and desultorily setting out chairs. The Basilica looked as if it were made from Turkish delight in the pink morning light. Lorenzo's arm was around her shoulders, his body big and hard and warm against hers, and he said, 'Later this will be so full of tourists that you won't be able to see the ground.' He pulled away from her, taking her hand and swinging her around until she was dizzy and laughing. 'But now it's yours. All yours,' he said, and then he drew her back into his arms and kissed her. And Sarah was so happy that she almost believed him.

They were both quiet on the flight back to Pisa, and as the car wound its way through the verdant Tuscan hills and ochre villages back to Castellaccio Sarah felt her happiness dim a little, as if a cloud had come over the sun. She was desperate to see Lottie, and deeply touched and grateful that Lorenzo had understood this morning how she needed to get back to her as soon as possible, but as they sped through the sun-baked green and gold of Tuscany, Venice in the diaphanous light of dawn seemed as insubstantial as a dream.

Beside her, Lorenzo steered the car effortlessly around alarming hairpin bends, one hand resting on her knee. But already he seemed remote and unreachable, lost in his own thoughts. She longed to ask him what they were, but didn't dare. He had said that it wouldn't be over when they got back to the *palazzo,* but somehow, no matter how she tried, she couldn't imagine them picking up where they had left off this morning once they were back there. In Venice she had become a different person: the kind of woman who wore designer dresses and had a team of experts to get her ready. The kind of woman who made passionate, uninhibited love in lavish hotel suites. Now she was bare-faced and back in her scruffy supermarket clothes, ready to return to being a mother. A housekeeper.

How could he possibly find her attractive with her arms full of washing, she thought sadly, the smell of cooking in her hair? Last night had given her a glimpse into his life, and the film had given her an insight into his phenomenal creativity and skill. His talent and vision and brilliance. How could an ordinary girl like her interest a man like that?

All the doubts were temporarily pushed to the back of her mind when they pulled into the drive of the *palazzo*. Lottie and Dino had been waiting by the gates with Lupo, and they all ran alongside the car, Lupo galloping madly at the children's heels as Lorenzo pretended to race them. He let them win, of course, and Sarah got out to greet them as they jumped up and down in victory by the front steps to the house.

She hugged Lottie close, breathing her in.

'Did you have a good time?' she asked as Paola appeared, smiling and drying her hands on a tea towel.

'Oh, *yes,*' Lottie cried, her eyes shining. 'We ate hot dogs and *gelato* and Alfredo played the guitar and taught me an Italian song, and we stayed up until it was really late and there was a *full moon,* and it was huge, so it didn't really get dark and the garden was all silvery, and Lupo slept in our tent...' She broke off for breath, then shrugged and said simply, 'I had the best time *ever.* Did you?'

'Yes,' Sarah said quietly, catching Lorenzo's eye for a dizzying moment. 'I saw the moon as well. In Venice, shining on the water. And I missed you, but I had the best time too.'

Paola and Alfredo stayed for supper. Sarah made a very simple dish of tagliatelle with pesto and they all sat out in the courtyard until dusk had fallen and the children's heads were drooping with tiredness.

After they'd gone, in a flurry of *arrivedercis* and *grazies,* Lorenzo hoisted a half-asleep Lottie into his arms and carried her upstairs to her little room with the starry ceiling. Following a moment later, Sarah stood at the doorway watching him as he laid her gently in bed. She said something to him that Sarah didn't hear, and he smiled, stroking her hair back from her forehead, but as he straightened up again his face wore an expression that was almost like pain.

She remembered the bleakness in his voice when he'd told her last night that he couldn't have children of his own, and her heart ached. She longed to say something to him—to reach out to him and reassure him—but when she had said goodnight to Lottie and came out of the room there was no chance to say anything as he took her hand and led her through the summer twilight to his room. They undressed each other with trembling, tender urgency and she could only show him what she couldn't say in words.

The edges of the room had retreated into blurry darkness as she lay in his arms afterwards, her body still pulsing and wracked with pleasure. She could hear his heart beating beneath her cheek, steady and reassuring, and felt the gentle rise and fall of his chest as he breathed.

Emotion swelled and hardened in the back of her throat, stopping her breath and making her dizzy. She suddenly felt as if the world was spinning, faster and faster, and that there was nothing to stop her from being flung off and falling, spinning, hurtling down into nothingness.

Just as she had fallen in love with him.

She hadn't meant it to happen, but in the end she was as powerless to stop it as gravity. And she stuffed her knuckles in her mouth and prayed that she wouldn't wake him up with her stupid, irrational crying. Because then he would ask her what the matter was and she'd have to tell him that she was happy. That she was so happy that it scared her.

In the few brief, sunlit days that followed Sarah felt as if she was living in a bubble; one of the delicate, iridescent bubbles that Lottie blew through a wand, which wavered and shimmered over the lawn before vanishing in a shower of rainbow droplets.

She and Lorenzo made love in the early mornings, in the tranquil hour before dawn when the air was cool on her skin; and in the sultry purple dusk, when Lottie was asleep. They would come together on the stairs, in the garden, on the chill tiles of the kitchen floor, satisfying their craving for each other quickly and hungrily, before falling into bed and doing it all over again. Slowly and luxuriously.

On Wednesday morning she woke early, twisting gently from the circle of his arms so she could turn and look at his face as he slept. The dewy light made his dark skin look unnaturally pale. Asleep, he seemed to inhabit somewhere completely beyond her reach, and she wondered what dreams were playing across his brilliant, endlessly fascinating mind.

In spite of the warmth of his body next to hers she felt suddenly cold and regretted moving out of his embrace. But then his thick, dark lashes fluttered and his mouth widened into a slow, sleepy, unmistakably sexy smile.

'I was just dreaming about you,' he said huskily, pulling her against him.

There was something more intense in their lovemaking that morning, something that touched her more profoundly even than before, when he'd taken her so high that she felt as if she was soaring with the angels. But this time there was no sense of blissful abandon. Lorenzo leaned over her, his dark, compelling gaze never leaving hers as he filled her, slowly and deeply, and it felt as if he was saying goodbye.

*I'm being completely ridiculous,* she told herself sternly, clattering crockery in the kitchen as Lottie's bright chatter filled the silent spaces that lay over the breakfast table. Lorenzo listened patiently, smiling enigmatically as she tried to extract clues from him about the birthday treat he had promised, while Sarah busied herself clearing plates and giving herself a strict talking-to.

What happened to the girl who used to pride herself on her independence? she thought disgustedly, tossing her untouched toast to a grateful Lupo. Weeks had used to go by without her hearing a word from Rupert, and she barely gave it a thought.

But then she hadn't loved Rupert.

Not as she loved Lorenzo.

He wouldn't let her drive him to the airport, so they said goodbye in the bright sunshine outside the *palazzo.* Throwing his bags into the car, he bent down to give Lottie a hug.

*'Arrivederci, tesoro. A presto.'*

*'A presto, Lorenzo,'* she said in a small voice. 'Why do you have to go?'

'Because I have some work to do.' He smiled. 'And because I have some arrangements to make for a certain someone's birthday treat.'

She threw herself into his arms, and Sarah had to turn away as Lorenzo stroked her hair and said, 'Look after Lupo for me. And your *mama.*' God, she wasn't going to cry, that would be too pathetic for words, but seeing her little girl enfolded in Lorenzo's huge arms was almost too much.

He set Lottie down and stood up, taking her hand and pulling her towards him. Since their return from Venice by some unspoken mutual agreement they'd kept the shift in their relationship secret, making sure Lottie didn't have any reason to suspect that anything had changed. Now, gripping her hand tightly, he looked straight into her eyes.

*'Mi mancheri.'*

She laughed, because it was better than crying. 'Why can't my Italian be as good as Lottie's?'

'I'll miss you. But I'll be back very soon.' Clenching his teeth, he turned his head away so she could see the muscle flickering in his cheek, and the shadowy anxiety that had been stealthily stalking her for the past few days closed in on her a little.

'Lorenzo?' she whispered.

But whatever it was she had seen on his face had passed, and he turned back and kissed her hard, on the mouth, while Lottie looked on, her eyes as round as saucers. And then he got into the car and drove off quickly, the tyres throwing up clouds of dust from the drive.

The big old house felt very empty without him. It wasn't the only one, Sarah thought with a sigh as she trailed through the hallway with a basketful of washing. He'd only been away for—she glanced at the huge old grandfather clock beside his study door, and frowned. An hour? It felt like much longer.

And then she gave a shaky laugh as she noticed that the clock had stopped. Of course it was more—three hours at least—but without him she felt pretty much like the clock. Stopped. Waiting.

Beyond pathetic, she thought with a disdainful sniff, hitching the washing basket up on her hip and heading for the stairs with renewed purpose.

She was stopped in her tracks by the ring of the telephone. Dropping the basket at the bottom of the stairs, she ran across the hall and into Lorenzo's study to answer it, her pulse quickening at the thought that it might be him. Would he be there yet? In London? Perhaps he was ringing to tell her he'd just landed...

'Hello?'

'Oh, hi,' said a voice on the other end. English, female and surprised. 'I was bracing myself to struggle with my basic Italian, but you're English, right?'

'Yes,' said Sarah, choking back her disappointment.

'Great, that makes it easier. Are you Mr Cavalleri's PA, by any chance?'

Through the open door Sarah could see the washing spilling out of the basket onto the hall floor. 'I work for Mr Cavalleri, yes,' she said wryly. 'I'm afraid he's not here at the moment.'

'No, I know that,' the girl said easily. 'I'm Lisa, Jim Sheldon's PA. Jim's got a meeting with Mr Cavalleri later on this afternoon, so he's gone to check out the location for the project and he's just phoned in to say he's lost. Honestly, it's typical. Mr Cavalleri's not answering his phone, so I assume he's still in the air, and I've got Jim calling me on his mobile from the middle of darkest Oxfordshire having a complete meltdown. I just wondered if you could help me point him in the right direction.'

'Oh,' said Sarah, faintly. Her pulse was drumming so loudly in her head she had to press the phone very hard against her ear to hear the breezy cockney voice at the other end. 'Oxfordshire. Right. I'll do my best. Where is he heading for?'

There was the sound of papers rustling at the other end and Lisa's voice was distracted. 'Um...well, I gave him directions to the village, but now apparently he's looking for some pub or other. Mr Cavalleri said it was important in the book...'

Sarah lowered herself abruptly into the chair in front of Lorenzo's desk. She was finding it hard to breathe, and her legs felt suddenly bloodless.

'What book?'

'Oh, sorry.' Lisa, whoever she was, sounded surprised. 'Jim's talked about nothing else for weeks, so I assumed it would be the same at your end. *The Oak and—*'

'*The Cypress,*' Sarah finished hoarsely. Dark spots danced in front of her eyes.

'That's the one. Jim's so excited about it, especially since Damian King's on board now. All very hush-hush, of course, but we've just got to keep our fingers crossed that Mr Cavalleri manages to pull off all the legal stuff. Anyway, the pub—do you know what it's called?'

'The Rose and Crown.' Sarah's swollen throat ached with the effort of sounding normal. 'It's off the main road, about a mile or so outside Lower Prior on the road to Stokehampton.' *Or less, if you cut through the fields...*

'Oh, that's brilliant. Thanks so much. I'll phone him back now and...'

Sarah didn't listen to the rest. The phone had slipped down onto her shoulder and she held it there for a while, staring straight in front of her as her mind inched slowly back over the last month, blindly groping over everything that had happened and suddenly understanding.

Why he'd taken such an interest in her. Why he'd asked her to stay on, and why he'd taken her to Venice and bought her the necklace and...and...seduced her so very, *very* thoroughly. Oh, God. It must have been him who had applied for the rights to the book. And after she had refused he had set out to do all he could to guarantee success...

'*No!*' The cry of anguished denial was torn from her and she jumped to her feet, dropping the phone back into its cradle with a clatter before yanking open the drawer of the desk and pulling out piles of papers with shaking hands. And as they slid onto the desk she fanned them out and saw photographs of the fields she knew so well, fields she had walked across since she was a child, the pub where Lorenzo had kissed her that night, the river where her father had taken her to fish for trout, and where he had taken his life.

There was no need to look at any more. The evidence was all there. Clumsily she bundled the papers back up and shoved them into the drawer, then leaned on the desk for a moment, breathing hard.

So that was it. The silent, stalking beast had pounced. She was caught in its claws, her heart ripped out, and the stupid thing was she wasn't even surprised.

She had known it was too perfect to be real.

Men didn't notice Sarah Halliday; she just wasn't that kind of girl. In a crowded room their eyes slid over her without interest as they looked for the next slim blonde. In particular, powerful, successful men like Lorenzo Cavalleri didn't notice her, and they certainly didn't single her out, take her out to lunch, look after her when she was tired, feed her cake and champagne, make her feel like a goddess, *unless they had a reason.*

Tears were running down her face, swiftly and silently falling onto the cluttered surface of Lorenzo's desk. Closing her eyes, she took a very deep breath, holding it for as long as she could, struggling to control the shadowy beast that now threatened to annihilate her. Her lungs burned and strained, and she exhaled slowly, then did it again.

There. It wasn't so bad. In and out, that was all there was to it. Now she just had to keep it up for the next sixty years or so.

The thought made her feel eerily calm and blank. Her face was wet but composed as she sat stiffly down on the chair again and picked up the telephone with numb fingers to book herself and Lottie on a flight back to England.

And then she took a blank sheet of paper from the tray on the desk and put it on the blotter in front of her, biting her lip hard as she began,

*Dear Lorenzo...*

# CHAPTER SEVENTEEN

'HAPPY birthday, darling! Oh, goodness me, I hardly recognised you, you look so very grown-up now that you're *six!*'

Lottie turned her cheek resolutely away from her grandmother, so Martha's kiss missed it and ended up somewhere above her ear. Sarah gave an apologetic shrug and smiled wanly.

Martha gave Lottie a robust hug. 'Go and find Grandpa in the other room and see what goodies he's got for you,' she said in a hearty, encouraging voice. Lottie said nothing, but walked listlessly to the door and disappeared.

'Sorry about that.' Sarah turned away and absent-mindedly rubbed at a stain on the cracked Formica worktop with a cloth. 'It's not personal. Not to you, anyway. It's just me she hates.'

'Oh, darling.' Martha's tone was both gentle and reproachful. 'She doesn't hate you, but it's understandable that she's upset. She was so happy at Castellaccio, and she loved Dino and Lupo, and Lorenzo...'

'Yes, well,' Sarah rubbed harder, 'that's the trouble with love, isn't it? It makes you happy for about five seconds and then it all goes horribly wrong. Perhaps the one good thing that'll come out of this is that she'll learn that at an early age. Love hurts. It's a useful lesson.'

Martha came to stand beside her and gently took the cloth

from her hands. 'Sarah, what happened? I thought you were happy there too.'

The mark was still there, but Sarah dimly remembered that it always had been. Funny how in a few short weeks she'd forgotten the grimness and squalor of her own flat. It seemed incredible now that at one point she'd genuinely believed she might not come back here.

Ha. *And they all lived happily ever after...*

'I was,' she said in a low voice. 'I was happier than I thought it was possible to be.'

'So, what went wrong?'

The compassion in Martha's eyes was almost more than Sarah could bear. Clenching her jaw, barely moving her lips, she said, 'It was based on a total delusion. I thought he...liked me, for *me*.'

'So what makes you think now he didn't?'

Sarah had to laugh at that. It was a harsh, ugly sound in the small, shabby kitchen. 'It was all going so well up until the moment I found out he was banking on me giving him the film options to Dad's book. He did a very good job of making it look like he cared for me...' She stopped for a moment, horror closing in on her as her mind scrambled back over it. Again and again, she did this. Remembering things he'd done or said that all made sense now. Like the night in the temple when she'd been so touched that he'd held her and talked to her about her father. God, she'd even thought that it meant *more* that he hadn't tried to get her clothes off...

Her eyes burned as she looked back up at her mother now. 'I can even tell you the exact moment when he realised. It was that first night, after the disaster with the roof and everything, and you introduced yourself.'

Bewildered, Martha shook her head. 'What are you talking about?'

'He knew who we were. He knew all about us. He'd been planning to make this film for ages.' She gave a strangled sob.

'I thought it was such a coincidence that we'd seen him in The Rose and Crown, but it wasn't. He was there checking out the location, and then when we all turned up on his doorstep I bet he couldn't believe his luck. No wonder he let Angelica get married there. No wonder he singled me out especially. He knew that I held the rights to the book. He knew...' she faltered, and took a gasping breath '...he knew my *real* name.'

'Oh, Sarah...'

'So you see, I couldn't stay. I know it was cowardly to run away without talking to him, but it would have been just too humiliating and painful, to have to face him and tell him that I knew it was all lies...'

Martha's shoulders sagged with the enormity of it all. 'Does he know yet that you're gone? Have you heard from him?'

'No. Not from him. I got a call yesterday from someone called Jim at this film studio. He's a friend of Lorenzo's, and he was very nice and very gentle and sympathetic and told me that Lorenzo had organised this treat for Lottie today, and that he hoped we would still be able to come "despite what had happened".' Sarah couldn't keep the sour sarcasm from her voice. 'So Lorenzo might not have spoken to me, but it seems he's spoken to this Jim.'

'He got in touch with us last week about today,' Martha said flatly. 'Guy and I were saying how much trouble he'd gone to, and we were so happy because we thought it must mean—'

'I know,' Sarah cut in harshly. 'I did too. But it didn't, did it?'

At that moment the door burst open and Guy appeared with Lottie on his back. He was wearing a sequinned tiara and was carrying a fur-trimmed wand, which he was waving around frantically as he pretended to look for her.

'Has anyone seen the birthday girl? Because unless I'm very much mistaken we have to leave in a moment for a birthday surprise at a mystery location, and if I can't find her she's going to miss it.'

'Here I am!' Lottie cried with something of her old sparkle as she waved her arms in front of Guy's face. But when Sarah caught her eye and smiled she looked away.

'*Grazie,* Jim. I appreciate this.'

Jim took the package that Lorenzo handed him and gave a small shrug. 'Hey, anything to oblige. I know how important this girl is to you, and if I can smooth the path of true love *and* secure us the go-ahead for the film, then, man, I'll do anything.'

'She's given me the rights,' Lorenzo said tonelessly. 'And her blessing.'

Lorenzo turned away. The letter was in the inside pocket of his jacket, and he touched it with his fingertips now. For reassurance. There was no need to read it again; he already knew it virtually by heart.

*The rights to the book are yours. You seem to be able to take the most unpromising, easily overlooked material and turn it into something that feels special, so I know that you'll treat it with respect and tenderness. I know this because it's how you have treated me, although you were never honest about your motives for doing so.*

'That's great! Isn't it?' Jim clapped his hands and rubbed them together.

Lorenzo winced, pressing his temples and trying hard to control the savage desperation that was tearing his insides apart. 'I don't just want the rights on paper. I want them morally, emotionally...' he said through gritted teeth. A yawning abyss lay in front of him, and he couldn't bring himself to look into it. 'I can't make this film unless she's with me.'

'But you said she gave you her blessing. What more do you want?'

Lorenzo turned round, and his face was a frozen continent of despair.

'Her.'

Film studios, it seemed, were like so much else in life. Glamorous and exciting in theory, but disappointingly scruffy and dingy in reality.

They walked across the car park to a building that looked unpromisingly like a warehouse. Not the kind of setting where you could imagine dreams were spun into happy endings. Sarah hung back, relieved to hand over the burden of Lottie's happiness for a while. Guy and Martha held each of Lottie's hands, swinging her high, but hearing her laugh and seeing other people succeed where she had failed again made Sarah's cracked heart ache.

A pretty girl wearing a tight hooded sweatshirt and trainers greeted them at the door, her blonde pony-tail swinging as she bent down to say hi to Lottie.

'I'm Lisa, and I'm going to be showing you round today.'

As she spoke Sarah recognised her cheerful voice with its London twang from on the phone, and felt almost dizzy for a second as the horror rose up around her again, sucking her down. She turned away, fighting back nausea, and caught sight of her reflection in a big plate-glass window.

God, she looked awful; ashen and hollow-eyed. The shimmering vision in the raspberry-pink satin dress who'd walked up the red carpet in Venice a week ago seemed like a character from a dream.

'Come on, darling, we're going in,' Martha called from behind her, and Sarah turned to find that everyone else had disappeared through a small doorway.

Wearily she followed them. The room in front of them was big and dark like a cinema, and they shuffled hesitantly forward into the muffled blackout. As soon as they were all in, the lights suddenly went up and a shrill voice shouted out,

*'Sorpresa!'*

Sarah caught a glimpse of the incredulous joy on Lottie's face as she leapt up and threw herself at the small figure who had sprung from out of the shadows.

*'Dino!'*

Incandescent with happiness, the two children hugged and danced around together, and Sarah's sore eyes stung with the last drops of her reservoir of tears. When at last they let each other go Paola and Alfredo came shyly forward, their faces wreathed in smiles as they bent to kiss Lottie on both cheeks. There were other people there too—Hugh and Angelica, enviably tanned from their honeymoon, Hugh weighted down with an obscene amount of presents and a huge balloon shaped like a rocket—and, bizarrely, Fenella, looking slightly out of place at a children's party in her gold high heels.

Lottie was dazed with happiness as everyone gathered around to wish her happy birthday. All the time her eyes kept darting back to Dino, as if she couldn't quite believe that he was here. Or that he wouldn't disappear again.

Which, of course, he would. Sooner or later.

Sarah leaned her head back against the wall, light-headed with the effort of holding herself together. Her shredded heart swelled and throbbed with gratitude to see Lottie so happy, while her mind struggled to assimilate the fact that that happiness had been brought about by the same man who had caused her such pain. Lorenzo, with his unique way of understanding exactly what people wanted and needed, had done this, bringing together the people Lottie loved most to make her feel special and cherished on her birthday.

There was only one person missing, she thought, and was suddenly seized by a wild, irrational hope that Lorenzo would be here too. Before she could stop herself she had turned her head, looking round for him, before her brain caught up and remembered that it was over. She had let him go. Released him from any further obligation to pretend.

Lisa stepped forward, clapping her hands and beaming

round at everyone. 'Right, now that everyone's here, we're going on a journey. A very special birthday trip. Can you guess where...?'

The lights dimmed. The velvet drapes around the walls glided back and from out of the darkness all around them stars began to emerge. Thousands of stars; on the walls and on the ceiling, tiny points of light and bigger, luminescent orbs.

'The moon!' shrieked Lottie, clapping her hands. She was standing up, her face dimly illuminated in the bluish light, an expression of absolute wonder upon it that made Sarah's heart turn over. On the screen in front of them the tiny crescent of a new moon appeared. Sarah saw Lottie and Dino look at each other with wide eyes, linking hands and screwing up their faces intently as they made a wish.

The moon got bigger. It felt as if you were there, standing in space, staring out into the vast, starry expanse of eternity. Sarah recognised some of the shots from the Galileo film, and that above all else seemed to bring Lorenzo painfully close. His vision. His amazing creative talent. She was taut as a bow string, her hands balled tightly into fists as the film continued its journey around the heavens, and she was desperate for it never to end. She just wanted to keep watching the vision that Lorenzo had created, because the moment it was over he would be gone and it would be like saying goodbye to him all over again.

But it did end. The stars dimmed. The room went dark and she felt herself collapse inside a little, breathless and dejected.

Then a white square leapt across the black screen in front of them, numbers scrolling across it, like on an old-fashioned movie reel. The music that Sarah recognised from hearing so many times floating out from Lorenzo's study at the *palazzo* suddenly filled the small room, and Lottie appeared on the screen. Lottie, in her bridesmaid dress, stepping daintily down the stairs at Castellaccio.

The footage was jerky, deliberately naïve, the camera zooming in on her face as she flashed a mischievous smile into the lens. A little murmur of appreciation went round the room at this surprise, and at Lottie's sweetness, and, glancing at her, Sarah saw the delight on her face at being the star of her own film.

And then the screen blurred and the music slowed and quietened, until it was just one unbearably poignant violin. Instead of Lottie, Sarah found she was looking up at herself. A black and white image of herself, wrapped in a towel, her hair wet around her shoulders as she leaned over the banister at the *palazzo,* spread across a twelve-foot screen.

Anguish sliced through her. Her hands went up to her face, half-covering her eyes. She felt paralysed with horror, pinioned with shame at the thought of everyone watching her, and willed the moment to be over and the camera to shift to something else.

But it didn't.

It lingered on her face, closing in, picking up the play of emotions there as she watched the scene below. Sarah remembered it clearly; Angelica leaving for her wedding with Lottie, solemn and exquisite at her side, and she saw her own wistful joy, her pride in her daughter. The film slowed, the camera clearly picking up the tears that shimmered in her eyes as she blew a kiss down.

More. There was more. She was walking across the lawn in her lilac dress, her feet bare, her hair loose. Running down the stairs at the *palazzo,* saying something over her shoulder and smiling. Getting out of the car, her arms full of shopping, the keys clamped between her teeth. And there were still photos of her too, bending over and talking to Lottie; laughing with a glass of wine in her hand, sunlight slanting across her face; blowing a bubble from Lottie's bubble wand, her lips pouting as if in a kiss.

Of her in Venice, a Press shot from the red carpet. Hand in hand with Lorenzo as they got out of the car.

Another, taken a few seconds later. A close-up of her looking up into the sky as he leant close and whispered in her ear.

Oh, God.

It was like a love letter. A love letter in images.

Around her everyone was very still; every pair of eyes in the room was trained on the screen.

Another shot. Close up at first. Very close. Eyes closed, lashes sweeping down over her cheeks, then moving out to show her mouth, her lips slightly parted, her hair spilling out across the pillow. Oh, dear lord, Lorenzo must have taken it when she was in his bed at Castellaccio. She was sleeping and she looked peaceful and happy and...almost...yes, almost...

'Now can you see it? Now do you understand?'

She gasped. His voice was a broken rasp of despair beside her in the darkness, and he was taking her hands, squeezing tightly as he said so quietly that no one else could hear, 'You're *beautiful,* Sarah, you're so beautiful...can you see it now?'

'Oh, God, Lorenzo...'

'Shh,' he moaned, pressing his fingertips to her lips. 'You have to let me apologise. You have to let me explain, please. About the film.'

Around them everyone else was still watching the screen, oblivious. Tears spilled down Sarah's cheeks, blurring the images in front of her eyes. 'It's all right,' she whispered, 'you don't have to.'

'I do,' he said in a low, fierce voice. The dark enfolded them, so that she couldn't see his hands holding hers; could only feel the strength of his grip and sense his despair. 'I wanted to do it before I met you. For years. It was a dream...' He broke off, and in the flickering light from the screen she saw the abject torment on his face. She gave a sob, pressing her face into his chest to muffle the sound, not wanting to draw anyone's attention.

'Why didn't you tell me?'

His mouth was against her hair, his voice cracked with

pain. 'At the beginning it was because I wanted to work out the best way to approach you. But as time went on it became so much more important than that. I was so scared of not getting it right. Of letting you down. I wanted to show you how brilliant your father was, in the hope that it might help you to see how brilliant you are...'

Against the darkness of his chest she closed her eyes and breathed him in, wanting to absorb his essence and his strength into herself. Gently he took her face between his hands and tilted it up towards him. His eyes were wet with tears and full of agony.

'And you are brilliant. You fill my head and you make things make sense and you inspire me, so that I don't care if I never make another film again, just as long as I can have you and tell you every day for the rest of my life how beautiful you are and how much I love you.'

Weak with relief and joy, scarcely able to take in that he was there, never mind what he was saying, she grasped blindly at the collar of his jacket. He bent his head and kissed her with a ferocious, bruising tenderness, crushing her against him while his lips moved across her trembling mouth, her wet cheeks, her eyelids, her jaw...

The film had ended and the lights slowly came up again. Martha and Paola were hastily brushing tears from their cheeks, grinning self-consciously at each other. Lottie, thrilled and mellowed into forgiveness, instinctively looked round for her mother after three days of freezing her out, and gave a sudden, heart-rending sob.

'Lorenzo! Oh, *Lorenzo!*'

She hurtled towards him, and he and Sarah pulled apart just in time for him to catch her and hoist her into his arms. 'That's what I wished for when I saw the new moon!' she cried. 'I wished for *you*. And Lupo. Did you bring him?'

Lorenzo shook his head and caught Sarah's eye, with an expression that made her heart turn over. 'I thought I'd planned everything, but you thought of the one thing I'd forgotten.' He kissed her cheek and buried his face in her hair. 'Is there anything else you wished for that I could give you instead?'

Lottie put her head on one side and gave a coy, dimpled smile. 'A new daddy? And to live next door to Dino for ever...'

Lorenzo laughed, pulling Sarah into his arms so that both of them were folded into the strength and safety of his body. He dropped his head so he could look into Sarah's eyes, and she caught the low note of hope and longing in his voice as he said, 'Well?'

'Yes.' She was crying and smiling as she pressed her mouth to his. 'Oh, yes, please.'

# EPILOGUE

*'It was widely agreed that the wife of director Lorenzo Cavalleri, who was awarded Best Director for* The Oak and the Cypress, *easily outshone many of Hollywood's more polished stars with her lustrous natural look...'*

Smiling broadly, Lorenzo leaned back against the pillows and stroked a leisurely hand down Sarah's bare back as he turned the newspaper over and read further down the column:

*'Sarah Cavalleri was radiant in a midnight-blue Valentino dress that looked slightly more crumpled than when it appeared on the catwalk in Milan last month, and the trademark necklace of diamond stars that she has worn at all her public appearances. The 31-year-old's naturally curly hair was loose about her shoulders, and it appeared to be still wet as she walked up the red carpet hand in hand with her husband. Experts also speculated that her glowing skin had more to do with diet and exercise than make-up...'*

'Oh, God,' Sarah yelped and buried her head in the duvet. Lorenzo laughed and carried on.

*'Her seemingly effortless beauty has been rapturously heralded as the start of a backlash against increasingly extreme A-list perfection.'*

'Stop!' she croaked, moving the corner of the duvet back so she could look at him from beneath it. 'It doesn't really say that, does it? About my dress being creased and my hair still being wet?'

Lorenzo let the paper drop as he kissed her bare shoulder. Thin spring sunshine was pouring through the windows of the hotel's penthouse suite, glinting on the gold statuette that stood on the dressing table and illuminating the chaos in the luxurious room. The midnight-blue dress was now discarded on the floor, along with Lorenzo's white evening shirt and bow tie, and Sarah's shoes.

'Oh, yes, it does,' he murmured appreciatively against her warm skin. 'You're famous, *tesoro*.'

Sarah groaned. 'Famous for being the woman who was so busy being thoroughly seduced by her multi-talented husband, *in her award-ceremony dress,* ten minutes before the car came that she didn't have time to put on make-up.'

'No. Famous for being beautiful. And they were right about the exercise,' he said huskily, trailing a finger across her collar bone. 'You do realise you're going to be inundated with requests from magazine editors wanting to know your beauty secrets now?'

She propped herself up on her elbows, smiling wickedly into his eyes. 'The trouble is that none of them are remotely suitable for publication. What else does it say?'

'Nothing important.' He kissed the hollow beneath her jaw, and the newspaper slid from his fingers. Sarah caught it before it fell to the floor.

'Uh-uh, not so fast,' she said huskily. 'I want to hear the bit about how brilliant you are...'

Lorenzo carried on kissing her as she sat up properly and started to read.

*'Collecting the ceremony's most prestigious award, Lorenzo Cavalleri paid tribute to Francis Tate—author of the book on which his film is based and his wife's late father—thanking him for "giving the world an extraordinarily beautiful book" and for "giving me my extraordinarily beautiful wife and daughter..."'*

Sarah's voice cracked and she faltered for a second, before carrying on in a choked voice.

*'Cavalleri, who is known in the industry for his inscrutable calm, seemed to struggle for a moment to keep his emotions in check in what was, despite its unusual brevity, undoubtedly one of the most moving speeches of the evening.'*

She stopped, her eyes shimmering with tears, remembering the moment when her husband had stood in front of the packed auditorium and a worldwide television audience of millions and gazed down at her, lost for words, the huge screen behind him magnifying the expression of profound love on his face.

'It was...wonderful,' she sighed softly, running her fingers through his hair with infinite tenderness.

'I didn't mean it to be quite so brief,' he admitted gruffly, capturing her hand in his and dropping a kiss into the centre of her palm. 'There were lots of other people I should have thanked. Most notably you.'

'You don't have to thank me for anything.'

He took her face between his hands, his eyes searching hers, searing into her soul as the smile died on his lips. 'I have you to thank for...*everything*. If I'd started it would have taken all night.'

There was a pause, a heartbeat, as the atmosphere between them shifted and intensified and their locked gazes darkened. 'As I recall,' Sarah breathed, 'it pretty much did...'

'Hmm,' Lorenzo murmured as he pulled her into his arms, 'and I've barely even scratched the surface...'

\* \* \* \* \*

# MILLS & BOON

## Book of the Month

**ABBY GREEN**
*One Night With The Enemy*

## We love this book because...

Against the stunning backdrop of Argentina's vineyards, Nic and Madalena's passionate, intense, and evocative story of a forbidden young passion reignited unfolds...and this time they'll finish what they started.

On sale 3rd August

*Visit us Online*

Find out more at
**www.millsandboon.co.uk/BOTM**

# Special Offers

Every month we put together collections and longer reads written by your favourite authors.

Here are some of next month's highlights—and don't miss our fabulous discount online!

Nora Roberts
Luring a Lady
On sale 3rd August

Hot nights with a SPANIARD
CAROLE MORTIMER    INDIA GREY    LYNN RAYE HARRIS
On sale 3rd August

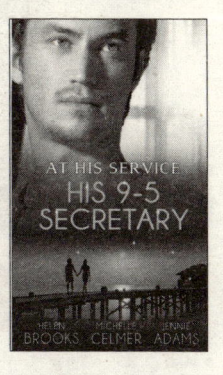

AT HIS SERVICE
HIS 9-5 SECRETARY
HELEN BROOKS    MICHELLE CELMER    JENNIE ADAMS
On sale 3rd August

## Save 20% on all Special Releases

Find out more at
**www.millsandboon.co.uk/specialreleases**

Visit us Online

0712/ST/MB381

# New York, Hollywood... Pregnant?

**P.S. I'm Pregnant**

*Secrets, scandal and finding true love*

Heidi Rice

If her landlady's cat hadn't gone missing and Connor Brody had bothered to return her messages asking for help in the search, Daisy Dean wouldn't have been sneaking around his garden at night—and he would never have caught her in her underwear!

But Connor's quite pleased with his scantily clad intruder. His business deal is about to fall through—maybe Daisy could make it up to him by accompanying him to NYC?

What's the worst that could happen?

**www.millsandboon.co.uk**